SANDS

Barbara Erskine is the author of *Lady of Hay*, which has sold well over a million copies worldwide, *Kingdom of Shadows*, *Encounters* and *Child of the Phoenix*, which was based on the story of one of her own ancestors. *Midnight is a Lonely Place* and *House of Echoes* were short-listed for the W H Smith Thumping Good Read awards of 1995 and 1997 respectively and were followed by *Distant Voices* and *On the Edge of Darkness*. Her most recent novels, *Whispers in the Sand* and *Hiding From the Light* were both *Sunday Times* top ten bestsellers. Barbara Erskine's novels have been translated into thirty languages.

Barbara Erskine has a degree in mediaeval Scottish history from Edinburgh University. She and her family divide their time between the Welsh borders and their home near the coast of North Essex.

Praise for Barbara Erskine:

'Barbara Erskine's storytelling talent is undeniable'   *The Times*

'Her forte is mood, atmosphere and toe-curling frisson.'

ELIZABETH BUCHAN, *Sunday Times*

By the same author

LADY OF HAY
KINGDOM OF SHADOWS
ENCOUNTERS (Short stories)
CHILD OF THE PHOENIX
MIDNIGHT IS A LONELY PLACE
HOUSE OF ECHOES
DISTANT VOICES (Short stories)
ON THE EDGE OF DARKNESS
WHISPERS IN THE SAND
HIDING FROM THE LIGHT

BARBARA ERSKINE

Sands of Time

HarperCollins*Publishers*

These stories are entirely works of fiction. The
names, characters and incidents portrayed in it are
the work of the author's imagination. Any
resemblance to actual persons, living or dead,
events, organisations or localities is entirely
coincidental.

HarperCollins*Publishers*
77–85 Fulham Palace Road,
Hammersmith, London W6 8JB

www.harpercollins.co.uk

This paperback edtion 2004
1 3 5 7 9 8 6 4 2

First published by HarperCollins*Publishers* 2003

ISBN 0 00 651209 7

Chapter head illustrations by Rex Nicholls

Set in PostScript Linotype Meridien with Photina display by
Rowland Phototypesetting Ltd, Bury St Edmunds, Suffolk

Printed and bound in Great Britain by
Clays Ltd, St Ives plc

If poets' verses are but stories, so are food and raiment stories.
So is all the world a story. So is man of dust a story.

St Columba

CONTENTS

PREFACE

This third collection of short stories has allowed me to fulfil, at least in part, my ambition to write a sequel to *Whispers in the Sand*. One of the hardest stages in the writing of a novel is finishing it. For weeks, perhaps months, I will have been looking forward to writing those two magic words, *The End* – words that mean a conclusion to obsession, to long hours, to RSI at the keyboard and to saying no to invitations I would so much love to accept. When the moment finally comes, however, saying goodbye to the characters, reconciling the urge to give them a happy ending with the temptation to leave the reader on a knife edge – after all, real life doesn't provide neat endings – and parting with the characters, people who have become closer in many ways than family or friends, and whom I will miss enormously, is the most difficult and painful time. The close of a book leads to a few hours of euphoria and relief, then to intense post-natal depression! One way of getting over that feeling is to consider, if only for a short time, the possibility of resurrecting the story by writing a sequel – something I have actually gone on to think about seriously with only two of my novels, *Midnight is a Lonely Place* and *Whispers in the Sand*.

The result of these thoughts as far as *Whispers* is concerned is presented in this short story collection. There are two long stories, one of which picks up Louisa Shelley's life some seven years after we leave her at the end of *Whispers*. The second continues the tale of Anna and Toby, in this case only days after the end of the novel. It has been a fascinating exercise and not nearly as easy as I thought. I had the novel sewn up pretty well and it was quite hard to unpick a loose end to carry on the narrative. I hope you find that the resultant unravelling and re-ravelling fulfils your expectations and leaves you – well, wait and see . . .

To be putting together another collection of short stories is an indulgence, an enormous pleasure. Reading through the stories that I have written over the past five years I see the mood has changed. The themes move on, reflecting my own preoccupations and those of the world around me and many of my contemporaries. Almost inevitably most of the stories involve ghosts – partly because they interest me, partly because once one has a reputation for writing about a particular kind of subject that is what magazines ask one to write! In case this is seen as something of an obsession I should point out that many months separated most of them in the writing! And I see I have been travelling by train more than I used to – I have always loved writing on trains; that womblike abstraction from the world is the perfect place to lose oneself in the narrative of the imagination. Although the silence and isolation have alas been spoiled by the advent of the mobile phone, even so the strange hypnotic quality of train travel continues to fascinate. And most of these train stories are based on events that have actually happened to me on my travels. Trains lead to adventures.

In this collection I have for the first time included one or two short poems. I have written poetry since I was at school and have occasionally over the years published individual poems, but on the whole I have always felt poetry too intensely personal a medium to show to people. It is time, I felt, that I came out of the closet.

I hope you enjoy *Sands of Time*.

The Legacy of Isis

1

'No!'

Louisa Shelley's anguished denial was instantaneous. 'I don't want to see them!'

The maid's message had been so innocuous. She had come in carrying a steaming ewer of water as Louisa was standing staring out of her bedroom window.

'My lady said I was to tell you that we have a treat this evening, Mrs Shelley. Unexpected guests. She understands they are old friends of yours. Mr and Mrs David Fielding?' The girl smiled, clearly delighted with her news. 'They arrived while you were out painting.'

Her eyes widened as she registered Louisa's horrified reaction. She had been somewhat overawed at first by their guest's fame. Louisa Shelley was an acclaimed water colourist. Her drawings and paintings of her travels in Egypt in the mid 1860s had been exhibited in London galleries, so she had been told, and besides that, Louisa's elegance and beauty had stunned her. Her hair was glossy chestnut, the colour emphasised rather than spoiled by the threads of silver appearing at her temples. She wore graceful flowing dresses in bright jewel colours quite unlike those of the lady of the house, Sarah Douglas – in fact unlike any dresses Kirsty had ever seen. Her awe had quickly turned to worship as Louisa's easy charm won her over. But there were no smiles now. None of the eager excitement she had expected. Louisa's face had gone white. Her features had lost their vivacity.

'But –' Kirsty was shocked into indiscretion. 'Lady Douglas will be heartbroken. She is so excited. She's ordered a special meal and cook is over the moon. It's not often we get the chance to entertain properly.'

Glen Douglas House had once rung to the sounds of music and laughter, but Sir James did not care much for company now that the five children were grown up and gone and in the last few years Sarah had found herself often alone. It was on a visit to her eldest daughter's home in London that she had met Louisa, a friend of a friend, and the two women had taken an instant liking to each other. Sarah had impulsively asked Louisa to come to Scotland for the summer to paint. So far the visit had been a resounding success.

Louisa turned away from Kirsty, defeated. It would be unforgivably discourteous not to come down to dinner. It was only after the little maid had curtseyed and left the room that she gave vent to her true feelings, throwing herself onto the bed, smothering angry tears in her pillow. The very mention of the Fieldings' names had brought it all flooding back, the memories she had tried so hard to bury of that visit to Egypt seven years before when she had met – and lost – the only man she had ever truly loved.

It had all started after the death of her husband, David.

Nothing but her grief and despair at the seemingly needless suffering of such a good, kind man, of whom she had been so extremely fond, and her own increasing ill health, would otherwise have persuaded her to leave her two beloved young sons with their grandmother to travel in search of the warm climate and relaxation which would, she hoped, hasten her recovery.

Her subsequent adventures, her meeting with Hassan, her love for whom had completely and overwhelmingly eclipsed that which she had felt for her adored David, the gift Hassan had given her of a small bottle, an artefact from an ancient tomb, and the cataclysmic events which had followed that simple generous act, had combined on her return to London to bring back a reoccurrence of her ill health. Her restless sleep had been more and more frequently dogged by nightmares. Nightmares about the ancient bottle and the two ghostly spirits who guarded it; and nightmares about the safety of her two sons.

Sarah Douglas's invitation had come at an opportune moment. It was an excuse to send the boys to their grandmother's house – somewhere they needed no second invitation to go, away from the heat and smells of a London summer – and allow her to leave for a complete change of air, in Scotland.

*   *   *

Outside her bedroom window the hot sun beat down on the terraced lawns, driving the aromatic oils from the pines and cedars scattered around the ornamental lake and turning the heather on the distant hills to purple fire. Wearily drying her tears she climbed to her feet. She glanced down at her sketchbook and paintbox lying on the table by the window. The open page showed a delicate watercolour of the eighteenth-century folly, built by her host's great-grandfather. This summer her sketchbooks and canvasses were full of the colours of Scotland, the purples and greys of the moors and mountains, the dark greens of the forests and the deep peaty browns of river and loch. Seven years before they had been full of the golds and creams and yellows of sandstone and the pinks and rose of arid rock and the incredible, ever changing, colours of the River Nile.

Hassan had been her dragoman, her guide, her interpreter, her mentor and, at the last, her lover. His handsome face and tall figure had featured in many of the paintings she had exhibited in London. None of the captions told his story or named his name and no one asked. He was, after all, only a native, part of the scenery. On the two separate occasions when gentlemen, who were captivated by Louisa's charm and beauty during these last few years, had plucked up the courage to ask for her hand, both had retired from the field disappointed. They did not know that they were competing with a dream. Neither imagined for a single second that the heart of the beautiful woman whom they so desired was still captive to the tall dark figure who appeared so enigmatically in her paintings.

The Fieldings had known Hassan's story. They had

known who he was and what he meant to her. Their dahabeeyah had sailed in convoy with the Forresters' boat on which she travelled with Hassan as her servant and they knew how he had died. They had been kind to her – indeed Katherine had named her eldest son Louis after her, following that desperate night on the Nile when she had assisted at his terrifying premature birth.

When they had all parted at Luxor and Louisa had left the Forresters and the Fieldings to take the steamer north at the start of her journey back to England it had been with many tears and hugs and promises to meet again. Augusta Forrester had written to her often over the past years but not once had she mentioned Egypt. She had been tactful. Her letters were full of reassuring gossip and pleasantries and for that Louisa had been thankful. The Fieldings had never contacted her and she had not expected them to. Too much had happened; the memories were too painful to recall.

And now this. With no time to prepare herself, to seal down the emotions which had been reawakened by their name, to rebury the memories and arm herself against the past, she was about to be catapulted back into a storm of reminiscence and nostalgia and grief. Glancing down at the sketchbook again she bent suddenly to the painting, ripped it from the book and tore it across the middle.

The Fieldings were seated in the great drawing room of Glen Douglas House when Louisa finally forced herself to go downstairs. Katherine saw her first. Rising awkwardly to her feet she smiled. Then she held out her hands. 'Louisa! Dear, dear Louisa, how are you? I couldn't believe my ears when Sarah told us you were their guest!' She kissed Louisa on each cheek, her awkwardness explained on closer inspection by the fact that she was expecting a child.

Louisa returned her smile and turned to greet David Fielding. 'How are you both? I see the family continues to flourish.' A gentle acknowledgement of Katherine's condition.

David nodded. 'We have three children now. They are upstairs with their nurses. And as you see, we await a fourth.' He glanced fondly at his wife who nodded a little smugly. 'You must see Louis, my dear. He is the most beautiful child.'

Louisa nodded. 'I would expect no less.' She hoped they were not going to launch into a long explanation of how they knew one another for the benefit of their hostess. But Sarah, it appeared, already knew the story of Louis's dramatic birth. Either out of great tact or by accident she adroitly changed the subject.

'The gentlemen are going out on the hill with the guns tomorrow, Louisa. So I thought perhaps we would spend a quiet day in the gardens or maybe take a short carriage drive?' She raised an eyebrow at their newly arrived guest. 'Only if Katherine feels like it, of course.' A well-built, attractive woman with elegantly dressed greying hair, Sarah surveyed her guests calmly, her blue eyes shrewd.

Before Katherine could respond to her suggestion the door opened and another woman walked into the room. David Fielding's sister, Venetia. Louisa sighed. The younger woman's figure had thickened slightly in the last seven years in spite of her tightly laced corset, her face had hardened, the corners of her mouth were drawn down, the eyes were a trifle deeper set, but she was still a beautiful woman. In spite of herself, as she stepped forward to greet her, Louisa glanced at her hand. No wedding ring. Obviously not, if she was still trailing around after her brother and his wife.

Venetia's smile did not quite reach her eyes as she greeted Louisa. Her kiss was perfunctory and did not do more than brush the air beside Louisa's cheek. 'How are you now?' Four innocuous words, but loaded with innuendo and dislike.

'Well, thank you.' Louisa smiled and turned to find a seat. A dozen spirited questions and retorts flashed through her mind. All were instantly rejected. Silence was the most dignified route.

Venetia sat down next to Sarah Douglas and smoothed the flounced silk of her skirt over her knees. 'So, your curiosity got the better of you, Louisa. You couldn't keep away from Glen Douglas.' Her smile masked considerable venom. 'You know, of course, that he's not here. He's travelling abroad.'

Louisa frowned. 'I'm sorry? About whom are we talking?' She glanced at their host who was engaged in animated conversation with David Fielding by the fireplace. Both men held whisky glasses in their hands. The huge hearth behind them was filled with an arrangement of bog myrtle and heather.

'Lord Carstairs, of course.' Venetia's cheeks coloured slightly.

Louisa stared at her, her own face growing so pale her hostess sat forward anxiously, afraid Louisa was going to faint. 'Roger Carstairs lives near here?' Louisa whispered.

Sarah Douglas nodded. 'So you know him as well? But, of course, you must have met him in Egypt. Our estates march together, my dear. Carstairs Castle is but two miles from here.'

Louisa found her mouth had gone dry. For a moment words failed her totally in the rush of emotions which assailed her. Roger Carstairs: the man who, in Egypt, had asked her to marry him, who had tried to seduce her, who had seen and recognised the little bottle Hassan had given as being something of supreme supernatural importance and who, when he was refused the bottle, had finally been responsible for her beloved Hassan's death. A man so imbued with evil that his very name sent a shiver of distaste through the households of the British aristocracy amongst whom he used to socialise. A man whom Venetia had liked very much indeed.

Somehow Louisa found her voice, aware that Katherine's gaze was as full of sympathy and kindness as Venetia's was of spite.

'I had no idea this was where he lived.' She took a deep breath. 'How extraordinary. But I had heard that he never returned to Britain after –' She found her voice growing husky. 'After our visit to Egypt.'

Sarah walked over to the table and poured a glass of ratafia. Handing it to Louisa she smiled. 'He has a certain reputation, I have to admit. And he doesn't come home often. But he has two sons who live at Carstairs. They have a tutor who is their guardian, I believe, in their father's absence. And he does return to see them from time to time. We haven't met him lately. He does not visit his neighbours.' She glanced from Venetia to Katherine and then back to Louisa, her face suddenly alight with mischief. 'I have an idea!' She plumped down on the ottoman next to Katherine. 'We could drive over to the castle tomorrow. He has a museum. In the stable block, I believe. A friend of ours went to see it. Lord Carstairs's servants would show it to us. I understand it is very interesting. He spent a year in India quite recently and after that he was in America. He has a collection of fascinating artefacts from the American Indian tribes. Feathered head-dresses. Peace pipes. All kinds of things.' Her eyes were sparkling. 'Would you like to go?'

Louisa was torn. Part of her shrank from the prospect of going anywhere near the castle. But another part of her was intrigued, both to see where Roger Carstairs lived, and to view the curiosities he had brought back from his travels. Curiosities presumably like the ancient bottle Hassan had given her, which Carstairs had so wanted for his collection that he had been prepared to kill to obtain it; the bottle which lay hidden at this very moment in the secret compartment in the desk of her London home. Oh yes, she would be interested to see it all, just so long as it was certain, beyond all possible doubt, that he was not there himself.

Carstairs Castle was a grey stone edifice, with turrets and battlements surmounting small windows in thick ancient walls. As their coach rumbled up the curving drive through the rhododendrons, brought by his lord-ship from India and already growing in profusion, the

9

four ladies stared out with eager curiosity. The messenger who had ridden over the previous evening to see if their visit was convenient had returned with an assurance that Mr Dunglass, Lord Carstairs's factor, would greet them and personally escort them round his lordship's gardens and museum.

The factor was waiting on the steps at the foot of the main tower. A small, red-haired man wearing the kilt, he stepped forward to greet the visitors.

Louisa climbed out of the coach last and stared round nervously. The place had a prosperous well cared for feel. The paths and driveway were neatly weeded and raked and there were flowers in the beds around the walls. She glanced up and the skin on the back of her neck prickled slightly. Were they being watched? So many narrow deep-set windows, dark and shadowy on this west-facing side of the castle, looked down across the drive and towards the hills. A hundred pairs of eyes could be watching them and they would not know it. She became aware that the others were walking away, following Mr Dunglass around the base of the tower, and she hurried after them, shrugging off her unease. Lord Carstairs was once more in America, so his factor informed them. He was not expected home until next year at the earliest.

A modern stable block and carriage house had been constructed in the early part of the century by Lord Carstairs's grandfather on the eastern side of the castle. The buildings surrounded a courtyard – a line of loose boxes, all empty as his lordship's horses were out at grass, on one side, a line of double doors concealing no doubt his lordship's carriages on the other, while between them, on the south side, rose a small pedimented coach house surmounted by a clock tower. In this building all the windows had been barred. Mr Dunglass headed towards it now, groping in his sporran for a large iron key.

'This way, Mistress Shelley.' The man had ushered the others up the steps and through the door as Louisa lagged behind and now he was waiting for her, his eyes boldly on her face. How did he know her name? Standing below him in the cobbled yard she looked up and met his gaze. He did not lower his eyes; his expression was carefully blank but behind the facade there was something else. Insolence? Triumph? The moment passed and he looked away. 'The others are inside, Mistress Shelley. If you would like to join them I'll explain some of the items you can see in there.' His tone was respectful. Even friendly. Surely she had imagined that momentary expression on his face?

The room into which they had been led was large and dark. Standing still they waited while their guide opened the shutters allowing the bright sunlight to flood the room. As they stared round there was a moment's stunned silence, then at last it was Venetia who spoke first. 'My goodness.' She gasped with a nervous laugh. 'How amazing!'

The items on display nearest to them, the bows and arrows, the huge beautiful feathered head-dress, the beaded jewellery, the bison skins, had been brought back so they were told by Lord Carstairs the previous year. 'He went right across America,' their informant told them, clearly awe-struck. 'He lived with the various tribes he encountered. The Sioux; the Cheyenne.

11

They made him welcome and he smoked the peace pipe with them.' He indicated the large pipe decorated with coloured bands and feathers. 'He has been studying their religion and their beliefs. He witnessed the Sun Dance.' He paused, obviously expecting them to look impressed. 'Beyond the American exhibits you will see those his lordship brought back from the Indian sub-continent in 1870. Beautiful silks and brocades as you will notice; items from Hindu temples and gifts he received from the maharajahs and British dignitaries with whom he stayed.'

Louisa was not listening. She had wandered past the American items and the Indian, past a huge glass-fronted bookcase and display cabinets of every shape and size, to the back of the room. In the corner, standing upright in the shadows, was the unmistakable painted face and body of an Egyptian mummy case. She closed her eyes, steadying her breathing with an effort.

'Ah, Mistress Shelley. You have discovered Lord Carstairs's Egyptian collection.' The voice beside her was soft and ingratiating.

She gave a nervous smile. 'He has a great many interesting items.'

'Indeed.' The factor glanced over his shoulder. The other three women were gathered around a glass case, staring down at a mass of beautiful shells. 'Wampum,' Venetia repeated, baffled, reading from a card inside the case.

Louisa stepped away from him. His presence beside her made her feel uncomfortable. She walked over to a table nearby and stared down at the items displayed on it. One stood out from them all. A small carved statue

12

of a coiled snake. Without thinking she picked it up and examined it. 'Solid gold, Mistress Shelley.' The factor was still there at her elbow.

She stared down at the item in her hands, holding her breath. Almost she could hear Roger Carstairs's voice in her head. 'So, Mrs Shelley. You came to find me after all . . .' The sound was so real she glanced up, shocked. But it was her imagination. Hastily she set the item back in its place and walked away. She glanced again with some distaste at the mummy, then moved on and stopped, staring at the wall. Framed in ebony with a deep terracotta mount she found herself looking at one of her own watercolours. A painting of the temple at Edfu.

She gasped.

The man beside her nodded. 'You recognise it, of course.'

She spun to face him. 'Where did he get that?'

'He bought it, Mistress Shelley. In London.' He bowed. A minimal movement betrayed a touch of mockery beneath the respect. 'He has attended all your exhibitions, Mistress Shelley.'

Her stomach tightened with fear as she met his eyes. 'Indeed, Mr Dunglass. I'm flattered at his interest.' She managed to hold his gaze unwaveringly.

He looked away first. 'So, madam, have you seen the next exhibit?' He smiled again. 'An example of one of the most poisonous of Egyptian snakes –' He broke off as her hand flew to her mouth. In the case in front of her on a bed of pale dry sand lay a coiled snake, its head with spread hood rising out of the dry skin, its tiny button eyes fixed balefully on some imagined desert distances.

Louisa turned away with a cry of distress. It was so like the snake that had killed Hassan. The same shape, same length, same colour – its eyes were similar. Unblinking. Beady. Missing nothing.

'It's dead, Louisa.' The hand on her arm was firm. Katherine was beside her. 'Come away. Don't look at it.'

'Katherine –'

'I know, my dear. They told me all about it. And the way he conjured a snake onto our dahabeeyah. Magic snakes. Evil magic.' She glanced round the room. Nearby was a wooden statue of a child holding a snake in its hand. The inscription underneath said, 'Horus of the Snakes'. She shuddered. 'Dirty magic. All his efforts to make himself a so-called master of the occult, and what for? A small room in the back of beyond and a few boxes of stolen mementoes.'

'I beg your pardon?' Mr Dunglass had overheard her. He was bristling with indignation. 'Nothing here has been stolen. Everything was bought or given freely.'

'Really?' Louisa looked at him bitterly.

'Really!' The man glared at her.

Katherine shuddered. 'Well, I don't envy him this. I really don't.' She reached over and thumped the glass case with her folded parasol. The snake moved infinitesimally.

Louisa swallowed. Clutching her shawl around her shoulders she moved away from the Egyptian corner of the room to stand in front of the American head-dress with its regal glossy feathers, concentrating on the exquisite workmanship, the detail, the tiny beads.

Katherine moved on too, standing beside Sarah and

14

Venetia, staring at some clay pots, laughing softly as Venetia, oblivious to the earlier exchange, pointed out some detail in the swirling decorations.

The hiss was so quiet Louisa barely heard it. For a moment she didn't react, then she spun round staring back at the case. From where she was standing she could see an almost invisible film of dust on the glass. Nothing moved. She clenched her fists. Stupid. It was her imagination. Her idiotic, feverish, over-active imagination.

Behind her she heard Venetia's voice. 'And Lord Carstairs's darling boys? Are they at home at the moment?' and Dunglass's grunt. 'Aye. They are.' He did not sound impressed.

'We would so like to meet them, wouldn't we, Sarah?' Venetia clung to her hostess's arm for a moment.

Louisa saw the factor's eyebrow rise almost to his hairline. 'I have no idea where the boys are, Mistress. You'd have to be speaking to Mr Gordon, their tutor, about them.' His tone implied that their whereabouts was something he for one would rather not look into too closely.

'We'll do that.' Venetia simpered at him. 'We know dear Lord Carstairs so well, I'm sure he would wish us to enquire after his sons. Are they not at Eton with your elder boy, Louisa?' She turned and raised an eyebrow.

'I don't think so,' Louisa returned sharply.

Dunglass shook his head. 'They've been expelled from every school in the country! I doubt his lordship could find one to hold them. That's why they have a tutor.' His lips tightened. 'Believe me, ladies, I doubt you'd want to meet them.' He folded his arms firmly.

Sarah and Venetia looked shocked. It was Venetia who voiced what was going through both ladies' minds. 'I don't think you should speak like that about Lord Carstairs's sons, Mr Dunglass.'

'No?' The man snorted. 'I'm thinking their father would agree with me!'

'Really?' Venetia simpered at him. 'Oh my goodness! In which case –' She fluttered her eyelashes at the man in apology and Louisa turned away sharply. Was it possible that Venetia still had hopes of the odious Carstairs? Surely not? But here she was, still unmarried, still travelling with her brother and his long-suffering wife. Still hankering after a rich titled husband. She gave an involuntary shudder. No doubt the handsome Lord Carstairs would fit her imaginary ideal in every particular. She did not, after all, know what the real man was like!

'Louisa dear? It's time we made a move for home.' Sarah's gentle hand on her arm made her jump. 'Have you seen enough?'

'Quite enough.' Louisa glanced towards the back of the room where the case containing the stuffed cobra was standing in a patch of sunlight from the high window. There was no movement; nothing at all in that corner of the room. So why did the very stillness make her feel uneasy?

In her dream she was standing at the mouth of the cave, staring into the darkness, anxious to escape the glare of the sun. Hassan was beside her, his handsome face eager, gentle, so very loving. He turned with that serious smile she loved so much and held out his hand. 'Come, my Louisa; we will go in out of the heat.'

She reached towards him. She only had to speak to save his life. All she had to say was, No, come back. Don't go in. But the words would not come. Her throat was constricted, her mouth full of sand. There was a roaring in her ears like the waters of the cataract in flood and then it happened. In slow motion she saw the sinuous movement of the snake; saw it head towards Hassan, saw it rise up, its hood spread, its mouth open –. Her scream this time, as always, came too late; her waking, alone, in her bed, desolate.

She sat up, sobbing, aware of the moonlight flooding through a crack in the curtains. The room was very quiet. Not a breath of air stirred the wisteria on the wall outside. The night was very hot. Her face still wet with tears, she climbed out of bed and went to push back the curtains. The tall windows opened out onto the balcony which ran the entire length of the first floor of the house overlooking the gardens. Pushing them open she stepped outside and leant on the stone balustrade. The countryside was as bright as day. She could see every detail of the garden with its formal hedges and beds and its vistas across the parkland and the loch to the mountains beyond.

'So, Louisa. You came to visit my house. You couldn't resist seeing where I lived. I saw you pick up my golden snake. I felt you call me.'

Lord Carstairs was standing on the balcony half hidden by one of the clipped potted bay trees near her window. Tall, handsome in the moonshadows, his eyes were strangely colourless in the strong contours of his face. He was dressed in a loose white shirt and trousers. Over one shoulder he wore a tartan plaid, fastened in place by a Cairngorm brooch.

Her heart almost stopped beating. 'I never called you! I thought you were abroad!' She stepped back towards the window, feeling acutely vulnerable in her night-gown, with her feet bare and her hair loose on her shoulders.

He smiled coldly. 'And I never thought to see you in Scotland, Mrs Shelley. I am flattered you should come. Very flattered.' He emerged from the shadows and the moonlight glinted on the yellow stone in the brooch on his shoulder.

She frowned. 'Don't take a step nearer. I have only to call out and people will come. What are you doing here?'

He laughed quietly. 'What if I were to tell you that I am not here, Louisa, I am four thousand miles away, eating peyote buttons with the men of the Cheyenne in a tepee under an arid western sky.' He took another step forward and reaching out his hand touched her hair with his finger tip.

She shuddered and took a rapid step backward. 'I don't understand. Are you trying to tell me that this is a dream?' She clutched behind her at the heavy curtains of her bedroom window.

'Just a dream.' His voice was mocking. 'Nothing but a peyote dream.'

'What is peyote?' If it was a dream she wanted to wake up now. End it. Banish this man back to the depths of whatever hell he lived in.

'Peyote, Louisa, is a sacred plant; a way of life; an entrance to other worlds where one may travel unencumbered even into the bed chamber of a sleeping woman.' He moved forward again. She could smell a strange muskiness about him; the scent of woodsmoke and flowers, of bittersweet tobacco and an acrid hint of desert wind.

She took another step back, aware that they were now on the threshold of her bedroom. The moonlight flooded in through the open curtains illuminating the white bedlinen and lace-trimmed pillows. He smiled. He was very close to her now.

'Aren't you going to scream?' His eyes were insolent. Challenging.

'Oh yes, I'm going to scream!' She tried to stop the treacherous trembling of her limbs as she raised her hand towards him, ready to fend him off if he came any closer. 'If you don't leave now I shall scream the place down and your reputation, my lord, will be destroyed forever.'

'My reputation, Mrs Shelley,' he returned the formality like a tennis partner volleying a ball, 'was gone long since. I did not value it. It was of no consequence to me. While yours, I feel sure, though blighted by your dalliance with a native –' he raised his hand to silence her protest – 'Your reputation, as I was about to say, probably survived at least in Britain, thanks to the

19

loyalty of your friends.' He narrowed his eyes. 'Scream, Mrs Shelley. See if you can make yourself heard. Remember you are dreaming. All this has been conjured by your mind.' He reached out and stroked her cheek. His hand was very cold.

'Don't touch me!' She backed away into the room. 'I will call for help.'

'Call then.' He reached out and caught her shoulders, pulling her against him. 'Beautiful Mrs Shelley.' His words were whispered into her hair. 'Oh, how much I have desired you. And how angry you have made me.' She could feel his heart beating against hers. 'And now I shall have you, Mrs Shelley. And perhaps I shall punish you for rejecting me. For not giving me what I wanted.' She did not know whether he meant her body or the tiny bottle he had so much desired, and which as far as he knew was lying at the bottom of the Nile. He smiled again. 'The interesting part of this experience is that you will remember none of this in the morning, Mrs Shelley. None.'

His lips against hers were fierce and eager. She could feel her breasts against his chest as he dragged her nightgown down to her waist. His eyes, so near hers, were slits of silver. 'Go on. Call, Mrs Shelley,' he murmured. 'Call for help. Why don't you?' His hands were all over her body now as her nightgown fell to the floor. To her horror she found herself responding to his touch. Her body refused to struggle; with a groan of pleasure she found herself pressing against him, reaching up for his kisses, caressing his back with fingers that had intended to scratch and maim.

Without further struggle she felt herself falling back

20

onto the bed, felt him groping for his belt buckle, felt his weight on her with eager excitement as she arched her body towards his.

He laughed exultantly. 'So, at last I have you, Louisa. And I shall make you scream.' He put his hand for a moment across her mouth. 'But it shall be with pleasure. It will be to beg for more.' He removed his hand and she felt it travel down her body as he stopped her mouth once more with his own.

She was powerless. Her limbs refused to obey her. The more she wanted to push him away the more she found herself pulling him closer. With a groan of ecstasy she closed her eyes, allowing herself to feel the touch of his skin, the caress of his lips and then finally the full thrust of his passion as he made her his.

The first light of dawn had dimmed the moonlight when she slept at last, lying naked across the bed amongst the trailing bedclothes.

The scream when it came was from Kirsty and was bitten off as soon as it had formed. 'Oh, Mrs Shelley, I'm sorry!' The girl had almost dropped the ewer of hot water she was carrying as she turned away, trying not to stare at the beautiful voluptuous body of the woman lying so wantonly on the bed.

Louisa lay still for a moment, not knowing where she was, still hazy with sleep, all memory of her dream gone, then she grabbed for the sheet and pulled it over her, inexplicably amused at Kirsty's stunned expression.

'Kirsty! Come in. Bring the water.' Sitting up she swept her hair back off her face with her hands. 'Forgive me. It was so hot last night I threw off the bedclothes.'

And her nightdress. She could see it lying in a crumpled heap near the window.

Kirsty had regained her composure. Her eyes fixed on the floor she set the jug down. 'Do you want me to help you dress, Mrs Shelley?'

Louisa shook her head. 'Not yet, thank you. I'll take a moment to wake up. I'll ring if I need you.'

Her whole body was alive and tingling. She felt younger than she had felt for years. Young and happy and excited.

She waited, swathed in the sheet, for the girl to leave the room, then she climbed out of bed and walked naked over to the open window. The morning air was cool and she shivered as she bent to pick up her night-gown. It was torn almost in two. She frowned, staring down at it. Had she caught it on something? Had she sleep-walked, restless in the heat of the night, and thrown it off without bothering to unfasten the ribbons which held it closed?

She glanced round the room, suddenly uneasy. She had had a strange dream, and in the dream –

But it had gone.

Walking over to the basin she poured some hot water and reaching for the embroidered wash cloth on the wooden towel rail she began to sponge her face and neck. When she reached her breasts she winced. Looking down at herself she realised suddenly that they were reddened and sore. With an exclamation of surprise she went to stand in front of the cheval mirror in the corner of the room and stared at herself in horror. There were bruises on her arms and breasts, her nipples were engorged and there was a mark on her neck which

22

looked suspiciously like a bite. She stood for several moments unable to move, her whole body numb with shock, then slowly she raised her hands and ran them gently over her cold skin. Her body tingled with anticipation. She stroked her thumb over the bruise on her hip and felt herself respond with a leap of desire so overwhelming that she gasped out loud.

She did not call Kirsty to help her dress. Painfully she pulled on her petticoat, her loose cotton drawers and one of her pretty aesthetic dresses, the kind which had so shocked her hosts in Egypt seven years before, but which were now blessedly a fashion item and approved even in *The Queen Magazine* as an acceptable alternative to tightly corseted waists and the bustle. Around her neck she fastened a velvet ribbon to hide the red mark.

It was as she was slipping on her shoes that she found the brooch on the floor, half hidden by the trailing bedclothes. She picked it up and stared at it. Deeply engraved silver surrounded a large golden topaz-like stone – a few strands of fine red wool were caught in the pin as though it had been torn from someone's shoulder.

She sat down, turning it over and over in her hands, then leaping to her feet she ran over and dragged the covers back off the bed, staring down at the sheets. They were spotless.

Lord Carstairs. The man who filled her with loathing and horror; the man of whom she was so desperately afraid; she remembered it all now; he had been there, in her room; he had hurt her. And yet – she hesitated even to address the thought – the touch of his hands, his lips – had given her pleasure.

For a long time she stood without moving, trying to understand what had happened. Her body ached; her clothes were ripped. She had his brooch. And yet this man was, as far as she knew, four thousand miles away in America. It had been a dream. But how could it have been?

She tried to force herself to confront what had happened. He had been there. In her room.

He must have been.

She shuddered. No. It wasn't possible

3

'We leave for Edinburgh this morning, Louisa my dear.' David Fielding smiled at her as she appeared at last in the breakfast room. 'And Katherine was wondering if you would like to accompany us. If Sarah could spare you for a few days I am sure you would enjoy it.'

Louisa found herself giving a deep exhausted sigh. Until last night this place had been a haven; a retreat from her dreams and nightmares. But now everything had changed. Even the thought of spending time with Venetia might be better than living with a dream like last night's. She turned from the sideboard with her bowl of porridge to take her place at the table, her mind almost made up to accept, but Sarah was already speaking.

'Bless you, David, for the thought, but I have already planned to take Louisa to Edinburgh later in the month. I'm afraid I can't possibly spare her now. We have so much planned. So many things to do.'

'I was right to say that, wasn't I?' she said to Louisa later. 'I could see you and Venetia do not get on. I'm so sorry. I didn't realise. I had thought we were all friends. But at least I could spare you the long journey in her company.' She paused. 'Are you all right, Louisa? You look a little feverish.'

Louisa and she had watched the Fieldings depart an hour earlier with their nurses and their children and were now seated on the bench in the shade of one of the great cedars on the lawn behind the house. Sarah had brought her embroidery outside with her, Louisa a sketchbook and a box of watercolours and the latest letters from her two sons. All lay untouched on the seat beside her. How could she tell her hostess she would rather have driven on with the others even if that meant tolerating the company of the odious Venetia; that she dreaded another night under this roof because of her dreams. If they were dreams. She pictured again the brooch, now hidden in her own jewel box, and the man who had been wearing it.

As though reading her thoughts Sarah went on, 'We haven't talked about our visit to Carstairs Castle. What did you think of the place?'

Louisa was staring down across the grass towards the distant hills. 'Very impressive.'

'Do I gather Venetia has a fondness for his lord-ship?'

'She has always found him attractive, I believe.' Louisa smiled grimly.

'Oh, but he is. Devilishly attractive!' Sarah giggled. 'If I were a little younger I might have set my cap at him myself.' She raised an eyebrow. 'You are still young enough to ensnare him, Louisa. How would you like a title and a fortune? It is such a long time since your husband died. Think what fun you could have. A man with a certain reputation!' She was setting her stitches with care, not looking at Louisa's face.

'He is in America, Sarah.' Louisa's voice was so taut that Sarah at last glanced up. Her guest's face was as white as a sheet. Their eyes met. 'He is in America.' Louisa repeated. 'Isn't he?'

'Yes, my dear. Of course he is.' Sarah put down her sewing. 'What is it? You look frightened.'

'I dreamed about him last night.' Louisa bit her lip. 'It was so real. I –' She hesitated, shaking her head. 'It was so real I found it hard to believe it was a dream.'

The brooch was not a dream. Nor were the bruises on her body.

Sarah was still studying her face, her embroidery lying discarded on her knee. 'And it was not a pleasant experience, if I read your expression aright.'

Louisa blushed scarlet. 'No.'

Yes. The treacherous word hung between them, unspoken.

For a moment Sarah continued her silent scrutiny. 'Were you – that is, did he pursue you when you were all in Egypt, my dear?' She leaned forward and put a gentle hand over Louisa's.

Louisa nodded.

'But you didn't encourage him.'

'Of course not.'

'Ah, I see the source of Venetia's jealousy.' Sarah sighed. 'Was he very persistent?'

Louisa nodded. 'He would not take no for an

answer –' Her voice broke. The memories were too powerful, too painful to bear.

For a moment both women sat without speaking. It was Louisa who broke the silence. She turned to her friend, her face tense with anxiety. 'Do you believe in magic? High magic, where people can put others under their spell and force them to do things they don't want to do. To have them in their power.'

Sarah stared at her. 'You think Roger Carstairs has put a spell on you?'

Louisa saw the conflict in the other woman's face. Disbelief. Amusement. And then finally horror. She shrugged. 'I don't know. It sounds crazy. Such strange things happened in Egypt. Evil things. Even now I don't know if they were coincidence or –' Her voice trailed away. She sat silently for a few more minutes, then she turned back to Sarah. 'If we could be sure he is in America I would like to go back to that museum of his.' She gave a tight smile. 'To lay a ghost.'

Sarah gave a nervous shiver. 'I am sure we have only to ask Mr Dunglass.'

'And you would come with me?'

Sarah nodded. 'Just try and stop me.'

Their excuse was that Louisa would like to sketch the great feathered head-dress which was the centre of Lord Carstairs's collection and it was arranged that the two ladies ride over early next day escorted by one of the Douglas's grooms.

Before that Louisa had to live through another night.

Kirsty had removed the torn nightdress without comment and replaced it with a fresh one from Louisa's trunk. It was lying ready on the bed when at last she came up to her bedroom that night. She had delayed her hosts for hours, begging Sarah to play the piano, asking James to tell stories of his time in India, and again when briefly he was member of parliament for the county. They both looked exhausted when at last they bade their guest goodnight at the top of the main staircase and headed towards their own bedrooms leaving her alone.

The lamp by her bed was turned low, the water in the ewer already cold. She had told Kirsty not to wait up for her; she could undress herself.

The windows were closed; the curtains drawn tightly together. Standing quite still she looked around the room, listening intently. There wasn't a sound.

The lamplight barely reached the corners of the room. Carefully, holding her breath, she searched every inch; the huge wardrobe, the alcove near the fireplace, the dark shadows behind the cheval glass, under the high bed, behind the curtains. The room was empty. Only then did she turn the key in the door, undress quickly and put on her nightgown then her dressing gown, pulling the sash tightly round her and knotting it securely. Outside, the night was velvet soft beneath the moon. Inside, the room was hot and stuffy and she longed to open the window; to step out onto the balcony. She could feel the perspiration running down between her breasts as she climbed into the bed and sat, her arms around her knees, staring towards the windows she couldn't see behind their heavy drapes.

After a while she began to doze.

She was awakened by a sharp rapping on the window

pane. She was hunched up against the pillows, still wearing her dressing gown, the sheets pulled up over her. Remaining quite still she lay staring round, her heart beating very fast, unsure what had awakened her; she had no idea how long she had been asleep.

There it was again. A sharp knock on the window. Her mouth dry with fear, she sat up and sliding her feet over the edge of the high bed she stood up. Tiptoeing towards the windows she stood immediately behind the curtain, listening intently.

By the bed the oil lamp flickered slightly and she heard a faint popping noise from the glass chimney. Oh please, let it not be running out of oil. Normally she would have turned it off long since. There was a faint murmur of sound from the window and she tensed. Could it be the slither of a snake? Something seemed to be scraping at the glass near her. Then she heard her name being whispered so quietly it could just have been the sibilance of the wind in the creepers.

Suddenly unable to stand the terror anymore she turned and flung back the curtains. The balcony was completely empty as the moonlight flooded past her into the room.

Mr Dunglass was waiting for them once more as they rode into the castle courtyard. He stabled their horses, showed them into the museum and, having confirmed that his master was most certainly still in America, left them with only the minimal of courtesies.

Sarah looked after him as he strode back across the cobbles.

'He's not feeling very sociable this morning, it seems.'

'No.' Louisa clutched her bag of drawing materials tightly to her chest as she looked round. 'Just as well. I don't feel very sociable either.' She swept off her tall hat with its veil and dropped it with her whip onto the chair by the door.

'So, what are we going to do?' Sarah whispered. Neither woman had moved more than a few steps into the room.

'I don't know.' Louisa was staring at the huge head-dress. 'I will have to sketch it. Mr Dunglass will expect to see something, but before I do –' She was staring towards the back of the room – towards the Egyptian part of the collection.

The eyes of the mummy stared, huge and blank, in a silence broken only by the sound of the skirt of her riding habit dragging on the stone floor, the tap of her high heels. She stopped by the case containing the snake and looked down at it for several seconds before rapping loudly on the glass. It didn't move.

'You didn't think it was real –' Sarah's whisper at her side made her jump.

'No. I didn't think it was real.'

'But you're afraid of it.'

'He used a snake for his magic, Sarah. In Egypt. It obeyed him. It killed for him.'

Sarah stared at her, horrified. 'And there was a snake in your dream?'

'No.' Louisa felt her face grow hot. 'But last night, on the terrace, I thought I heard something –' She paused. 'I will not be afraid, Sarah. I will not let him bully me. There must be a way of containing him.'

Sarah shuddered. 'I don't like it here. Not now. I'd

never have thought of this stuff as evil, not really, not before. But now . . .' She was looking over Louisa's shoulder towards the snake.

'Well, it is evil. Surely you've heard his reputation?'

Sarah looked abashed. 'I'm afraid I thought it rather daring knowing him. I never believed it all to be true. He has always been so utterly charming I thought that the talk of his interest in the occult must be exaggerated.'

Louisa pursed her lips. 'Charm is something that exudes from every pore of the man. But if you look closer, right into his eyes, then –' She broke off suddenly, staring round.

Sarah stepped back. 'What is it? What's happened?'

'He's here. I can feel him watching us.' Louisa caught the other woman's arm.

'Don't be silly,' Sarah whispered back. 'He can't be.' She too was staring round the room.

'He is. I can smell the pomade he uses; and that strange smoky scent I smelled in my dream.' She gave a shuddering sigh suddenly. 'Can you hear drums?'

'No.' Sarah shook her head adamantly. 'No, I can't. Come on. Let's get out of here.' She tried to pull Louisa away but Louisa tore her arm free and put her hands to her head. 'Drums! I can hear drums!'

'No, you can't. You're imagining it.'

Louisa was shaking her head, her eyes closed. 'He's trying to get into my head. I can see him. He's coming closer.'

Sarah was near panic. She pulled at Louisa's arm again, then she turned and ran towards the door. 'Mr Dunglass, come quickly!' She pulled at the door handle, but it wouldn't open. She pulled harder, rattling it desperately but again it wouldn't turn. 'Oh, my God!' She ran to the window but the windows were high up and barred on the outside. Spinning round she ran back to Louisa. 'Lou, are you all right? Lou, listen to me! It's all in your head. He's not here. He's not. He can't reach you. He's in America. It's your imagination. It has to be! Fight it, Lou!'

Louisa could see him clearly now. He was sitting in a circle of Indian braves. In the centre of the circle a fire burned, lighting the darkness of the prairie night. The men were passing a pipe one to the other, each taking a long slow draw of the aromatic smoke before passing it on to his neighbour. Like them, Roger Carstairs wore buckskin trousers and a loose shirt stitched with beads; his hair was long, swept back from his forehead and held in place by an embroidered band, hung with feathers and beads. His eyes were closed.

Louisa stepped closer to him, feeling the warm prairie soil under her bare feet, smelling the fragrant smoke, the sharp wind across the grass cold on her naked skin. Slowly he opened his eyes and he was looking straight at her.

'So, I have brought you to me, Mrs Shelley. How convenient.' He stood up slowly stepping away from the circle into the warm scented darkness beyond the reach of the firelight.

He held out his hand towards her. She stepped back quickly, aware suddenly that she was after all still wearing her green riding habit, the train now securely looped to her waist, out of the way, and her feet, a moment before bare, were encased in her high-heeled riding boots. 'Don't you touch me!' It was only in his dream that she was naked.

He smiled. 'I won't touch you. Not here, Mrs Shelley. Not in front of my brothers and – who is that with you?' He peered past her. 'Ah, Lady Douglas. My trusty and oh so incurious neighbour. So, you have drawn her into my web with you. No matter.' He reached towards Louisa and ran his finger lightly down the buttons of her habit. 'We will meet later, my dear, when we are both alone. You have to admit you will look forward to that as much as I shall. Our love-making was spectacular, was it not?'

'Louisa! Wake up!' She realised suddenly that Sarah was shaking her arm. 'Lou! Can you hear me?'

Louisa blinked. He had gone. There was no sign of him or the Indian braves or the camp fire. She was once again in the high-roofed room in the outbuilding at Carstairs Castle with Sarah.

'Louisa?' Sarah seemed near to tears. 'Please, listen to me!'

'I'm listening.' Louisa's mouth was dry, her head spinning.

'Oh, thank God! I thought you had gone mad. What happened? You were in some sort of a trance.'

'I was in America.' Louisa put her hands to her face. She took a deep shaky breath. 'I was there, where Carstairs is. Near his camp fire with lots of Indian warriors. He was dressed like them –' She was trembling violently. 'But I wasn't there, was I? I couldn't have been. It was all a dream. A horrible dream!' She caught Sarah's hand. 'How did he do it? He is using some kind

33

of trance-inducing drugs. Opiates. I don't know what. But I'm not! How did he make me go there, to him?'

The two women were staring round the room as they spoke. One wall was covered in books, safely encased behind glass, and for the first time Louisa became aware of their titles. Most were accounts of travel to distant lands, but some were about magic; drugs, shamanism, occult studies, in several languages. That was how he had done it. To Lord Carstairs oceans were no barrier. There was nowhere he could not go; nothing he could not do if he so wished.

They were suddenly aware of footsteps outside on the cobbles. Feet ran lightly up the steps to the door and it was flung open. 'Did I hear someone call?' A boy stood in the doorway – tall, red-haired, handsome, his eyes transparent grey. Louisa gave a gasp of recognition. This must be one of Lord Carstairs's sons.

'Indeed someone did call.' Sarah pushed in front of her and confronted him indignantly. 'I couldn't open the door. It was locked.'

'Locked?' He looked puzzled. 'Indeed no. I opened it just now without any bother, Lady Douglas.' He gave a gentle apologetic smile. 'Why would it be locked?'

'I don't know and I don't care.' Sarah stepped towards him. 'Would you ask Mr Dunglass to fetch our horses. We have seen enough.'

'But Mrs Shelley doesn't want to go yet.' The boy looked straight at her. 'Surely she hasn't had enough time to sketch the head-dress which she came to see. My father told me to come over specially and make sure she had everything she needed.'

'Your father,' Sarah drew herself up to her full height,

'is not here. I fail to see how he could have done any such thing.'

'I assure you he did, Lady Douglas.' The boy smiled, and suddenly Louisa could see the likeness to his father and understand, perhaps, Dunglass's obvious antipathy. The outward charm, the handsome good looks, masked an icy watchful control. This boy was dangerous.

It had taken her several seconds to compose herself enough to speak, but now she stepped forward. 'You are quite right, young man. I haven't had time to do all I wanted. Perhaps you would allow us a few more minutes and then we will call Mr Dunglass ourselves.' She took a deep breath. 'You are very like your father. He must be very proud of you.'

The boy looked startled, and for the first time they saw a hint of doubt in his eyes. 'I don't believe so, Mrs Shelley. He constantly complains of my behaviour and that of my brother.' He shrugged. 'It is only when we do small services for him, such as passing on this message, that he recognises our existence.' He looked so crestfallen for a moment that she felt quite sorry for him, but then the self-confidence returned and once again she saw his father's arrogance looking out from those young eyes. With a small bow, he turned and retraced his steps across the yard. To Sarah's relief he left the door open.

'Give me a few minutes. There is something I want to find,' Louisa whispered, 'and I must do a few quick notes which I can work into sketches later, then we'll go.' Leaving Sarah standing by the door she ran back into the Egyptian section of the room. There must be something there she could take. Something she could

35

use as a lever against him; something he would really care about. She glanced along the shelves at statuettes and pots, carvings and pieces of broken tile. It had to be something valuable but something that would not immediately be missed. Although Dunglass did not look like the kind of man who knew or cared about what was in his master's collection beyond the few show pieces he had described for them, that shrewd young boy would not be so easy to fool. She glanced at the glass cases around her. In one there was a selection of jewellery. Gold and enamel necklets and bracelets. Rings. She tried the lid of the case. To her surprise it wasn't locked. It lifted easily. Reaching in she took a heavy gold ring – small and half hidden by a larger item she doubted if it would be missed by anyone except Carstairs himself. With a grim smile she lowered the lid gently back into place, slipped the ring into the pocket of her habit and turned back towards the door.

4

It was late before Louisa made her way at last to her bedroom that night. Two neighbours of the Douglases had come to dine and entertained them at the piano with a succession of Scots songs before riding home at last under the brilliant moon. Tired and content Louisa let herself into her bedroom. The lamp as before had been trimmed and lit and the soft light fell across the bed where earlier Kirsty had turned down the bedclothes.

Curled up on the pillow was a huge snake.

Louisa's scream brought the Douglases running,

closely followed by several maids, a footman and the housekeeper. Sir James strode into the room, a silver-topped cane raised in his hand. 'What is the matter? What is it?' He was staring round enquiringly.

Louisa pointed at the bed. Her heart was thudding so hard she could barely breathe.

'What? Where?' Sir James marched across and stared down at the bedclothes as his wife put her arm around Louisa's shoulders.

'A snake!' Louisa could hardly speak.

'Snake?' Sir James took a step back.

'There.' She pointed, but already she knew they would find nothing. Carstairs was far too clever for that.

'Look, James.' It was Sarah, gently pushing Louisa aside, who stepped up to the bed 'There, on the pillows. You can see the indentation where it lay. And there –' She pulled the covers back. 'Sand.'

'Sand?' Sir James looked bewildered.

'Mr Graham.' Sarah turned to the butler who had appeared somewhat belatedly, his jacket awry as if he had hastily pulled it on. Judging by the slight aroma of whisky on his breath the disturbance had caught him relaxing in the servants' hall. 'Take two of the lads and search the room. How big was it?' She turned to Louisa.

'Big.' Louisa's mouth had dried. She could barely speak.

'We'll put you in another room.' Sarah hugged her again. 'Kirsty can make you up a bed, can't you, Kirsty? You can't possibly stay in here.' She shuddered. 'Oh, how horrible.'

'I don't understand this at all.' Sir James was staring round the room thoughtfully. 'The windows are shut.

How on earth could a snake get in here? What kind of snake was it, Louisa? An adder? A grass snake?'

'It was a cobra,' Louisa whispered.

'A cobra?' Sir James glared at her, clearly disbelieving. 'What nonsense. Are you sure you didn't imagine the whole thing? Perhaps you had fallen asleep and were dreaming.'

'She can hardly dream on her feet, James,' Sarah put in quietly. Behind them the servants were staring round, Mr Graham clearly of the same opinion as his master, the young women looking frightened. 'And we had said goodnight only moments before, if you remember.'

Sir James snorted. 'All right. Go and make up another room for our guest, girls, and the rest of you search in here. Carefully. If it's a cobra they are poisonous.' His glance heavenwards was not missed by the others in the room. Clearly Sir James did not believe in the creature's existence.

It was an hour later when Louisa found herself alone once more. She was in another of the plentiful guest rooms, comforted by two lamps and a cup of hot milk and the knowledge that the room had been searched as had the rest of the house. Nothing had been found in her original room, nor anywhere else, save for those few enigmatic grains of sand.

Before she returned to her room Sarah had caught her hand. 'Will you be all right?'

Louisa nodded. 'He took me by surprise. This time I shall be ready for him.'

'Be careful.' Sarah eyed her doubtfully.

'I will.' Louisa leaned forward and kissed her. 'Goodnight.'

Once the others had left her, Louisa glanced round nervously. This room too looked out over the back of the house. This room too had tall windows opening onto the long balcony. Taking a deep breath she walked over and throwing back the curtains she pushed open the casement. The moon was shining across the garden and parkland throwing deep shadows under the tall trees. Nothing moved.

'So, my lord,' she whispered. 'Have you used the last of your strength with that performance? Have you nothing else to frighten me with?'

In the distance she heard the eerie cry of an owl. She shivered. The night was uncannily still. She held out her hand, touching the stone balustrade. On her forefinger she was wearing the heavy gold ring she had taken from the case in Carstairs Castle. It gleamed softly in the moonlight.

'I have one of your treasures here, my lord, do you see? It's very beautiful. Very valuable no doubt.'

There was no response from the darkness. There was no sign that anyone had heard her challenge.

Taking off the ring she weighed it in the palm of her hand. 'Do you remember my little scent bottle? The one you wanted so badly for your collection? You thought it contained the tears of Isis and I threw it in the Nile to stop you getting it.' She paused turning the ring over in her hands. 'But someone rescued it, and it came back to me. I still have that little bottle. And now I have your ring as well. And tomorrow perhaps I shall return to the castle and take something else. And then something else. And then again.' She paused and smiled, staring out into the darkness. 'Checkmate, my lord.'

The stonework was cool under her hands, fragments of lichen catching against her skirt as on a far away plain a white man stepped out of his tepee and bowed to his hosts before sitting down by their fire. The elders of the tribe bowed back and silently resumed their scrutiny of the flames. This was a man with whom they felt at ease. A walker between the worlds like themselves, a medicine man of extreme power. A man comfortable in the presence of the Great Spirit. They did not know where it was their guest travelled under the influence of the peyote god nor did they care. That was his business and his alone.

He wasn't coming. Leaving the windows open onto the hot night Louisa went back inside the room. She drank her milk, then, turning off the lamps which were surrounded with fluttering moths she began to undress, half of her relieved that all was peaceful, half angry and tense with nervous anticipation. Pulling on her nightgown she unpinned her hair and reaching for her hairbrush she wandered towards the window, attracted by the beauty of the moonlight. She had put the ring on the table by the lamp; it lay there, gleaming gently as she stood drawing the brush through her long hair.

This time when she saw him his chest was bare. He wore the buckskin trousers and there were strings of beads around his neck as he stood staring in through the double windows with those strange colourless eyes. He bowed. 'Tonight you were expecting me, I think.'

The ring. She had taken off the ring. Squaring her

40

shoulders she looked him in the eyes. 'Why did you send a snake to my room?'

He smiled. 'To act as your body guard should you need one. You knew it wouldn't hurt you.'

'So, you still serve Isis? For all your wanderings in India and in the Americas, your heart is still in Egypt?'

He was watching her intently, his eyes probing. 'As is yours, I suspect, or have you at last forgotten your native paramour?'

Clenching her fists, she took a deep breath. 'I shall never forget Hassan, my lord. Nor the fact that you killed him.'

He laughed, the sound quietly chilling. 'He was killed by a snake, Louisa. Even my worst enemy would find it very hard to believe I could have arranged such a deed, and you surely are not my worst enemy.'

'No?' She looked at him through half-closed eyes. He wasn't real. This man, solid as he appeared, was some kind of phantasmagoria conjured by his mind and perhaps hers in a strange drug-induced union. His body was far away in the Americas, or perhaps in Egypt or India. Wherever it was, his soul had learned to step outside it and travel around the earth. And his soul was nothing but a shadow; a ghost; a dream.

She smiled, reassured by the thought.

He raised an eyebrow. 'Something amuses you, Mrs Shelley?'

'It does indeed. I was reminding myself of your insubstantial nature.' She drew herself up to her full height.

'Insubstantial, but nevertheless satisfying,' he said. There was a mocking gleam in his eye and she felt herself blush violently.

41

'A dream, my lord. Nothing more.'

'But what a dream!' He took a pace forward and reflexively she stepped back away from him. 'A dream of ecstasy and abandon,' he went on, 'one would find very hard to resist.'

'Don't take another step!' She put up her hand to ward him off and her fingers met hard smooth skin.

He looked down into her eyes. 'An excellently real dream, Mrs Shelley, you must acknowledge.' He was so close now she could feel the touch of his breath on her cheek and smell the bittersweet smokiness of that distant ceremony. 'You enjoyed our encounter last time, did you not?' His hand came up to stroke her hair and suddenly she found herself unable to move. Desperately she tried to step away from him, but she couldn't. She wanted nothing so much as for him to touch her, to hold her and pull her close once more. Slowly she felt her ability to fight him die. She raised her face to his and closed her eyes as he bent to kiss her. Her whole body responded to the touch of his lips with a thrill of excitement; her knees grew weak; she longed to give herself to him, to throw herself down and pull him with her, to abandon herself totally to the ecstasy of his love-making.

His quiet chuckle as he sensed how close he was to victory brought her to her senses. With a small exclamation of alarm she ducked away from him and ran to the bedside table. Scooping up the ring she turned with a cry of triumph. 'No, my lord. Winning me over is not that easy. Do you see this? One of your treasures, my lord. Egyptian gold. Something no doubt you value highly.' Behind him the moonlight had moved from behind the great cedar on the grass outside her window. It streamed in across the floor throwing his shadow before it, a shadow that was as substantial as hers.

'So?' He looked amused. 'My treasures are at your disposal, my dear.'

'Indeed.' She was taken aback. 'Yet you were prepared to kill for my little bottle.'

His eyes held hers for a moment. 'That was not quite the same, Louisa. The tears of the goddess, prepared by her temple priests, were irreplaceable. You destroyed not only a piece of history but a powerful link to the goddess herself. Something of inestimable value; something of power so great that it would have given its owner the keys to the world! It was an unforgivable act.'

'But you seem to have forgiven me now?' She raised an eyebrow.

'No, I haven't forgiven you.' His voice hardened. 'You amuse me. It is always a pleasure to take a beautiful woman; the more so if it makes her despise herself.'

She closed her eyes for a moment, blanking out the sudden hatred she saw in his face; shocked at how much the knowledge that he had merely been playing with her hurt. 'What if I told you the tears of Isis still exist?'

He froze, staring at her. 'What do you mean? I saw you throw the bottle in the Nile.'

So. He was not all-seeing. The confirmation of the fact comforted her. 'The bottle was wrapped in a piece of cloth which floated. My servant saved it and returned it to me.'

She saw how every muscle in his body tensed. 'And where is it now?'

It was her turn to smile. Her weakness of a moment before had turned to something like triumph. 'Nowhere you could find it, my lord. That is my secret.'

His cry of fury was cut off short as he grabbed her wrist and pulled her violently against him. 'If that little bottle still exists, I will have it. This time, Mrs Shelley, I will have it.'

She found she could look up at him almost unafraid as she spat her defiance at him. 'No, and that is my revenge, my lord. For Hassan's death. You say you were not responsible for killing him, but we both know you sent the snake to that cave. It will give me enormous pleasure to know you realise the bottle still exists, but that you will never, never see it again. If I choose to destroy it, I shall. If I choose to keep it, I shall. But you will never set eyes on it.'

She gave a small cry of fright as he pushed her violently backwards onto the bed, and climbing onto it after her, straddled her body with his knees. 'I think I know how to persuade you.'

'I don't think so.' She was still clutching the ring. 'I'm not afraid of you any more, my lord.' To her surprise she realised suddenly that it was true. 'And I have discovered your weakness. You say your treasures are at my disposal, my lord, but I doubt if you would be happy to see them lost or destroyed. In fact I think that would make you very angry. And very sad. And I suspect, if you are really in America, they are beyond your reach. You see this?' She thrust her clenched fist up into his face. 'Your ring. I am going to throw it into the loch. See how easy it was to steal? And you can't stop me, because as you have said you are not really here. And tomorrow I shall go back to your museum and I shall simper at your Mr Dunglass and flutter my eyelashes at your son and ask to paint more of your collection and they will let me in. And one by one I shall destroy your treasures. Your gold and silver. Your feathered head-dresses, your fragile mummy, and above all, that dry hollow skin which was once a snake! And you will be able to do nothing. Nothing! Because you are four thousand miles away!'

He was staring down at her, his face impassive. Only his eyes seemed alight in the shadowed sockets. He smiled coldly. 'So, don't you believe I can communicate with my sons or my factor to warn them? Believe me, I can. Not easily, I grant you with Dunglass – the man is an idiot – but my sons have promise. They are receptive. They will listen to me.' He was still, looking down at her almost thoughtfully. 'But on the whole I prefer to deal with you. You are so open, so –' He paused. 'Eager.' Releasing her wrist he put his hand to the ribbon at the neck of her nightgown and gently pulled it open. 'You are still beautiful, for an ageing woman.' He said it almost absent-mindedly then his expression changed to a cold sneer. 'But your charms have suddenly diminished. You have revealed yourself to be a spiteful witch. And witches have to be dealt with.' His hand dropped away and he sat staring down at her thoughtfully for a moment. 'I wonder how. There are so many possibilities. So many ways to contain that spite.' His weight held her immobile. She could feel the muscles of his thighs gripping her legs. He touched her cheek lightly. 'Did you dream of revenge, Louisa, as Hassan died in the dust? Did you watch the poison from the snake bite spread through his veins and think of me? How gratifying.'

Unable to bear his gloating expression for another instant she tried to wrench herself free, throwing herself sideways, but she couldn't move. Smiling he reached down and grabbed her chin, forcing her to look at him again. 'I have an idea. You like my museum. I think we will visit it together. Would you like to travel with me through the secret byways of the medicine man, the dark tunnels of the shaman, the hidden paths of the witch doctor? I know them all.' He laughed quietly. 'I know how to enter them and I know how to leave them and I know how to entrap someone's soul forever in the mists and shadows of their darkness. All I have to do is to suck your soul into mine with the time-honoured seal of possession, the traitor's kiss.'

Desperately she tried to wriggle away from him, pushing frantically at his chest, but he grabbed her wrists in one hand and with the other again forced her to look at him. Slowly, smiling all the time, he leaned forward and pressed his lips once more against hers.

She held her breath, fighting him, trying frantically to squirm away from him, kicking, wrenching, but it was no good. Her strength was failing; the world was starting to spin and at last, unable to stop herself, she drew in a long gasping breath of the smoky essence of the man above her and immediately she was whirling away into the dark.

When she opened her eyes all was black. Her head was throbbing and she was very cold. She tried to speak but no sound came and all around her the silence was

46

profound. Cautiously she tried to move her limbs. Her body felt stiff and bruised and she was very afraid.

'So, you came with me.' The voice in her ear was very close.

'Where is this? What's happened?' She managed to speak at last.

'I have brought you to see my museum.' She heard a movement beside her. 'Wait. I'll light the lamp.'

She sensed him move away, heard the rattle of matches, saw a flame. Seconds later a gentle light filled the room as he settled the glass chimney over the wick.

'How did we get here?' She found she was standing in the middle of the floor near the case of Egyptian artefacts. A glance down told her she was still dressed in her nightgown. The ring was still on her finger.

'We flew.' The sardonic look in his eyes did not escape her.

'I see.' She pursed her lips. 'I'm dreaming. I know I'm dreaming. Did you drug me?'

He put his head on one side. 'All it would have taken was a few drops of laudanum in your milk.'

She groaned. 'And you've been here all along? Skulking somewhere in this great castle playing games? No! I don't think so!' She was suddenly furious at her own fear. 'So, what are you going to do with me now? You've made it clear you see me as ancient and ugly so no doubt my virtue is not in danger.'

'I seem to remember that your virtue is already lost.' He raised an eyebrow. 'But I would be more inclined, Louisa, to wonder if there is a threat to your life.' He folded his arms. 'No one knows where you are. And I am in America.' He gave a laconic smile. 'Should you disappear no one would ever find you. No one would even know where to look.'

She stared at him. His eyes were like clear glass, the pupils pin pricks in the lamplight, the sensuous mouth set in a thin hard line. 'Are you saying you want to kill me?' Her brow creased with puzzlement but her fear strangely had eased a little. She felt distanced from him; unreal.

'Your life or death is a matter of indifference to me, Louisa. As it should be to anyone who understands the nature of the soul and its journeyings. The thought of death merely serves as a lever to lesser mortals who value this transitory life.' He gave a cold smile. 'I am prepared to bargain. The tears of Isis for a human life.' He was watching her carefully. 'The gods of the under-world may not take my bargain so lightly when they weigh your soul in the balance and find it was you who stole the sacred ampulla.'

'I have stolen nothing.' She managed to straighten her shoulders. 'The tears of Isis as you call them are safe. As is your ring. So far. You on the other hand appear to be planning robbery with violence. Something which I would have thought would weigh heavy when your turn comes.' She turned away from him and walk-ing towards the case of Egyptian treasures she lifted the lid and stared down at them. 'And your threat means little to me, my lord. You forget that if you kill me, you send me to join Hassan. I can think of no greater joy.' She glanced up at him and it was her turn to smile. 'You care so little for human life. That makes you funda-mentally evil, in my book.' She turned away again. 'Take care, my lord, for your soul. I can see demons hovering round you ready to drag you screaming down to hell.'

He threw back his head and laughed. 'Well done, Mrs Shelley. You are learning fast.' He stepped towards her and stood for a moment looking down at the artefacts inside the case. Gently he ran his finger over a small statue, a smile on his lips. Then he moved back and carefully closed the lid. 'Alas, I can't spend much longer debating this point with you. Where is the ampulla?'

'In London.' She returned his smile. 'In safe keeping.'

'We'll go there. Now.'

'Now?' She stared at him. 'I don't think so. How do you propose to transport us there?'

'The same way we came here.' His voice was grim. He reached for her wrist, but she jumped back. 'No. No more. I'm going nowhere with you.' She grabbed at the lamp base and lifted it high. 'Stand away from me, or I will throw this in amongst your precious collection. I mean it. Stand right away.'

His face went white. 'Be careful! Some of these things are priceless. Please put that down.'

'I don't think so.' The lamp was heavy. She wasn't going to be able to hold it much longer.

As he lunged towards her with a cry of fury, she half dropped half flung it into the glass topped cabinet. The glass shattered and a stream of burning oil ran between the priceless artefacts in the case. In seconds the more fragile had caught alight and a sheet of flame shot up. She heard Carstairs shout, saw him leap towards the flames, then she turned and ran towards the door.

It was locked. Dragging at the handle she heard

herself beginning to sob as the heat engulfed her and slowly, for the second time that night, all went black.

'Mrs Shelley? Mrs Shelley! I've brought your hot water.'

The voice was persistent, dragging her into wakefulness. 'Mrs Shelley, it's late. Lady Douglas was worried.'

Opening her eyes Louisa stared into the anxious face of the little Scots maid who, having pulled back the curtains, was leaning over her bed.

'Kirsty?' Her head was thumping, her eyes and throat sore. 'I'm sorry. I had such a nightmare.' Somehow she managed to lever herself into a sitting position. She stared round the room. Outside the sky was overcast.

'There is a storm coming.' Kirsty reached down and picked Louisa's dressing gown off the floor. 'Thunder, can you hear it? That's the nice weather gone for a while.' She glanced at Louisa's face. 'Would you like me to bring you something, Mrs Shelley? You look terrible.'

Louisa managed a painful smile. 'I feel terrible. I expect it's the storm. And the bad dream.'

She was remembering more and more. Carstairs. His threat to kill her. The fire. She stared down at her hands clutching the sheet. The huge gold ring was still there on the forefinger of her right hand.

'Louisa?' Sarah's voice in the doorway made both women look up. Sarah bustled in, took one look at her guest and turned to the maid. 'Would you bring some coffee please, Kirsty.'

Kirsty bobbed a small curtsey and disappeared as Sarah pulled herself up onto the bed. 'Well? How did you sleep? Not well, judging by the look of you.' She leaned forward and pushed Louisa's hair back off her flushed face. 'Did anything happen?'

'Oh yes.' Louisa gave a grim smile. 'I dreamed about him. He came here and threatened me . . . and then . . .' She hesitated. 'We were back in the museum. He said he was going to kill me and I overturned the lamp and set fire to his precious collection.' She put her face in her hands. 'Oh, Sarah, it was awful. I can't tell you how awful.'

'My poor dear.' Sarah squeezed her hand, then she stood up and walked over to the windows. 'Look, it's beginning to rain. I'll shut the windows for you.' She paused. 'How strange. Look at this.' She was unhooking what looked like a necklace from the wisteria around the door. 'Is this yours? How pretty. It's all made of shells and beads.'

Louisa slid from the bed. Padding barefoot across the floor she took it in her hands, staring down at it. 'It's his. He was wearing native American dress.' She glanced up at Sarah. Her face was white. 'It's his, Sarah.'

The two women looked at one another.

'So, he was here?'

Louisa bit her lip. 'He can't have been.'

'Then it was a dream.'

Louisa looked up, her eyes huge and frightened. 'I don't understand it. I thought it was a dream, but . . .' She paused looking at the necklace. 'He said he had drugged me with laudanum. He could have bribed Kirsty –'

'Rubbish!'

'In my milk. She could have put it in my milk.'

'Absolutely not. She wouldn't. She is completely loyal.'

'Then it was a dream. All of it. But where did this come from?'

They stared at each other in silence. Louisa was remembering the brooch. 'When I see him he is always dressed in strange garb,' she said at last, thoughtfully. 'In Egypt too he always affected the dress of the natives. And last night he was dressed in skins and beads.' She shook her head. 'Why does he do it? Is it to frighten me?'

'I've never seen him wear anything other than formal dress,' Sarah said. She gave a wry smile. 'He's a good-looking man.'

'I suppose he is.' Louisa's reply was reluctant. They both glanced at the door as Kirsty came in with the tray of coffee. She set it down on the table then turned to them, her eyes bright. 'My lady, have you heard? The news is all over the servants' hall. There was a fire at Carstairs Castle last night. Lord Carstairs's museum and all the outbuildings and stables were burned out. There were no horses hurt, but all his wonderful things are gone!'

Louisa gasped. She staggered back to the bed and sat down. Kirsty stared at her. 'Are you all right, Mrs Shelley? Of course!' She clapped her hand to her mouth. 'You were both there only yesterday. Oh, my lady!' She turned to her mistress, distraught. 'It's so terrible. I don't know what his lordship will do when he finds out.'

'The servants would know, would they not, if he had returned unexpectedly?' Sarah asked with a thoughtful glance at Louisa.

Kirsty nodded. 'Oh yes, we'd know. Catriona has a great fondness for his man, Donald, who went with him to America. They are not expected back until next spring. Mr Graham says they are blaming the factor, Mr Dunglass. He left a lamp burning in there and it was knocked over in the night.'

'How?' Louisa asked sharply. 'How was it knocked over? Was there someone there?'

'I suppose there must have been. I don't know, Mrs Shelley.' Kirsty shrugged.

As the girl closed the door behind her Sarah went and sat next to Louisa on the bed. 'Your revenge at least was real, it seems.'

Louisa nodded. 'And I escaped, Sarah. But did he?'

5

For the next few days the countryside could talk of nothing but the fire at Carstairs Castle. As far as could be ascertained no one was hurt in the catastrophe; no one had been found amongst the wreckage, but the collection itself, estimated to be worth countless thousands of pounds, had been totally destroyed. Urgent messages were despatched by telegraph and by letter to Lord Carstairs himself, but no one it appeared knew quite where he was. He had left New York in the late spring, travelling west, and no one had heard from him since. Mr Dunglass was interviewed by the police, as were his lordship's two sons and their tutor. All denied ever having taken a lamp into the museum, never mind lighting it, and Louisa's hastily drawn sketches were scanned as evidence of what had been there. She pointed out that she could hardly have bothered to paint such an everyday item as a lamp – but then before the police could question her and Lady Douglas further about their visits, news came that Mr Dunglass had packed his bags and fled. His panic confirmed his guilt in many eyes.

Louisa moved back to her original bedroom and continued to paint the gardens and the moors as the storms passed and the good weather returned. Her dreams remained untroubled. She had no nocturnal visitors. But the fear was still there. She had locked the ring and the string of beads away in her jewel case with the topaz brooch and tried not to think about what had happened. Until one morning she received a letter. It was from George Browning, her sons' tutor. 'I don't want to alarm you, but we seem to have had an intruder in the house. A very thorough, I would say almost professional, search has been made of every room. I cannot ascertain that anything is missing – certainly nothing obvious, but I am worried that a particular search was made of your studio and some sketches and paintings may be lost. Also there appears to be something there of which I have no recollection. I have checked with the boys and they do not recognise it either. A small paperweight of what looks like solid gold carved in the shape of a coiled snake was left on the table in your studio. Beneath it was a paper inscribed with hieroglyphics of some sort. The boys feel it is a message from some person you met on your Egyptian travels and are much excited by it. I should reassure you that they have not been in the least alarmed by these occurrences and are indeed very reluctant to return to their grandmother's care next week . . .'

Louisa passed the letter to Sarah. 'I have to go home. Today. He's back. He's left me a message.'

Sarah went with her. On Louisa's urgent instructions George had removed the boys at once back to their grandmother's house so it was to a depleted household that they made their way from the station in a hansom cab. Louisa's cook housekeeper, Mrs Laidlaw, and one maid, Sally Anne, were there to greet them.

Louisa went straight to her studio. There on the table as George Browning had said sat the gold serpent. She had last seen it in the museum at Carstairs Castle.

'Am I never to be rid of him?' Louisa turned to Sarah in anguish.

They had taken off their hats and coats and settled into chairs in the pretty drawing room overlooking the small garden of Louisa's terraced London house.

'Has he taken anything?'

'I don't know.' Louisa was staring round the room. 'I haven't noticed anything. There is only one thing he wants.'

'And is it there?'

Louisa shrugged. Standing up she led the way back into her studio and stood in front of the davenport where she did her correspondence. The studio was very cold; there was a strange smell in there she couldn't immediately identify – not paint. Not linseed oil, or charcoal. Something sweet and slightly exotic. She shivered. 'I put it in there. In the secret drawer.'

'See if it's there.'

Louisa put her hand out to the polished wood of

the desk lid. Then she shook her head. 'Supposing he's watching me.'

'Watching?' Sarah glanced over her shoulder uneasily. 'How could he be watching?'

'How could he do any of the things he does?' Louisa replied crossly. She moved away from the desk. 'He has been in this room. How else could the snake have got here? It is a message. A warning. Oh, Sarah what am I to do? Can't you feel it? There is something here. Someone.' She picked up the piece of paper with its strange illegible message and stared at it, then with it still in her hand she turned on her heels and swept out of the room with Sarah behind her.

In the drawing room where Mrs Laidlaw had brought them a tray of tea Louisa threw the piece of paper with its scrawled hieroglyphics down onto the table.

'What does it say? Can you read it?'

Louisa shook her head. Bending over it she ran her finger lightly over the symbols which had been inscribed there, then drew her hand away sharply.

'What is it? What's wrong?' Sarah's blue eyes were fixed on the paper.

'Nothing. It felt hot. My imagination.'

Sarah glanced up sharply. 'Are you sure?'

Louisa shrugged. 'I'm sure of nothing. I don't know why he's left this. He must realise I can't read it.'

'He's just trying to frighten you. Tear it up.'

Louisa shook her head. 'Supposing it's important. These symbols. They have power.'

'Exactly.' Sarah stood up. She reached for the paper. 'If you won't destroy it, I will.' About to throw it into the fireplace she stopped with a gasp.

The figure in front of them was no more substantial than a wisp of mist but both women saw it. Both shrank back. The paper dropped from Sarah's hand and she fell back into her chair, white-faced.

'Dear God!' Louisa's whisper was barely audible. 'The djinn. The evil djinn!'

Already the figure had gone. It had been no more than a shadow.

'What was that?' Sarah's voice shook.

'Hatsek. The priest of Sekhmet. Two priests follow my ampulla and fight over it.' Louisa's voice was dreamlike. 'Hassan called them djinn. The paper that came with the bottle was inscribed with their names. I don't read hieroglyphs but I suppose this is what is written here.' She took a deep shaky breath.

She bent and picked up the piece of paper. 'You were right. It must be destroyed.' Without giving herself time for second thoughts she walked across to the fireplace and threw the paper down. Then she reached for the box of Vestas on the mantelpiece. In seconds the paper was a pile of ash.

She gave a deep sigh. 'I hope that is the last we shall see of him!' She shuddered.

Sarah gave a shrill laugh. 'You hope! Louisa. Do you realise what happened just now? We saw a –!' She paused, at a loss as to how to describe it. 'A ghost? A spirit? An ancient Egyptian! And you *hope* it won't come back!'

'It was a warning.' Louisa shrugged.

'So, will the fire stop it coming again?' Sarah stared down at the small heap of ashes.

Louisa nodded. 'I think so.' She gave a grim laugh.

'Fire would appear to have a cleansing effect on most things.'

And so it seemed. In the days that followed the household settled into calm. Louisa unpacked. She forced herself to check the house minutely. There was no sign of anything missing. The only place she did not look was the davenport. There was no need.

News came from Scotland that Mr Dunglass had been arrested in Glasgow. He had, it appeared, been quietly salting away a fortune in cash and valuables from the castle and the authorities looked no further for a cause of the fire. The case was closed. The two Carstairs boys, they heard, had been sent to a distant relative in the far north of Scotland for the rest of the summer. There was still no news of the absent lord.

In October came a letter from Augusta Forrester. The Fieldings had returned home, it said, with the wonderful tidings that Venetia had met a widower in Edinburgh and agreed to marry him. He had both a title, although not one as exalted as that of Lord Carstairs, and a small fortune as well as a goodly estate and she was content. Reading the letter Louisa smiled. Poor Venetia. If only she knew the fate she had been spared had she won her noble lord.

With many hugs and kisses and promises that they would meet again in Scotland the following year Sarah said her farewells and left and Louisa's two boys returned from their grandmother. Her eldest son David was beginning his second year at Eton; his brother John returned to the schoolroom with George Browning. The staff was completed by the return of Louisa's man servant, Norton, from a holiday with his family in Hertfordshire.

The day after Sarah left, Louisa's nightmares about Egypt returned. But this time she did not dream about Hassan. Instead she was standing on the banks of the River Nile, the scent bottle in her hand, about to throw it into the water, when she realised there was a man standing in front of her. A tall, swarthy man dressed in the skins of a lion. 'Do not dare to throw it!' His mouth did not move but she felt the strength of his thoughts as though he had screamed them at her. 'Do not throw! What you hold is sacred.'

She woke up with a start and sat up, shaking. The priest of Sekhmet had returned in her dream. His face was stern and forbidding, his eyes piercing, as he stood over her. The following night she was not on the banks of the Nile; he was here, in her room, bending over her bed.

Her screams brought Mrs Laidlaw and Sally Anne running from their bedrooms, just above hers in the attic. Luckily John and George Browning had not heard her and were not disturbed.

The next morning she went into the studio and stared at the davenport. Why had he returned? What did he want her to do? The answer to that came very swiftly. Two nights later she was preparing for bed, standing dreamily in her room, brushing her hair by the light of a bedside candle, when she became aware of someone standing near her in the shadows. The brush fell from her hand as she turned.

'Egypt. Take it back to Egypt.' The voice rang in her

ears. 'The tears of Isis belong in her own land; the ampulla must return whence it came.' She could see him in the shadows.

'How can I? How can I take it back?' she stammered, but already he had gone.

As the autumn nights drew in Louisa felt her strength waning. She found it hard to eat and coughed incessantly, but she returned to her painting. Day after day she retired to the studio and embarked upon a new series of pictures of Scotland. The magic of loch and mountain could not however drive her demons away and at last she found herself painting the priests of ancient Egypt, Hatsek and his one time colleague and eternal enemy, Anhotep, who haunted her dreams, as though by capturing them on canvas she could exorcise them from her brain.

It didn't work. Still they returned, sometimes apart, sometimes together, arguing with each other, arguing with her, every time coming closer, appearing more threatening, more inexorable. In her misery she wrote to Sarah, to the Forresters, even to the Fieldings. Then one night as sleep failed yet again to come and she sat up in bed reading, the one person who had not haunted her dreams in London appeared once more. Carstairs came back.

She looked up from her book to see him standing at the end of the bed watching her. He was dressed in an open necked voluminous white shirt and baggy trousers with a broad sash into which was thrust a scimitar.

'So, clever Mrs Shelley. So devious. So cunning. You have hidden the ampulla from me, set a priest to guard it and you have destroyed my life's work into the bargain. But don't think you can continue to outwit me. I shall have that bottle. I know it is here.'

Louisa clutched her wrap around her shoulders, shivering. 'If you have not found it by now, my lord, I think it unlikely you ever will,' she said defiantly. She held his gaze. 'So, where have you been? Where are you now? Still in America? Or have you returned to Scotland? Or are you really here, in the flesh, having walked up the stairs like a mere mortal? Did you ring the bell and ask Norton to show you up? I must confess, I did not hear a knock at my door.'

'A walker between the worlds does not knock.' He folded his arms. 'Anymore than does a priest of the old gods.' He narrowed his eyes. 'When I leave here I shall set something to guard the sacred bottle from you and from the priest. Wherever it is my serpent will protect it. I cannot guarantee the safety of your household or your children, Mrs Shelley. Please do not sacrifice another life for the sake of something so trifling. You have no interest in my bottle save to thwart me. Is that not so?'

She shrugged. 'You are probably right. It is just that I cannot rid myself of the notion that whatever power lies in that bottle should be used for good, if it is used at all. And you, my lord, intend to use it for your own evil purposes.'

'So, you would risk your sons' lives?'

'There will be no risk.' She continued to hold his gaze defiantly. 'I can send John back to his grandparents at any time. He will be safe there –'

He shook his head. 'Do you still underestimate me so grievously, Louisa?'

'I don't underestimate you. Far from it. But I have realised that I can fight you. Remember your priest of Sekhmet, my lord? Remember the lion goddess? The lioness is invincible in the protection of her children. You threaten my children and I will unleash more rage than you can ever contemplate.'

Without realising it she had risen to her knees on the bed. He took a step backwards. 'If there is a snake in my studio I will banish it. If there is evil in this house I will destroy it and you with it.' She paused. 'Where are you, Lord Carstairs? Are you still in America with your Indian braves?' And now she realised that she recognised the costume he was wearing. 'No, of course, you are in Egypt.' She smiled. 'Is the call so strong?'

'The priest of Sekhmet wants his ampulla returned. Tell me where it is and I will leave you in peace.'

'No! Hassan gave me that ampulla. It was his gift. It contains all I have of his love. So, you will never set eyes on it. Never!' Her voice had risen desperately almost to a shout and seconds later there was an urgent knock at her door. 'Mrs Shelley? Is something wrong, madam?' It was Norton's voice. 'Shall I call Mrs Laidlaw?'

'Thank you, Norton. I am all right. I am sorry to have woken you. Please go back to bed,' she called over her shoulder. When she turned back towards the room. Lord Carstairs had gone.

And so had the golden snake. The next morning when Louisa went downstairs into her studio the statuette had vanished from the shelf where she had put it above the table where she worked. She did not even bother to call the staff to enquire as to its whereabouts. She knew who had taken it.

She searched the studio from top to bottom, not for a golden snake, but for a live one, alert every second to the possibility of the sound of scales slithering on the floor or over the shelves. None came and slowly she settled down to her day's painting, conscious of the sounds around the house – the servants going about their business, John and George working in the small morning room which had been set aside for their studies, the distant rattle of wheels and hooves upon the roadway outside and the rustle of wind in the golden leaves in the garden.

The figure of Lord Carstairs cast no shadow as he stood between her and the sunlight flooding through the window. 'Where is it?' His voice was a hiss of fury.

She did not make the mistake of glancing at the davenport. Slowly she stood up, the paintbrush still clutched in her hand. 'Nowhere you will ever find it!'

She realised suddenly that they were not alone. Two other figures hovered in the room. Two priests. The guardians of the bottle. He spotted them almost as soon as she did and whirled to face them. 'So, the moment of confrontation has come! I am sure, my lords of the ancient world, that you are as anxious as I to return the sacred ampulla to the place it rightfully belongs. I can take it there. I can transport it over time and space.' He stepped closer to Louisa. 'Only one person stands between us and our hearts' desire, my lords.'

'Do not touch her!' The voice seemed so loud it appeared to fill the spaces of the room, the house, even the sky outside.

Carstairs shrank back. Then he put his hand to his belt

and Louisa realised that a wickedly curved broad-bladed sword hung there. As he pulled it free she dropped her paintbrush and fled towards the door. Her shout for help died on her lips. Glancing round as she groped for the doorknob she saw the raised scimitar catch the sunlight in a blinding flash. There was a huge crash. It was not her he had attacked, but the two priests, spirits from another world, and as suddenly as they had come, all three men disappeared.

Shaking with fear she took a step forward. Then another. Nothing in the room appeared to have been touched. The only sign of the interruption was the small splash of bright colour on the thick watercolour paper, where her hand had smudged it, and the paintbrush lying on the floor.

She never saw Lord Carstairs again. Nor the priests, and if a snake appeared in her studio to guard the sacred ampulla she was never aware of it.

That wasn't the end of the story of course, for the ampulla remained in her desk. She never forgot it, but neither did she think about it. If one day her sons or one of their descendants wanted to take it to Egypt that would be up to them. The portrait of the two priests she pushed into a dark corner. It was not shown in any of her exhibitions. It never occurred to her that someone, some day long after her time, might think the little bottle a pretty trinket suitable to give to a child.

What Price Magic?

'Why move?' they had said. 'Let him be the one to go. He's found a new life, a new woman; let him find a new home somewhere else.' But she knew she couldn't do it. The house was their house; the garden their garden; the furniture mostly their furniture that they had chosen together. She wanted to move on, to start again with nothing to remind her of the past and how happy they had been.

It had been very hard when she knew she was losing him. Shock, pain, outrage, anger had all taken their place in the queue with loss of self-esteem, but she had forced herself to come through it, and now here she was in a small Victorian terraced cottage instead of a large modern house, in a town instead of the country, with new furniture and even – especially – a new bed. She had defiantly chosen a huge king-size bed. It took up most of the bedroom and came with a gloriously comfortable mattress – not the iron-hard orthopaedic job Steven had needed for his back. She smothered it in a bright duvet and dozens of pillows, and had a TV in the bedroom.

That part of being divorced was good. She could watch her choice of programmes all the time and take her supper to bed if she felt like it. Or breakfast. Or lunch. And she had independence and freedom. And a new-found ability to make decisions and realise that they were perfectly valid. And time for herself. And money.

It might have been better had she needed to work, but Steven had been generous – guilt, she supposed – and that was the problem. A delightful town, a picturesque street, pleasant neighbours, but no friends. She was lonely. She should have stayed where she was, where her friends had been supportive and sympathetic and angry on her behalf. But they had been too angry. Angrier than she was. They kept on about Steven and what he had done, and they wouldn't let her move on. She wanted new friends who hadn't known him. People who would show her how to get over that one last hurdle: the feeling that she hadn't been good/beautiful/successful/young enough to keep her man. But how to meet them? And how to feel a different person?

She stood naked in front of the bathroom mirror and surveyed herself critically. Figure – not bad. Skin – quite good. Legs – still definitely an asset. Eyes – beautiful, or so Steven used to say, and presumably they had not changed. Hair – neat, quite attractive. But even naked the overall effect was demure. How could one look demure naked? She tried a few un-demure poses. No, she had to admit, demure seemed to come naturally.

She went into her bedroom and threw open the cupboard. Smart/pretty. Mid-length hems. Court shoes. Demure. And – she had to face it – middle-aged! But she wasn't middle-aged! It came out as a wail inside her head. Was she?

Steven obviously thought she was. The new wife was twenty years younger than she was. But also, to her astonishment when she had finally seen (not met, not allowed to meet) her successor, she, too, was demure. So that proved that she had been the wife Steven had wanted her to be. The wife he had conjured out of the malleable young girl she had been. He had made her demure, and she, Janet, didn't want to be demure any more. She went back to the bathroom and stared at herself again. What could she do about it?

Strangely, it hadn't occurred to her to throw out her clothes when she began her new life. They had escaped the blitz intact, to every last Jaeger sweater and Jacquemar scarf. The trouble was, how did she want to look? She wasn't sure.

She put on some clothes – a sensible skirt, tailored shirt, double row of cultured pearls – brushed her hair neatly, and slotted her handbag on her arm. She set out purposefully for the centre of town, where she veered away from the stores she usually frequented and headed for the network of medieval lanes behind the cathedral, looking for the smart 'little shops'.

Meeting Annette was providential.

Janet was staring at a strikingly attractive narrow window display on the corner of St Anne's Lane, featuring a dress of the kind she secretly coveted but had never had the courage to buy, when she noticed another woman apparently rapt in admiration of the same dress. She gave her a shy glance. 'It's pretty, isn't it?'

The other woman was, Janet saw in the quick scrutiny she allowed herself, stunningly attractive. She was slim, dressed in a style not dissimilar to the clothes in the window, and had an enviably relaxed elegance. Janet gave her another surreptitious, admiring look. The woman smiled. 'I'm glad you like it. I've just finished arranging it. That's why I was checking what it looked like.'

Janet felt herself blush. 'It's your shop?'

The woman nodded. 'I'm Annette.' She indicated the sign on the fascia. 'Do come inside and look round if you like.'

It was the first shop Janet had entered on her quest for a new identity and she looked round curiously, made an instant assessment of Annette's obvious grasp of style, and, as the shop was small and empty at that moment of other customers, and the smallness and emptiness fostered a feeling of confidence and confidentiality, she told Annette everything.

And found herself trying on long, soft dresses with plunging necklines, shoes with platform soles, ropes of beads and fringed scarves. She was made to bend from the waist and comb her hair up the wrong way until it stood round her head in a wild ruff which made her look – and feel – twenty years younger. She was bullied into trying new eye-shadow and lipstick out of Annette's own cosmetic bag, and at last she was allowed to look at herself in the full-length mirror. She was speechless.

'Pleased?' Annette tried to hide her own delight. The transformation was stunning.

Then Janet hit a problem. The trouble was she couldn't bring herself to wear her lovely new clothes outside the house. However much the image was one she had dreamed of, she just didn't have the courage to step outside dressed like that. Disparaging phrases like 'mutton dressed as lamb' floated through her head, phrases which she was sure no longer made sense in a world where everyone, except perhaps her, could please themselves as to how they looked. The image just did not fit her, however much she longed for it to.

She did wear the dress when Annette came over to see her – their bond in the dressing-room had gelled instantaneously into friendship – and she felt exotic and free in a world full of new possibilities. But when Annette and her bubbling enthusiasm went home Janet, crossly aware that this was Steven's legacy but finding herself incapable of overcoming her inhibition, guiltily crept back into the boring anonymity of her demure image.

On one visit Annette showed Janet how to rinse her hair with nettles and rosemary and how to scent her skin with rose and jasmine (making herbal potions was her hobby when the dress shop was shut), but when she had gone home Janet angrily brushed her hair back into its neat, permed order, and with the neatness came her old submissive, demure personality. And it made her furious with herself.

* * *

Her life might have gone on like that were it not that one Saturday Annette persuaded her to go to the natural healing exhibition in the town hall. It was not at all the sort of thing Janet would normally have gone to, but Annette was selling some of her prettily bottled mixtures there. Janet desperately wanted to wear her new dress and was perplexed as to why it felt so wrong. She took it off and decided that, as it was so hot, Annette wouldn't find a floaty summer dress – demure, but cool – too odd. But she went convinced she wouldn't enjoy herself.

The place was packed. She began to wander around and was soon lost among the crowds whose dress, she noticed, was completely eclectic. Jeans, dresses, skirts. Long, short, mini. Anyway, you could hardly see what people wore because of the crowds. Comforted by the lack of conformity and the general bonhomie, she forgot to be demure and soon found she was enjoying herself enormously. She loved the sheer dottiness of it all. She loved the people and the things. She bought herself a beautiful ring with a healing amethyst set in knotted silver, a book of cookery recipes to keep her young, and, when at last she found Annette in a small corner stall between a man selling biorhythm charts and another selling runes, she bought herself some bath-oil in a blue bottle tied with a pale pink ribbon. She watched demonstrations of Tai Chi, yoga and Japanese sword-fighting, and stood absorbed by an Adonis who was practising inversion therapy by hoisting a beautiful woman, mercifully clad in jeans, upside down into the air and balancing her on his hands while he lay on his back and peered up into her cleavage with a look of serene transcendence. She had a cup of herbal tea and a flapjack with sufficient roughage to pave the town square, and then wandered over to look at the Buddhist stand.

The tall man in charge sported the ubiquitous pony-tail favoured by many of the stall holders, but his face was a contrast to the rest of his appearance. There was an aesthetic set to his features that intrigued her. She watched him surreptitiously for a moment. He was being assisted by a pretty young girl. Unconsciously, Janet ran a wistful hand through her hair, ruffling it from neat and demure to wild and untidy before she drifted closer.

'Are you interested in singing bowls?'

She suddenly realised he was talking to her. She blushed and looked down at the small pinky-pewter-coloured bowl he was holding out to her. 'Go on. Have a go.' He smiled, a grave, soul-searching smile which seemed to link his eyes to hers. She felt a flicker of sexual excitement in the pit of her stomach – something that had not happened for years, even with Steven.

She smiled back. 'How do you have a go at a bowl?'

He shook his head. 'I knew you weren't listening.' He produced a short wooden baton and, balancing the bowl on the palm of his hand, tapped it smartly. It gave off a deep bronze note like a bell. Then, as she watched and listened in amazement, she saw him draw the baton around the rim of the bowl, stroking the metal until the note caught and rose and steadied, on and on and on, weird and wild and beautiful.

She listened, enchanted.

He stopped abruptly, silencing the bowl with his other hand. 'Do you want a go?'

'You mean I could make it sing?' She felt breathless and strangely emotional.

He nodded. He handed her the bowl and the stick, and for a moment she felt the warmth and power of his fingers over hers. And then the bowl was singing. She could feel the vibration of the metal through her palm, up her arm, into her very soul. She went on and on, stroking out the different sounds, until at last she was too tired to go on and she let the singing die away.

He was watching her again, having served another two customers in the interim. 'So?' He smiled.

She wasn't sure whether the spell had been cast by him or his bowl. 'I want to buy it.'

Instead of looking pleased, his expression clouded. 'Are you sure?'

'Yes, I'm sure.' It was expensive – she had glanced at the price on the little sticker – but not that expensive. Anyway, what price that kind of magic?

'What did it do for you?' He still seemed doubtful.

'It transported me. I could see oceans and mountains. Snows. Skies. Towering clouds.' She paused, embarrassed, wondering why she had said all that, and then realised it was true. For several long minutes the noisy, stuffy hall with its crowds of people and mingled smells of incense and vegetarian hot dogs and talking and laughter and music and Tannoy announcements had faded into non-existence. She shrugged. 'It would be coming to a good home.' Why did she feel she had to justify wanting to buy it?

He had put out his hands for the bowl but she didn't want to let it go. She cradled it against her chest possessively.

He laughed. 'It's all right. I was only going to wrap it for you. Look, they come in their own special bag.' He glanced up and their eyes met again.

That was all. He put the special striped bag inside a white carrier bag. She signed the credit card slip, filled in her name and address for his mailing list and at last, with no excuse to stay longer, fled the exhibition, exhausted but strangely triumphant.

The bowl was alive. She stood it on the chest in the corner of her living-room and looked at it in awe, then, gently, tapped it with the wooden stick. The note rang on and on, vibrating down through the wood of the chest, up into the air, into the very walls of the cottage. She sat looking at the card which had come with it, describing its history in Tibet and how it was made of a secret amalgam of seven metals, then she picked up the bowl, held it on her hand and made it sing. Later she put on her new dress, ruffled her hair, kicked off her shoes and danced alone in the vibrating silence of the room.

It was almost no surprise when he knocked on the front door. 'I'm sorry to call round. My daughter forgot to give you back your credit card. I thought you'd like it back at once.'

He paused, eyeing her, and she realised he had been expecting to see the demure ex-housewife who had bought his bowl. She laughed in delight. The woman he was seeing instead was barefoot, beautiful, exotic, a confident goddess with eyes that shone and skin that glowed.

There was a moment of silence. He couldn't see the bowl but he could feel the vibrations in the air. It had been singing to her. Ten years before, when his wife died and he had made his first trip to Nepal, he had felt that excitement himself for the first time and he had been hooked.

He held out his hand with the credit card. As she took it their fingers touched.

'You looked so . . .' He floundered. 'So unlikely a person to own a bowl. But now . . .'

She laughed. 'But now you've caught me as my real self. Thank you for bringing me my card. It was silly of me to forget it.' She couldn't leave it at that. Not now. 'Can I offer you a drink to say thank you?'

He hesitated. For a moment she thought he was going to say yes, then, regretfully, he shook his head. 'Perhaps another time. There's so much packing up to do.' He stepped towards the door, then stopped and turned round. 'May I say something?' His smile was gentle. 'You should dress like that all the time. It suits you.' He smiled again and was gone.

She stared after him, then slowly pushed the door shut. Picking up the bowl, she carried it to the mirror and, her eyes fixed on her image, began to make it sing.

She was seeing herself as he had seen her. Confident. Attractive. A complete whole. Slowly, sensuously, she began to dance again.

When the doorbell rang she knew that she had called him back. That was how it would be in the future. She had liberated something in her soul. She liked men. She might even like this one very much indeed. But her destiny was in her own hands now. And from now on she would call the tune.

Between Times

Heat fell across the garden like a blanket. Sighing with relief Helen turned her back on the now spotlessly tidy chalet and carrying her cup of tea, a fat paperback novel and a rug she stepped out of the French doors onto the grass. Tim had taken the children to the beach. Ahead of her lay two or three hours of perfect peace.

'Come too, Hen.' Tim had dropped a kiss on the top of her head. He tried bribery. 'I'll buy you an ice cream?'

No contest. Two hours alone – completely alone – versus thousands of people, shouting children and, the final turn-off, runny ice creams dripping stickily down sun-sore skin. No thanks!

She spread out the rug in the shade under the small cherry tree, kicked off her flip-flops and sat down cross-legged, the mug on one side of her, the book on the other. The silence was total.

She adored the children – there were three of them, Jack, Felix and Polly – and she adored her husband, but they were all so noisy, so demanding, so overwhelmingly *there* all the time, that moments like this were almost non-existent now. Thoughtfully she picked up her mug and sipped at the tea. It was delicious; cooling, even though it scalded her mouth. Cupping her hands around the mug she gave a wry grin. Had she really forgotten how to savour tea; how to sit down in silence?

This was their first real holiday all together and Tim was being marvellous. Putting thoughts of the office for once behind him and ordering her to do the same, he had marshalled the children; they had tidied their toys, helped wash up, each found towel and bathing costume, and then suddenly there was silence and there was nothing – blessed nothing – to do!

She took another sip of tea and gazed lazily around her, unwilling even to make the effort to pick up the book. Each of these chalets had their own garden and they had been there long enough to have established hedges and flower borders, ornate trees, neat handkerchief-sized lawns. Nearby she heard the sharp alarm call of a small bird and she screwed up her eyes, trying to see it. The neighbouring gardens were totally silent too – no doubt the other families also on the beach. And then she saw it, the tiny brown bird with its ridiculous pert tail and bright eyes watching her from its hiding place in some ivy clinging to the fence near by. She smiled. Finishing her tea she lay back on the rug with a sigh of blissful contentment.

Did she fall asleep then? Afterwards she always wondered. But of course she had. How else was it all possible?

As she lay looking sleepily up through the lacework of the leaves, feeling the sun dappling her face, she realised there was someone in the garden with her.

'Tim? Have you forgotten something?' Her initial reaction was extreme irritation. Could they not allow her just this one small window of peace?

There was no answer and she turned her head, her arm shading her eyes against the glare of the sun.

From where she lay she realised suddenly that she could see through a gap in the hedge into the next door garden. A man was standing there watching her. She sat up hastily, knocking over her mug as she did so.

'Sorry. Did I startle you?' He stepped forward between the laurels and she saw that he was a man of middle height, handsome, tanned, his hair bleached almost white by the sun. 'The children are on the beach and Mary is asleep. How are you?' He sat down opposite her on the grass and leaned across to lay his hand for a moment over hers. It was a curiously intimate gesture. Not in any way threatening. He smiled at her and she found herself smiling back. Her initial indignation at his presence had disappeared. He wasn't a stranger. She knew him well.

'It's blessedly peaceful without them for a while, isn't it?' she said quietly. Her eyes were, she realised, still staring into his; she was drowning in his gaze. Drowning. She had read that expression in one of her novels, and not quite understood what the cliché meant. Now suddenly she knew. She could see into the depths of his soul and she could see that he loved her. He loved her with tormented, agonising, passion.

'My dear.' She turned her hands upwards to meet his and their palms touched, their fingers intertwined. 'How long will they be away?' She couldn't remember his name, this man whom she had loved forever and to whom she realised suddenly she was going to make love, here in the back garden of a rented holiday chalet in a place she had never been to before.

He smiled at her. 'Long enough.' His hand strayed to her shoulders and he twisted a strand of her hair around his finger. 'I go back tomorrow. This will be our last chance to be together. Perhaps for ever.'

'Don't say that.' Her eyes filled with tears. 'You'll come back; we'll both come back.'

He was wearing an open-necked shirt, the sleeves rolled up above the elbows, and she found herself reaching for the buttons, unfastening them one by one. Her hands, resting on the hot skin of his chest, encountered a rough, newly healed scar. She touched it gently and leaning forward, kissed it. 'My poor darling. I had hoped it was bad enough to keep you here. Safe.'

He shook his head ruefully. 'Let's not talk about it. Let's make the most of the time we've got.'

As he drew her to him she remembered thinking with some distant part of her brain, How strange. I still don't know his name, before she surrendered to his urgent kisses, pushing his shirt back from his shoulders, helping him undo the leather belt and the buttons of his trousers, slipping down the straps of her own brief sundress, until they were lying together naked on the grass. Once or twice she seemed to glimpse a huge tree overshadowing them, sensed its shade, its privacy, then she was lost in the ecstasy of their love-making. When at last they lay exhausted side by side she looked up into its spreading branches with a long contented sigh and realised she was smiling. Her body felt heavy and unutterably content.

'Helen?'

The voice seemed to come from hundreds of miles away.

'Helen, darling?'

She turned her head lazily towards the man beside her. Her hand touched the closed pages of her book, lying on the grass.

'Helen! For goodness' sake!'

It was Tim's voice she could hear, and then the children's giggling. 'Mummy's got no clothes on!' It was Felix. She heard the rush of feet.

'Mummy, you're getting burned.' It was Polly, solicitous, a little embarrassed, gathering up Helen's dress and pushing it at her. 'The man in the next chalet could see you!'

Grabbing the dress, Helen pulled it over her head. She didn't remember taking it off. She must have been sunbathing, taking the opportunity in the solitary little garden for an all-over tan. She glanced at Tim and shrugged, but Tim was staring at her strangely. He looked angry. She looked back towards the hedge, and suddenly she remembered. The man in the next chalet, Polly had said. The man to whom she had been making passionate love only minutes before. Was he still there? Had Tim seen him? Or had the whole thing been a dream?

The hedge looked solid from here. There was no possibility of someone seeing into the garden from the windows of the single storey building next door, nor of coming through the hedge without doing both themselves and the hedge considerable damage.

'You said there was a man?' Helen pushed the hair back from her face. She frowned at her daughter. 'What man? No one can see me from here.' She was agitated. Uneasy.

'The man next door. I saw him walking away from the gate.' She pointed at the hedge.

'There's no one there, Pol,' Tim said sternly. 'Your mum was asleep. No one could see her. I was just worried she would be sunburnt, lying spread out like that.' He held Helen's gaze for a moment and she saw the puzzled hurt in his face.

'Polly's making it up.' Felix could sense that something was wrong. He pinched his sister's arm. 'There's no gate there.'

'Well, I saw him!' Polly stamped her foot, rubbing furiously at the spot her brother's small fingers had so expertly tweaked. 'He was getting dressed; he put on a white shirt and brown trousers and he had blond hair like mine!' She was by far the fairest of the three children and Helen found herself staring at her daughter. No, the little girl was wrong. He had been fairer than Polly. Much fairer.

'Who was he?' It wasn't until the children were in bed that evening and the dishes washed and put away that Tim broke his tight-lipped silence.

'There wasn't anyone, Tim.' She had pulled a cotton shirt on over her dress as the sea breeze, coming in through the window, turned cooler.

'Don't give me that!' Tim's voice was hard. 'If you could have seen yourself lying there, your legs apart; it was disgusting. You reeked of sex!'

She shook her head. 'Tim! It's not true. There was no one there. I swear it.'

'So, Polly was lying?'

'She has a good imagination, Tim. You know there's no gate. How could there have been anyone there?'

But Polly had described him.

'It was so hot and peaceful in the garden I thought I could sunbathe. What's so wrong with that?' Suddenly she was indignant. 'No one could see me! If I hadn't fallen asleep I would have made sure I was dressed before you all came back. Not that it matters. The kids have seen me with no clothes on before –' They both wandered round the house at home nude in front of the children from time to time. They had discussed it and decided that probably it was the right thing to do – to demonstrate modesty, but no shame in the human body.

'You had love bites on your neck, Helen.' His voice was so cold she felt herself shiver. 'I didn't put them there.'

For a moment she stared at him in silence, then she walked over to stand in front of the mirror which hung over the sideboard. Pushing back the shirt she lifted her hair off her neck and stared at herself in the glass. The two flaring red marks were obvious and unmistakable.

Charles.

Charles Douglas.

The name came to her suddenly out of nowhere.

'He was going back to the front,' she said, frowning, puzzled by her own sudden unexpected remembrance. 'It was our last meeting. He was killed three weeks later. On the Somme.' She turned back to Tim. 'I remember now. He was so young. So handsome.' She shook her head, dazed, aware of the anger and incomprehension on her husband's face. 'It was a dream, Tim. I was dreaming about him. It wasn't real.'

But the marks on her neck were real. Silently she turned back to the mirror and raised her fingers to touch them. They felt bruised. Painful.

'And you dreamt those into being I suppose.' He was still angry.

'I suppose I must have.' She shrugged. 'Tim, please. You know there's no one else. I love you!'

'I thought so.' The hurt in his voice was palpable.

But she had known she was cheating on him when she had turned to Charles and unbuttoned his shirt even as Charles had known he was cheating on his own wife and children.

She sat down, realising suddenly that she was shaking. 'It was so real.' She shouldn't talk about it. She shouldn't say any more, but suddenly she couldn't stop herself. 'He was so frightened. So lonely. He knew he was going to die. They must have all known they were going to die. He was living on borrowed time and his wife didn't understand him. She was a stupid, vain woman, who was only interested in herself and her own imagined ills. She wasn't there for him, Tim, when he needed her. When she saw the terrible scars on his body she shuddered and turned away.'

How did she know all this?

Tim was staring at her. His face was white. He said nothing as she went on: 'There was no one there for him. That was why he came. Just to talk. Just to describe a little of what it was like; to try and defuse some of his nightmares. It was so harmless at first. He was little more than a boy and he loved his Mary so much, but she was lonely too. They married just before he was posted overseas and when he left she was pregnant. She didn't see him for more than a year. He came back on leave to a stranger with a young baby. When he came back again a year later on a stretcher she had another child. That one wasn't his. She said it was his fault. She stormed and raged at him and tried to justify herself. What was he to do?'

'That seems to have been some dream!' Tim said drily as she lapsed into silence. 'So, exactly where do you fit in?'

Helen shrugged. 'I was the other side of the hedge.'

'A neighbour?'

'I suppose so.'

'And you comforted him.'

She looked away. 'So it would appear.'

'And he left you radiant. Sated. Covered in love bites.' He moved towards the door.

'Tim, please. You have to believe me –'

But he had gone. She heard him open the door, pull it closed behind him and walk away down the quiet road towards the sea.

She sat still for a long time, staring out of the window. Slowly it grew dark. She didn't bother to turn on the lights, aware that the tears had long since dried on her face. It was all so stupid. A dream. How could they

84

quarrel like this over a dream? Then she touched the bruises on her neck again and she sighed. They were not part of a dream.

There was no sign of Tim. Where had he gone? She pictured him walking miserably on the beach, alone in the dark and she ached to follow him, comfort him, explain. But how could she when she couldn't explain it herself?

It was nearly midnight when, still sleepless, she pushed open the door and stepped out into the garden. The moon had risen, bathing everything in silvery light. Faintly she thought she could hear the gentle shush of the sea on the sand in the distance. She could smell the sharp salt of it over the soft sweetness of the honey-suckle and roses in the flowerbeds near her. The grass was wet with dew as she stepped down off the step. She could see the china gleam of her mug lying where she had left it. No one had thought to pick it up. Or her book, which was lying open, the pages damp and wrinkled.

Quietly she walked towards the hedge. The gate was there as she had known it would be. She put her hand out to the cold wood and pushing it open she stepped through. The house across the lawn was large, imposing in the moonlight. A cedar tree stood in the centre of the lawn, throwing stark black shadows slanting over the grass. The silence was intense. She could no longer hear the sea.

She walked slowly towards the house, staring up at the windows. They all looked strangely blank, blinds shutting out the moonlight in every one. Beyond the house more hedges bordered a deserted country lane. There was no sign of the row of little holiday homes which in her world lined the road to the sea. She turned round in sudden fear, looking for the gate through which she had come. It was there, standing open as she had left it. Beyond it she could see the huge oak tree under which she and Charles had lain. There was no chalet there now. No cherry tree. No washing line with small swimming costumes and brightly coloured towels hanging where she had forgotten to take them in.

And suddenly she was crying. Crying for her dead lover, buried so long ago somewhere in the mud of northern France, and for her husband walking in lonely misery on the beach in the moonlight and for her children who had gone to bed puzzled and unhappy at the sudden atmosphere between their parents on what had up till then been a holiday of total happiness.

Almost as though the thought had conjured her out of the night Helen was aware suddenly of a small girl walking towards her across the grass.

'Don't be sad, Mummy.' Polly slipped a small warm hand into her cold one. 'Is it that house that makes you sad?' The little face looked up at hers earnestly. 'I don't like it. The windows can't see.'

So, Polly was aware of it too, with its blinds and its aura of unhappiness.

'Someone has drawn the blinds, darling. That is why the windows can't see. It is a sad house because some-one has died.'

'The man I saw kissing you?'

Dear God! What else has she seen.

'He was an old friend, darling. From long ago.'

'Why did he die?'

Helen frowned. Her mind was wheeling between times and she didn't know how to answer. 'He lived a long time ago, Polly, and he had to go to fight in the war.'

'So he's a ghost.' The child was still staring up at her trustingly.

'I suppose he is. Yes. At first I thought he must be a dream, but if you saw him too then he can't be.' Helen glanced back over Polly's head towards the neighbouring garden and suddenly it was as it had been; the large house was gone. The great trees had vanished. In their place the line of small holiday bungalows with defining hedges and fences once more stretched away in the moonlight.

'That's better.' Polly sounded more confident suddenly. 'It's all gone back to normal now. Silly dream.' She reached out for Helen's hand again. 'I'll tell Daddy and he won't be cross any more.'

'You think so?' Helen smiled sadly. 'I hope you're right, darling.' She glanced back over her shoulder in spite of herself. The garden was as it should be still.

When they walked back into the house Tim was standing just inside the front door. He appeared to be lost in thought.

'Tim?' Helen went over to him. Hesitantly she put her hand on his arm.

He frowned. 'Where have you been?'

'In the garden, Daddy.' It was Polly who answered. She threw her arms around her father's waist. 'I saw the dream house where the ghost lived. It looked all strange in the moonlight. The man Mummy saw is dead. He's gone now. He was a ghost!'

'A –' Tim stared at Helen.

'I seem to have got mixed up in someone else's tragedy, Tim; someone else's life, long, long ago. You have to believe me at least about that one thing. It wasn't real.'

For a long moment they stared at each other in silence, the little girl looking anxiously up first at one then the other.

'We're never going to understand what happened, Tim. It was a slip in time.'

Tim sighed. 'I suppose I'm going to have to believe you.' He shrugged. 'Largely because I can't bear the alternatives.' He walked past her into the room and sat down. Putting his elbows on his knees he ran his fingers through his hair. 'As I walked up and down that beach I realised I couldn't live without you. You mean everything to me.'

Helen smiled uncertainly. Kneeling in front of him she reached up and put her arms around his neck. As she kissed him Polly jumped onto the sofa next to him and burrowed between them into the shelter of their arms.

Outside in the moonlight Charles stood on the lawn staring towards the lighted windows of the bungalow unseeing. In his own time he was standing under a spreading tree in the dark. Behind him the house of his dreams lay shuttered and empty. His wife and the children had gone. Only one person had ever made him feel loved and happy and in his cold, lost loneliness he drifted across the grass looking for her, the warm gentle kind woman he had found lying in the sunlight under the tree. He was resolved, if necessary, to search forever until he found her again.

Sea Dreams

How was she going to tell him? Rachel looked across the table at Alex, watching fondly as he poured out his breakfast cereal and reached for the milk jug. No children, they had said. Or not for years. Too busy. Too poor. Too stressed. Too soon.

He glanced up and grinned back at her. 'OK?'

She nodded. 'OK.'

How had it happened? Well, she knew that. Gastric flu. She'd puked up the pill. As simple as that. And now she was feeling sick again.

Alex stood up and, dropping a kiss on her head, made for the door. 'You'll be late for work, Rachel.'

She nodded. 'Just going.'

The door closed behind him and she put her head in her hands. Perhaps it was a false alarm. Perhaps it was still the flu after all.

That Saturday was the second time Rachel went to the yoga class. Alex, seeing her tenseness, her strange, unaccustomed unhappiness, had suggested she go. Slowly and gently Eileen took her twelve pupils through the series of asanas and breathing exercises then, as before, at the end they all lay down on their mats, covered themselves with blankets and closed their eyes for a period of relaxation.

'Picture yourself in your favourite place in the country.' The deep, melodious voice seemed further away than the low stage of the hall. 'Feel your bare feet in the grass, hear the birds, the wind in the trees, smell the flowers.'

Except that Rachel, trying hard to put her worries out of her head, was suddenly, violently standing on a beach. The rattle of pebbles was deafening as the waves sucked back, she could smell the raw, cold tang of salt and seaweed and ice.

'Find yourself a nice secluded spot under a tree –' Eileen's voice was barely audible now. 'Sit down and imagine you can feel yourself leaning against its trunk.'

Another wave crashed onto the stones and Rachel realised that she had jumped backwards to avoid the spray, her feet slipping on the pebbles.

It wasn't supposed to be like this. They were relaxing – warm; safe; preparing to empty their minds for the meditation.

'If at any time you feel at all uncomfortable,' Eileen said suddenly, 'just open your eyes.'

'Open my eyes.' Rachel was sure she had said it out loud. 'Open my eyes.' The next wave broke higher up the beach and suddenly she could hear footsteps slipping, laboured, crunching towards her.

'Just open my eyes.'

But they were open. She knew they were open. They must be. She could see clearly.

'Maddy!' The young man was beside her now, looking straight at her. 'Maddy, you must come. They've found him.'

'No!' She wasn't aware that she had spoken this time.

'You have to come, Maddy.' The wind was tearing at his hair, almost dragging the shirt from his shoulders. 'You have to come –'

'– and slowly come back to the room, and when you're ready, open your eyes.' Eileen's voice was right in her ear. With a start Rachel sat up. Her head was spinning. She stared round. The others were still lying flat on their backs beginning to open their eyes, to stretch.

Eileen was sitting on the edge of the platform, swinging her legs. She saw Rachel and her pale angular face shadowed. She slipped off the platform and tiptoed over on silent bare feet. 'Are you OK, Rachel?'

Rachel shrugged. She felt as if she were going to cry.

'You sat up too suddenly, my dear. Breathe slowly.' Eileen patted her shoulder then she straightened and turned away. 'That's all for today,' she called to the class. 'I'll see you next week.'

'You all right, Rachel?' The tall, willowy young woman next to her was rolling up her blanket. 'Did you fall asleep? It's very easy to do.'

'No. I'm fine. I'm OK.' Somehow Rachel managed to scramble to her feet. She groped for her blanket and began to fold it.

'Coming for a coffee?' Susie was persistent. She swung her bag on her shoulder. 'Come on. You can only do so many things that are good for you in one day!'

It was easier not to argue. Silently Rachel followed her out. They called their farewells to the others, threw the rugs into their cars and strolled up the village street towards the tea shop.

Susie ordered coffee and tea cakes for them both at the counter then she came and sat down opposite Rachel. 'Are you going to tell me what's wrong?' she asked gently.

Rachel shook her head. 'Nothing. Honestly.'

'Then why were you crying?'

'I wasn't. At least –'

But she had been. It was all too much. On top of the worry about pregnancy the scene on the beach had for some reason left her devastated. Leaning forward she pushed aside the small vase of pinks which stood between them on the table. 'Something weird happened. When we were supposed to be visualising a wood or something I found myself by the sea.'

'You fell asleep. You were dreaming.'

'No.' Rachel shook her head vehemently. 'No. I wasn't dreaming.'

The ice cold wind. The pounding waves. The fear.

They were real.

'What happened?' Scrutinising her friend's face Susie's voice had dropped to a whisper.

'That's it, I can't remember. There was someone there.'

'Two tea cakes. Two coffees.' The brisk arrival of their order distracted her. By the time the waitress had tucked the bill under the vase of pinks and walked away, swinging her empty tray, Rachel had lost the thread again.

Susie waited expectantly. 'Was the someone a he?'

Rachel smiled and shrugged. 'I honestly can't remember. It's gone. It must have been a dream after all.'

That evening Alex bought them a take away. And he was full of plans. 'A holiday, Rachel. We haven't had one since our honeymoon. We deserve it, sweetheart.'

She smiled. 'Where did you have in mind?'

'I don't know. How are you enjoying your yoga? What about Tibet?' He was joking, of course.

At three in the morning she sat up suddenly in bed, shaking like a leaf.

'Rachel, what is it? What's wrong?' Alex reached for the light switch, fumbling in the darkness. He put his arms round her. 'Sweetheart, calm down. It was only a dream.'

Only a dream! The thundering waves, the long shingle beach with the wind screaming in her ears, tearing at her long skirt, her shawl, her hair flying round her head.

'Oh, Alex.' She pressed her face against his chest. 'It was awful!' She put her hand to her head. Her hair was neat, short, chestnut. In her dream it had been long, dark and wild.

'Bad dreams.' Alex hugged her hard. 'Cup of tea help?'

She clung to him for a moment then almost reluctantly she nodded. She didn't want him to leave her. She wanted to tell him everything, but at the same time, she realised suddenly she needed to be alone, to make some sense of the inexplicable fear which had woken her.

She took a deep breath and uncomfortably she pressed her hands against her ears.

'*Maddy!*'

The voice was in the room with her. Pulling the bed covers up to her chin she stared round, terrified.

'*Maddy!*'

'Alex!' she called out desperately

But he couldn't hear her. He was downstairs listening to the increasing rush of water boiling in the kettle, sleepily staring out into the moonlit garden. The kettle switched off automatically and in the sudden silence he heard an owl hoot. A shiver ran down his spine. For a moment he stood quite still, listening, then with a small irritated shake of his head he turned and reached for the teapot and caddy.

'Here's the tea, Rachel. Now we're awake, let's plan the holiday.' He pushed open the bedroom door with his elbow and carried the tray in. 'Rachel?'

The bed was empty.

'You have to come, Maddy.' He was holding out his hand. Icy rain was soaking through his shirt, stinging his eyes.

'I can't!' She took a step back, aware of the huge waves crashing onto the beach behind her. 'Please, don't make me look at him.'

'But he's alive, Maddy!' His face broke into a smile. 'They pulled him out alive!'

She could feel the hot rush of joy, then hope, then disbelief and then the sicker terror flow over her like a tide. He was alive. He would tell her secret. His life meant her death.

Ralph had reached towards her and caught her wrist. His hand was ice cold, slippery with salt spray and rain.

'Over here.' He was pulling her with him.

She could see them now. Four men bending over the body of a fifth. They were covering him with cloaks, chafing his hands.

'Francis!' She stood staring down at him. He was sitting up now, his face white, his teeth chattering, his expression mirroring hers: relief and love, then wariness and last of all, fear. 'Maddy! I thought you'd gone. The boat sank. I was trying to follow you.'

There was a long silence, then, suddenly she had to tell them the truth. 'We were going to run away together. To France. To a new life where no one would know –' Without realising it she had rested her hand on her stomach. Ralph, following the gesture with his eyes saw the slight swelling as the wind and rain flattened her gown against her belly. His eyes widened incredulously. 'You are with child?' The fury in his voice was vicious. 'You, my wife, are carrying my brother's child?'

'Ralph –' Francis had scrambled to his feet, throwing off the cloaks which had been wrapped round him. 'Listen, brother, you must not blame her!'

'Must I not?' The wind was whipping away their words as they confronted one another, shouting. 'Then who do I blame? My own impotence, perhaps, or you, who in your generosity, came to her aid?'

The men with them had drawn back out of earshot, muttering uneasily, glancing from one man to the other, then surreptitiously at Maddy.

Tears poured down her cheeks. 'Ralph! Francis –'

They ignored her. This was men's business.

Slowly she turned towards the sea.

Behind her, Ralph stepped forward. He laid hold of his brother's shirt and pulled him close, glaring.

The cold of the waves snatched her breath away. She took one step, then another, staggering under the power of the water. There could be no looking back. When at last the waves swept her off her feet she held out her arms to embrace the water as though it were the lover she had found such a short time before and now irretrievably lost.

At first Alex thought she was hiding. He hunted for her, laughing while the tea grew cold. Then he sat down on the bottom step of the staircase and put his head in his hands. His initial emotions – puzzlement, curiosity, even bewildered anger, had been replaced by just one. Fear.

He glanced at his watch. At last it was growing light.

It took only three minutes to put on his shoes and find his car keys. At least, touring the streets, he would be doing something. Supposing she was sleepwalking? The front door was locked, their keys still there on the sideboard, but supposing she had somehow found a spare front door key, opened the door, relocked it? Supposing she had walked out into the moonlight barefoot – her slippers were still where she had kicked them the night before, under the bed. Supposing she had walked, still fast asleep, down the road, silent and empty in the pre-dawn dark, through the village and out into the network of lanes between the moors and the sea.

He turned out of their road and into the next, putting

the lights on full beam, scanning the hedgerows with their strange irregular shadows.

'She's gone, Francis!' The voice was in the car with him.

Alex slammed on the brakes. The engine stalled and in the sudden silence Alex found himself holding his breath as he stared ahead at the deserted road. He groped for the ignition.

'Look! There. In the sea!'

Icy perspiration drenched his shoulders as Alex's hand fell away from the key.

'Quickly man, if you love her!'

The sea? How could Rachel have reached the sea? It was three, four, miles away. Almost in a daze he groped in the glove pocket and reached for the mobile. Rachel's friend Susie lived by the sea. On the esplanade, in a small pink cottage, idyllic in summer, in winter soused in spray and reverberating to icy winds.

'Yes, I know what time it is!' The line crackled; the battery was very low. 'Please, Susie, go and look. I beg you. I'm on my way.' He was sobbing as the connection went dead.

'Maddy!' The voice was lost in the rush of wind and tide. 'Maddy, come back!'

The instinct to swim was too strong. She flailed out wildly with her arms and legs, feeling the entangling skirts pulling her down.

'Francis!' The water was in her mouth, her eyes, her nose. 'Francis –' A wave caught her and lifted her, sucking her back towards the beach, closing over her head as she felt the sudden rasp of sharp stones beneath her feet. She scrabbled frantically for a hold and lost it again and then her head was above the water and she saw them near her, both of them, her husband and his brother, struggling through the waves towards her.

'Maddy! Hold on! Hold on, my love.' It was Ralph. He was close to her now. She could see his head on the smooth green pillow of water. She could see his hand stretched out towards her, so close she could almost touch him. Beyond him, further out in the tide race she could see Francis. He was swimming desperately.

'Francis!' Her scream was cut short by the wave. She felt it close over her and pull her down. In the green depths it was quiet, strangely peaceful. She could see Francis now, near her. He was smiling, holding out his arms . . .

'Rachel! For Christ's sake, Rachel, breathe!'

Someone was thumping her back. She felt herself slither on the pebbles and suddenly she was bitterly cold. Retching frantically she managed a breath, then another as she pulled herself onto her elbows.

'Thank God!' There was a blanket round her now, and arms, hugging, shaking. 'Rachel, what on earth were you doing?'

It was Susie, a raincoat over her nightdress, her bare feet pushed into heavy shoes, her long hair loose and wet, strung over her shoulders. 'I couldn't believe it when I saw you. I couldn't.' She was pulling at her. 'Come on, up. You've got to stand. You've got to come inside.' The beach was deserted, lit by a cold light reflecting on the clouds from the sun still below the horizon. 'Come on!'

Rachel staggered to her feet and somehow Susie managed to lead her up the beach across the narrow road and into the cottage. Out of the wind it was eerily quiet.

'Save the explanations. Strip off those clothes and put on my dressing gown.' Susie pushed her onto the sofa and heaped rugs and cushions round her.

'What happened?' Rachel took the proffered hot water bottle and hugged it to her. Her teeth were chattering.

'Don't ask me. You were the one in the sea!' Susie threw driftwood from a basket onto fire lighters and watched it blaze up. 'Where's Alex? He rang me then we were cut off.'

'Alex's in bed. We were both in bed –' Rachel was crying suddenly. 'Susie –'

'I think I'd better phone for an ambulance –'

'No! No, don't do that. I'm fine. I want Alex.' Tears were streaming down Rachel's face. 'I don't understand. It was a dream.'

'A dream?' Susie echoed. 'That's what you said before. A man on a beach.'

'Francis.' Rachel nodded slowly in confusion. 'He was called Francis. And the sea took him.' Her voice broke. 'His brother Ralph was there. He tried to follow Francis. He tried to catch hold of him but he had gone.' She sat up, pushing her wet hair out of her eyes. 'He was very kind. He let them think the child was his,' she went on urgently, suddenly clutching at Susie's hand. 'He raised her. He loved her as his own. No one ever knew. But he never forgave Maddy. Never.'

Behind them the door opened and Alex peered in. They hadn't heard his car draw up outside for the roar of the fire in the chimney. In two strides he was on his knees by the sofa. 'What happened? You're all wet! For God's sake! What happened, Susie?'

'You tell me.' Susie shrugged. 'You rang, Alex. You told me what to do.'

Rachel stared at him. She freed her hand from the cocoon of blankets and reached out to touch his face. 'How did you know where I was, Alex?'

'There was a voice – in the car.' Alex shook his head uncomfortably, clearly embarrassed. 'It said you were in the sea.'

Quickly man, if you love her!

Rachel was frowning. 'I remember you getting up. You went downstairs to get tea, then suddenly I was in the water –' She pulled one of the cushions to her and hugged it desperately. 'I must be going mad.'

'If you are, Rachel, so are the rest of us,' Susie put in gently. There was a long silence. She was frowning. 'I think Rachel has had a glimpse into the past.' She looked at them both and shrugged. 'It breaks all the rules of time and space that you and I were taught at school, but it doesn't mean we're mad. I think we are privileged.'

Scrambling to her feet she turned back to the fire. 'It occurs to me,' she said, looking down into the flames, 'from what you said, Rachel, that this is really all about a baby.' She paused and turned round. 'You're not pregnant, are you?'

The question had come out of the blue. Alex gasped. He turned to his wife, scanning her face.

She bit her lip. 'I haven't had a test, but I've been wondering –'

'Rachel' Alex leaned forward and hugged her. 'Oh my darling, that's wonderful!'

'But we hadn't planned –'

'It doesn't matter. Nothing matters but that you're safe.'

'You mean it, Alex?' Rachel clutched his hand. 'You really don't mind?'

'Of course I don't mind. Sweetheart, we'll manage. We always have.' He leaned forward and kissed her then he turned to Susie. 'How did you know?'

Susie smiled and shrugged. 'I guessed.' There was a short silence, then she broke suddenly into giggles. 'Sorry, but if we look for a rational explanation for any of this we won't find it. You know my philosophy of life. I've always thought that we question too much. You can't spend the rest of your lives worrying about something you will never ever be able to explain.' She bent to throw some driftwood onto the fire. 'Time for a hot drink. Then later I suggest Rachel goes to see the doctor so that at least you know that for sure.'

'If I am pregnant and it's a girl I want to call her Maddy.' Rachel lay back frowning. She was staring into the distance. 'You know what I think? I think this is my opportunity to put the past right. I – we've been given a second chance. But why?' She turned to look at Susie by the fire. 'Why me? Why Alex?'

Susie shook her head. 'Why not? All that matters is that the three of us know that in our very ordinary lives in our very ordinary world a small miracle has happened and that you are happy about it.'

Rachel squeezed Alex's hand. 'OK?' she whispered.

He nodded. 'OK. When I think how I nearly lost you – ' He shuddered.

'But you didn't.' Rachel smiled.

'I think you've found each other,' Susie put in quietly. 'I think you've found each other after what is possibly a very long time!'

The Footpath

It was Doreen Oldfield who first realised there was a problem. A group of strangers was standing the other side of her garden fence staring along it towards the field. One of them held a map in his hand. He spotted her as she limped across her back garden towards them.

'Excuse me,' he called. 'Where is the path?'

'It's up on the far side of the post office.' Doreen stared beadily at them. She didn't smile. She didn't know them.

'No.' The man stabbed at the map with his forefinger. 'It's here. I'm standing on it.'

'Why ask then?' She glared at him.

'Because it's too overgrown to use, and I can't see where it goes from here. According to the map it should go straight across the field.'

Doreen sighed. 'Maps!' she said in disgust. 'You don't want to pay any attention to them things. No one uses that path nowadays. It's moved. It goes along the edge over there.' She waved her arm vaguely. 'Has done since they had the hedges out after the war. This one doesn't exist any more.'

They did not listen. Before her outraged eyes the group set off. Forcing their way through the undergrowth, they headed out into the middle of the field, beating a way through the lush corn with their walking sticks.

It was the first hint of the war to come.

The footpath did indeed in theory run between Doreen's cottage and the side garden at Copthorne's. Bordered on one side by a magnificent laurel hedge and on the other by Doreen's rickety picket fence with several slats missing it was now overgrown with brambles and nettles. Unpopular with people in the village and seldom if ever used by any but the local boys on their mountain bikes and the occasional horse rider, it had all but disappeared because of the broad pleasant track everyone liked much better a hundred yards up the road. That path was a popular route into the fields and woods. Dog walkers used it, and local people going for an afternoon stroll, and kids wanting to sneak into the old farm buildings behind Osbecks. Over the years the path had moved. It was as simple as that.

Joe Middleton was sitting at his breakfast spooning his cornflakes into his mouth several days later with his own copy of the very same map that the strangers had used spread out on the table in front of him. 'The inspectors are right. The path has been deliberately blocked, here and here and here.' He put down his spoon and reached for his fluorescent marker.

His wife Maureen sighed. 'I think it's a lovely walk just as it is, Joe. It hasn't been blocked at all. One can walk the whole length of that path. It is just that it has been rerouted once or twice. But that's nicer. One can see the birds and flowers in the hedges . . .' She broke off almost guiltily as her husband gave an exasperated sigh.

'We do not go for walks to see birds and flowers,' he said firmly. 'You know that. That is the whole point of joining the Association. We walk to make sure that rights of way are not being abused.'

'Boring!' She said it under her breath. There was no point in arguing with him. She knew that from long experience. No point at all.

As she expected once he had finished his breakfast he headed for the phone. 'Footpath 29,' he said urgently, into the mouthpiece. It was like a code word, signalling the start of the D-Day landings. 'Your inspectors were right. I checked yesterday. There are four deliberate obstructions, two fields with unsprayed, unmarked paths, a great deal of untidiness and a village of yokels who couldn't care less!' There was a pause. Whoever was the other end of the line at headquarters in London was rustling a reciprocal map, trying to fold it open without spilling his cup of coffee or getting jam from his doughnut onto the paper. 'Saturday? OK. Perfect. I'll contact everyone on my list and you bring your team. And by the time you come I will have checked every path in the parish.'

Maureen could hear the eagerness in his voice and the excitement and, she had to admit this, the spite.

Slowly she began collecting the dishes and carrying

them over to the sink. She knew exactly what would happen next. The group would descend on the selected footpath, they would walk it slowly and determinedly. They would scatter little yellow arrows, hammering them on other people's gates and telegraph poles and trees, they would rip off private signs, destroy all *keep out* notices and *no trespassing* signs they came across, whether or not they actually referred to parts of the right of way, all the time maintaining expressions of self-righteous zeal worthy of seventeenth-century Levellers. Then, exhausted and much empowered by their day in the country, they would all return home to compose letters which would flood down onto the doormats of local councils – county, district and parish – and landowners, and finally, the press, local and better still, national, and then sit back to watch the chosen community tear itself to pieces. It was a sport to people like Joe and she hated it. Even more so now because for the first time this was a footpath on their own doorstep.

He was worried about that too. Embarrassed. 'I have been too busy with other projects, Mo.' He kept looking at the map and shaking his head. 'How could I have missed it? This is my own village! Right on my patch. What must the Association think of me? I won't be able to hold up my head when they come over.' He sighed mournfully. Then he glanced at her. 'You'll be coming too, won't you, Mo?' He walked over to the sink to begin brushing his hiking boots even though he knew she hated him doing it over her cooking space. 'I thought we could have cheese and pickle sandwiches this time. There isn't a pub round here that I can recommend to the members. Not the sort of thing they're used to, anyway.'

'There's a lovely pub, Joe.' Maureen was indignant. 'For goodness' sake. These people are supposed to be coming out to enjoy the country, not replicate their posh London bistros!' She knew it was a pointless comment. She had learned by now that enjoying the country was not actually on these people's agenda at all. She heaved another deep sigh. 'I'm not sure if I can come. I might go over and see the kids. I promised our Primrose I would.' That would take her safely out of the loop for the whole day with a bit of luck. She glared down at the sink, now covered in a fine dust of dry earth. What she had said was tantamount to treason and she knew it, but she had also known for a long time that she was going to have to put her foot down one day and today was as good as any to start. One did not mess in one's own village. What Joe was about to get involved in was going to have repercussions.

It wasn't until three days later that it began to dawn on the inhabitants of Winchmoor that they were the target of a well-orchestrated, nationally-advertised invasion. It was Doreen who saw the first sign. Someone had ripped out several of the sagging pickets of her fence and tossed them into her garden. The rambling rose whose weight had caused it to collapse had been viciously hacked back and someone had nailed a small bright yellow arrow to her gate post pointing down the footpath, which from being a gentle rose-scented overgrown lane had turned since mid-morning into a broad, naked track. On the other side to her own garden

Colonel Wright's beautiful laurels had also been sliced back into a hideous torn caricature of a hedge through which she could now see clearly right into his garden.

'Oh my lor!' She stared round, her heart thudding with fear and anger. 'We've been vandalised.' She picked up a piece of her fence. It had been lying out across the path and she had meant to fix it sometime, but no one had ever made a fuss about it, not even the kids on their mountain bikes, so she never thought anyone minded. And now. She surveyed the wreck of her roses in dismay and suddenly her eyes filled with tears.

Colonel Wright did not cry. He contacted the police. They agreed with Doreen that it must have been vandals. Neither the local constable, nor Bill Cartright, chairman of the parish council, had noticed the small yellow arrow and if they had they would not have realised that it was a declaration of war. No one did until the letters began to arrive – from all over England! It appeared, to the amazement of the inhabitants of the village, that members of the Association had been coming on a regular basis from every corner of the country to this particular spot and that they had regularly, if unnoticed, been walking this beautiful and important track, a vital link in the national footpath highway, and had suddenly found it unacceptably and deliberately blocked.

Stung by the attack the various council departments went into action, now fully and indeed painfully aware that they had been remiss in the maintenance of several rights of way in the Winchmoor district. First they contacted Ted Ames, the farmer. He must spray off the crossfield paths immediately or face heavy fines. No, they wouldn't wait for the few short weeks until the harvest. No they wouldn't agree that as the villagers had walked around the field for fifty years instead of across it the path had been changed by custom. No one had applied for a proper diversion according to the bylaws. And that was that. An ugly brown gash appeared across the field as the crops died. Poison was what the enemy wanted. Now. Poison was what they got.

'You know who's behind this, don't you?' Sally Murphy from the pub had phoned Julie Ames the day after her husband had given up arguing in the name of common sense and sprayed the field. 'It's that odious little man from Dyson Drive.'

'Not Mo's husband?' Julie was shocked. 'Surely he wouldn't do this. Not to his own village.'

'He would. You know the kids have been banned from riding their bikes up the path now? Apparently they are not allowed on the footpath as it's only for people on foot. There's a notice gone up. And horses can't go up there any more either. They all have to go on the road through the village and you know how dangerous that is!' She paused as they both considered the flow of lorries hurtling off the bypass to cut a few minutes off their journey towards the motorway link. 'I heard he walked straight through Bill Riley's back garden the other day as well. Said it was an ancient right of way and no one was going to stop him.'

'But that's crazy. No one has used that path for years. There's a whole estate of houses built across it now.'

Sally gave a hollow laugh. 'Apparently he's been on to the parish council and is demanding they run a path behind the whole line of houses, cutting them off from their gardens. Either that or pull the houses down because the builder hadn't checked properly about rights of way.'

Julie was stunned into silence for a moment. 'He can't do that!'

'He can apparently. It only takes one person to insist on the letter of the law.'

'What is the matter with the man? Why would anyone want to walk up there anyway? It doesn't go anywhere.'

'I don't think that's the point.' Julie sighed. 'These people have no idea. No idea at all.'

It was Colonel Wright who opened the *Sunday Times* first in the village, exactly two weeks later. 'Village torn apart by footpath row,' he saw as the page two headline. 'Lone local hero fights to re-open rights of way against a barrage of local resentment. Entrenched landowners determined to break the law . . .' And there was a photo of Joe Middleton standing by . . . The colonel squinted at the photo in astonishment and fury. It was his own decimated laurel hedge! He felt his blood pressure mounting dangerously high as he reached for his coffee cup and then put it down again untouched. His hands were shaking violently. That was his own beautiful hedge and it had been blocking nothing! Nothing.

Doreen surveyed the pile of timber that had been her fence. A man from the council had come over with a measuring tape and fussed and measured and tutted and told her that it encroached fifteen centimetres onto the public right of way – the footpath. So the whole thing had to come down. As did the remains of the rose. She stared at her once beautiful little garden miserably. Completely open down its entire length it was unprotected from children and dogs and litter. All had done their worst. How was she ever going to replace the fence? She couldn't even afford a new rose. Bewildered and unhappy she stood and watched as Marjory Cockpen's Jack Russell skipped in off the path and proceeded to squat almost at her feet. Marjory, walking along the now broad and ugly path, eyes front, ignored the dog's indiscretion. Doreen wasn't to know that the old woman was as unhappy and embarrassed as her neighbour. It had never occurred to Marjory to take a bag for her dog's do-dos – hitherto deposited out of harm's way in the hedge, and even if it had with her arthritis she could never have stooped to pick it up.

Crying silently Doreen turned back into her cottage and closed the door behind her. As far as she was concerned she had just lost a friend.

Maureen was standing at her kitchen window staring out at the road. Two reporters were there from the local paper talking to Joe by their front gate. The whole world knew by now that this was the local HQ of the war.

'This is the third footpath I have campaigned about.' Joe's words would appear on page three the following morning. 'The other two were in neighbouring villages and are now fully open and accessible. They are tidy and neat and though I say it myself would do credit to a proper garden!' What he didn't expect when he proudly read the piece the next day was the sharp little editorial two pages further on.

'Joe Middleton is a representative of an increasing phenomenon in the countryside these days; a retired townie determined to turn the country into a mirror image of the town he has forsaken. He appears to have no real concern for the accessibility or the beauties of the landscape, obsessed instead, in an all too familiar way, with small detail rather than the greater picture. Interviews in the villages whose footpaths he has so proudly fought to clear all tell the same story. Neighbours once friends, now enemies, beautiful countryside fractured, hedges and trees trimmed neatly back to conform to some notional norm, while flowers and berries die. Fields are blighted by the now familiar ugly poisoned scars which dissect them with the precision of a ruler rather than gently following ancient contours and byways. All to provide access for armies of seemingly angry walkers who it is rumoured actually measure the length of grass blades to ensure that they comply with footpath regulations, rather than raise their eyes to enjoy the God-given glory of the countryside they are traversing. Communities do exist where members of different countryside groups have managed to get together to settle such matters as the rerouting of old rights of way amicably and sensibly. Would that this could happen everywhere. Alas, as long as people like Joe Middleton see it as their duty to regard common sense as a dirty word and live by a Pooterish insistence on the value of small print for its own sake, this country will continue to slide into a morass of red tape and mediocrity, turning its back on the spirit of independence combined with neighbourly compromise which once made this country great.'

'I'd give a good deal to know who wrote that!' Ted Ames read the leader out to his wife as she dished up the potatoes for lunch. 'That makes me feel a whole lot better, that does!'

'Well, you won't when I tell you the latest thing this man wants.' Julie sat down opposite him and shook her head. 'I think it's probably the last straw. You know where the footpath emerges from Dines Wood and crosses the heath?'

Ted nodded. He picked up his knife and fork.

'Well, apparently the footpath has moved a few feet from its old position. The hedge has widened over the years and parts of the wood are bigger now. They've made the whole thing into a nature reserve. There's a lovely old holly on the edge of the wood. This man says it has to be cut down as it's on the footpath.'

Ted dropped his knife and fork, his food still untouched. 'But can't they go round it?'

Julie grimaced. 'Oh come on, Ted. You know better than that by now. This man won't go round anything. He knows his rights. He's obsessed!'

Ted stared up at the ceiling. 'What's the council say?'

She shrugged. 'No idea. They seem to be caving in to his every demand. He's got the law on his side, it seems. Colonel Wright is demanding some kind of legal enquiry about some of the things that have happened, but I don't suppose anyone will be interested in this. It's right out in the country.'

Ted shook his head. 'A holly, you say?'

She nodded.

'Well, that's going to be an interesting one.' He gave a wry grin. 'I'm glad it's not on my land, that's all I can say.'

'You are not seriously insisting that they cut down a tree when there is a sixty-acre field out there for people to walk in to go round it!' Maureen was watching her husband with something like awe. She had been listening to him lambasting some poor man in the council highways department over the phone.

'It's on the footpath, Mo.' Joe sat back, exhausted. 'I don't think you understand how important this all is. I'm not doing this to upset people you know. But someone has to take a stand. These landowners think they can walk all over the rest of us just because they've got money and big houses. One day all land will be accessible to everyone, but until then they have to be made to toe the line.'

'Poor old Doreen Oldfield doesn't have a big house or any money,' Maureen said quietly. 'I was hearing at the post office that she hasn't been seen outside her cottage in weeks. She just sits and cries because her garden is ruined.'

'That's hardly my fault.' He folded his arms across his chest. 'She should have checked her boundaries. There's nothing to stop her putting up a new fence.'

'Except money. And anyway, they were saying that her fence is on the old building line that goes back hundreds of years. It's hardly *her* fault.'

Shrugging he gave a testy sigh. 'Well, that's not my problem.'

He had pinned an Ordnance Survey map to the wall now. It was covered in highlighter and pins and flags. Each footpath was marked and where they were blocked or deviated by so much as a foot from the official line he had flagged the spot. There were dozens of flags on the map. Dozens of campaigns ready to go once this one was finished. He gave another sigh, this time of contentment. Just one tree and footpath 29 would be clear and neat and ready for inspection by the committee when they came down from London to admire his handiwork and pose – this was his idea – for press photographs to celebrate yet another victory. That unfortunate editorial had been glanced at and immediately forgotten. It had obviously been written by some romantic hayseed with no idea of the realities of country life.

Maureen however was not prepared to let that one last detail go. 'You are not actually going to force them to cut down a tree on the edge of a wood which is a nature reserve and standing by the side of a huge field?'

He nodded briskly. 'They can always grow another tree if they want one. It's the principle of the thing, Mo. I would have thought you would realise how important this is by now. We can't make any exceptions.'

'Why not?' She stood looking at him with something like dislike. 'Why not, just this once, make an exception?'

'Because it's breaking the law.'

'The tree is breaking the law?'

He nodded.

116

She took a deep breath. 'I gather it is a very beautiful tree, Joe. And old. There will be a lot of ill feeling if you insist on this.' As if there wasn't already. She sighed.

'It's not just me. It's the council. It's their job to enforce the law.'

'And judging by your conversation with them just now they thought you were overstepping the mark. This isn't some snooty landowner, Joe.' The hated word. Red rag to a bull. 'This tree belongs to a nature reserve. It belongs to the birds. To us all.'

'It belongs to no one. It's on a public right of way. It has to be removed just as it would be if it was a nettle or a bramble.' He had his own secateurs for just such purposes. They always went with him on his walks. 'No, Mo, I'm sorry. You are being sentimental. There is no place for sentiment in this campaign. None at all.' And he set his jaw in a way she knew well. There would be no diverting him.

The argument on this particular tree lasted longer than most so far. People spoke about tree preservation orders; they contacted the tree warden, the Woodland Trust, the RSPB and Greenpeace; even the local druids, who promised to send someone to sit in the tree until they realised it was a holly, after which they felt a magic circle around it might be more helpful. Joe would not relent and eventually the council sent a truck laden with chainsaws and two men in hard hats. The van bounced up the footpath towards the tree and stopped. The holly was at its most glorious; laden with berries, a beacon in the dead winter landscape. The two men

117

climbed out and stood staring at it. One took off his hat and ran his fingers through his hair. 'Seems a shame.'

The other shook his head. 'I'm not touching that. Not a holly. Bad luck that.'

They nodded in unison, climbed into the truck and drove away.

A week later the council rang Ted Ames. 'If one of your farm workers could take down that holly we'd much appreciate it.' There was a loud sigh the other end of the line. 'It's got to be done. We'll pay, of course. We'll never have any peace if we don't get it sorted.'

But none of the farm workers would touch it.

Two lots of contracting tree surgeons from neighbouring towns found themselves too busy to do it before the spring at the earliest. The odd job man from Dyson Drive turned down two hundred quid. 'Unlucky to chop down a holly, mate,' he told a by now almost incandescent Joe.

In the village people were beginning to smile to themselves quietly.

No one had actually turned their backs on Maureen. Most were sorry for her. But still, people stopped talking when she went into the shop. They stood back and let her go first and waited until she had closed the door behind her before they resumed their conversations. It was on one such an occasion, after she had gone and the long silence was suddenly broken, that Colonel Wright's wife heard from Julie Ames about Doreen's heartbreak. 'Why didn't anyone tell us that she couldn't afford a new fence?' she asked, horrified. 'That's awful.'

The other women in the shop shrugged. How could they explain? The colonel and his wife were part of the village, but not of the inner cadres. Their large house and their money and their posh accents set them apart.

Two days later however the village watched with deep approval as a lorry arrived at Doreen's cottage with new fence timbers to erect a smart fence on the correct line along the footpath. This gesture was followed by the colonel's own gardener laden with young rose bushes and a mandate to restore Doreen's garden. From then on the colonel and his wife became part of the village at last – a village where their ancestors had lived for two hundred years!

It was from the gardener that Doreen heard about the stand-off over the holly. She smiled, by now almost restored to her former benign self. 'Silly man. After all he has done, doesn't he realise to cut down a self-sown holly is to court bad luck for the rest of his life?'

The gardener shrugged. 'He's a townie, Dor. He doesn't care.' He shook his head. 'And I don't think he's going to give up.'

He didn't. Hiring a chainsaw from the tool hire company, with all the protective gear to go with it – goggles, hat, gloves, trousers – Joe took the holly down himself four days before Christmas. He sawed up the tree and carted loads of berried branches in his car boot back to Dyson Drive where he proceeded to sell them to all his neighbours who did not realise where they came from.

The village waited with bated breath. The footpath was now clear over its entire route. Not a branch, not a weed, not a blade of overlong grass obstructed it. A drift of arrows pointed the walker from one end to the other, finger posts announced the start and the finish and it lay across the countryside like an unhealed scar. No walkers came of course from the town in winter, not even the committee. They spent the cold wet months planning next year's onslaughts and had no intention of actually setting foot in the countryside if they could help it until the spring; and they wouldn't be returning to Winchmoor anyway. They had no interest in the place now they had done their bit. The locals didn't walk it either. Not as it was now. It had lost its charm; and the muddy tracks across the open fields, without the shelter of the hedges which made the winter walks tolerable, were universally shunned. They followed the paths they always had and ignored the neatened corners, the dead straight miles. Who wanted their dog to walk over poisoned ground anyway? So footpath 29 lay for the most part unvisited – except by Joe.

Thus it was that he was quite alone when he strode the path two months after Christmas on a clear bright day after a week of violent February gales. He walked slowly along the muddy track alongside the nature reserve, admiring its neatness, the straight clean edges of the ditch where someone after his own heart had trimmed the dead wood back neatly and removed the unsaleable remains of the holly which Joe had tossed over the ditch into the wood to make sure that the path was unencumbered. Standing under the overhanging branches of an ancient oak, safely rooted on the far side of the ditch, he did not look up to admire its grace and stature and thus did not see the huge bough, detached by the gales, hanging precariously over his head. That it chose just that exact moment to fall was of course complete coincidence.

Maureen was visiting the kids that weekend so there was no one to miss him. He came round once or twice, lying on the path, gazing up at the beauty of the huge tree under which he lay. It swam in a mist, from time to time seeming to dance slowly in a graceful pirouette, and from time to time he thought he saw faces peering at him from among the branches. It grew dark early at that time of year and as the hazy sun set below the rim of the field the temperature began to drop sharply. With a smile he closed his eyes. In the morning he would have to see to it that the fallen bough was sawn and the path tidied otherwise someone might trip over and hurt themselves.

It was three days before they found him. The village was sorry for Maureen of course. One by one they called to see if they could help and almost immediately she found herself at the centre of conversations in the post office. Once she began to get over the shock she mourned Joe, of course. But the man she mourned was the man she had married before the obsessions set in. She was, she had to admit, secretly glad to be free of him. And suddenly she felt for the first time at home in her own house. She began to feel as though she had lived in the village forever and at last she was confident that she could ask people home. When they came for coffee or tea there was no sign of any Ordnance Survey maps; no flags or pins or fluorescent pens. Around the lawn she had planted a holly hedge and that spring, out on the fields, nature began to grow back. The tree stump in the middle of the path near the nature reserve had already thrown out one or two small green shoots. No one would ever cut it back again. It's unlucky to cut down a holly.

Sacred Ground

Somewhere in this field there is sacred ground.
Beneath the plough, the hooves,
the combine harvester,
the uncaring plodding feet,
there is a place where our ancestors
six thousand years ago
buried their dead
within a circle
sained by their priests
for all eternity.

There is no sign now of what went on.
Of the ceremonies or the prayers,
except
for a slight catch in the air,
a silence,
a space around which pipits circle.

123

High above, the jet plane does not know it is
    dissecting sacred space.
Thousands of feet up, the prayers have dissipated
whisked onwards to the stars;
or whipped to nothing in the wind.

The gods have been down graded.
They have decamped to the edge of the field,
to a tiny copse which overhangs a stream.
Drowned by the gurgle of water
and the rustle of leaves
they are unheard by all
but those who look for them.
And listen.

Damsel in Distress

For the first ten miles she had still been crying, angrily scrubbing the tears from her cheeks with her sleeve as she swung the heavy old car around the narrow bends of the country lanes, thoughts of Murray and what he had done reverberating round and round in her brain.

It had not occurred to her to wonder, when she reached the lochside cottage in the early hours of the morning, just whose was the MGF tucked so tidily into the layby behind Murray's Saab. She had cursed that her customary spot was taken and driven a few hundred yards on down the lane to the next field gate and left her own car there. That was why, when she arrived, hefting her overnight bag over her shoulder, they hadn't heard her. Why, when she pushed open the gate, turned up the path, let herself in, and run up the narrow wooden stairs no one had realised that she was coming.

She dropped her bag in the doorway and headed in

the dark for the bed. 'Murray! Surprise! I managed to get away!'

It was only as she held out her arms and threw herself towards him that Murray had woken and gasped and reached for the light switch. The woman in bed with him was blonde, at least ten years younger than Ruth and even in that state of surprise, dishevelment and fear, a stunner.

For what seemed like a whole minute the three of them stared at each other in silence, then all three moved at once, the unknown lady to pull the sheets over her head, Murray to reach for his dressing gown and Ruth to turn and run back down the stairs.

Outside a huge full moon had risen over the hill behind the cottage. The silver light flooded the garden and the lane and down across the loch as she ran back towards her car.

'Ruth!' Murray's voice was close behind her. 'Ruth, darling, wait. I can explain!' – the words used so often over countless generations by husbands who thought they would never have to say them.

She ignored him, blundering between hedges full of honeysuckle, alive with pale moths, and grabbed at the handle of the car door. For a moment she struggled with it, forgetting she had locked it, then she fumbled in her pocket with shaking hands for her keys, realising as she did so that she had left her bag she had dropped it on the bedroom carpet.

With a sob she dragged open the door and letting herself in she stabbed the key into the ignition. Behind her Murray had found some shoes for his bare feet and was running up the lane towards her. She slammed down the door locks as the engine caught and throwing the car into gear pulled away, leaving him clawing at the empty air behind her.

The highland cottage, with its whitewashed walls and low slate roof had been her dream. Away from the hurly-burly of their busy lives in Edinburgh, packed diaries, continually ringing phones, e-mails, deadlines, stress and exhaustion, it was a place of sanctuary, a place of peace, a place which, even if they found time to go there together only twice a year, remained vivid and special in the imagination – there always as a dream. Ruth had photos of the cottage pinned up around her desk. There was a beautiful sparkling stone from the shore of the loch on the table as a paperweight, there was a jar of dried heather from the brae behind the honeysuckle hedge on the filing cabinet.

It had been a year earlier that Ruth, suddenly having to cancel a trip to the cottage because of an unexpected conference in Amsterdam, had suggested Murray go on his own. He had demurred, said he wouldn't enjoy it without her; said they could postpone the visit. But in the end he had gone and enjoyed it and finding that he with his job as a fund manager had far more free weekends than she, with hers as a conference organiser, began to go more and more often without her. 'I find myself liking the solitude,' he said. 'I prefer it when you're there, sweetheart, of course I do, but on my own it allows me to recharge my batteries in a way I can't do in the flat . . .'

'I'll bet!' She slammed her hands on the steering wheel as the car thundered through the darkness. 'Bastard! How could you! How *could* you!'

Automatically she was heading back across country towards the flat; her only refuge. Home. On the dashboard a red light was winking. She glanced at it and drove on. Hurling the car into a bend too fast she only just managed to haul it round with difficulty and she slowed at last as adrenaline kicked through her system. She had almost come off the road there. She must drive more slowly. The red light stayed on this time and she squinted down at it. Shit. It was the fuel gauge. Her car ran on diesel. She mustn't run dry or she'd never get it going again. Normally she filled up in the village before the return trip. Where was she? She had no idea. Her internal drama had been preoccupying her so much she had been paying no attention to the road as it flashed by in the darkness. Even if she had passed a garage it would have been closed. She hadn't passed another car in what seemed like hours. Was there a spare can in the boot? Murray had warned her to carry one on these long cross country trips but she didn't even know if the can was there, never mind if it was full. She sniffed hard, trying to fight off another flood of tears, looking for somewhere to stop. The road was narrow, bendy and steep. It would be dangerous to run out here. Even as the thought crossed her mind the car began to jolt over a rough surface and she realised that in her panic she had missed the bend in the road altogether and was hurtling down a rutted track. She braked sharply and the car skidded to a halt. The engine stalled and she saw to her horror that the fuel gauge needle hovered a whisper from empty.

It was a long time before she moved. Aching with fatigue and misery she pushed open the door and climbed out. The air was cold and spicy with pine resin and apart from the narrow strip of moonlit sky above the track it was very dark. She listened. The silence was intense. She had come only a short way off the road but it felt as though she was a thousand miles from anywhere. She could hear no night birds, not a breath of wind in the trees on either side of her. Nothing.

With a shiver she went round to the rear of the car and threw open the boot. There in the dim light was the box of food she had packed so excitedly only a few short hours before, champagne for the midnight feast she had planned as part of the surprise for Murray, champagne to celebrate the fact that she had wangled a few days off to spend with him. Champagne because tomorrow – today – was her birthday!

Blindly she reached past the boxes, rummaging through rugs and tools, maps and all the detritus of years of driving up and down in the old car when Murray had the Saab, searching for the fuel can as slow hot tears rolled unchecked down her face, dripping onto her hands. It wasn't there. She closed her eyes and said a short prayer. When she opened them it still wasn't there.

Slamming the boot shut she went back to the driver's seat and, climbing in, she put her head back against the head rest and closed her eyes. Her mobile was in the bag she had dropped on the floor of the bedroom. As was her money. And her credit cards. Everything but her keys. Her whole bloody life!

She sighed; perhaps she should try and get some sleep. It was – she squinted at her watch – 2.30 in the morning. In a few hours or so it would be light and she could walk back to the road and try to hitch a lift to the next village.

Sleep refused to come. Shivering, she peered through the windscreen into the dark. Trees crowded close to the track on either side, but in the distance where they thinned she could see the luminous night sky. She sighed. Climbing out of the car, she slammed the door and stared round. Perhaps if she walked up the track to where the woodland gave way to open hillside she would be able to see some lights. Unlikely at this hour of the morning, but she had to do something. Sleep was not going to come now.

The night air was soft and cool and very still. The track climbed steeply as she walked, until she found herself out on the open hill. Here the countryside was bathed in silver moonlight. She could see two huge lone pine trees standing nearby, smell their sharp resin, see the vivid moon shadows on the heather. Somewhere in the distance she heard the call of an owl. She stopped, glancing round. It was incredibly beautiful; soothing. Her hurt and anger dulled into a quiet ache. At the top of the rise the country fell away before her and in the distance she could see the sea. If she held her breath she imagined she could hear the restless murmur of the waves on the distant rocks.

The man was standing watching her quite openly about twenty-five feet away. She hadn't seen him arrive; hadn't heard his footsteps. Hadn't had any warning of his presence at all. She drew in her breath sharply, part of her mind doing a lightning calculation as to how quickly she could get back to the car and lock herself in, if indeed she could outrun him at all, the other part searching out his face, half turned towards her, and finding no threat there at all.

She took a deep breath. Help was after all what she had been looking for. Maybe he had a phone that worked. Maybe he had come from a nearby croft and had a can or two of diesel stashed away that she could borrow.

She smiled uncertainly. 'I didn't expect to see anyone out here,' she called. In spite of herself her voice sounded nervous. She took a deep breath and moved a step towards him. 'It's a beautiful night, isn't it. Except that I've been stupid and just about run out of fuel . . .'

He didn't move. His eyes, she realised, were looking past her down the hill towards the sea.

She took another step forward. 'Is there any chance you can help me?'

Shadows were chasing across the heather towards her. She glanced up and saw a wrack of cloud moving tentative fingers across the moon's face. In another moment it would be hidden. She looked back at the man, but he had gone. Where he had been standing there was nothing but empty road bordered on either side by grasses and rocks and heather. Behind her the two Scots pine were the only landmarks in the empty landscape.

She gasped in dismay. 'Where are you? Come back! Please, I need your help –' Her voice trailed away. Had he ever been there at all? Had he been a mere trick of the light? But she had been able to see him clearly, his face, his loose open-neck shirt, the sleeves rolled up above the elbows, his rough trousers, tucked into serviceable boots, his untidy hair, his gentle expression, the high cheek bones, the sad shadowed eyes.

'Please, come back!' She found herself turning round, staring out into the distance.

And then she saw him again. He had moved away from her into the heather. He turned, and she saw him nod his head as if urging her to follow. She shrugged and cautiously she stepped after him, finding a narrow deer track through the tangled heather stems.

The croft nestled in a hollow out of sight of the road. Single-storeyed, roofed with turf, it lay quietly in the moonlight, inside a square of dry stone walling. At right angles to it stood a byre. He moved ahead of her through the gap in the wall and led her round behind the byre where someone had parked an old tractor. Next to it there were a couple of rusty cans.

'Is it diesel? My car takes diesel.' But of course it would be if it was for the tractor. Stooping she lifted one of the cans and shook it. It was empty. She shook the other and there was a reassuring splashing from inside. After a slight struggle she managed to unscrew the rusted top and she sniffed. Diesel.

'Thank you so much. I promise I'll return it.' She turned back towards the croft.

He had gone. The door was closed, the windows dark. She frowned, then she shrugged. Obviously he did not want thanks for his good deed.

Retracing her steps with difficulty through the darkness she lugged the rusty old can back towards the road, struggling through the tangled heather and soft lumpy grass until her feet once more found the rough metalled track. Behind her the shadows were lightening. The cloud had gone. The moonlight returned. Somewhere a fox barked once and was silent.

The fear when it hit her was all encompassing. Suddenly she was ice cold and shaking; her stomach lurched and her throat tightened. The palms of her hands were clammy with terror. Something was terribly wrong. The whole landscape was out of synch. In the cold moonlight it had lost its velvet softness and was hard, two-dimensional. Threatening. For a moment she couldn't move; she couldn't breathe; and then it was all over. She felt a breath of wind on her cheek and then another and behind her the trees began to whisper reassurance. She was almost back at the wood when she glanced over her shoulder one last time. The countryside was empty.

With shaking hands she unscrewed the fuel can and praying that it was indeed diesel and that it wouldn't be too rusty, she began to pour. When it was empty she put the old can in the boot. She intended to refill it and return it but in the meantime she wanted to go home.

The phone was flashing a message when at last Ruth let herself into the flat. It was daylight, although it was still early, and sunbeams were warming the polished floor as she threw down her keys and punched the message button.

'Ruth, darling, I am so sorry. It was a huge mistake. Not what you think. Please. We must talk. Pick up the phone.'

She shook her head sadly and walked across the room towards the bedroom. It was empty. The whole flat was empty. So, Murray was upset, but not so upset he had jumped in the Saab and driven after her. What had he done? Gone back to bed? Sat up discussing the wife who didn't understand him? Chased after a furious girlfriend who hadn't known he had a wife at all?

Exhausted, she sat down at the kitchen table and put her head in her hands. She was beyond tiredness. Beyond coherent thought. The phone rang but she ignored it. She heard the click and whirr of messages recorded and listed. She didn't register if it was Murray's voice or not. She didn't care.

Eventually she climbed stiffly to her feet and walking into the bedroom she threw herself down on the bed. She slept at once. When at last she was awoken by the sound of a key in the door it was already late afternoon.

They made up the quarrel in the end. She tried to make herself believe his excuses, tried to see his meaningless dalliance through his eyes as her fault, tried to believe it wouldn't happen again. But it was only three weeks later that she saw him with his arm around the woman's shoulders. They were standing at the traffic lights in Hanover Street and gazing into one another's eyes as though there was no one else in the whole world but them. No reconciliation could survive that look. There was no point in even trying.

As though acknowledging her change of attitude and recognising at last the depth of her hurt, Murray accepted a relocation to his firm's New York office. There would not be another unexpected glimpse of his happiness with someone else. That at least he would spare her. Ruth did not ask if the new lady was going too and he did not volunteer the information but it seemed a certainty. The divorce was, if not amicable, at least civilised, and sheepishly, perhaps regretting what he had lost as much as looking forward to what he had gained, Murray gave her his half of what was, after all, her cottage so that it would not have to be sold as the flat would have to be sold. 'Remember the happy times!' he whispered with a wry shrug as he gave her his key. 'Don't let me have spoiled this for you as well.'

He hadn't, but it took a long time. It was winter when she went back at last and there was a new man in her life. Their relationship was still delicate, gently explorative, a slow unfolding of possibilities and it had been several weeks before she suggested they go to the loch. On the way she wanted to drop off a can of diesel to say thank you to her midnight rescuer.

She had thought about him often, wondering what he had made of his strange nocturnal visitor; wondering why he had not spoken to her or acknowledged her thanks, and her telling of the story had been a way of letting Edward know about her pain, about the tenderness and vulnerability she felt each time she saw him; explaining her reticence about a relationship which was in so many ways just right.

'I'm not Murray, Ruth,' Edward said gently as yet again she withdrew suddenly into some safe centre deep inside herself. 'I am not going to hurt you.'

She nodded. 'I know. I want to believe you. I want to believe in love and trust, I really do. It's just –' She hesitated miserably. 'It won't happen. Not yet.'

And he smiled and kissed her gently, like a brother. 'Give it time, love,' he said. 'That's all you need. Time. I'll wait. I'll be there when you want me.'

She pored over the map, trying to decide where it was she had been on that fateful night. She traced with her finger her flight back along the main road, remembered where the car had flashed through the village and up the long slow hill beyond the brae and then she saw it, the right angle bend where she had in the dark driven straight on, doubling back unintentionally towards the sea. On the map she could see it was an unmade track which led onto the hill and then stopped; she could see the wood and the moors and the tiny black square which was the croft.

Edward was a good driver and she sat back, enjoying the way he handled his car, content to act as navigator, and tolerantly amused by his raised eyebrow when she missed the turning she wanted him to take. Murray would have fumed and criticised and argued impatiently. But then Murray wouldn't have wanted to bother to return the diesel at all. Edward merely slowed the car and found a place to turn and they approached the corner again. Again they missed it. The track, if it was there at all, was obviously harder to see in daylight than it had been at night. They consulted the map, heads together, hands almost touching, then he engaged gear and once more slowly they edged towards the place. And there it was, scarcely more than a path, overgrown and muddy, heading into the centre of the wood.

'I don't see how I could have thought it was the main road!' Ruth frowned as the car bumped over the ruts.

Edward shrugged. He threw her a quick smile. 'You were upset and angry.'

'But not blind drunk!' She grimaced as his car

grounded and the wheels slithered sideways. 'Look, maybe this isn't a good idea. I'm not sure it's right at all.'

But it was right. Around the next bend they came to the place her car had finally stopped. She recognised the skyline, the hill, the two Scots pine. Leaving the car they walked along the track, Edward carrying the new can of diesel. He was laughing. 'Remind me never to make you angry. The adrenaline which carried you up here thinking it was the main road must have been formidable!' He put down the can and stretched his arms. 'It's worth it, though. The view is amazing.' From the path they could see across the moor towards the sea and the islands beyond.

Ruth frowned. 'There wasn't a fence here before. There can't have been.'

'No?' He glanced at her. 'But this has been here for ages, Ruth. Look.' It was rusty, threaded with dead bindweed and bracken, the posts in places rotted half through, hanging drunkenly from the very wire they were supposed to be supporting.

Ruth walked on. There was the rock where she had spotted the mysterious man. And there in the heather the sheep track they had followed. To reach it she had to climb through the wire.

'I don't understand it.' She shook her head. 'This doesn't feel right. Everything is where I expect it to be. The track, the rocks, those trees, but there was no fence.'

'Well, we'll soon know. If the cottage is there.' He put down the heavy can again and reached out to take her hand. The wind was cold and there was a scattering of sleet in the icy sunshine, but there was something else as well. 'You look scared.'

'I am scared.' She was shivering. How Murray would have mocked her. 'And I have just remembered. I was scared last time, too. Really scared. For no reason. Suddenly. It felt odd. Lonely. Threatening.' She bit her lip. 'I'm glad you're here.'

'So am I.' For a moment their eyes met. He smiled. Picking up the can again he began to walk. 'Come on. Over this rise and we'll see if we've got the right place.'

The croft was there, but there were no white walls, no shaggy turf roof. A few piles of stones, a ruined gable end, the footings of the byre walls surrounded by nettles was all that remained of the place now.

Ruth stared, open mouthed. 'I don't understand.'

Edward glanced at her. He had put the can down again. 'Where did you find the diesel?' he asked quietly.

'There. Round the back of the byre. There was an old tractor –'

Leaving her standing where she was he pushed his way through the weeds and thistles.

'Don't bother, Edward. It's the wrong place. It has to be,' she called. Ramming her hands deep into her coat pockets she followed him.

The tractor was still there. What was left of it. A pile of rusting metal. And the remains of the other old can stood by the crumbling wall. She had picked it up and shaken, hadn't she? A rowan tree was growing through it now.

'No!' She shook her head and backed away. 'This is all wrong!'

'There must be a simple explanation.' Edward put his arm round her again. She was shaking. 'I suspect you are right. There are probably several old cottages and crofts around here and they all look much the same. I'm sure they all had ancient tractors and they would all keep a bit of spare fuel, living so far from civilisation.'

She nodded. 'You're right.'

There had only been one track on the map. One tiny square to represent a dwelling, amid thousands of empty acres of moor and mountain.

'If we went into the shop in the village on the main road, maybe they'd know,' she said hopefully.

He nodded. 'This must have been a beautiful place, but bleak in winter.' It was his turn to shiver. 'The ground is very poor. The tractor must have had a job doing anything at all.'

They stood for a few more minutes, staring round, then they began to retrace their steps towards the car.

The old lady in the post office stared at them over her spectacles. 'You must mean Carn Breac.' She shook her head. 'That place has been empty since before the war. Michael Macdonald stayed on there a year or two after his parents died, then he upped and left. He settled in Canada I believe.' She frowned, searching her memory. 'If you hold on now, I've a photo here.' She came out from behind the counter and disappeared for a moment into the sitting room which opened out of the shop. When she came back she was carrying an album. 'Yes, see here.' She opened it and stabbed at a faded photo with her finger. 'That's Michael, and Donald, his father, next to him.' The sepia shadows showed some half-dozen men ranged against a wall, staring ahead at the camera. The one called Michael had a wooden rake in his hand.

Ruth felt her mouth go dry. For a moment she thought she was going to faint.

'What do you want with him?' The post mistress slowly closed the book.

Ruth couldn't speak. It was Edward who said quietly, 'We have something of his we want to return.'

'I don't know his address.' She shook her head. 'It's so long ago. You could maybe ask the minister. He's only been twenty years or so at the manse, but I think there are records there. If anyone knows where he went, it will be him.'

'You think he might still be alive then?' Edward probed gently.

She shrugged. 'I've no idea.'

The minister knew the family. Michael James Macdonald had died in Prince George, British Columbia on 24th July that year, at the age of eighty-nine. It was the day Ruth had seen him leaning on a rock by the croft where he had been born.

Edward poured them both a glass of wine and joined her by the fire in the cottage by the loch. 'Are you OK now?'

She nodded. 'I still can't believe I've seen a ghost!'

'You're a lucky lady. Not only to see one, but to be rescued by him.'

She sipped the wine. 'How is it that the diesel worked? You'd think it would have gone off. Rusted. Evaporated. Something.'

He stared into the depths of his glass. 'The other can had disintegrated completely.'

'Perhaps a farmer had left it there recently?' She looked at him hopefully.

He smiled. 'Perhaps. I don't think you are ever going to know the answer to that one.'

'And, if it was him, why did he appear as a young man and not the age he was?'

'We can't answer that either.' He leaned back and put his arm round her shoulders. 'One thing you can be sure of though. He must have loved that place. It must have been very hard to leave it forever. Perhaps he promised himself he would go back one day.'

'At least he had a happy life, and a wonderful marriage.' The minister had told them that. She didn't realise how wistful the words sounded until they were out of her mouth.

Edward didn't answer. He was staring into the fire.

'Have you ever been married?' She realised with a shock she had never even asked him.

He shook his head. 'Nearly. We thought better of it. Just as well as we haven't seen each other for five years. Since then I haven't come close.'

'Oh.' Her voice was bleak.

'Until now.' He hesitated. 'This is going to sound very corny, but when you find something precious you need to hang on to it otherwise you are going to regret it all your life. Our relationship – Sarah's and mine – just wasn't that precious.' Once again he paused. 'Why did you and Murray end yours so quickly?'

She thought for a long time. 'I suppose I wasn't that precious to him. Not in your sense of the word. And perhaps –' She paused thoughtfully. 'Perhaps after all he wasn't that precious to me. I gave him a second chance. I wasn't prepared to give him a third.' She shrugged. 'That doesn't show me in a very good light.'

'It shows you as a realist. And your Michael Macdonald. Presumably he was as well. He knew the croft couldn't sustain him. In his eyes he had no choice.'

She stood up and went to sit on the floor by the fire. 'It's a sad little story.'

'No.' He followed her. Kneeling down he reached over and kissed her gently. 'It's actually a wonderful story. Why are we letting it make us sad? It had a happy ending. He came home. And he helped a damsel in distress. He made choices, but they seem to have been the right choices. After all he had children and grandchildren and even great-grandchildren to succeed him. No doubt one day they will come home and stand where you stood and stare at the tiny croft which is their heritage. But I wonder if they will see him as you did?' He raised his glass. 'Let's drink to his memory. And to our future.' He grinned. 'Who knows, maybe I'll come and haunt this place when I'm eighty-nine!'

She laughed. 'Perhaps you will. And maybe you'll still be coming here in the flesh!' She clinked her glass against his. 'Who knows?'

The Last Train to Yesterday

Chloë awoke with a start and stared up at the ceiling, her heart thumping. Dusky pink curtains across the window intercepted the harsh red glow from the eastern sky and filled the room with a warm eerie half-light. With a groan she rolled over and groped for the alarm clock, peering at it myopically as her sleepy brain tried to work out the time. Five minutes before the alarm. Pressing down the knob to pre-empt the angry buzz she put it back on the bedside table and swung her feet to the floor.

Drawing back the curtains, she sighed.

Red sky in the morning
Shepherd's warning

Already threatening bars of cloud were hovering above the fields beyond the garden. By the time she left for the station it would be raining. She was peering into the mirror, trying to put on her eye liner before inserting her contact lenses when she heard the first rain pattering down on the leaves outside the window.

'Damn!' London was never fun at the best of times for a rushed business day. The smart sandals she had planned to wear would have cheered her up. In the soupy dirt of wet pavements they would never work.

She tucked in the lenses and carried out a quick survey of the face that zoomed suddenly into focus. Short reddish-brown curls, artfully casual. Eyes – not bad – a deep hazel green. Skin good. Still fairly unmarked by time. Nose, small and ordinary – not what romantic books would call tip-tilted – more of a small conk really. Mouth, definitely a bit big, but Edmund used to say that was attractive. The expression in front of her degenerated into a fearsome scowl. Edmund and his opinions were no longer to be considered. Off the scene. Out of the plot. Finito.

She claimed one of the last spaces in the car park – the regular commuters long gone, before dawn – and hauled her briefcase out of the car. Behind her: cottage, garden, and two tolerantly patient cats who would welcome her home, if not with the gin and tonic she might have liked, then at least with expectant glances towards the tin opener! It was better than no one. In front of her lay noise, bustle, meetings, rush. She loved the contrast.

A spatter of September leaves whirled into a puddle near her. She grimaced. Mud on her boots already and she had twenty yards to go to the footbridge which led up and over the line to the ticket office which was on platform two, the only platform still in use.

Behind her, hidden by a skimpy hedge liberally threaded with old rusty wire, lay the old railway hotel, derelict behind its boarded windows. On fine days the pigeons cooed and strutted on the roof and basked on the broken tiles. Today they sat disconsolately, their feathers puffed, while a loose hoarding banged in the wind. She shivered suddenly and pulled up the collar of her coat.

'Good morning, Mrs Denver.' The figure beside her raised a hand. She had barely noticed him park next to her and climb out beside her. 'One of your days in town?'

Chloë smiled at him. The new man who had bought the Beeches on Thorney Road. She groped for a name and came up with a blank.

He grinned. 'Miles. Miles Rowton.'

'Of course.' She smiled. He had a nice face. Square, almost ugly, deeply lined between nose and mouth and at the corners of his eyes, but nice. Probably in his forties. Once she might have been interested. Not now. What she wanted now was the peace and stability of her own company.

They reached the footbridge in silence and he paused with old-fashioned courtesy to allow her to go up ahead of him. The wind and the sweeping rain precluded conversation. She climbed, trying not to be aware that he was close behind her, concentrating on the steep metal treads, her hand on the cold wet rail, its black paint dimpled with rust.

Afterwards she supposed she had stumbled. The world seemed to do a strange somersault and for a moment she thought she could hear music carried in the wind. Then it was gone and she was standing near the top of the long flight, panting, clutching the handrail with both hands.

'Are you all right?' He didn't touch her. He merely stood there, two steps below her, so his face was level with hers, registering surprise and mild concern. Apparently he could not see how her heart was pounding or the sheen of sweat on her face.

She took a deep breath and shook her head slightly. 'Sorry. I must have tripped.'

Mary! Mary wait!

Where had the voice come from? Her head was swimming. She glanced down the flight of steps and clutched more tightly at the rail, knuckles white.

'It's a bit slippery in this rain.' Miles Rowton was beside her now. Then in front. 'Shall I lead the way?'

Hadn't he heard it? She shook her head a little, trying to clear the sound from her brain. There was no one near them. No one else anywhere in sight. He glanced over his shoulder at her and smiled encouragingly. She must look perfectly normal then, or surely he would have stayed at her side.

Stop! Mary, wait!

The words must have come from somewhere in her head.

Help me, someone. Mary!

She didn't know what was wrong. She was still clinging to the rail, shaking.

Please, don't leave me!

This couldn't be happening. Miles had walked on. He paused to glance back. 'Coming? The train has been signalled,' he called. She could see his hair lifting boyishly on his forehead in the wind. The words were being whipped from his mouth.

Somehow she forced herself to take a step forward.

Then another. Then suddenly it was easy. She was hurrying after him, the wind tugging at her hair. Behind her, on the roof of the old hotel, the pigeons lifted as one, whirled high above the station and settled back onto the old broken slates.

On the train, still shaken by her experience, she ordered a coffee from the trolley. Miles Rowton had seated himself opposite her, across the aisle. Too far away for easy conversation, but close enough not to appear rude. Once their eyes met as she sipped the scalding liquid and they smiled. Then both looked away back to their respective laps, his covered in papers, hers the newspaper she had grabbed at the village shop as she drove past.

London was all Chloë had feared. Crowded, wet, taxis impossible to find and when she did, gridlocked in the traffic. She was late for her first meeting, then the knock-on effect came into play and the whole sequence of the day slipped back first twenty minutes, then forty, and by the time she reached the end of lunch she was running an hour and a half late. Moving her design consultancy to the country at Edmund's behest still worked best for her most of the time. It was on days like this when she wondered briefly whether the hassle of commuting and serving many masters was worth it all. Thankfully they did not happen that often.

In the end she caught a very late train home. The cats would be livid, showing their displeasure by sulkily shunning their food and refusing to climb into bed for a goodnight cuddle. She smiled at the thought. Was she so devoid of human relationships these days, that she was worried that her cats would be cross with her? Settling back in her seat, exhausted, she unbuttoned her jacket and kicked off her shoes. There was barely anyone else left in the carriage.

With a sigh she fought back a longing for a huge baguette, the kind it is impossible to eat without doing an impression of Quasimodo, and which, when bitten, empty their contents down one's front. She had had to run to catch this train and at this hour, when she needed it most, there would almost certainly be no trolley on the train. She hadn't even had time to buy an evening paper. Closing her eyes Chloë dozed.

It was dark when she stepped onto the deserted platform and took a deep lungful of the cool fresh air. It had stopped raining at last and she could see the stars. There was no one else on the station. Even the ticket office was closed. There would be only one more train that night.

With an exhausted sigh she gripped the handle of her briefcase more tightly and set off for the footbridge. Halfway over she realised she could hear, above the ringing echo of her own footsteps, the sound of music drifting on the wind across the car park. She stopped and listened. Below in the dark the car park was deserted. Only three cars remained from the huge crowd this morning, their bodywork gleaming gently in the darkness. She could barely see over the tall parapet, but standing on tiptoes she gazed into the dark with sudden misgivings. The station was down a quiet lane some half-mile from the village. There were no houses near by. Yet she could see lights. They seemed to be coming from the direction of the derelict hotel. And again, faintly, in the distance, the music drifted up towards her.

Nervously she began to move forward, trying to silence the sharp echo of her heels. At the top of the downward flight she stopped again, reaching out for the handrail.

Mary, please come back!

The man's voice sounded so close to her that she recoiled.

She peered down, expecting to hear the echo of footsteps running up the metal steps. There was nothing. Far away, on the main road she heard a car engine rev away into the distance.

Straining her eyes into the darkness ahead of her she gripped the handrail and put her foot on the first step.

Mary, for pity's sake, my darling, listen.

The words were caught by the wind and whisked away over the tracks and into the darkness.

She gripped the handrail more tightly and moved down another step.

The door to the Station Hotel banged in the wind and the sound of music escaped into the night. Mary had stood there for only a second, staring into the smoky bar, looking round, but she had seen him at once, his arm around the red-haired girl. For a moment she stared. Very few bothered to turn to look, fewer had noticed the expressions which crossed her face in quick succession. Shock. Disbelief. Anger. Misery. And then that final despair as her husband raised his hand to a titian ringlet and, laughing, wound it around his finger. Mary made no sound. In that split second when her world spun and came apart she was silent. And he heard the silence. His hand fell from the girl's cheek and he turned slowly towards the door.

For a long seemingly endless second husband and wife stared at one another and he read in her eyes what he had done.

Mary! Sweetheart! Wait!

He slid from his bar stool and began to move towards the door. But his limbs wouldn't move fast enough. He felt as though he were swimming through the smoky air, the noise, the laughter.

Mary, wait!

The girl with the red hair tossed her curls and turned back to the bar. The married ones were the most fun. Their reluctance before, their guilt afterwards, made them more exciting. But what matter. There were plenty more fish in the sea . . .

Mary!

He had seen it in her eyes. Her love for him had been total. Complete. With a careless, meaningless flirtation, he had destroyed everything.

Mary!

He stood outside in the wind, staring round as the swinging door closed and cut off the smoky lamplight leaving him in the dark. And then he saw her running towards the bridge and in a flash he knew what she was going to do.

Mary, no! His voice broke as he started to run. *Mary, my darling, please, you must wait!*

He saw the swirling white of her petticoats below her coat as she ran towards the bridge, even as he heard faintly the hollow rumble of the train as it started across the viaduct in the distance, puffing purposefully towards the station.

Chloë stopped halfway down the steps, clutching the rail with both hands. Her briefcase fell, teetered beside her for a moment on the step, began to rock and slowly slid out of sight. She did not notice it had gone. She too now, could hear the train wheels rattling hollowly in the distance.

'No,' she whispered. 'No.'

Suddenly the footsteps were behind her, running. Clenching her teeth against a rising scream Chloë forced herself to take another step down. She could hear the train getting closer, the clackety-clack of the wheels on solid ground now, the sound of the steam coming in powerful rapid gusts.

Reaching the bottom of the stairs she stood for a moment staring round into the dark. The platform was lit by one faint lamp near the small entrance, beyond which lay the car park. She felt the ground beneath her feet shake as the train drew in with screaming brakes.

Clapping her hands over her ears she stared at it in horror. The windows were welcoming, warm behind her. The train seemed empty. She heard a single door bang. Then silently it began to draw away from the platform. Under the tall fluorescent lights she could see it clearly now. An ordinary four-carriage train. There was no engine. Certainly no steam engine.

Behind her she could hear the footsteps again. 'I'm going mad!' She groped at her feet for her briefcase, swung it up and turned towards the entrance.

'Hello there!' The cheerful voice from the top of the flight stopped her dead. 'I didn't see you on the train. How was your day in London?' He was running down towards her now. Miles Rowton, his own briefcase grasped firmly in his left hand, his right lightly skimming the handrail. At the bottom he stopped and she saw his cheerful smile turn to a look of concern.

'I say, are you all right? You didn't fall?' His hand was on her arm. 'What's wrong? Can I do anything?'

Numbly Chloë shook her head. 'It's so silly,' she whispered. 'I don't know. I don't know what happened . . .'

She stared at him, her eyes on his for several seconds as though trying to convince herself that he was real, then reluctantly she looked back up at the bridge. 'She was running. I was sure she was going to throw herself in front of the train . . . I could hear her – hear him – following. I heard the train braking.'

His arm was round her shoulders now, supporting and consoling, his own briefcase beside hers on the wet ground. 'Mrs Denver – Chloë – what are you talking about? There's no one there. Look for yourself. The platform is empty. The train has gone. No one is hurt.'

'Are you sure?' Confused, she was clinging to him.

'I'm sure.' He rather liked her helplessness. Always when he had seen her before, in the distance, she had seemed so calmly confident, so much in total control of herself he had felt a little in awe of her.

A similar thought had obviously occurred to her. He could feel her self-consciousness returning as she realised she was standing on the platform more or less in the arms of a man she hardly knew. She stiffened and then slowly she pushed him away.

'I'm ... I'm sorry. I must have imagined it. I don't quite know what happened.'

He smiled down at her. 'One's eyes and ears sometimes play tricks when one is tired, especially in the dark like this. Let me walk with you to your car.' He had let go of her arm when she pushed him away, so now he stooped and picked up both their cases. Sensing that she was just about enough recovered to object he moved ahead of her under the small 1970s ugly brick entrance arch and out into the car park where his car was parked next to hers.

When they reached the cars she stopped and stared at the dark silhouette of the deserted hotel. 'When did this place close down, do you know?'

He followed her gaze and shrugged. 'A long time ago, judging by the shape it's in.'

She did not tell him she had seen it with lights pouring out of the open door, that she had heard music from one of the bars as the wind carried the noise of talk and laughter up to her on the bridge.

With a smile at him and a few polite words of thanks she climbed into her car and let him close the door on her as with a hand which she found was shaking slightly she inserted the key in the ignition and switched it on. As the headlights came on, illuminating the ruined building behind its wire fence, the sleeping pigeons on the roof moved restlessly, complaining quietly to themselves before settling once more to their roost.

She gripped the wheel and closed her eyes. When she opened them again his car was drawing backwards away from her. With a small polite toot on his horn he swung the car away and in a moment he had gone, his red tail lights vanishing into the lane.

'Mary.' She murmured the name as she peered at the dark, gaping windows. 'What happened?'

There was no answer. As she engaged the reverse gear, her eyes were still on the broken windows and sagging door and it was slowly and almost reluctantly that she pulled away and turned out into the lane herself.

The cats were surprisingly forgiving. Perhaps sensing something of her melancholy they settled down, after wolfing down their supper, one on either side of her, as she sat curled up on the sofa in front of the open fire.

She sipped at her mug of coffee staring at the glowing logs.

Mary.

The man's anguished voice echoed in her ears and she shivered as she stared down at the heap of papers and sketches on the floor beside her. She had two reports to read and a whole heap of notes which should be written up before tomorrow. When, by rights, she should go up to town again. She sighed, one hand playing gently with a pair of silky pointed ears.

The sound of the phone made her jump. She reached for it over the arm of the sofa carefully, anxious not to upset feline equilibrium.

'Mrs Denver? Chloë? It's Miles Rowton. Forgive me. I just wanted to make sure you had got home safely. I felt very guilty after I left you that I hadn't offered to drive you –'

'Don't be silly.' Her voice was sharper than she intended. 'I'm perfectly all right.' The cat beside her stood up, stretched, and curled round more comfortably. It knew about telephones. People sat satisfactorily still for hours once they had a receiver in their hand. Chloë smiled to herself, understanding its body language. How wrong it was on this occasion. 'I'm sorry. That sounds so ungrateful.' Her voice had softened. 'I'm not sure what happened to me. As you said, probably tiredness and too late at work. I started hearing voices, of all things!'

Mary, wait!

'I thought for a moment I must be going mad, and then I suppose I slipped on those stairs –'

'They are slippery.' He paused, not knowing quite how to continue the conversation. 'Well, if you are sure you're all right –'

'I am.' She hesitated. 'Thank you, Miles. I appreciate you phoning. It is a bit bleak coming back here on my own sometimes.' She needn't have said that. 'Particularly if one has reason to doubt one's sanity.' The lightness of her laugh reassured him.

'I'm sure you're perfectly sane,' he said gallantly. 'But look, if you are worried at all, or you need anything, don't hesitate to give me a ring. I didn't realise that you were on your own.' Liar. The whole village gossiped about Chloë Denver whose husband had run off with another woman. They all liked her well enough, and were sorry for her in their way. They had seemed such a devoted couple. But she sort of half commuted to London, which made her an outsider, and she kept her grief or her relief – for who knew how she really felt about her husband's departure – to herself.

'Are you going up to town again tomorrow?' he asked suddenly.

She shrugged and then realised he couldn't see the gesture. 'I'm not sure. I should be in theory, but –'

Mary, please, my darling.

She grimaced, her knuckles whitening on the phone. He misunderstood her hesitation. 'I know. In this weather it's grim, isn't it? You are lucky not having to go regularly.'

'How do you know I don't go regularly?' She was intrigued by the comment and a touch of amusement showed in her voice.

'I'm sorry. I don't. I suppose I assumed I would have seen you at the station before if you did.'

'That's probably true.' The cat stretched luxuriously, secure that the conversation was well under way.

'So you will ring me if you need anything?'

'Yes, I will. Thank you.'

'Chloë –' He was anxious not to end the conversation. His own life was unbearably lonely. Moving to a new area had seemed sensible after his wife died. Now he knew it had been madness. 'The voices. What did they say?'

She laughed. 'Aren't the voices in people's heads confidential?'

'It depends. If they are internal voices, voices from God, then yes, perhaps they are. But if they are external, real voices, then perhaps not.'

'What do you mean, real voices?' She couldn't tell him she was still hearing them. The voice did not sound like God to her. It sounded like a desperate young man with a local accent.

'Ghosts?'

The icy shudder which swept over her body was totally involuntary. For a moment she couldn't say a word.

'Chloë, are you there? I was only joking.'

'The trouble is –' She found there were tears in her eyes, 'I think that you might be right.' This was mad. She was letting him wind her up. 'Look, Miles. Thank you for ringing, but I've actually got quite a lot of work to do tonight. Perhaps we can talk about this some other time?'

She didn't work though. After she had hung up, all too aware of the disappointment behind his apologies for having taken up her time, she sat for a long while gazing into the fire. She was wondering what his name was, Mary's young man, and what he had done to make her threaten to throw herself under a train. She thought she could probably guess.

She had felt like killing herself when she first found out about Edmund's affair. Only it wasn't just an affair. It turned out that it was the great love of his life and it was she who had been the mistake. She stroked a silken purring tummy gently and was rewarded by an ecstatic stretch. Was that why she had heard the voices? Because she understood?

It was very late when she at last went to bed and, exhausted, she slept dreamlessly, aware of two small solid bodies curled up on her duvet. It was only at dawn that they awoke and crept out into the garden to create mayhem amongst the birds, leaving her to turn restlessly over and bury her face in the pillow.

She did not go to London. Partly because her reports

were not written, her sketches not finished, partly because, she had to admit, she did not want to go near the station. It was the perfect autumn day, warm, glowing, the air sweet with berries and nuts and damp leaf mould beneath the trees. She took her lap top and her phone out to the small summer house in the back garden with all her books and papers and she spent the morning there engrossed in her work.

Miles had been standing there for several minutes before she looked up and saw him. Instead of his city suit he was wearing an open-necked shirt and a heavy knitted sweater. He smiled apologetically. 'I didn't want to disturb you.'

She stretched her arms above her head and switched off the lap top. 'You haven't. You have rescued me from all my good resolutions.'

'I too work at home sometimes.' His eyes were silvery grey, startlingly alert in his tanned face. She wondered why she hadn't noticed how good-looking he was. 'In fact in about three weeks' time I shall be giving up the day job altogether, so I thought today was too good to spend on the eight-fifteen. I did go to the station though.'

'Oh?' In the orchard a light breeze had got up and she felt a small shiver tiptoe across her shoulders.

'I wanted to get a good look at that old hotel in daylight. Normally in the morning when I go for the train I'm comatose.' He grinned. 'It was a beautiful building once. I asked Peter at the ticket office what he knew about it. He said if I wanted to know I should go and see the old father of one of his colleagues whose own father was on the railway before him apparently and he can recall all sorts of stories about the station in the early days.'

The wind had grown stronger and she was shivering. 'And did you go?'

'I thought you might like to come with me.'

Mary wait for me.

'I don't know. I'm not sure I want to know.'

She led the way into the kitchen and brought a bottle of wine out of the fridge. 'Her name was Mary. She threw herself under a train. He was running after her. Trying to save her.' She shook her hair back out of her eyes and he saw the glint of tears.

'How do you know?'

'I don't really. It sort of fits.' Behind her one of the cats had come in from its hunting. It was sitting on the dresser carefully washing its face with its left paw. He accepted a glass of wine and stared round. The kitchen was pretty, attractive, cosy. All the things his own was not. 'If you don't want to come I'll go and see him on my own. I'm just curious about what happened. I won't tell you if you would rather not.'

She smiled. 'I don't think I would be able to contain my curiosity. I'll come. If I don't I won't be able to stop thinking about her.'

Or get his voice out of my head.

Jim Maxell was ninety-four. His memory was as clear as crystal. But he shook his head at their request. 'People have jumped, of course. But not a young woman. Not as far as I recall. The Station Hotel closed in nineteen fifty-four. It sort of went down hill, became less and less popular because the line was used less and less then when they closed the maltings up the lane that was the end of it. It used to be packed before the last war. Village people used to take the train in to market and then come back with money in their pockets. I can remember it just as you described it, love, noisy, smoky, the lamplight spilling out across the pavement. There were quarrels a plenty.' He gave a chuckle. 'I can remember many a woman fetching her man a slap across the face for one reason or another – and vice versa!'

And with that they had to be content.

Over a ploughman's in the pub in the village Chloë and Miles discovered they had more than an interest in a possible rail tragedy in common. Both alone, both in their own way bereaved, they felt their way cautiously forward: music, painting, books, gardening, cats. Exchanging a shy glance of complicity as they decided to consult the old newspapers in the library they even found they shared a taste for the death by chocolate pudding which was the pub's speciality. And they were both, did they but realise it, now the centre of the village's latest and hottest gossip.

The town's modern library had the local paper on microfiche. Without names or dates it was not going to be easy to find out the truth – if there was a truth – behind the story. And secretly neither wanted to, not too soon. Further visits to the library would, after all, inevitably require further visits to small local restaurants to fuel the energy needed for research.

But before they could do that Chloë had to visit London again.

She promised him that she would tell him when she went, but something stopped her. The phone call from her largest client had come quite late. They needed the sketches the next day and the sketches were ready; there was no need to spend more time on them. All she needed to do was deliver them herself. Promising to be there by ten she sat on the sofa staring at the fire. Outside it was raining again. The wind had risen and she could hear the branches of the trees thrashing in the wind. The two cats were coiled together, yin and yang, in the old armchair that Edmund used to consider his own. She stared at them, remembering how they would vie for the favoured place on his knee and every night compromise in a love knot just like the one which they had made tonight. And like tonight excluding her.

She should have seen it coming. His distance from her; his smart new shirts of a bright hitherto untolerated colour, the change of aftershave and the rejection of her presents on his birthday. Nothing rude or unkind. It was just that they were quietly jettisoned at the back of his cupboard and never referred to again. She was glad he had not wanted to take the cats. Technically they were his but he said, trying to make a joke of it, that she could have custody. There was no place for cats in his new life. They, like her, had been rejected.

And suddenly she no longer minded.

She liked her new independence. And she liked Miles. A lot.

But that did not mean she could not function without him. Never again was she going to allow herself to rely on anyone else. And it was a matter of pride that she should climb the footbridge alone.

The storm had blown itself out next morning, and the sky was a delicate blue streaming with rags of crisp clean cloud. She parked the car in good time and stood staring at the old hotel. A new section of the tiles had been stripped off in the night and there was a gaping hole now, showing the stark roof ribs. Amongst the grey pigeons were a pair of exotic white doves, blown away from their home territory, slumming it happily with their cousins.

Gripping her briefcase tightly she walked towards the bridge. There were several people waiting on the platform already and she could see a short queue at the ticket office as she set her foot on the first step.

Halfway up she stopped, straining her ears. She could hear nothing but the wind, barely more than a breeze now, soughing gently in the tangled hedge on the far side of the line. Glancing over the parapet at the old hotel she could see the white birds clearly on the roof. They seemed unperturbed, preening in the sunshine, sheltered from the wind by the chimney stacks.

She moved on, reached the top, walked slowly across the bridge and then began to descend.

'Chloë, dear!' The oh-so female voice behind her was loud and very real. 'Going up to town? How lovely. We can travel together.'

Glancing round, Chloë caught sight of the two white doves, in the distance, wheeling now above the station. She smiled at the owner of the voice, a woman she usually tried to avoid, and resigned herself to an inquisition from which there would be no escape. At least it would deflect the disappointment which she realised suddenly she was feeling that there had been no voices in her head, no music floating in the sky above the hotel.

The business dinner, the result of the prompt personal delivery of the sketches, had been unavoidable and because of it she had to catch the last train. When she at last stepped out of the empty carriage the ticket office was closed as she had known it would be. There was no one else on the platform.

The footbridge rose against the starry sky, a black silhouette in the total silence. The lonely station light did no more than throw pools of black shadow under its high arch.

Her briefcase tightly clasped in one hand Chloë took a deep breath and walked towards it. The steps between its walls formed a canyon of darker black. The one light at the top of the stairs had long ago been broken by vandals, the damaged fitting left to rust. Almost without realising it she was straining her ears for voices; for music from the hotel across the tracks, but the night was perfectly silent save for the call of an owl in the fields on the far side of the lane.

Resolutely she put her foot on the lowest step of the bridge. Her mouth had gone dry, and she told herself not to be a fool. What, after all, was there to be afraid of? A voice? The echo of running feet? Some nameless tragedy from the past which had barely touched the history of time.

She had taken two more steps up when she heard in the distance the rumble of a train. She froze, listening. The tracks had begun to whisper behind her.

Mary, my darling, wait. Let me explain.

She glanced up ahead, suddenly wishing she had brought a torch. The darkness of the steps between the walls was impenetrable.

She could hear the wheels now as the train reached the viaduct, their note hollow, inexorable, and above it the snorting of the steam.

Mary.

The footsteps were so close she flinched and ducked back against the wall. Turning she fled back onto the platform. Her hands were shaking as, her resolution gone, she pulled her mobile phone from her bag.

Please let him be in. 'Miles? I'm at the station. Please come.'

Switching it off she slipped it into her pocket, her eyes on the bridge. He had not questioned her. There had been no recriminations that she had come alone as once Edmund would have done. She stiffened. Had that been the flash of a pale skirt she saw out of the corner of her eye at the top of the flight? Holding her briefcase in her arms, across her chest like a shield, she slipped around the corner of the small ticket office and pressed close against the cold wall.

The train was getting closer. On the bridge the shadows grew if anything more black.

Mary.

His voice was very faint this time.

Mary, my darling, forgive me.

Her mouth dry, Chloë peered around the corner. The car park was silent. Please hurry, Miles. Please hurry.

But it wasn't Miles who needed to hurry. If only she knew the young man's name.

The sound of the train was louder now. The hollow ring of the wheels changed note as it passed across the viaduct and reached the solid ground. It was coming very close.

Mary, wait.

Chloë could hear running footsteps. They were coming across the bridge. *Mary, my darling, listen.*

White petticoats frothed in the darkness, descending the stairs and suddenly Chloë could hear a woman's broken sobs near her, on the platform.

Mary.

His voice was still on the bridge, far away. The noise of the steam engine was deafening. Pressing her hands over her ears, Chloë closed her eyes.

In the lane the car broke all speed limits as it tore towards the station forecourt and came to a halt. The door opened and Miles leaped out, leaving the engine running and the headlights shining full across the track.

'Chloë,' he shouted. 'Don't move. Don't go near the edge. I'm coming!'

She didn't hear him. Her eyes were on the rails.

'Mary,' she whispered. 'Please, don't do it. Listen to him. Believe him.'

'Chloë!' The whole bridge vibrated to Miles's heavy footsteps as he ran.

Chloë had dropped her case. She took a step forward. 'Mary!' she called.

She could see her quite clearly. The pale face, the dark curly hair, the dark dress and heavy, long coat, pulled straining across the huge belly. And the eyes. The huge eyes, blank with despair. For a moment the two women stood facing each other as the train drew into the station with a scream of wheels on metal.

'Chloë!'

Mary.

As Miles grabbed her shoulders and swung her away

165

from the edge of the platform Chloë caught a momentary glimpse of the young man who had thrown his arms around Mary and dragged her away. He was tall, his face shadowed beneath his cap. And then they had gone. The platform was empty and suddenly, shockingly, silent. There was no train. Never had been a train. Only the wind soughing across the fields and the lonely call of the peewits disturbed the night.

Chloë was trembling as she clung to Miles. 'It was all right. He saved her. Perhaps *we* saved her.' She found she was sobbing gently. 'That was why it wasn't news. There was a happy ending.'

'I'm glad.' He smiled down at her. 'Come on. Let's take you home. We'll come and get your car in the morning.'

As they climbed back over the bridge Chloë glanced over the parapet towards the hotel. Lights spilled out of the doors across the grass and in the distance she could hear the cheerful notes of a honky tonk piano. She stopped.

'Can you hear that?'

He nodded.

'And see the lights?'

He nodded again.

'Do you think they lived happily ever after?'

She needed him to say yes, but he laughed.

'Oh, my darling sweet romantic. And I thought you were a hard-boiled business woman! No, I don't suppose they did. They probably had happy bits and sad bits. I expect they quarrelled and they made up and they had four or five children and lived to become fat and staid and boring. But I expect he always remembered that passionate wild gesture of hers, and she always remembered that he saved her life, whatever it was he had done before. And that was the secret they never told their children and they never spoke of again. A secret which when it happened caused them both to feel such pain and such fear that it was imprinted on time itself. I think that is what ghosts are. They are not the spirits of dead people; they are emotions so intense, so raw, so deeply felt that they become locked into the place where they happened and sometimes, if the time is right, other people see and hear them.'

He took her hand and tucked it under his arm. To her surprise she did not move it.

'Come on, I can feel a philosophical drink by the fire is in order,' he said firmly. 'Will you let me drive you home and propose a toast to Mary and her Joe.'

'How do you know his name?'

Below them the car park was suddenly dark. The music had stopped and the wind was blowing through empty, ruined rooms.

'I don't. I guessed.' He smiled. 'Come on, my dear. Let's go home.'

Party Trick

'Have you ever tried dowsing?' Morgan Conway looked across at Pippa and smiled.

He had arrived to spend the weekend at the cottage with her and Colin, but now Colin was out on call, attending a calving two miles away, leaving them facing each other over cups of strong coffee, running out of small talk after only a few minutes. The trouble was that Colin had told her nothing about their unexpected guest. 'We were at school together. Lives in London. Nice chap.' And that was all, for God's sake! Nothing about where he had been up to now and why she hadn't met him before. Things were difficult enough between her and Colin at the moment. They had only lived here a few months and she loved the cottage, but unable to find a job, any job, let alone the busy administrative post she'd had before, she was as bored as he was happy and fulfilled in the new practice.

Their latest row was a direct result of her own

personal angst. It had been about babies. Why not? Colin had said. The implication being that it would give her something to do; something to fill her time; keep her out of mischief. Her anguished refusal even to contemplate having a child had appalled him and their quarrel had escalated terrifyingly. Her misery at his apparent lack of understanding, at the crassness of the timing of the suggestion, made her say things she didn't mean – that she never wanted children, that a baby would be an admission of defeat, that there were enough children in the world already.

Since the argument a couple of days ago they had barely spoken. It was not a good time to try and entertain a stranger.

Except, perhaps sensing her hostility and her embarrassment, he was obviously intending to entertain her.

'By dowsing, you mean water divining?' She stood up and went to the stove. This would be her third cup – he had declined her offer of a refill – and already her nerves were jumping.

He glanced at her, noting the smartly cut blonde hair, the intense blue eyes, the tight nervous smile. She was good looking, Colin's wife, but obviously highly strung and, if he was any judge, utterly miserable.

He nodded. 'It's my party trick. Weekends in the country with vets and doctors. They take one look at me and retreat immediately to deal with emergencies leaving me with their poor wives who would much rather be out shopping with their friends.'

She was glad she had her back to him, to hide her confusion. Was she that transparent? Well, he was wrong about one thing: she had no friends down here yet. None at all.

When she turned, coffee pot in hand, he was watching her, his eyebrow raised. He had a nice face, kind, rugged, if a bit lopsided, and she realised as she met his gaze, he wasn't teasing. He was perfectly serious about his party trick. 'Have you got any wire coat hangers?'

She produced them and watched while he bent, snapped and twisted them into two right-angled rods.

'OK. Here's where I earn my lunch. What have you lost?'

'Lost?'

He nodded. 'Engagement ring? Wedding ring?' So, he had noticed the bare third finger of her left hand. A silly gesture, taking it off. They had got married, hadn't they, and they weren't divorced. Not yet. 'Have you mislaid your car keys? Rolex? Pension book?' He stood up holding the rods loosely in front of him. They remained still, but she had the feeling that they were quivering slightly like dogs waiting for a command. The idea made her smile.

Sitting down again she found she had relaxed for the first time since he had arrived. 'If you're serious, I lost a little gold cross soon after we moved here. My godmother gave it to me and it really upset me. I searched everywhere.'

He nodded. Moving away from the table he held the rods out in front of him. 'OK. Let's ask a few questions.' He concentrated for a moment, then addressed the rods. 'Is the cross in the house?'

The two bent coat hangers quivered and sprang apart.

He glanced up at Pippa. 'Which room? We'll ask one by one. Tell me what rooms you have.'

Within seconds they had established that the cross was – according to the rods – in the small conservatory behind the kitchen.

'But that's ridiculous. I never took it in there!' Pippa found she wanted desperately for him to be right. She had never seen this done before and it intrigued her enormously. Once when she was a child, her grandfather had shown her and her sisters how to dowse for water, walking up and down the back lawn with a hazel twig in his hands. It was a bit like that. He had found the main water pipe into the house but they had all known it was there anyway and so they had not been impressed.

'Is it in the flower beds?' Morgan asked the rods.

No.

'Pots?'

No.

'What else is there?' he asked Pippa. It was as though he were interpreting at a conference – or a police enquiry.

'Paving stones?'

No.

'Plants, I suppose. Perhaps they ate it!'

Her frivolous remark did not even need to be relayed. The rods sprang apart.

Yes!

'OK. Which plant?' Morgan was frowning with concentration.

'Geranium.'

No.

171

'Busy Lizzie?'

No.

'Cactus?'

No.

'Oleander?'

YES!

She laughed. 'Oh please! Not possible. Those skimpy old things at the back? This I have to see!'

They made their way into the conservatory, leaving the rods on the kitchen table. It wasn't really a conservatory worth the name, just a small glassed-in area behind the kitchen, smelling strongly of damp earth and rotting flowers, the mossy paving stones only a pace or two long and scarcely that wide. In the corner a pile of old clay pots spilled out stale dried earth. From one a pretty fern arched over a discarded trowel.

Against the back wall of the house there was a small bed in which were a dozen or so straggly geraniums and behind them two tall oleanders, their dusty leaves eclipsed by cascades of red flowers.

'We should take care of this place better.' Pippa stood beside Morgan, staring ruefully at the plants. 'They survive in spite of me, poor things. I never even water them. It's Colin who looks after the garden when he's got time, which isn't often. He's practically never here.' She reached up to remove a dried shrivelled flower and gave a faint gasp. Entangled in the stem was a fine gold chain. 'I don't believe it!' Cautiously she unwound it and in seconds the cross was in her hand. The chain had broken near the clasp. 'It must have caught as I walked by and then the plant grew and carried it up with it!' She looked at Morgan in astonishment. 'You've earned your lunch! Is it always so accurate? What else can we ask it? Who taught you to do it?'

He sighed. Always the same questions. Always the same curiosity. The trouble was, this particular party trick had the potential to end in tears. The rods never lied. The temptation to ask the unaskable was too great. Perhaps he shouldn't have started this.

'It's all right, Morgan.' Pippa had read him like a book. 'I won't ask you about Colin. I suspect I already know the answer. She's the receptionist at the practice. And the strange thing is, if it's true I don't think I'm going to mind that much. Not any more. Not after our last quarrel.' They moved out of the conservatory onto the small back lawn. 'I suppose we never really loved each other. Not properly.' Her face was wistful. She had loved Colin. She still did. But she was not about to tell his friend that. 'It was wishful thinking. For both of us,' she ploughed on, 'but moving here, I think, crystallised things. We saw more clearly. We couldn't hide things from each other any more. It was as if the house was some kind of catalyst. It had such a lovely atmosphere and we were somehow spoiling it.'

'That's sad. What will you do?'

She shrugged. 'Move out, I suppose. Go our separate ways. With no hard feelings, though. I hope we'll stay friends. We won't embarrass you with screaming rows or anything like that while you're here, I promise.'

Morgan raised an eyebrow. 'I'm glad to hear it.'

'I'd like to know about the house, though.' She turned to look at it thoughtfully. It was a pretty cottage, smothered in late roses, small windows opened to let in the autumn sunlight and warm grass-scented air, the old clay tiles a faded red, touched here and there with lichen. 'I think someone who lived here knew about love,' she said so quietly he had to strain to hear her. 'Is that something you could ask your coat hangers?'

For a moment he didn't respond, staring at the cottage in silence. Then at last he nodded.

The questions were laborious, each answered only by a yes or a no, but slowly a story emerged, teased carefully out of the air as they stood in front of the smouldering apple logs in the low-ceilinged sitting room.

'Can we talk to the person whose love still fills this house?'

Yes.

'First, how old is the house. Three hundred years? Two hundred years?'

Yes.

'Which year did you come here? Was it in the 1700s?'

No.

'The 1800s?'

No.

'The 1900s?'

Yes.

'1901? 1902? . . .'

It was 1911.

'Were you newly married?'

Yes.

'What did your husband do?' They were assuming it was a woman. 'Was he a farm labourer – a gardener – a shepherd – a smith?'

A smith. He was the village blacksmith.

'I know what's coming!' Pippa put her hand on Morgan's wrist as though to stay the restless movement of the rods. 'Oh God, he was killed in the Great War, wasn't he.'

NO! The rods had crossed, their tips trembling. No, not the war.

'What was your name?' Pippa asked the rods direct. Then realised that was stupid. How could they answer her? They could only say yes or no.

My name is Hattie.

The words were so clear Pippa could not believe Morgan hadn't heard them too, but he gave no sign. He merely shrugged. 'We can't ask that, I'm afraid. So many names to choose from. It would take too long –'

'Hattie. Her name was Hattie.'

He frowned. 'How do you know that?'

'I heard her . . .'

He lowered the rods. 'Speak to her. See if she'll answer.'

Pippa was staring round the room. 'Oh my God, is she a ghost? Where is she? I can't see her.'

'Ask her.'

She hesitated. 'Can you hear me, Hattie?' she whispered. She was suddenly apprehensive and not a little self-conscious.

I can hear you.

The voice was as soft as the wind across the grass.

'Were you happy here?'

Oh, I was happy. So happy.

Behind her, Morgan sat down in one of the fireside chairs. Quietly he laid the rods on the floor at his feet. She couldn't tell if he could hear the voice or not.

'How long did you live here?'

A long time.

Pippa hesitated. 'Was your marriage happy?'

So happy.

'Did you have any children?'

There was no answer. She glanced at Morgan. 'I think she's gone.'

'Maybe.' He raised an eyebrow. 'Do you mind the idea that you might have a ghost in your house?'

She hesitated, then she shook her head. 'She doesn't seem frightening.'

'I'm sure she's not. Ask your question again.'

Pippa repeated her question and waited, staring thoughtfully into the fire.

I had ten. Ten beautiful babies. We were a happy family!

'So many children!' Pippa exclaimed.

This house loves children! The voice was growing fainter.

A log shifted, scenting the room with apple smoke.

'Hattie? Hattie, don't go,' Pippa called.

There was no reply.

She sat for a long time without moving, aware that if she spoke she would cry. Morgan wasn't looking at her. When she glanced at him she saw his eyes were closed.

'Did you hear what she said?' she asked at last.

He nodded.

'She was so lucky.' She whispered the words to herself.

'So could you be.' His eyes were open now and he was watching her with concern.

She shrugged. 'I was happy when we first came here.'

'This is about Col?' Bending down, he picked up the rods.

'Don't ask them!' Pippa spoke more sharply than she intended.

Dropping them at once, he raised his hands in surrender. 'I wasn't going to.'

'Sorry.' She put her head in her hands. 'Yes, of course it's Colin. He loves someone else.'

'No, Pippa, he doesn't. He loves you.'

'You don't know anything about it!'

'I do. He told me.' He stood up uncomfortably and bent to throw a log on the fire.

'So this was a set up!' She was furious suddenly. 'All this. Coming here. Your rods. Your party trick!'

'No, Pippa –'

'Did he hide my cross and tell you where it was?' Her tears were very close again. 'Hattie. That was all pretend!' Suddenly she was furiously angry. And disappointed.

'No.'

'Did he tell you what we quarrelled about? But of course he did! That was what this is all about. Children. Keep me occupied. Distract me! Good old Morgan can talk her round.' She bit back an angry sob.

'I'm not a ventriloquist, Pippa. I can't throw my voice. And if I could it wouldn't be a woman's. I didn't know about your cross. All he told me was that you were both very unhappy and he was terrified he was going to lose you.' Morgan stood up, irritated and uncomfortable. 'Look, I'm sorry. I didn't intend to become involved in all this. I came because Col sounded so miserable when I spoke to him I thought maybe he could do with a sympathetic ear.' He paused, seeing her indignation.

'I'm sorry. I know there are always two sides to every quarrel, but I can tell you honestly that he loves you. He really does.'

She was biting back tears. 'Maybe he lied to you.'

'He wouldn't lie about that.'

'How do you know?'

He hesitated. 'I just know. It's a bloke thing!' He gave a shrug, half humorous, half rueful.

'I don't think so! Blokes are not renowned for their mutual confidences.' She shook her head wistfully.

There was a moment's silence. 'Maybe I should leave,' he said at last. 'None of this is my business and I've managed to put both my feet well and truly in it! I'm so sorry.'

She didn't reply. Suddenly she wasn't listening. He paused for a moment, trying to hear whatever it was she could hear. The only sound in the room as far as he could make out was the gentle crack and shift of the fire in the hearth. Quietly he moved towards the door.

It was only when he had picked up his overnight bag and walked sadly out to his car that he realised he didn't have his keys. He must have dropped them on a table somewhere as he walked into the house just as he did at home. He glanced back at the cottage, cursing under his breath. He had messed up completely. He didn't want to go back and confront Pippa and he particularly didn't want to see Colin. 'She might talk to you, Morgan. See if you can turn on a bit of the old charm. She's not got many friends round here yet, and I don't know if there is anyone she can confide in. I can't ring one of her old London friends, they wouldn't tell me. You know what women are!'

Oh indeed. He was the expert on women. No question. That was why he hadn't noticed his own marriage coming apart; why Sheila had left him for someone else. After all, it was because of their divorce that he was so often at a loose end at weekends, free to dispense his invaluable advice, while his married friends were tied up with their families. With a sigh he leaned on the gate.

Inside the house Pippa was staring at the rods, lying on the carpet where Morgan had left them. For a long time she didn't move, then at last she picked them up. For a moment they hung inert between her fingers feeling exactly what they were, bent coat hangers, then almost cautiously she changed her grip, holding them as he had, by the short side, extended in front of her, and as she did so something strange seemed to happen. They seemed to come alive. She could feel them suddenly taut, almost trembling, attentive, as she looked at them. For a second she stood watching them, willing herself not to throw them down. Then, her voice husky, she whispered her question. 'Did Colin tell Morgan the truth? Does he love me?'

The pieces of metal almost wrenched themselves out of her hand as they sprang together and crossed. She stared. That meant no. She had seen it so many times in Morgan's hands. Apart: yes. Crossed: no.

'Did you ask them to show you a yes?' The voice behind her made her jump.

'I thought you'd gone!'

'I forgot my keys.' He had already spotted them, lying on the coffee table.

'They say he doesn't love me.' She turned away to hide her tears.

'Ask again.' He sounded very stern.

'But they said –'

'Ask them. They move in a different way for everyone. You have to establish what the code is for you.'

For a moment he thought she was going to refuse, but she did as he asked and when she whispered, 'Show me a yes,' the rods sprang across in front of her.

'There you are!' He nodded, satisfied. Scooping up the keys he turned back to the door. 'Tell Col I will ring him, OK? Sorry to miss him.'

It was the second time he had exited without her noticing. He shrugged as he let himself out of the house. Better this way. Give them some time to themselves and if they couldn't talk to each other before, perhaps now they could, with their little wire go-betweens. The idea cheered him up as he climbed into his car and set off on the long lonely drive back to London.

'Hattie, are you still here?' Pippa laid aside the rods at last.

There was no reply.

'Hattie? I need to talk to you.'

But the rods had told her what she wanted to know. Yes, Colin genuinely wanted children. Yes, he wanted them soon. No, he wasn't having an affair. No, he had never even contemplated it and, yes, he would love her whatever happened; whatever she decided.

'And me,' she had asked at last, the final question, her mind tired, the rods more and more reluctant to respond. 'Do I really, deep down, want children? Do I want a baby?'

She had always thought not. She stared at the two motionless rods in her hands, almost willing them not to move. Babies meant loss of freedom, exhaustion, the anguished juggling of job and family, the need for everything and the achievement of nothing. She had seen it again and again, in her friends, her two sisters. She remembered her own mother, struggling to look after them all and keep working at the same time till she dropped with exhaustion. Oh yes, she had two successful friends who had managed it in London. One with the help of buckets of money and a nanny, the other with a willing house husband. But even they were not completely happy; they were missing so much of their children's babyhood. One couldn't win! She glanced back at the oracular coat hangers.

Yes. The rods had snapped across. Yes, she wanted a baby.

No.

Did she?

Really?

Of course she did. She wanted one so much it hurt. She dropped the rods and went to stare into the fire.

What on earth had happened? What had changed her mind? It was as though she had suddenly been given permission to confront the truth. Had the relentless time clock she had heard so much about suddenly ticked another second on its inexorable round and pushed her into biological panic or had it got something to do with Hattie? Hattie who had loved her man and loved her babies and who had died with so much love still in her

181

heart that it was imprinted on every timber and every inch of plaster in this cottage.

She was still sitting staring at the fire when Colin came home. She hadn't heard from Hattie again, but she had heard laughter, children's laughter, in the distance. Perhaps it had drifted in through the window from the village.

Colin looked down at the dying ashes. 'Pippa? Where's Morgan?' He ran his fingers through his untidy fair hair. Unbuttoning his wax jacket he dropped it over the back of the chair.

She bit her lip. 'He went back to London.'

'Why? What happened?'

She smiled 'He's a very nice tactful man, your friend Morgan. He thought we should spend the weekend on our own.' Climbing to her feet she put her hands on his shoulders. 'I'm sorry I was such a cow this morning. Will you forgive me?'

He laughed. 'Nothing like the cow I had to deal with today, thank God!' He kissed the top of her head gently. 'I even forgave her in the end! Of course I forgive you. I always do, my darling.'

'It's more than I deserve.' She took a deep breath. 'I have learned a few home truths about myself today. In-depth analysis, you might say.'

'From Morgan?' He looked incredulous.

'From those!' She waved her hands at the truncated coat hangers.

'And what were these truths? Am I allowed to know?' He was staring at the coat hangers with a puzzled frown on his face, clearly not recognising the route they had marked into his wife's – and his own – subconscious.

182

'In a nutshell?' She paused dreamily. 'I love you. I'm sorry I accused you of being a cheat because I know you're not, and –' she hesitated, suddenly afraid to say it out loud.

'And?' Colin stared down at her, his face so clearly registering hope, anxiety, fear, concern, that she reached up and put her fingers against his mouth as though to still his frightened speculation. 'And – I want to have a baby.'

He stared at her. 'Just like that? After all we've been through, suddenly, you've changed your mind?'

'Just like that. And I want Morgan to be its godfather.'

Colin's mouth dropped open. 'Isn't that being a bit premature?'

She shook her head. 'No. Just well organised. I'm going to be very organised in future.'

'You're going to have to be.' He scanned her face tentatively. 'You know your dream job – the one you wanted so much? Well, it's yours if you want it. At the practice. 'Eve has left. I know once or twice you've come into the surgery and caught us together and I could see you wondering about us!' He gave a hoot of laughter. 'She was actually telling me confidentially how much better my predecessor was at everything. I got so sick of it! I think we can safely say we loathed each other by the end. I couldn't stand the woman. And it was clearly mutual. When I went back to the surgery just now I found she had left us a note that she's gone. No notice. No warning. I rang Bill before I came home and he agreed: the job is yours if you want it. It's a good job. You'd be perfect.'

'And if I was pregnant?'

'If you didn't mind, we certainly wouldn't. There's plenty of cover with the part-timers. And later, you can stick the baby in the back office.' He was watching her anxiously. 'You'd even be in the right place for emergency deliveries. We had a beautiful calf this morning. A heifer!'

She laughed out loud.

'Any other godparents lined up?'

She shook her head. She did have an idea, that was true, but she wasn't sure yet whether Hattie would qualify.

Putting her arms round Colin's neck she hugged him. This time, when she heard children's laughter, she was almost sure it came from their own garden.

Lost in the Temple

The first day of the cruise began so normally. The River Nile was bustling with boats of every size and shape. Palm trees stood sentinel on the far bank and a graceful minaret rose against the vivid blue sky. Emma glanced at Gill as they collected cereal and fruit from the serving table. 'I can't believe we're really here!'

Gill grinned. Tall, blonde and tanned from the sunbed, she had been noticed at once. The night before, at their first meal on-board, Emma, glancing round, had caught appraising looks cast in their direction by some of the men, not least the tour guide who, after doing the rounds of the tables, had finally settled in an empty chair next to them and introduced himself. His name was Mahmoud and, having established that they were without male escorts and so presumably potentially available, he hadn't taken his eyes off Gill.

Emma sighed. She was used to this. Small in stature, shy, her dark hair cut to a shoulder-length bob, she had years ago resigned herself to being outshone by her friend. Strangely, in the end, Emma was the one who had married – even if it hadn't lasted. And after all, it didn't matter here. They hadn't come to Egypt to meet new men. They had come to see the antiquities. Or she had.

Climbing onto the bus which was to take them from the boat through the teeming, noisy streets to the Temple of Karnak, she found herself sitting alone. Scanning the crowded seats in front of her she spotted Gill's blonde head. She had taken a place near the front. Next to Mahmoud. Actually, Emma was quite pleased. She didn't want to talk. She wanted just to look.

With a hiss of compressed air, the bus doors closed and it set off, lurching up the track from the river bank towards the road. On either side, mud-brick houses, adorned with brightly coloured rugs and blankets airing in the sunshine, alternated with groves of palm trees and exotic plantations. As the bus swung out to pass an old man perched perilously on the rump of a small donkey, Mahmoud stood up, holding on to a seat-back to keep his balance. Emma saw him glance down at Gill and wink as he launched into his running commentary. With a resigned smile, she sat back and turned towards the window. This was going to be the most wonderful holiday of her life and she was not going to allow anything to spoil it.

By the time they had disembarked and crossed the dusty car park to enter the Temple, Gill was once more at her side. Mahmoud was too busy, buying tickets and passes, ushering his charges through the gates and describing the avenue of ram-headed sphinxes, to pay her any attention. Emma smiled as she reached for her camera. 'It looks as though you've made a conquest.'

Gill shrugged. 'Isn't he gorgeous?'

Emma was just standing there, staring at the statue of Rameses in front of them and nodded dreamily.

There was a peal of laughter from her companion. 'Not that thing! I mean Mahmoud.'

Emma raised an eyebrow. 'Each to his own. It's the Pharaoh I fancy!'

Almost deliberately she found herself dropping further and further behind as Gill hung on Mahmoud's every word.

The heat was unbearable. The sun beat down on hats and dark glasses, reflecting from every stone surface. Huge stone columns rose around her, casting black heavy shadows between ribs of vicious sunlight. Emma stared up at a distant lotus-shaped capital which had once, presumably, supported a roof. A group of Italian visitors passed her and for a moment she was engulfed in noise and laughter, then they disappeared towards the next gateway. Wistfully she watched them leave. Now they had gone, she was surrounded by silence. Even the cheeping of the sparrows had stopped. There was no one else in sight. She shivered. But not because there had been any relief from the heat. On the contrary, it was hotter than ever.

She stepped out of the shade and stared around, trying to orient herself. Suddenly she wanted to be back with Gill and Mahmoud and the other members of the tour. The Temple was teeming with visitors; she hadn't strayed into some area that was closed. Only a moment or so ago, a tall, lithe Italian man clad from head to foot in Gucci had glanced back at her with a smile and lifted a hand with a soft *ciao* as he followed his compatriots out of sight.

She hitched her thumb determinedly into the strap of the day-sack on her back and walked straight down the avenue ahead of her.

It was so hot, it was hard to breathe, the air around her seemed almost solid. She stopped and stared around again. Although she had been walking for two or three minutes, she didn't seem to have moved. By some strange optical illusion, the same vista of columns appeared to stretch endlessly ahead and behind and to the left and right, but now, suddenly, there was more shade. She glanced up. She had, without noticing it, walked into an area that was still roofed. Here, the sand of the floor had been brushed aside to reveal smooth paving stones and it was cooler at last.

There was a movement in the distance. Emma's heart leaped. 'Hello?' Her voice sounded muted, strange. It hardly seemed to penetrate the vast shadows around her, but at that moment a young woman appeared, running towards her through the columns. She was wearing a long, white dress with a veil looped around her shoulders and neck and over her hair.

Emma smiled and raised a hand in greeting, then the smile froze on her lips. The woman stopped, glancing over her shoulder, every gesture and line of her body denoting fear. There was a man behind her. Pounding over the paving slabs in sandalled feet, he was dressed in the long, loose, everyday garb of so many Egyptians, the galabiya. In his hand he was brandishing a knife. He stopped. Even at that distance Emma could see he was gasping for breath, the hand which was not clasping the knife clamped to his side as if he was winded. The man and the woman stared at each other for an interminable moment as Emma watched. She could see the longing in his eyes and the regret as he raised his hand towards her, a hand that was smeared with blood. For a moment, the woman hesitated. She reached out to him in a gesture which spoke of poignant love and loss and then she turned and started to run again, towards Emma. She was so close now that Emma could see her face, her dark eyes, huge with terror, her long hair, torn free of the veil, streaming black behind her, streaks of blood on her dress, her breast, her hands. Her cheeks were wet with tears.

Terrified, Emma stepped back out of the way. Between one second and the next, she was there, close enough to touch, to see the detail of her torn, embroidered neckline, the shredded silk of the veil wrapped around her neck, the bare, slender feet soundless on the paving, and then she had run past. Emma spun round to stare after her, but she had gone. Trembling, Emma turned to where she had seen the man bending double to catch his breath. There was no sign of him either.

Hardly daring to breathe, Emma crept towards the spot and stared down. There must be traces of blood. Some sign of the man's anguish. Some sound. There was nothing.

She looked back to where she had been standing. The sun blazed down between the pillars onto the sand.

'Oh God!' Slowly she turned full circle, staring up. There was no sign of a roof now – only lofty columns towering above her. Beneath her, there were no paving slabs either. She was beginning to panic. She was imagining things. It was the heat. The exhaustion. The strangeness of it all.

'Gill?' Her frightened cry echoed for a moment through the silence. 'Mahmoud? Is there anyone there? Anyone?' She took a deep breath, then she paused, listening. A voice was answering. She strained to hear it.

'Hello?'

There it was again. Nearer, this time. A man's voice. She spun round, trying hard to locate the sound. It was deadened; strange.

And then she saw him. Tall, his shock of fair hair obscured by a wide-brimmed sun hat, his eyes a clear green, like a cat's, he appeared suddenly from behind a pillar only a few yards in front of her. For a moment they stared at each other in astonished silence, then his face relaxed into a grin. 'It's Emma isn't it?'

'Oh, thank God!' Confused and still unnerved, she almost threw herself at him. 'Did you see what happened?' To her embarrassment, she found she couldn't hold back the tears of shock.

His arms closed around her, holding her steady, then gently he pushed her away, his hands on her shoulders. 'I didn't see anything. What's wrong?' He could feel her trembling violently.

'I saw this woman.' She could barely get the words out between her sobs. 'There was a man chasing her. I don't know why, but I got the feeling he had tried to strangle her! She must have stabbed him. He was bleeding!' She was staring round wildly.

'And where are they now?' He frowned. For a moment she thought he was going to turn away, then she realised that his quick glance was as nervous as her own. He took off his hat and pushed his hair out of his eyes with the back of his hand.

'I don't know. I could feel their emotion. It was as if their love and their fear were tangible! Then it had gone!' She ground the heels of her hands into her eyes, suddenly conscious of the fact that nothing she said made any sense, and that she had thrown herself into the arms of a total stranger. A stranger who knew her name.

As though reading her thoughts, he asked, 'You don't remember me? I'm Patrick.' His voice was deep and mellow. 'I was at the next table on the boat last night. I saw you stray away from the party just now and I thought what a good idea to get out of the sun. I'm writing up the cruise for a travel mag. I was photographing the columns.' He had a camera bag slung over his shoulder, a Nikon around his neck. 'Then I heard you calling.'

She gave him a watery smile. 'I'm sorry I threw myself at you. I was so frightened. It was so strange. And after they disappeared it was as though suddenly I was the only person in the world.'

He glanced round. 'We still might be.' He frowned. 'There is an eerie atmosphere in here, I agree. Come on.' He held out his hand. 'We'd better find someone and tell them what you saw. I'm sure it wasn't as bad as it looked. Whoever they were, they seem to have gone now.' There was something about Patrick which she found comforting.

They walked several paces down the centre of one of the avenues between the columns, then Emma stopped. She shook her head. 'The roof was still there, where I saw them. And the floor was paved. Somehow, I've moved away from where it was.' She turned round slowly. On every side, all she could see were vistas of columns beneath the sky. She saw Patrick glance at her for one thoughtful second and she grimaced. 'You think I dreamed it up. Heatstroke or something.' She shook her head slowly. 'Am I going mad? But it was so real, so clear.' She bit her lip.

He stared past her into the distance. 'No, I really don't think you're going mad. Something does feel wrong.' He took a few steps away from her and, very cautiously, reached out to touch the column that was nearest them.

She watched, holding her breath as his fingers traced the lines on the carved stone. He withdrew his hand and stared at it thoughtfully, then he reached into his hip pocket for a well-thumbed guide-book. 'This doesn't look right at all. I think we should find Mahmoud. He'll know what to do.' He took a few paces forward and stopped, puzzled. 'There should be people. Crowds. I don't understand.'

'And the sparrows are quiet,' Emma put in nervously. Her voice shook. 'Did you notice?' Suddenly it seemed terribly important.

He turned back and put his arm around her shoulders. Somehow the gesture, protective and comforting, made her feel even more scared. She huddled against him, conscious that her mouth was dry with fear. 'This isn't in your guide-book, is it?' She stabbed at the open page with her finger. 'Look at all those columns. The hypo-style hall. It looks like this, but it isn't. This goes on forever! We're lost!'

'We can't be lost, Emma, it's not possible. The site is vast, but not that vast.'

'Then we've fallen through a trap door in time –' She broke off abruptly. She had meant the remark to be facetious but as their eyes met she saw that, for a split second, they both wondered if it were true. 'They were ghosts, weren't they?' she said at last.

There was a moment of silence. 'It's possible, I suppose.' His reply was cautious.

'So you believe in ghosts?'

'Not until now.'

'She was real, Patrick. She ran by me, only a few feet away.' But without a sound, without a movement of the air around her. She managed a shaky smile. 'Perhaps we'd better pinch each other!' She saw him grin. Saw him reach out towards her. Felt the tips of his fingers brush against hers. Then the world went black.

For a long moment she held her breath, unable to think, then the air around them exploded into sound. She felt Patrick grab her wrist, realised they were running, heard the echo of music and the noise of disembodied voices.

'What's happening?' She was bewildered. Terrified.

'I don't know. Come on. Let's get out of here.'

At least now there was noise. Light. He clapped his hands over his ears as the sound of trumpets and brass echoed around the Temple. Stopping, he pulled her into his arms in the shelter of a stone wall.

'It's all right, Emma! It's all right! It's the sound-and-light show. I don't know how, or why, but somehow we're in the middle of it! Look!' Bright lights flared up all around them.

'It's night. How can it be night?' Emma found she was still clutching his hand.

'I don't know; and I don't for the minute care. At least we're out of that place!' He caught her hand and they ran together, dodging between obelisks and statues, through columns and past walls, seeing spotlights playing on the stone near them, then swinging away to light another area.

There was no one on the gate; the car park was a sea of empty coaches. Panting, they stopped and stared around.

'We'll find a taxi.' Patrick glanced over his shoulder as one of the spotlights swung up towards the sky.

To Emma's relief he seemed to know where to find one, how to negotiate the fare with the driver, even where the boat was moored. As they rattled back through the streets of Luxor, she found she was still clinging to his hand.

'Patrick,' she said quietly. 'Whatever happened back there?' She glanced at him in the glare of the street lights as the taxi ground to a halt behind a sleepy man on a donkey. Their driver leant from the window with a string of good-natured invective. And the donkey moved over.

'I've absolutely no idea, but somehow we've lost about twelve hours!' Patrick glanced at his watch and frowned. 'What time is it, my friend?' He leant forward and tapped the driver's shoulder. 'This says 10.40.' He stared at it for a moment. It had stopped.

Emma frowned at her own wrist. '10.34. No one will believe us.'

'No.' He sat back in his seat with a sigh.

They sat in silence.

'Will they have reported us missing?'

He shrugged. 'I suppose so. Luckily, I'm here on my own. My ex-wife would have killed me if I'd disappeared for hours with a beautiful woman!'

She acknowledged the compliment with a smile. 'I'm divorced too. I'm here with a girlfriend.'

'I hope she won't be too hard on you for disappearing.'

'She probably hasn't even missed me, if the truth were known.' Emma shook her head wryly. 'Mahmoud will have, though. He counts everyone all the time.'

The taxi had reached the darker streets now, away from the town centre. 'We have several options,' Patrick said slowly. 'We can plead insanity. We can say one of us was ill. I can say I was following a story and forgot the time or got lost. We could say you came with me and we were sidetracked . . .'

In the end that was the story they chose. After all, it was in a way true. They stood side by side like naughty children as Mahmoud berated them for being late and causing him worry, then they went together to the empty dining room where, having relented a little, he ordered them a drink and some soup.

It was there that Gill found them.

'You sly old thing!' She sat down on the chair next to Emma. 'How did you hook the most handsome man on the boat?' She smiled dazzlingly at Patrick.

'I thought Mahmoud was,' Emma replied softly.

'He is. Okay. The second most handsome.' Gill giggled. 'We're leaving soon to set off up river. See you on deck.'

Patrick waited for the door to close behind her before he reached for Emma's hand. 'So, you've hooked me, have you?'

Emma smiled. 'You must admit my technique is original!'

He nodded soberly. 'Unique.'

'We're never going to know what happened, are we?'

Laughing, he shook his head. 'Probably not. But I'm going to have a good try at finding out! That's the investigative journalist in me.' He leant forward on his elbows, pushing aside his soup bowl. 'Will you help?'

She nodded. 'Of course.'

'You're not still frightened?'

'Aren't you?'

There was a moment's silence. Then he admitted, 'If I'm honest, yes.'

'I wonder if we could find out who they were. The man and the woman I saw.'

'One incident out of four thousand years?' He pondered. 'It won't be easy. But there will be records. The place is steeped in history. When the boat returns at the end of the week, we can make a start at the museum.'

Beneath their feet the engine rumbled suddenly into life. He stood up. 'Shall we go up on deck?'

They stood side by side leaning on the rail, staring at the reflections in the water and the stark line of the distant mountains against the stars. 'This is going to be an interesting holiday,' he said at last.

'That's one way of looking at it.' She glanced at him

196

sideways. 'I haven't thanked you for rescuing me. I think I would have lost my mind if you hadn't turned up when you did. I'd fallen through a hole in time.'

'And I fell with you.' He looked down and their eyes met for a moment.

Behind them the moon was rising, huge and serene.

'I wonder what their story was. Were they lovers, driven to despair by some sort of betrayal? Did he try to kill her and she defended herself, or did she start it? Or were they priest and priestess of the Temple, locked in battle over rival gods?' She shivered. 'I need to know.'

He put his arm around her shoulders and they stood together in silence, watching the silhouette of the palm trees slide by. Emma found herself very conscious of the solid warmth of the man at her side. The strange way they had met, the sudden intimacy of the experience, had brought them together with an intensity which made her feel she had known him forever.

She glanced up and found that he was looking down at her again. He smiled and she knew with absolute certainty that they would go back to the Temple. She shivered. But she also knew that whatever happened there and whatever tragedy they uncovered, she would follow him wherever he went, and that by some strange pact, born from the mystery of this eerie Egyptian night, their future together had been sealed in a Temple as old as time.

Random Snippets

Amanda loved travelling alone. She always had. Where her friends craved companionship and mutual support even on the shortest journey she did all in her power to avoid the hustle and endless chatter which was the inevitable result of someone else going along. She ducked and lurked on railway platforms; she studied shop windows with elaborate care as people she knew walked by, all for the sake of that blissful moment when the doors closed, the train drew away and she felt her spirit fly. She was not a woman who took a mobile phone wherever she went!

It was not that she was unsociable. Far from it. She loved people, enjoyed their company, adored her job as an advertising executive and threw parties and cooked meals at the drop of a hat. But travelling – and, at the end of the day, living – was something she felt she had to experience so absolutely fully that it had to be done alone.

Sex of course cannot be done alone. Well, it can, but Amanda was not a solitary player in that field. She had a lovely, attentive, understanding man who knew the rules of her particular life plan and was happy to abide by them. She knew he had another life. He worked in the City and it was unlikely he did not find solace there when she was away, and sometimes that knowledge saddened her. But she could expect nothing else, nothing more. If she wanted her private secret side, so would he.

Thus it was that he had gone with her to the airport when she had set off on her trip to Canada, joined her in a coffee after she had checked in, chatted amiably about her journey and waved her off with, had she turned to see, only the slightest touch of wistfulness in his smile.

Amanda settled into her seat in delight. She had a new paperback to read, a guide book to Canada and a new spiral-back notebook – the latter because, although she didn't realise it, Amanda was a writer. When she was born, amongst the thousands of genes she inherited from her parents was the writing gene. She had never actually manifested a desire to be a travel writer or a novelist or a poet. She had never attended writers' circles or author talks at Waterstones, nor had she ever kept a diary as such. But, and it has to be admitted this was done almost surreptitiously, some might say even secretly, she wrote all the time. She called these writings her snippets. Things she had done. Things she had seen. Things she had thought. And people she'd met. This was the real reason she liked to avoid people she knew on her travels. They distracted her from the people she didn't know. And from the endless stories which swirled in her head as character after character passed in front of her for her delectation.

Only this morning on the train to the airport it had happened. Admittedly Derek had been there with her, but buried in his *Financial Times* he had seen nothing and been no distraction. The scenario which caught her attention had been so small no one else had seen it, or if they had, they had ignored it. The woman sitting opposite them was pale and drawn, her eyes sunken and miserable. Covertly Amanda studied her face. She was, she could be, incredibly beautiful beneath the ugly baseball cap which had been pulled down to cover her hair. As she sat, staring into space, her mobile phone rang. The opening bars of the 'William Tell' overture (presumably chosen as ringing tone in more optimistic mood) rang out with increasing urgency and volume in the quiet carriage. At first the woman ignored it, pretending it had nothing to do with her, then as its insistence grew more obtrusive she pounced on her bag, rummaged, found the phone and, instead of switching it off, wrapped it in her scarf and buried it at the bottom of the bag. Rossini's electronic masterpiece diminu-endoed to an angry and still audible squeak. When at last it stopped the woman delved back into her bag, retrieved her phone, punched in a short number and returned it to its place. Two angry spots of colour had flared over her cheekbones. At the next stop she got off, leaving Amanda agog with curiosity. Presumably the number she had put into the phone would block the call from that person? But why not switch off the phone? And if not switch it off, who was it whose call she was hoping for? Who? What? Where?

As she settled into the seat of the 767, peering down over the dull panorama of West London, she reached automatically for her notebook.

Unless you have had a chance to study them in the departure lounge before you leave it is hard to get an overview of your fellow passengers on a plane. The one sitting next to you is of crucial importance – particularly if their personal habits are unpleasant or if they turn out to be an Olympic talker. Or if they are under the age of reasonable restraint. The rest are only glimpsed in tiny cameos if they stand up or move about or as they sit in serried ranks facing you as you pick your way to the loo, making the most of every second of blessed freedom before slotting yourself carefully back into place.

Amanda, on this the longest flight she had as yet made, unbelievably, grew bored. It was not as though she had a holiday to look forward to. The journey would end in a series of meetings. And tricky ones she was fronting for her cowardly boss. She was tired of the view of the seat in front. She could not see the screen with the film – which at any rate seemed to be about delinquent baseball players, not her favourite subject. She ate. She slept. She read. She studied cloud formations and she looked down at the beauty of the deep blue crepe which stretched on every side far below as they flew west over the Atlantic Ocean.

Her somnolent boredom was interrupted by the pilot. 'Ladies and gentlemen, we are just flying in across the coast of Labrador. It might interest you to know the temperature down there now is minus twenty-eight degrees.'

Amanda's eyes flew open. She leaned towards the window and peered down. The endless shining blue had disappeared. Far, far below the sea was grey and white and broken with ice and rock. Very soon there was no sea at all. All was ice. She shivered despite the fact that the temperature in the cabin must have been approaching plus twenty-eight degrees. The emptiness, the bleakness, the purity and wildness of that endless landscape was breathtakingly beautiful.

Across the aisle Amanda's neighbour stood up, stretching. Unnoticed he had been studying her on and off from behind his newspaper. He cleared his throat and hovered. 'Excuse me.'

She did not hear him. She was totally absorbed in the landscape below.

Smiling, he turned back to his seat nodding to himself. She was in a world of her own. The perfect place to be.

The plane was lower now. If there had been people there to see, she would have seen them as small black dots, indistinguishable from the stumps of felled trees or, she thought suddenly, bears. She craned closer to the window. She could see a road now, dead straight, cutting like a ruler across the landscape below. Lower and she could see that there was only one car in that whole desolate scene and near it she could see two small specks moving away from it. Who? Why? Where? The familiar mantra echoed in her brain. They were too far apart to be together and yet in that whole vast landscape how could they be separate?

In the seat across the gangway Amanda's neighbour glanced towards her seat and frowned suddenly. He hadn't seen her get up and leave her place. He turned, craning towards the back of the plane. No sign. Excellent! Smiling, he faced the front once more, wondering where she had gone and how long she would be.

The bite of the cold air and the crunch of snow beneath her feet, was so sudden, the moan of the wind so desolate, she was for a moment incapable of reacting. Near her she could see the woman. She was wearing a fur-trimmed parka and thick trousers but her gloves were gone, her hands like her face, chapped and raw. 'Help me!' Her breath was coming in tight raw gasps.

'What is it? What's happened?' Amanda could feel the ice riming her eyelashes. The wind tore the words from her lips.

'He's going to kill me!' The woman looked over her shoulder and following her gaze Amanda saw a figure in the distance labouring through the snow.

'Help me!'

There was nowhere to run. Nowhere to hide, just one chance as the wind whipped the top coat of snow from the road like spume from the sea. 'Down here – maybe we can hide in the snow.' She caught the woman's arm and pushed her down into a drift at the side of the road. A few frantic scoops and she was hidden.

No time to hide herself. Trembling she turned to face him; saw the angry, blotched features, the snarling mouth, the hair whipped free of his hood, beaded with ice. There was a gun in his gloved hand.

'Where are you, Mary-Anne?'

He ran towards Amanda without seeing her. 'All I wanted was that you loved me!' She could see the tears freezing on his cheeks, hear the despair in his voice.

'Was that too much to ask?' He staggered to a stop, staring round the empty landscape, still not seeing Amanda. His lungs were heaving, his sobs coming in raw anguished gulps. Suddenly hurling the gun out into the whirling whiteness he collapsed onto his knees.

Beside her there was a flurry of snow. 'Andy!' The woman was clawing her way back towards him. 'Andy, I'm sorry. I love you. I love you!'

He was holding out his arms. They were both crying now. The wind grew stronger. Behind them the car was out of sight.

'Go back! Get in the car!' Amanda pleaded. She squinted through narrowed eyes up at the sky. Was that her plane up there, silver against the billowing snow cloud? Panic knifed through her stomach. The couple were staggering up the road into the wind away from her. In a moment they would be out of sight and she would be alone. 'Wait!' Her voice was torn to shreds by the wind and spun away to nothing. 'Wait –'

She couldn't breathe. The air was hot. Stale. Her out-flung hand caught against the window next to her ear. She had been asleep. Dreaming! Disorientated she pulled herself to her feet and clambered over the empty seat next to her, intent on finding the loo. It may have been a dream, an imaginary interlude, but her hands and face were chapped and frozen, her breath still rasping in her chest.

The man across the aisle smiled. 'So, where did you get to then?'

She stared at him, puzzled.

'Looks as though you popped out for a breath of air.' He was looking at her feet.

Following his gaze she gasped. Her shoes were wet with melting snow. Snags of ice clung to the bottom of her trousers.

Looking up she met his eyes and he saw the first dawning hints of fear. 'Go and freshen up,' he said. 'I'll order you a drink.'

When she came back to her seat he had ordered her a whisky and ginger but he did not move to the seat next to her. Instead he leaned across the aisle. 'OK?' His smile was gentle. Unthreatening.

'What happened to me?' Her hands had begun to shake.

He shrugged. 'A dream? Out of body experience? Lucid trance? Writing your own script?' He nodded at her book of snippets still lying open on the seat beside her, the pen cradled against the wire spiral at its centre.

'You make it sound quite normal!'

'Who is to say it isn't?'

'It's never happened to me before.' She was still very shaken.

'Perhaps only in your dreams.'

She took a sip from her glass, feeling the bite of warmth through her veins and looked at him properly for the first time. Before, she had noticed him of course. Had seen he was about her own age – good-looking – had assumed he was trying to pick her up. Now she saw he was older than she had thought and she sensed genuine interest, kindness, in his glance.

'Was I really not here. Out of my seat?' She glanced down at her still-damp shoes.

He nodded.

'I don't want it to happen again.'

'I'm not sure you can stop it.' He frowned. 'There are things you can do to help. I could write down the titles of some books for you to read.'

'How come you know so much about it?'

'I lecture on these things.' He smiled. 'I'm giving a talk in Toronto on parapsychology.'

'What a coincidence.' She took another sip of the drink then a thought struck her. She turned in her seat and stared at him. 'It is a coincidence, isn't it? You didn't beam me down there or something.'

He laughed. 'If only such things were possible, my dear.'

'And those people in the snow. Did that really happen?'

He shrugged. 'What people? What snow?'

She slumped back against her seat, defeated.

There was a moment's silence then he leant across towards her again, raising his voice slightly against the roar of the engines. 'The snow was real. I saw it on your boots.'

'So I'm not going mad?'

He shook his head. 'Never worry about that. You have a talent – perhaps ability is a better word. Cultivate it if you dare. It could be exciting.'

'No one will ever believe me.'

'No. But you're a writer. Write about it. Tell the story. Let those who want to, believe. The others can read and enjoy and maybe even wonder.'

He had been looking at her notebook. She picked it up thoughtfully. He had assumed she was a writer and it was true. After all, she spent every spare second of her life writing. She would talk it over with Derek. Tell him what had happened. No, he would never believe her. Her unknown friend was right. If she was to write her snippet at all for general consumption it would have to be as fiction. As a dream in a magazine article perhaps. Or maybe as a novel? Already, without realising she had done it, she had picked up her pen.

But deep inside her something has changed. Without knowing it she has become afraid of travelling alone. She has encountered passion and fear and she has realised how detached her own life has been. Her relationship with Derek when she gets home will be closer, more dependent. When he asks her to marry him in six months' time she will say yes.

Across the aisle Jack Kennedy smiled. He too had reached for his notebook. His was electronic.

Case 128: Subject's name: Amanda Jones. He had seen her name on the label of her cabin bag. *Estimated sensitivity: 7/10. Actual: 10/10. Verifiable facts: Maybe corroboration from two people on road? Check date and location.* He smiled quietly.

He had learned from experience to provide aftercare for his guinea pigs. Whisky and ginger for those visiting the snowy wastes. Iced gin and lime for those who landed in the Sahara. Chilblain cures or sunburn. And of course a signed copy of his own book on trans- and bi-location, with an e-mail address where they could reach him with news of life/career changes resulting from their experience and for advice when it happened again – as it always did . . .

Of course there was always a risk. Always the possibility one day one of them would fail to return to their seat near his on the aircraft. That would be interesting.

Probably unfortunate. Definitely worth an appendix on its own in his next book. A snippet. He smiled as he thought of the word scrawled across the cover of her notebook. It was funny how he often picked writers in his otherwise random selection of victims. Two novelists, a travel writer and four journalists to date. All travelling alone.

As he filled in the last detail and closed down his computer he lay back in his seat. Across the way Amanda was writing hard. He smiled thoughtfully. Perhaps he should ensure his next subject – no. 129 – did stay down there. His return flight to London in three days' time might be an ideal opportunity. Imagine the furore when they found a passenger had disappeared. Imagine the puzzlement. Imagine the sense of power as he selected someone who this time would be the victim of the perfect crime. Because, even if it was in the name of science, it would be murder. There was no doubt at all about that.

On the Way to London

They think I'm sitting on the train
But I'm not.

I'm walking in the woods
With the wind caressing my face.
The sound in my ears is
The sough of the breeze in the branches.
The click of the wheels
The constipated tinkle of phones
Blur and fade
As do the voices round me.

The woman opposite me stares.
She can't understand
The dream in my eyes.
Perhaps she thinks I'm mad.
Or asleep.

Or just vacant. Not at home.
She's right. I'm not sitting on the train.
I'm walking on the shore.
The crash of the waves
The rattle of shingle
The cry of the gulls
Drown out the sound
Of the rails.

I think I'm sitting on the train.
I don't realise that I have gone.
The woman opposite me screams.
The seat is empty.
I am not there.
They think she's mad
Or perhaps she dreamed.
They pat her hand and offer counsel
And no one – ever – looks for me.

I am there, on my imagined shore.
Trapped between times.
Between existences.

And I am late for my appointments.

Second Sight

There was a time tunnel at the stately home. Corinne knew it well because she had been there before. A dark leafy passage, it ran between the car park and the open area of gravel in front of the house. She paid her fee and walked through it, moving from the present into the past as she stepped from a cloak of green shade and into the sunlight. At once she saw the crowds milling around: tourists like herself wearing ordinary clothes and the people around them, who purported to come from Tudor times, wearing ornate velvets and silks or home-spun rags – some barefoot, some with intricate ruffs and elaborate jewellery.

She loved it. It was so easy to imagine yourself in the past. If it wasn't for the ordinary people who had just climbed out of cars and coaches, she would find it totally convincing. And she wanted to be convinced; to lose herself in the past; to forget her loneliness and anger for an afternoon at least. It had worked last time she came. For several hours she hadn't given a single thought to him – the man she had thought of as her lover, until she had caught him cheating.

She wandered towards the moat where a narrow bridge led towards the house itself and turning right, instead of going on into the dark, panelled rooms, she walked alongside the water where a peacock strutted and flirted its tail proudly, enamoured by its own reflections. A group of Tudor people stood there. They were playing some kind of Elizabethan game on the grass and seemed unaware of her curiosity. They were there, after all, to be stared at. One of them, a man, looked up suddenly and caught her eye. He doffed his velvet cap and gave her an elaborate bow, smiling impishly. She laughed.

That was nice. It was friendly. She felt attractive – something her lover's insults had made her doubt – but not threatened. There was no way he was going to talk to her, not unless she approached him more closely and even then he would talk that wonderful mock-Shakespearean language which these people managed to improvise.

She was very impressed with the way they did it. It showed how talented they were, how completely they had entered into the parts they had chosen to play. Something she needed to learn to do. To play the cool, independent, confident woman of the world. Then, with or without a man, she could hold her head high.

Still managing to smile cheerfully, she walked on, leaving them to their game. Round the back of the house it was all very busy. She was heading towards her favourite places: the dairy, the kitchens, the dimly lit, dusty barns where they wove and spun and dyed their wool and did all the everyday things of life when lives were real and proper and self-sufficient, in a time when people made everything themselves. The dark shadowy areas, lit by candles and stray beams of sunlight from the high windows, filled her with excitement, inspired her. She loved to see the people chatting, gossiping, laughing round the smoky fires. She spent a long time staring at them as they worked. Then at last, overwhelmed with sudden, unexpected sadness that she was not part of a community such as this, she turned away, threading a path out of the crowd, and headed up towards the orchard to the part of the garden which was deserted. No tourists came here, because nothing ever happened. There was nothing to watch. It was empty, a place to think.

Slowly, trying to imagine herself wearing a long velvet gown instead of her usual trousers and loose sweater, she walked into the trees – and stopped in surprise. There were things going on here after all. She could see a group of Tudor-dressed people in the distance. They were talking together quietly, urgently, and she found herself wondering if she was going to catch them out talking modern English or did they, even here away from the crowds with no one to watch and listen, still keep to the parts which they had so carefully constructed for themselves?

The grass was soft and damp under the trees. They didn't hear her coming. She walked slowly, not hiding her approach, but drawing near to the group she began to feel inexplicably nervous. There was no one else around and they were clearly talking about something

213

personal and secret. She wondered suddenly if they would welcome someone watching them. She paused, pretending to examine the leaves on a damson tree nearby, trying to look casual, wondering whether to bring out the sketch book which she always brought everywhere with her. She groped in the haversack on her shoulder and produced the small pad and pen and, perversely perhaps, given her suspicions about their preoccupation with themselves, began to move towards them.

The group shifted. There were five men. They were talking, then shouting. Two of them walked apart, throwing insults at one another. She couldn't hear them properly. In fact she couldn't hear quite what language they were using, but if it was acting it was a very persuasive show of a quarrel.

She stopped, leaning against the trunk of a tree, regretting that she had come so close, wanting suddenly to turn back towards the house to the noise of ordinary people talking and laughing, to the children screaming as they chased the peacocks. It was growing very hot. The sun beat down between the trunks of the trees, but her eyes kept being drawn back to the scene ahead. She was as trapped by it as were the participants, and in a way as involved. The voices grew louder. She could almost feel the heat pouring off the men. One of the two was waving his arms about. She watched his face growing red as he gesticulated, fascinated by the way the feather on his jaunty cap shuddered around his face, curling beneath his chin. Even as she thought about it, he tore off the cap and threw it to the ground, seemingly beside himself with rage.

The man next to him suddenly had his hand on the hilt of the sword which had been hidden by his cloak. She caught her breath.

Stepping away from the tree a little to show she was there, she moved closer still, hoping that one of them would catch her eye and acknowledge her presence, perhaps with another good-humoured bow to defuse the atmosphere around them. But they didn't see her. Two of the men lunged towards the one who had the sword, as he drew it with a rasp of metal from its sheath. They pulled at his arms, his clothing, trying to restrain him, but his anger had overwhelmed him. He swung the sword for a moment over his head and the man who had broken away stepped back, his red face suddenly white. 'No,' he shouted. 'No!'

The blade entered his body through the velvet and through the white shirt. Red spilled down his front. Corinne caught her breath. She tried to remember that this was make-believe. He would have something secreted under his clothes to contain the blood – some kind of bladder they wore to hold the gore; Kensington gore, that's what they called it, didn't they? It was very convincing.

The man clutched the sword, plucking at the blade as his assailant pulled it out, his fingers stickily trying to hold together the hole in his clothes, to stop the blood, the gore, seeping out. With an awful expression on his face, he fell to his knees on the grass. The others looked round. They seemed horrified. Stunned. And the one whose sword it had been looked at the bloody weapon in his hand for a moment as though he couldn't believe that it were there. Then he dropped it on the grass and ran, passing within a few feet of her as he headed towards the house and out of sight among the trees.

Embarrassed, Corinne waited. Did they expect her to applaud? What did people do under these circumstances? What was supposed to happen next? Her mouth had gone dry. She couldn't move. She wanted to go back to the house, have tea and surround herself with people, but was trapped.

The three remaining men stood huddled over their companion, awkwardly hunched on the ground. There was a moment's silence, then one looked up at the others. 'He's dead.' The words, stark, modern or ancient, without embroidery, echoed in the quiet of the orchard. She held her breath. What were they going to do now? The man who had spoken bent over his fallen friend, touched his shoulder and rolled his body over. It flopped, convincingly inert, and sprawled at their feet.

As she watched, the three of them lifted him clumsily. He was heavy. His cloak dragged on the ground. One shoe fell from his foot. They heaved their awkward bundle up and began to run with it towards the trees in the distance. In a moment they had gone.

Released at last to move, Corinne hesitated. She wasn't sure what to do. Suddenly she didn't feel like being with other people after all. She had been caught up for however short a time in the drama of the moment. Openly now, she walked forward, composing herself.

She went quickly to the spot where they had been. It would be there – the great red stain – and she would be able to tell now that it had all been an act, part of a play. She looked around in the grass. It must be the wrong place. She moved forward, looking for the shoe which she had seen fall from the man's foot. There was no sign of it. She went to the next tree and the next, but the ground was untouched, the long grass uncrushed; there was no sign of the sword, no sign of the shoe, no sign of the blood which had so copiously flowed from the man's chest. There was nothing.

A strange shiver swept over her and she realised that she was feeling very cold. This was odd. Nothing felt right.

Almost without meaning to she followed the way they had gone, away from the path through the nettles and the long grass. There was no sign of anyone having come this way, never mind three men, encumbered by cloaks, dragging a heavy burden. She stared into the shadows beyond the boundary hedges. Where had they gone? She saw now that there was rabbit fencing round the orchard, and on the far side of the hedge an electric fence and beyond that a field of grazing cattle. Of course the men could have vaulted the hedge and fences. Once out of her sight they could have put down their burden, and he, miraculously alive again, could have run with them lightly tiptoeing, probably laughing, out of sight of their audience.

She walked back again, searching meticulously, more thoroughly now, determined to find at least a trace of them. There was a tiny core inside her, growing steadily more afraid. She walked up to the corner of the orchard, along the back hedge, looking at each tree, quartering the ground. She did the whole thing twice, gridding backwards and forwards beneath the tall, old-fashioned, ancient apple trees heading back towards the house. Of the sword, the shoe, anything at all in fact, she found no trace. There was nothing in the orchard.

She began to retrace her steps back towards the open sunlight and the tourists and the people in their costumes, enacting scenes from a Tudor past, and looked at them suddenly with different eyes, knowing in some inner part of herself that she alone of all the people there had had a glimpse of the real thing . . .

'Corinne?' The voice behind her stopped her in her tracks. 'I've been looking for you.'

She turned.

The lover. Repentant. Charming. Rueful. 'Please?' He held out his hand.

She was still a little shocked. Still slightly shaky, she realised, suddenly. Had it not been for that, she might not so easily have decided that she needed someone to have tea with.

Anyone, as long as he belonged to the present.

The Cottage Kitchen

When Roz first saw Fen Cottage it seemed like home. The kitchen was the only thing which stopped her from making an instant offer. The rest of the cottage was idyllic. It had low beams, thatch, three small charming bedrooms with tiny windows, a pretty sitting room which looked out onto a flower-smothered terrace and a dining room with a large inglenook fireplace. The kitchen was a lean-to. It was long, narrow, dark and basic. She thought, made a few sketches, did some calculations, crossed her fingers – the numbers didn't quite add up – and made an offer. It was accepted at once.

It was eight weeks after that first enchanted viewing that she closed the door for the last time on her London flat, took a deep breath and headed for the country. It was only six months before that, that she'd first realised she wanted to leave London at all. Thanks to modern technology – she worked from home as a PR consultant

– she could live where she liked. Nothing was keeping her in town except habit. Certainly not men. Her last relationship had gone the way of the others before it – fun while it lasted, but somehow not completely satisfying. She had not, she supposed, met her true soul mate yet, and perhaps now she wasn't going to. The thought, to her surprise, did not worry her. In fact, she felt a sudden sense of freedom.

She turned one of the bedrooms – the nicest – into an office. It had a view across the wild, tangled garden (a future project, that) and over the hedge towards the fields. She established contact with the rest of the world via phone, fax and modem, and in the evenings began work on the dining room. It was going to be the new kitchen.

It obviously had once been the kitchen of the house, or so she thought. She could see the vestiges there. In the inglenook, behind the electric fire, was the bread oven, a salt box, even the iron upright of the sway which had once held a pot over the fire, all invisible beneath an encrustation of centuries-old soot.

She began on the floral wallpaper, the top layer of about six, pulling it off in great flapping wedges. Then, to tackle the Edwardian brown-painted cupboards, the Fifties light fittings and the damp floor, she decided to call in the help of a local builder. She had already had two quotes when Edwin Fosset appeared.

'I hear you want some work done.' He looked down at her gravely from gentle grey eyes. He was tall and thin with a kind, lived-in face, attractive in its way, the kind of face she trusted instinctively. In fact, within seconds she felt she had known him all her life. She found herself showing him inside and went to fetch her sketches.

He looked at them critically. 'It could be a nice room. No problems as far as I can see. I can get started straight away.' He shivered. 'It's chilly in here. Perhaps I should start by opening up these windows and letting in some sunshine!'

That was one of the problems. The room was extra-ordinarily cold. And depressing. When she stood in it she could feel all her buoyancy and energy draining out of her, as though someone had pulled a plug in the soles of her feet.

She mentioned it to her first guests, her new neigh-bours, Bob and Julie, who lived up the lane. They admired the living room and the bedroom, came with her into the kitchen while she made coffee and agreed with her that it was too small, then carried their cups with her into the old dining room. 'This is such a nice room. Potentially,' she added.

'Ah,' Bob said. 'Potentially.'

'And what does that mean?' Julie said, as she stood looking round. 'Potentially!' She echoed his voice. 'It's a lovely room! Look at the view across the orchards.'

Roz had her eyes fixed on Bob's face. 'Don't tell me. Someone died in here.' She tried to make it a joke, but it was a thought that kept on occurring to her with depressing regularity, one that had been suggested by several London friends who, on agreeing to visit at some time in the future and promising to bring food parcels as though there were no Sainsbury's outside the M25 ring, invariably asked with mock caution if there was a ghost and, if so, was it friendly?

Bob shrugged. 'I've never heard of anyone dying in here. But the Grahams, who you bought it from, never used this room. Betty said it was always cold, even in the summer. One of Jim Fosset's boys is going to work for you, isn't he? He would know.'

'Boy?' Roz giggled. 'He must be heading towards forty!'

Bob smiled. 'But this is a village, Roz. People are defined by generations. And the Fossets have been here hundreds of years. The boys' grandmother ran the village school, and their great-grandmother was cook up at the hall in the old days. And their great-great grandmother was –?' He hesitated, glancing at his wife.

'Don't tell me. She was a witch?' Roz looked from one to the other expectantly.

Julie shrugged. 'Not that I've heard. I haven't any idea what she was. I wonder where your builder fits in. He sounds older than the sons, so he might be the cousin who went off and made good. The one who went to university and is reported, by village gossip, to have made a lot of dosh. If that's true, why is he back here doing work as a jobbing builder?'

'I got the impression he is a craftsman,' Roz put in defensively. 'Perhaps he likes being a builder.' She had a sudden depressing vision of her newly-acquired friend leaving her amid piles of hammers and dust-sheets to go and attend to his investments. She was intrigued nevertheless.

She found herself thinking often about Edwin's strong brown hands as he handled his hammer and shovel. His quiet, reserved charm appealed to her more than that of the more extrovert men who had come and gone in her life up to now. She had to admit she found him very attractive. But she was not in the market for a man. What she wanted was a kitchen.

Only two days later Edwin climbed up the stairs to Roz's study and tapped on the door as she finished a phone call to New York. 'Can you come down?'

'What is it?' She felt a twinge of anxiety.

'There's something I want you to see.' More than that he would not say, and she had to follow the enigmatically silent figure down the twisting staircase into the dining room where he had been digging up the floor to lay a damp-proof course.

'You haven't found a body, have you, Edwin?' She tried to make it a joke. 'I've been waiting for you to unearth something in here.'

He grinned and his face lightened visibly. 'No, it's not a body. Look.'

She peered into the earth and dust. 'What exactly am I supposed to be looking at?'

He sighed. 'Look. Here.' He squatted on his haunches and scraped at the loose soil.

She crouched beside him and stared. 'It looks like old brick.'

'It is.' He smiled up at her. 'Well, tiles, actually. This house is supposed to have medieval foundations, and this is the old floor.'

She knelt to touch the red tiles. 'I had no idea the house was that old. They are beautiful. Can we expose them and use them, do you think?' She glanced up. 'Do you mind my asking? Is it true that you have a degree?'

'I have.'

'Am I allowed to ask what in?'

'History of Architecture.' He frowned. She had touched on forbidden territory.

She retreated to more neutral ground. 'So, you would know if we have to report it or anything?'

He relaxed. 'Yes, I would know.'

Encouraged, she dared to ask the question she had been brooding on. 'I am going to be nosy. Can I ask why, if you have an architecture degree, you are working on my kitchen?'

He shrugged. 'It's a job.'

'Not a very academic one.'

'I'm not an academic.' He picked up the trowel with which he had been digging. 'Did you mention a cup of tea?'

'You know I did not.' She smiled again. 'But I can take a hint.'

It was half past two in the morning when she was awakened by the sound of shouting. Struggling up from an exhausted sleep, she stared round the room, disorientated. It was silent now, but she was sure the noise hadn't been part of her dream. Climbing out of bed, she tiptoed to the door and listened. The cottage was completely silent. Outside the open window she heard the call of an owl hunting along the hedge behind the hollyhocks, then all was silent again as the smell of roses drifted up to her.

Pulling open the door as silently as she could, she stepped out onto the landing and crept on bare feet to the top of the stairs. The tiny hairs on her arms, she realised suddenly, were standing on end and she shivered in spite of the warmth of the night.

She could see the moonlight shining from the window of the dining room across the black chasm of the floor and out across the hall towards the staircase. The silence was suddenly oppressive. She took a deep breath and, plucking up courage, forced herself to go down. At the bottom she stopped again, staring into the room as she realised that there was an indistinct figure standing by the fireplace. She stared at it in astonishment.

'Edwin?' Her voice came out as a breathless croak.

The figure turned to face her and she was conscious of the pale, drawn face, gentle grey eyes and the worn brown jerkin. Then, as she watched, the figure seemed to fade and disappear. Not Edwin, but someone so like him.

For a moment, total silence still surrounded her, then she became aware of the usual cottage noises. The clock in the hall was ticking, she could hear a tap dripping from the kitchen and suddenly, from the window, came the pure delicate notes of a nightingale.

Abruptly, she sat down on the stairs and buried her face in her arms. She was shaking but it was, she realised, with shock rather than fear. There had been nothing at all frightening about him.

'I'm dreaming.' She spoke the words out loud. Taking a deep breath, she stood up and went to the door of the dining room. It was completely empty, the moonlight lying like a silver carpet over the dust and bricks and soil and scatter of tools. She took a few steps into the room, looking round. The figure had been standing in front of the fireplace, staring down into the earth in front of him. She looked down as well. There was nothing there.

When Edwin arrived next morning she was in her office on the telephone. She stood looking down at him as he walked up the path from his van, her concentration only half on what she was saying. Without realising it, she shivered.

When she finally went downstairs, half the floor had been uncovered.

'Good morning.' He smiled at her without stopping work.

'Edwin.' She hesitated. The face in her dream – if it was a dream – was still haunting her, but how could she admit to dreaming about someone who looked so like him?

'How long do you think it will take?' she finished lamely.

'Not long.'

And with that she had to be content.

Three nights later she was woken up again by the sound of laughter and shouting from downstairs. She stared round in the darkness. There was no moon tonight and she could hear the gentle patter of rain on the roses below her window, filling her room with the sweet scent of wet earth. She lay still for a few seconds, her heart thumping with fear, then slowly and unwillingly she sat up, swinging her legs over the side of the bed.

At the door she paused and frowned. She could smell beer. The sound of talk and laughter grew louder and she could hear the clinking of glasses coming from the dining room.

Creeping downstairs, she tiptoed across the hall and, taking a deep breath, she pushed open the door.

The silence was immediate and total. The room was empty.

She stepped in and looked round. It was as Edwin had left it. The floor was finished and neatly swept, the walls stripped and the window frames repaired. All that remained to be done was to fix the chimney and paper the room before the arrival of the Aga and the sink and the old dresser she had found in the antique shop in the village.

Reaching for the light switch, she turned it on. The smell of beer had completely gone.

'Do you think Fen Cottage was ever a pub?' she asked Julie when she met her in the village shop that morning. Edwin had gone to fetch a load of bricks.

'I've never heard it was. Why?' Julie was stacking her purchases into a basket.

Roz shrugged. 'Just something I heard.'

'It was an inn, yes,' Edwin said later. He sat back on his heels for a moment, a wedge of pale lime mortar on his trowel. 'A couple of hundred years ago. Why?' He looked at her hard.

She shrugged. 'I just wondered.'

When she heard the sounds again that night she almost didn't go down. She lay for five minutes, her head under the pillow, then reluctantly she climbed to her feet.

This time the noise did not stop as she pushed open the door. The room was full of people. She saw the smoke from the fire, and from the men's clay pipes. She saw the bar and the plump red-faced woman pulling beer from a barrel set up behind it. She saw the pretty fair-haired barmaid sashaying between the

227

drinkers, squealing as they flirted with her, slapping back their impertinent hands. And she saw the man she had seen before.

He was standing, his back to the wall near the roaring fire, his eyes fixed on the girl. As Roz watched, he slipped his hand into his pocket and brought something out. A small silver charm on a thin, filigree chain. She saw him catch the girl's hand as she whisked past him and she saw him speak, his longing clear in every movement of his body as he shyly pressed the charm into her hand. As the girl glanced down at it she saw the love and hope in the young man's eyes.

Then the girl laughed. She tossed her pretty curls and flounced her hips and tucked the charm back into his pocket.

He looked stunned. As Roz watched, he stepped away from the wall, his face scarlet with embarrassment as the jeers of the other drinkers told him they had missed nothing of the exchange. With one quick gesture he snatched the charm out of his pocket and threw it into the fire, then he turned and walked out of the door into the lane.

As the door banged shut, Roz found herself standing in the silent cottage staring into an empty room.

That evening, Bob dropped by to lend her a catalogue of light fittings and they went out onto the terrace to have a glass of wine. 'I hear you were asking about the house's history,' he said. 'You were right, it was a pub. And there is a story to go with it. One of the village men went away to London and made his fortune. He came back and fell in love with the barmaid here. She rejected him and the story goes he went out and hanged

228

himself.' He took a sip of wine and then caught sight of her face. 'Sorry, Roz. Perhaps you would rather not have known.'

'No.' She turned away so he couldn't see the tears in her eyes. 'No, I'm glad you told me.'

The next morning she asked Edwin if he had heard the story. As he turned away from repointing the chimney, she watched his face intently. He stood still for a moment staring into the distance, then slowly he shrugged. 'Yes, I think I might have heard it somewhere.'

And that was all.

But that evening he came out to the terrace where she was reading. There was something in his hand.

'I found it under some mortar.'

The silver charm was tarnished, almost black. For several moments she looked at it, then slowly she held it out to him again. 'I think it's yours.'

Their eyes met.

'That is what you came back for, isn't it?' she said.

He looked down at it and slowly he nodded. 'You say he looked like me?'

'Yes.' She hesitated. 'She didn't deserve his love. She wasn't worth it,' she insisted, more vehemently than she'd intended.

'I've dreamed about this house since I was small.' Glancing up he gave her a sheepish smile. 'I don't believe in reincarnation or anything like that. It's just that sometimes, if you let yourself listen, you can hear the echoes, feel the ripples of sorrow as they reach you over the years. I thought studying architecture would take away the pain, would make the past rational, cool, sensible. And that building would bring it under control, make it safe.' He looked down at his hands. 'When I heard you wanted a builder, it just seemed like fate. Like something I'd been waiting for.'

'And now you've found it,' she said gently, reaching out to touch the fragile silver where it lay on his palm and feeling the warmth of his hand as it slowly curled around hers.

The Room Upstairs

'Andy, I've found somewhere to live!' The tousled red hair was if anything more vibrant than usual.

Andy looked up from his books at the whirlwind hovering by his desk in the library, her arms full of files and notes, canvas bag dangling from her shoulder. He shrugged a weary hello. 'Can we afford it?'

Getting kicked out of their digs ten days before the end of their first term at university had been the last straw in a pretty foul week.

Jill nodded vigorously. 'Big attic room. A bit far out of town, but walking distance. Just.' She grinned. She held out two large keys. 'Coming to see it?'

'Now?' He glanced down at his desk with regret. It was warm and secure in the library. Outside there was a gale blowing, sleet hit the windows like machine-gun fire and the thought of a long hike through the dark filled him with about as much enthusiasm as facing a firing squad. Still, it had to be done. Out at the end of the week their landlord had said and Andy knew why. The bastard had found someone who would pay more, no questions asked about leases and things.

Jill walked fast, head down, her face screwed up against the cold, her collar high around her ears. He wondered what she would do if he put his arm round her shoulders and pulled her close. Just for warmth of course. They were room mates out of necessity. Or fate. Not lovers. He had met her on the doorstep of the digs back in October, and they had viewed the double room together as rivals. Both were seeking someone to share with. They tossed for the room. He won. He chose her. Simple as that. No sex. No dirty socks on public view. Her rules. Fine by him.

He glanced around him as they walked. The streets were empty in the rain, viscous puddles reflecting the street lights. From time to time he could see a Christmas tree in a window. Otherwise the houses had withdrawn behind their curtains. He half wished he could reach for Jill's hand. Just for company. In a lonely world. But that would be against the rules too.

As though half sensing his thought she grinned at him from the shelter of her collar. 'I did say it was a long way.'

'How did you hear about it?'

'Chap I met at the Union.' She was vague about the detail. 'Said he'd been going to stay there himself but he'd found somewhere better.'

'Sounds as though it's not much cop.'

'Cheap though.' She fished a piece of paper out of her pocket and stopped for a minute under one of the street lights. A rain drop hit the paper and smudged the ink. 'Next left. Then about half a mile.'

'Half a mile!' He was appalled.

She caught his eye and shrugged again. 'Cheap!' They said it together and laughed.

It was hard to find. The number had fallen off the gate and the front path was overgrown. They worked it out by the numbers on the other houses on either side. They were small and neat, with well-manicured gardens. Number 40 was overgrown, the paint on the door blistered. And it was huge.

'There's no one in.' They stood side by side in the gateway looking at the darkened windows. 'Shit!' Andy was shivering with cold. 'Now what?'

'We've got the key. The chap I spoke to said the room was at the top. He said he never saw the people who live here at all.' Jill looked down uncertainly at the keys in her hand. They were tied together by a piece of stringy red ribbon. 'Come on, let's check it out, then we'll go and get some fish and chips at that place we passed about ten miles back.' She was trying to jolly him along. And herself. 'It's not as though we've much choice. This end of term there's nothing left in town.'

The gate was stiff. The hinges creaked loudly as she pushed it open and walked quickly up the path. They knocked and rang the bell, reluctant to go in uninvited, but there was no answer.

The hall was long and narrow and smelled faintly of cooking. They sniffed. 'Cabbage.' Jill was groping for the light switch. 'Why is it always cabbage?' The single bulb with its pleated orange shade showed a narrow strip of flowered carpet and an ornate mahogany hall stand with a built-in mirror. On it was a rumpled lace mat the colour of cold tea.

'Hello!' Jill raised her hand to knock at the only door leading off the hallway, on their left. Its brown paint was badly scuffed and it looked as though it had been forced open at some point in the past. There was no reply and gingerly she turned the knob. It was locked.

They stood looking up the staircase. 'The top you said?' Andy put his hand on the huge wooden swirl at the bottom of the banister rail. It seemed too large and imposing for the narrowness of the hall. 'Come on then.'

The landing on the first floor revealed five more doors. One was a bathroom, basic, old-fashioned, without towels or mats or even – Jill noticed at once – lavatory paper. The other four doors were locked.

On up and they found three more doors. One, a small loo (also without paper) the other two locked, then a small uncarpeted staircase led even higher. They stood looking up into the darkness. *'Chez nous?'* Andy raised an eyebrow.

'I suppose so.' Jill grimaced. 'It's pretty quiet isn't it.'

'As the grave!' He put on a hollow voice, and then rather wished he hadn't. 'Here, let me have the key. I'll go first.'

She hadn't said anything but he could sense she was uncomfortable. So to be honest was he. The house was too bloody quiet by half.

The key slipped into the lock easily and the door swung back. It revealed, once they had found the light switch, in the orange glow of another pleated shade, a long low-ceilinged room with four mansard windows. Two looked one way over the street, the others looked presumably over the garden. When he knelt on a

234

window seat to stare out at the back Andy could see nothing.

The room was furnished with two beds, two chests-of-drawers, two cupboards and a table. The floor was bare linoleum. In the corner behind a blue flowered curtain they found a small scruffy sink, a gas cooker and another cupboard.

'Paradise!' Andy sat down experimentally on one of the beds and gave a cautious bounce. He glanced up at her. 'You OK?' She was awfully pale.

'Sure.' She said it too quickly. 'It's fine. So, who do we tell?'

He shrugged. Standing up he went over to the window. 'I thought I heard a car.'

They ran downstairs to find an elderly man on the threshold, opening and shutting his umbrella to throw off the rain. He looked up at them, a puzzled frown on his face.

'We came to see the room.'

'Are you the landlord?'

The simultaneous explanation and question seemed to confuse him. He put his umbrella carefully in the square compartment clearly intended for that very use at the end of the stand, then, slowly he began to unbutton his overcoat.

'Is it all right if we bring our things over later?' Jill smiled at him, not above wheedling when she had to. He reminded her a little of her grandfather and it had always worked with him.

He hung his coat on the stand and stood for a moment adjusting his tie, seemingly lost in thought, staring at the speckled mirror.

'Is it your house, mate?' Andy thought a man to man approach with a touch of familiarity might be appropriate.

The old man smiled to himself gently. He tweaked his jacket straight and stood back, turning towards the door behind him which Andy had tried earlier. They watched in silence as it opened and he walked into the room. As it closed behind him Andy gave a soft whistle. 'Did he even see us?'

Jill shrugged. 'Not very sociable, was he?' She tiptoed towards the closed door and put her ear to the panelling.

'Jill!' Andy was shocked.

'It's so bloody quiet. Too bloody quiet!' She turned to face him. 'I don't like it here, Andy.'

Secretly he agreed with her. 'What choice have we? We're not going to find anywhere else by tomorrow.' He shrugged. 'He looked pretty harmless. Quite nice in fact.'

She smiled at him in fond exasperation. 'Optimist. OK. Here goes.' She raised her fist and rapped on the door. 'At least he must know who we should contact.' She knocked again.

'Or, again, he won't.' After a pause Andy grimaced. 'As I said, not the world's most sociable.'

'Oh, come on!' Jill took a deep breath and smacked the door with the flat of her hand.

'Steady.' Andy put his hand on her arm. 'Perhaps he just doesn't want to talk to us.'

'Well I want to talk to him!' She shook him off and to Andy's surprise he saw that she was close to tears. 'I only want a word. I want to get it sorted, Andy. I want to move in and have somewhere to stay! Come on, you silly old fool. Answer.' She grabbed the door handle and shook it hard.

'Jill, don't –'

'Wait! Listen! I can hear him.' Jill held up her hand. 'He's coming.' Her relief was palpable.

Andy had heard it too now. Footsteps were approaching them on the far side of the door. He glanced at Jill, then he stepped forward and knocked again, politely this time. It opened almost at once.

'Yes?' The old man stared at them from mild, pale blue eyes.

'I'm sorry to bother you –' Andy found himself staring past the man's shoulder into the room. It was softly lit and from where he was standing he could see the fire crackling brightly in the grate, the corner of a blue sofa, a table with on it a vase of red anemones. He took a deep breath. 'We were wondering if we could rent the top room –' For some reason he was finding it hard to collect his wits.

The old man smiled. 'Of course.'

'You are the landlord?' Andy's glance shot back into the room as he heard a woman's cough.

'I am.' The old man inclined his head. 'You are very welcome to rent the room, young man.'

'What about references and things?'

'Tomorrow.' With another bow he stepped back from the door and pushed it gently shut in Andy's face.

For a moment he stood staring at the brown wood then he turned to Jill. 'Well. What do you think?' He was speaking in a whisper.

'I suppose it will do. Temporarily. We could always look for somewhere closer in, next term –' She broke off as behind them suddenly they heard the sound of raised voices from behind the closed door.

'Andy –'

'Wait.' He was listening again. 'They are having an awful row. I can hear someone crying –'

Suddenly the sound was reverberating around the hall. They could hear a woman shouting, then there was a scream. There was a loud crash from behind the door and then silence.

Andy and Jill stared at each other. 'Should I see if they're all right?' Andy was frowning.

'I don't know.' Jill was backing away towards the front door. 'Andy, I really think we should go.'

He glanced at her. Her face was white. He bit his lip. 'Look we've got to check. It's gone awfully quiet in there.' He raised his hand and knocked softly. There was no reply. He looked over his shoulder at Jill and knocked again. 'Hello. Is everything OK? Can we help?'

With a slight click the door swung slowly inwards under his hand. Andy took a step back, surprised. He took a deep breath. 'Hello? Excuse me, are you all right in there?'

With a quick glance at her Andy moved forward and pushed the door open. 'Hello –' he called again. He stopped abruptly.

'What is it?'

'It's empty!' He stepped into the room and stood staring round. It was large and high-ceilinged with an ornate fireplace. There was nothing but cold ashes in the grate. The room was empty and dark, the windows shuttered, the floor uncarpeted.

'It can't be! We both saw him.' Jill was hovering in the doorway. 'There must be another door. He must have come through here and gone somewhere else.'

He swallowed. 'I saw him. You saw him. The fire was lit. The room was warm. There were lights –'

'I want to go.' Jill's voice was suddenly very urgent. 'I don't like this. Come on.' She was pulling at his sleeve.

'But it doesn't make sense –'

'I don't care!' Jill's voice rose an octave. 'I'm going.' She turned and ran out into the hall again and reached for the front door latch. Fumbling she pulled at the handle and dragged it open. 'Andy , come on!'

'Wait, Jill. Wait for me –' Andy was still standing in the middle of the room, staring round.

Jill didn't hear him. She had run out onto the path. Two cars had drawn up at the kerb and there were a group of men standing on the pavement. She couldn't see them properly in the darkness and she paused. 'Run, love. Get away from the house!' A voice came at her out of the dark. 'Quickly. You're safe now –'

'Andy, what about Andy?' She could feel the icy rain streaming into her face. The wind was lashing her hair. She looked up at the house, then she glanced back at the gate. 'Andy, my friend. He's in there –'

The street was deserted. The car and the men had gone.

She stared. Then she turned back to the house.

In the darkness all she could see were trees. On either side the neat small modern houses with their lighted windows stood square against the rain. In front of her the weeds grew shoulder high and rank. She could smell nettles and dead leaves. The house had gone.

'Andy?' Ice cold, her stomach churning with fear, she stepped forward. 'Andy, where are you?'

There was no answer. The only sound she could hear was the patter of rain on the shiny wet laurel leaves of the hedge along the road. In the house next door, behind the fence, someone flicked a switch and in the window she dimly saw the lights of a Christmas tree shining through the dark.

Moonlight

Turning on the bed-side light Chris sat hugging her knees, her head resting on her arms. The dream had come again, exhausting, terrifying, but oh, so exhilarating and she had awoken from it once more with the strangest feeling that it had not been a dream at all.

It was only a few months since she had moved into this cottage, so different from the house in which she had brought up the children and lived most of her married life. It was mad to move from everything she knew, but it was something she had to do – a sign of independence for a newly single woman, and besides the Sixth Form College in the nearby town was perfect for the twins. It had surprised her when they leapt at the chance of the change, but who understood children? Far from bemoaning the loss of friends and cinemas and urban delights without number, they had talked in a most unteenage way of fresh air and birds and flowers. She had wondered more than once if they had talked it over in that disconcertingly parental way one's children sometimes did, deciding that it would be a good thing for her to move, to get away from Paul and his new wife. Not that she minded, all that much, seeing them together. When a marriage is over it is over. She was enjoying her new found independence.

She lay back on the pillows and closed her eyes. In her dream she had walked down the path between the beds of herbs and cottage things like delphiniums and hollyhocks to the long grass at the end of the garden where there were three ancient apple trees. It was waiting for her there: the most beautiful white horse. Without saddle or bridle, its mane like soft silk, it walked up to her and thrust its velvet muzzle into her hands, blowing gently on her fingers. This was the strange part. All her life she had been afraid of horses. Not that she knew any well, but even from a safe distance, though undoubtedly attractive creatures, they looked strong and uncontrollable and dangerous.

Here her dream became stranger still. After flinging her arms around the animal's neck and kissing it as though it were an old friend she somehow vaulted onto its back, feeling the muscular flanks of the animal beneath her bare legs, winding her fingers into the mane and leaning forward to whisper in its ear. It listened, it raised its head and pricked its ears, then it turned and strode purposefully towards the open (open? it had never been opened) gate. In her dream she was not afraid. She leaned low, encouraging it to go faster as the horse moved smoothly from trot to canter and finally into a gallop, taking her down the fields, across ditches and through gates and on towards the Downs.

By the time they returned her face was flushed, her hair tangled and her legs ached, but she was so, so happy. Slipping off the horse in the garden she kissed its nose and tiptoed up over the dewy grass and in through the back door where the children, music quiet at last, lay asleep.

Staring up at the ceiling, disorientated, she lay still for a moment, then, throwing back the bedclothes she walked across to her dressing table. Turning on the lamp she peered at her face. It was flushed and her hair was wild and tangled, but surely she looked like that every morning? Everyone did when they awoke. She examined her hands. No sign. Of course no sign of their fierce strong grip on the mane, no smell – she raised them cautiously to her nose – of horse.

With a sigh she turned and climbed back into bed.

'You're nuts, Mum!' Mat reached for the cereal box and tipped a helping onto his plate. 'You can't take up riding at your age. Besides, you hate horses!'

'Shut up, Mat!' Lyn poured herself her own breakfast – a single cup of black coffee. 'Of course Mum can learn to ride. Everyone ought to take up something new at her age.'

'Thanks,' Chris's dry acknowledgement was lost in the twins' banter.

'She might fall off and break her leg or something.'

'Nonsense. She'd be brilliant.'

I will be brilliant. She didn't say it out loud. They weren't listening anyway. Smiling tolerantly she chivvied them out of the house and went to get ready for work. As a part-time receptionist at the local surgery she had found herself the most perfect job she could have wished for. She had met practically everybody in the village and already knew most of their life histories.

Her colleague behind the reception desk that morning, Anita, knew Sandra Hodge, the woman who ran the local riding school. In a lull between patients Chris rang up and booked her first lesson before she had a chance to change her mind.

The horse was brown, its coat muddy; it wore a saddle and bridle and when she reached out her hand to stroke its nose it put its ears back and shook its head. She listened intently to the instructions on how to mount, thankful that this first lesson was on her own and not in front of twenty small girls who rode like angels or demons. Even mounting the thing proved a problem. Her foot would not reach the stirrup – it was too high and each time she tried, the horse side-stepped away from her leaving her hopping frantically in space.

Sandra grew bored more quickly than the horse. 'Come over here to the mounting block.' In seconds, much chastened, she was on. This horse was far fatter than her own Moonlight, as she had christened him, the stirrup leathers cut her legs through her jeans and its action as she was led out into the ring was jerky and uncomfortable. All her confidence had long since oozed away.

'Sit straight. Relax. Hold the reins as I showed you. Sit down into the saddle. Don't lean forward . . .' The string of instructions assailed her like machine gun fire. Her legs began to ache long before the lesson was over.

When the time came to dismount she nearly collapsed as her feet met the oh-so distant ground.

'Not bad.' Sandra gave her a tight smile. 'If you want to persevere I'm sure you'll get the hang of it. In the end.'

Get the hang of it – she, who had galloped, bent low over her horse's neck, through the moonlit countryside, the wind in her hair, and guided the horse with nothing more than the gentle pressure of her knees! Angrily she fumbled with the buckle of her borrowed hard hat and vowed never to return.

She managed a long hot bath before Mat and Lyn arrived home. It wasn't easy to hide her crippling stiffness but smiling determinedly she staggered round the kitchen and was relieved that, engrossed in college gossip, they did not notice. If they had she would never have heard the end of it.

She was doing an afternoon shift the next day, so in the morning, after the twins had left for college, she walked down the garden towards the apple trees. It had been a wet warm month and the lush grass and leaves had grown like tropical jungle. The next thing she had to learn was gardening.

She stopped by the tree where she had first seen the white horse, staring round the sun-dappled grass. What had triggered her dream? Nothing that she could see as she walked on under the apple boughs towards the back gate. The latch was rusty and bent. It took her several minutes of determined rattling and shoving to release it and force the gate open a few inches. Outside the field of green wheat, fresh and rippling like the sea, stretched away for miles. Around the edge there was a narrow track. She stepped onto it, staring round, trying to identify the landscape of her dreams. But it was no use. It all looked different in the bright warm sunlight.

She was just turning in at the gate once more when her eye was caught by something at her feet. Staring down she felt her stomach lurch with surprise. Cut deep in the sandy soil of the path she could see the shape of a large hoof print.

Of course, people must ride round the field. Why else would there be such a well-marked path? She cast round for other signs of passing horses but in spite of the soft ground there were none and puzzled, she made her way back into the garden.

The dream returned that night and as though remembering her riding lesson she hesitated as they turned out of the gate and guiding the horse with her legs and her balance she headed off the path and into the field. Cantering circles in each direction as she had seen some of the other students do in the distance, she listened to the rustle of its feet in the long sweet corn and watched the moonshadows stretch and turn across the ground in front of her. Only when they had done that did she lean forward and whisper in the horse's ear and turn it for the gallop towards the Downs.

Her next lesson was very different from the first. Different instructor, different horse. 'I'm sorry, Mrs Hodge had to go to London for the day.' Horse and teacher this time were both attractive, slim, long-haired and kind. Chris giggled to herself as the comparison flitted through her head and forgetting to be afraid she ruffled the mane of her new mount. 'I'm sorry, Mrs Hodge

246

didn't say how much experience you'd had.' The girl walked over to the barrier round the indoor school and reached for the saddle she had left there.

'No. Please. Can I try without?' Chris, left holding the bridle, whispered to the horse, which hadn't tried to bite her. It twitched its ears attentively. 'I haven't had much practice, to be honest, but most of what I have done in the past has been with no saddle.'

The girl let the heavy saddle fall back on its resting place. 'Great. Good training for you. Bring her over here so you can get on.'

The same mounting block. No stirrups. Not letting herself think Chris threw herself upwards and vaulted lightly onto the horse's back, gathering up the reins.

'Great. Canter her round the circle.' The girl sat down on the mounting block and prepared to watch.

Chris took a deep breath. This felt more familiar, and it had been so easy in her dream. A gentle squeeze with her legs, a chirrup at the eager ears.

The horse broke straight into a canter, loping easily round the sawdust ring, responding to her every move. To her surprise and delight she loved it. It was easy, exciting – not as exciting as being outside, but still exciting.

The next two nights she dreamed of nothing at all. On the third she dreamed she was stacking supermarket shelves with biscuits she had made herself on a bonfire at the back of the surgery. Bitterly disappointed, she retraced her steps, next morning into the garden.

'Moonlight?'

She shook her head in despair. Losing her marbles, as Mat would say. Calling out loud to a dream horse from a dream world. Perhaps she shouldn't have ridden for real. Perhaps the experience had destroyed the dream.

She made her way towards the gate and out onto the path. The ground had dried out now. It was hard and dusty. Turning left out of the gate she began to walk along the track listening to the skylarks high above the field, screwing up her eyes so that she could see the tiny specks against the brilliant blue of the sky.

The horse was upon her before she knew it, galloping around the corner, its rider intent upon the path. With a scream Chris threw herself sideways into the corn as the animal reared up and skidded to a standstill.

'Are you all right? My God, I'm sorry. I never saw you!' The man was off the horse and at Chris's side almost before the animal had stopped.

Shaken, she lay still for a moment, then slowly she sat up. 'I'm OK. It's not your fault. I wasn't paying attention. I should have heard you.'

His chestnut mare had trotted a few yards away and stopped. It stood near them, its rein trailing, snatching greedily at the hedgerow grass.

'I'm Tom Ketch. From Saddlers farm.' He had taken her arm and helped her gently to her feet. He was tall, tanned, her age, or perhaps a bit older. He was dressed in jeans, leather jacket and boots. 'You're Chris Dean, aren't you? I've seen you around. Is your ankle twisted?' She had staggered slightly as she put her weight on it. 'I'm so sorry. Look, sit here. Let me look.'

'I'm all right. Really.' It was wonderful to be so fussed over. But at the same time it was embarrassing. What kind of an idiot must he think her, nose-diving into the wheat like that? She firmly removed her arm from his and planted her foot on the ground, stamping experimentally and resolutely hiding the answering needle of pain which shot up her leg.

'It's a wonderful place to ride,' she said. 'Please don't think you can't gallop round here because of me. It's my own fault. I was too busy listening to the skylarks.'

'And why not?' He smiled and she found herself smiling back suddenly, unable to take her eyes off his face. 'Perhaps we can ride together some time?' he went on.

She wanted to. Oh yes, she wanted to, so much. She had placed him now. Tom Ketch. Newly returned from living abroad to take up the family farm and stables. Handsome. Fortyish. Gossiped about. And single.

She sobered rapidly. 'But I don't ride – or at least, I've only just started –'

'Nonsense. You're good. I've seen you several times.'

She could feel herself reddening. He must have somehow watched her that last occasion at the riding school. But several times? No.

'I've no experience at all. Honestly. I wouldn't be very good company.'

'On the contrary. You look as though you'd be very good company.' He broke off, looking stricken. 'I'm sorry. That sounded like a really corny chat-up line.'

'And a very nice one.' His discomfort gave her a little confidence. How stupid to feel so at a loss. It was so long since she had been involved in a conversation like this – a relaxed flirtatious to and fro, with a good-looking man.

'So, where do you keep her stabled? I thought I knew

all the liveries round here. I know there's nowhere at your cottage.'

Chris frowned. 'I don't understand. I've been riding at Hodges.'

'My God, why?' He reached into the pocket of his jeans and produced a distinctly grubby-looking packet of peppermints. The horse immediately looked up and whickered at him hopefully, a long trail of wild grasses hanging from the corner of her mouth.

'Yes, greedy, for you.' He held one out for the animal and she came to him like an eager dog.

'She likes them?'

Nodding he gave the horse one and rubbed her nose, then as she had feared he offered one to Chris. With a hidden smile she shook her head.

'I didn't realise that the Hodges took in livery horses.'

'But they weren't mine, the horses I rode.' Chris glanced at him shyly.

'What, not that gorgeous grey?'

'Grey?' She stared at him.

'The one I saw you on a few nights ago.'

Her mouth went dry. For a moment she stood stock still, looking at him, her eyes intently searching his face, then she turned away. 'You have seen me riding at night?'

'Yes.' She heard the puzzled tone in his voice, the chink of the chestnut's bridle as it pushed at his pockets, eager for another sweet.

'On a white horse? In the moonlight?' She was staring out across the field.

'I wasn't spying, Chris.' She could hear the amusement in his voice.

'No. No, I'm sure you weren't.' Suddenly afraid, she found herself clenching her fists.

He noticed. Unseen by her, an eyebrow rose fractionally and a glint of understanding showed for a moment in his eyes. 'Whose horse was it? Did you take her without asking?'

'No!' Her indignation took him aback.

'Then I don't understand.'

'No.' She shook her head violently. 'No, nor do I. I'm sorry, Tom. I have to go. I'm late for work.' Sighing she shoved her hands deep into the pockets of her jeans. 'I'm sorry I can't ride with you, I really am.' She couldn't meet his eye. Turning away from him she almost ran back towards her gate and fumbling with the latch she let herself into the garden.

That night as she rode Moonlight out into the darkness she was not thinking about Tom Ketch, the riding school horses, the surgery, the children. In her dream she was one with the horse, leaning forward to rest her cheek against the warm firm neck before urging the horse faster and faster towards the horizon.

On the edge of the field in the shelter of the trees Tom Ketch watched in silence. Only when she was out of sight did he turn and make his way up the field path to her gate. It was closed and overgrown with weeds. In the beam of his torchlight he could see no hoof marks, no bruising of the grasses, no trampled corn. For a long time he stood staring through the apple trees at the sleeping cottage windows, deep in thought. Then at last he turned away. Smiling to himself he began to walk home through the darkness. Tomorrow he was going to ask Chris Dean once again if she would like to

251

ride with him. On one of his horses, the pretty grey Arab mare he had thought of selling. And perhaps, if he persevered, he would for the first time in his life be in a position to make someone's dreams come true. It was a wonderful thought.

The Girl on the Swing

Charlotte put her hand on the gate and pushed hard. In the soft twilight the air was cool and fresh after the heat of the road. 'Are you sure this is the right house?' she called over her shoulder. She couldn't bear it to be wrong. Already she loved the place. She could feel the weight of stress and exhaustion lifting from her as she stood there.

'I'm sure. It's just like the photo on the brochure.' Rob slammed the boot lid and followed her up the path, a case in each hand, a bag under his arm, and waited while she put the key in the lock and after a short struggle turned it.

The silence of the room rose at them, enfolding them, holding them momentarily still and speechless.

Rob dropped the bags on the floor. The sound broke the spell and suddenly they could hear the birds outside again, the ticking of a clock somewhere in the corner, the creak of the door as it swung behind them. 'It's a bit cold in here.' He looked round and shivered. 'Let's leave the door open and let in some warmth.'

Lilac Cottage was tiny. A living room, pink-washed between the heavy oak beams, with a large fireplace filled with dried flowers took up most of the ground floor with behind it a kitchen furnished in old colour-washed pine. Behind that a small modern bathroom had been slotted somehow into what must have once been a lean-to shed. Upstairs there were two rooms each with two single beds covered in brightly coloured eastern throws, the curtains flame cotton, the old boards covered in rag rugs.

Charlotte surveyed the beds quickly. Hardly ideal for patching a marriage. Four beds. Two rooms. They would not be thrust into one another's arms. She glanced at Rob ruefully but he was staring out of the window.

'Look at the garden. It's gorgeous.'

The riot of colour echoed that of the bedrooms. Scarlet and russet and violet and blue and pink and orange jostled and quarrelled in the beds outside. The result was exuberant and vividly cheerful.

'Food?' Charlotte grinned at him. That at least was an uncontentious suggestion. It would put off the allocation of beds.

He gave her a smile in return. 'Sounds good to me.'

They clattered down the narrow wooden staircase. The living room was full of sunshine now. Charlotte stopped, entranced.

Rob was immediately behind her. 'What's wrong?' He passed her and picked up a box of food. 'Come on. Last one in the kitchen does the washing up.'

Alone in the middle of the floor she glanced round.

She could hear a blackbird singing in the garden, hear Rob cheerfully crashing round in the kitchen. For a moment she didn't move. Then she followed him.

'Drink?' He had found the corkscrew and the glasses. 'I'm afraid the wine is a bit warm.'

'Doesn't matter.' She took the glass from him and raised it. 'Here's to us.' He was still very handsome, her Rob. His square, regular features set off by his startlingly blue eyes and dark hair, his figure kept trim by games of squash and sessions at the gym.

'To us.' Rob smiled and leaning forward, almost shyly, he kissed her on the cheek. 'Pax,' he said quietly. 'No more fighting.'

'Pax.' She nodded.

They unpacked the food and laid out a cold meal on the kitchen table. Rob heated some soup whilst Charlotte searched the drawers for cutlery. The crash in the next room made them both look up.

'What was that?'

'Only the door. We left it open, remember?' Rob turned down the hot plate and went to look.

Following him, she saw Rob staring round. 'What is it? What's wrong?' She was nervous about the room. It felt, she realised suddenly, as though there was someone there, watching them.

'The door is still open. I wedged it.' He gave her a sheepish smile. 'We mustn't let ourselves get spooked.'

'Who is spooked?' She sounded defiant. 'This is the country. It was probably a sheep or something.'

'A sheep!' He let out a yell of laughter. 'Oh, Carla, my love, there are no sheep for miles.'

She liked the laughter. She hadn't heard it for a long

time. Not since she had told him she knew about the firm's problems. And Serena.

It was over, he said. Long over. Over before it had begun. Only the stress of the take-over and the threat of redundancy had pushed him into it. Mutual comfort. Shared problems. Being thrust into each other's company long day after long day. He couldn't help himself. Sanity had returned. Serena had gone and he had come back to Charlotte.

But not totally. Something was still missing; some vital, central warmth had gone from their relationship and Charlotte still felt lost and miserable.

The holiday was his idea. Leave the broiling London streets, the car fumes, the hothouse claustrophobia of the city, and in the scented greenness of the country learn to trust each other again. She hadn't asked him what *she* had done to lose *his* trust – the betrayal, after all, had been his alone. But deep down she knew. It was because she had found out. Never again could he trust her to look at him with the same innocence. The same certainty.

That was his loss.

They walked out into the lush twilight of the overgrown garden, and turned as bats swooped round them, to look at the cottage.

'It's still warmer out here than inside.' Rob sipped his wine.

'You noticed?' Charlotte glanced at him. 'It's worst in the sitting room.'

'Damp, I expect. It's probably been empty all winter.'

'And all spring? And all early summer?' She shrugged.

Behind them an old apple tree was silhouetted against the green afterglow of the sky. Rob put up a hand to the bough rough with papery lichen. 'I love these old trees. These days fruit trees are about two feet high. You couldn't climb in them. Or swing.' His fingers had found the old chains, bitten deep into the bark. They had been cut off a few inches below the branch. Rust and cobwebs and old leaves had all but hidden them.

'This must have been an idyllic place to live as a child.' Charlotte leaned against the branch. She could feel the coldness of the dew on her sandals.

'Only in fairy tales.' Rob began to walk back towards the house. 'No sanitation. Disease. Poverty –'

'Don't spoil it, Rob.'

They moved the dried flowers and piled the hearth with logs. Charlotte cut roses from the pergola and they found a concert on Classic FM.

It was after eleven before they stirred and, seeing the fire a bed of ash, thought about going upstairs.

Charlotte went first, noticing that Rob had left both their cases on the landing. She sighed. 'Where are we going to sleep?' she called.

'Don't mind. You choose.'

She picked up her case and walked into the left hand room. It was the larger of the two and faced, like the other, across the garden.

'This one.' She put the case down on one of the beds.

'It's good there are two rooms. We can spread our-selves.' He had come upstairs behind her. He lugged his own case into the other room.

Charlotte stared after him. This was supposed to be a reconciliation; a new beginning. She had imagined him bringing small gifts, wooing her afresh, reassuring her and above all making love.

Biting her lip she sat down on the bed. For a moment she was afraid she was going to cry. After a while she lay down, her arm across her eyes.

Mat? Where are you, Mat?

The voice outside her door was young; very clear.

She sat up and stared across the room in astonishment. 'Rob? Is that you? Who's there?'

The cottage was silent.

'Rob?' She realised suddenly that she was scared. 'Rob? Where are you?'

It was as though someone were listening outside the door. Mustering every bit of courage she could find Charlotte tiptoed towards it and pushed it open. The landing was deserted.

'Rob?' She nudged open the other door with her finger tip. 'Rob, are you there?'

Rob's case stood in the middle of the floor. The room was empty.

Running downstairs Charlotte called again. There was no sign of him in the house, or again when she searched the dark garden. Standing on the lawn she gazed round puzzled.

And suddenly he was there behind her in the kitchen doorway, mug in hand. 'Tea?' he called.

'Where were you?' She stared at him, disorientated.

'In the kitchen.'

'No, just now. When I came downstairs.'

'I was in the kitchen.' She saw impatience flicker across his features. 'You walked right past me.'

'I didn't.' She tried to make it a joke.

He shook his head. 'Never mind. Forget it. Have a cup of tea.'

He had washed the dishes, she discovered, and tidied everything away. He had put new logs on the fire and it was smouldering gently again.

Throwing herself down on the sofa, Charlotte sipped her tea. She watched him.

'I wasn't sleepy,' he answered her unasked question. He stood up, his back to the flames. 'It's nice here, isn't it. Incredibly quiet. I hope we don't get London-withdrawal symptoms.' He gave her one of his lop-sided grins, half humorous, half quizzical.

'So do I.' She hadn't meant her reply to sound so dry.

'It is over, Carla. I swear it.' He immediately looked guilty. 'I was a total idiot and I shall regret it all my life. Please try and forgive me.'

She stared down into the depths of her mug. 'I want to.'

'But?'

One word could convey so much. Uncertainty. Fear. Hope. Resignation. Anger.

She glanced at him. 'But you have to show me you still love me.'

'Carla, you know I do.'

'No, Rob. I don't know anything any more. Words are so easy. They are not enough. You have to show me. Tell me. Reassure me. Every minute of every day if necessary.' She paused and then tried to lighten the remark a little. 'At least until I'm convinced.'

'I see.' For a moment she thought he wasn't going to move, then at last his expression softened. 'So you won't hit me if I kiss you?'

She laughed. 'No, I won't hit you.'

She made it easy for him. She stood up and put down her mug and held out her arms.

'Carla –' He came towards her. His hand caught hers. Then he froze.

Mat? Where are you, Mat?

The call came from upstairs on the landing.

'Who the hell is that?' He dropped her hand and strode to the staircase.

'It sounds like a boy.' Charlotte was peering over his shoulder.

'Come on. We heard you. We know you're there.' Rob ran up the stairs two at a time.

Charlotte remained at the bottom. 'Be careful –'

He was out of sight now, in her room. Then she heard his footsteps cross the landing and he was in his own.

'There's no one here,' he called. 'Take a look outside. He must be in the garden.'

'How could he be? He couldn't have gone past us –' Her voice died away and she shivered. 'Forget it, Rob. It must have been someone outside in the lane.'

He was clattering down now, shrugging, heading for his mug of tea and the fire. 'I could have sworn the voice came from upstairs.'

He sat down and leaning over the arm of the chair he drew his briefcase towards him. Unfastening it he drew out some papers and then settled back with a comfortable sigh, the incident apparently forgotten.

Charlotte stared at him in dismay. What had happened to the kiss? 'Rob? You're not working?'

'No, of course not.' His eyes did not leave the pages on his knee. 'Just reading for a few moments while I finish my drink.' He looked up suddenly. 'You don't mind, do you?'

'No, of course not.' She sat down on the opposite end of the sofa gazing into the fire. Then she stood up again restlessly. 'More tea?'

He did not hear her.

Shrugging she walked out into the kitchen and opened the back door. The garden was sweet scented beneath the moon; almost as light as day. She stepped down onto the grass and wandered across the lawn. The apple tree cast a hard shadow in the moonlight. Beneath it, it was black. Somewhere near by an owl hooted.

Mattie, where are you?

The voice was further away now at the end of the garden. He sounded young and very sad.

'Hello!' Charlotte called.

She took a couple of steps forward. 'Hello? Don't be afraid.'

There was no answer. In the silence she found she was shivering.

Behind her in the cottage a light came on upstairs. She didn't notice. She stepped further into the shadows. 'Where are you?'

Above her the apple tree branches were dark.

In the cottage the light went out.

'I know you're there. Come out, so I can see you.' It was dark all round her now. The ground was damp underfoot, the air suddenly cold and bitter with rotting leaves. She knew there was no one there. She could sense the emptiness of the night.

Suddenly frightened she turned back towards the

house. The back door was half open as she had left it. In the living room one small lamp burned by the fireplace. There was no sign of Rob.

Climbing the stairs she glanced into his bedroom. His curtains were open. She could see him in the moonlight, lying on the bed.

'Rob!' she whispered.

He slept on.

In her own room the smell of lavender and roses drifted in through the open window. She dug in her case for her washing things and her nightdress and crept downstairs to the bathroom.

She woke suddenly a couple of hours later and lay looking up at the ceiling. The moon had gone and the room was dark. For a moment she didn't move, then she stood up and went to the window. The moon was behind the house now and the garden was still bright with its glow. There was someone under the apple tree. She frowned, straining her eyes. A girl in a white dress. She was sitting on a swing, gently rocking herself backwards and forwards with one foot.

As Charlotte watched the girl swung higher. She grasped the chains more tightly as she pushed harder, her head back, her long hair tumbling behind her as the momentum of the swing carried her higher, and she was pointing her toes now, her white dress flying in the moonlight.

Mattie, where are you?

The boy's voice was right behind Charlotte as though he too was looking out of the window.

Mattie, no!

Charlotte spun round, her heart thumping.

The room was empty.

'Rob, did you hear that?' Her voice was husky. She found she was shaking. Turning back to the window she glanced out. The garden was deserted. Under the apple tree the shadows were dark and empty.

'Rob? Rob!' Running across the landing Charlotte threw open his door. 'Rob? Did you hear him?'

Rob groaned. Turning over onto his back he opened his eyes and blinked. 'What time is it?'

'I don't know. Three-ish, I think. Rob, he was here, in my room.'

'Who?' Rob sat up. He was bare-chested, wearing only his shorts, and Charlotte was aware suddenly of how much she wanted him.

'I don't know who. The boy. The one we heard earlier. The one calling for Mattie.' She broke off. The girl. The girl on the swing. Had that been Mattie?

But she had been a dream. Surely, she had been a dream.

'Rob, I'm scared. Can I come in here with you?'

For a moment she wondered if he would refuse. He said nothing, looking at her, then he held out his arms.

'Why did you go to bed on your own?' she asked as she snuggled in beside him.

'You disappeared. I thought maybe you felt it was too soon.' He reached out and kissed her forehead gently. Then his arms slid round her waist and he drew her close. 'I'm so sorry, Carla. I've missed you so much, my darling. I just didn't dare hope that everything was going to be all right.'

*   *   *

'I think the cottage is haunted.' Spooning boiled eggs into egg cups, Charlotte set them on the table and reached for the toast rack. She was pink and scrubbed from the shower and glowing with happiness.

Rob nodded. 'I wondered when you would finally come to that conclusion.'

'You think so too?'

Spreading marmalade on his toast, Rob shrugged and shook his head slowly. 'I can't think of any other explanation.'

'But you don't believe in ghosts.'

'I know.' He grinned.

'Does it scare you?'

'No.' He reached for his coffee. 'It sounded like a child. Worried. Lost. Frightened but not frightening. I think this is one of those places where events have been recorded in the house walls. Like a video. It plays the same sequence again and again.'

'But there must have been a reason for it to have recorded that bit. He has lost someone. He is desperate to find her.'

The girl on the swing.

She sat down opposite him. 'Poor boy. I wish we could help.'

'Videos don't need help.' He began to tap his egg.

'I suppose not.' She wasn't convinced.

He glanced up. 'This isn't going to spoil the holiday for you?'

She shook her head and smiled. 'After last night? After all, he brought us back together.'

'He did, didn't he?' He lifted the top off his egg neatly. 'What shall we do today?'

She didn't answer. When he glanced up again he saw that she was smiling.

Later that morning they strolled along the lane to the village shop. It was the old man in the queue for the tiny post office counter who recognised them. 'You the folks from Lilac Cottage?'

Rob nodded.

'I thought so. You seen young Matilda yet?'

Behind them Rob heard Charlotte's quick intake of breath.

'Who's Matilda?' he asked.

'Now, Bill Forrest, don't you go scaring folk!' The post mistress leaned forward and tapped the glass partition between them sharply. 'Take no notice of him, my dears. He's an old fool.'

'No.' Charlotte stepped forward. 'No, wait. Tell us please.'

The old man glanced at her. His eyes were hazy blue, but they were very keen. 'You seen her, then?'

'On the swing. Yes.'

'Matilda Drew, that was. Her brother, he unfastened the swing for a prank. Thought it would dump her on the grass, he did, poor lad. Never occurred to him that a fall could kill her.'

'Oh God, that's awful.' Charlotte stared at him.

'When did this happen?' Rob put his arm round Charlotte's shoulder.

'Years ago. Long before my time.' The old man tucked his pension deep into his pocket. 'You go and look in the churchyard if you want to know about them. The grave is there, near the gate.'

* * *

265

They pushed open the lych gate on the way back to the cottage. The old stone, covered in moss, had leaned over slightly. The words were badly weathered.

> *Matilda Drew*
> *born 1753 died 1827*
> *May her spirit fly free as a bird on the wing*

There was a picture of a dove beneath the words, then under that again a smaller, less ornate inscription said simply:

> *And here lies also her brother John*
> *born 1750 died 1841*

Rob frowned. 'That can't be right. That means she was in her seventies when she died and he was over ninety. It must be the wrong grave.'

'No, it means John changed his mind. He got there in time.' Charlotte ran a finger over the rough lettering. She glanced at him. 'That's what I think happened. He realised what he had done and he ran out into the garden as she began to swing and he saved her.' Somehow she knew she was right.

'And his panic was so great that the house has remembered it all these years?' Rob nodded. 'They must have been very close, to be buried together like this. Neither of them married.'

'Do you think they were happy in the house?'

'Of course they were.' Rob grinned at her. 'I think there is a lesson here somewhere, don't you? Even if it does come right in the end one can still regret a mistake for eternity.' He pulled her against him gently and kissed her, then, stepping away, he leaned across to pick a wild rose from the hedge. Laying it at the foot of the headstone he stood for a moment in silence, then he turned and reached out again for Charlotte's hand. 'Come on, he said. 'Let's go home.'

An Afternoon at the Museum

For a few blessed moments the gallery was quiet. Too quiet. Stephanie glanced over her shoulder towards the doorway. The Egyptian rooms at the British Museum were usually packed with children at this time of day. Neat groups walking two by two in uniform speaking in hushed, respectful voices or chaotic hordes, rushing about uncontrolled, screaming; either way, this was one of the places they headed for first. And they all looked at the mummies. The ghoulish fascination exerted by a real dead body passed none of them by, from the most repressed scholar to the loudest, most rebellious thug.

She noticed one of the museum attendants standing near her. He had folded his arms and was watching the doorway, a quizzical expression on his face. He too was waiting for the next noisy flood of children. With a grin she turned back to her sketchbook. She had better make the most of the peace while it lasted. The magazine wanted the illustrations by tonight, 6 pm latest. She would deliver them by hand as soon as they were finished and then she would go home to the empty flat. She sighed. She couldn't even remember how the row had started, but it had been bad enough for Dan to leave. And not come back.

She glanced down at the neat black pen and ink sketch on her page and frowned. She had been working for about twenty minutes in the gallery, producing a series of sketches – a mummy case, a bandaged body, artefacts from the tombs, an intricate necklace of gold and lapis. This sketch was the last, the mummy of a child, impossibly moving in its poignancy, and she found it hard to concentrate on it. Taking a deep breath she gripped her pen more tightly and began to draw again.

Behind her the noise levels were building once more. She could hear the excited shouts, the thud of thirty pairs of trainers heading her way. On the page, the Egyptian child too was running. His head thrown back, a lock of hair flying loose behind one shoulder, long straight limbs rejoicing in the sun.

With an exclamation of annoyance she stared at what she had drawn. She had been doodling without realising it, wasting precious time. And now she re-membered what the quarrel had been about. Having children. Dan wanted them to get married. He had been hinting for months. It had come to a head when she said she didn't want a baby. Didn't even like them. He had stared at her as if she had said she was planning a murder and from then on things had gone from bad to worse.

'What you drawing, miss?' The voice at her shoulder

was breathless, cheeky. 'It don't look like no mummy to me.'

She glanced at the boy. Perhaps eight years old, or ten – with no experience of children herself, and few friends who had them, she found it hard to tell their ages. He had a grubby, freckled face, intensely blue eyes, an almost-shaven head and trouble oozed out of every pore. It was a reflex action to check her bag was closed and safe.

'You see that mummy there?' She pointed. 'That was a child. A boy like this.'

Like you.

She didn't say it, but the age would have been about the same, now she came to think about it.

'No chance!' He wasn't going to believe her. 'They were old geezers, the mummies. Dead.'

She glanced at his face again and saw long sandy lashes, impossibly cherubic on the rounded cheeks, and felt her hostility diminish. 'They mummified everything,' she said with a grin. 'Animals. Birds. Crocodiles. Old people. Young people. Even babies.'

'Babies!' He looked up at her. The cheeky combative tone was gone. She saw horror lurking there. 'That boy –' he stabbed at her pad with a filthy finger. 'He is running about and playing, right? Football and that, right?'

She nodded, aware that the rest of the kids were moving on towards the far end of the gallery. 'My picture is only pretend,' she said gently. 'I was wondering what he looked like before he –'

Died. She was about to say it, but something in the blue eyes stopped her.

'Where is your teacher?' She found herself smiling at him again. 'You don't want to lose the others.'

He touched the drawing lightly for a second time then he turned to look at the mummy. 'They did this so their bodies would be OK to use again, right?'

'Something like that.'

'What happens if they don't save the body? What happens if it gets incinerated? What does the person do when they come back and it's not there?' The intensity of the questioning, and the sudden anguish in the blue eyes made her catch her breath.

'We don't believe in the same things as the Egyptians did,' she said carefully. 'We don't believe we need our bodies to be preserved. We don't believe we need to take things with us to the grave like they did.'

This was too deep for her suddenly; the rest of the party had moved on into the next room. The gallery was quiet again.

And then the insight came. She put out her hand and took his. For a moment she thought he'd pull away but he didn't, he moved a step closer and she realised suddenly that a tear was trickling down his cheek. 'My little sister. She died.' He strangulated the words, ashamed of the need even to speak them out loud. 'My mum put her teddy bear in with her. In case she needed it.' Another tear spilt over. 'Then they burned her in the box.'

Stephanie was appalled. She didn't know what to say. Ducking down she leaned the sketchbook against the glass case and put her arms round him, feeling the shoulders, belying the rounded cheeks, painfully thin beneath the grey sweatshirt. 'They shouldn't have done that, should they, miss?'

'It's what we do, in our culture,' she whispered awkwardly down into the soft short-cropped hair. 'We believe we won't need the same body again. We believe we'll get a new one in heaven.'

'Then they were wrong?' He nodded towards the mummy.

'I think they were wrong.'

He was trembling and she tightened her hold on him, desperately seeking to give comfort.

'But we don't know. We might be wrong. I don't want to be burnt!' It came out as an anguished whimper. 'I'm older than her. A lot older, so I could die, couldn't I? Like that boy –'

She hugged him closer. 'I think you look fine to me. I think you look like someone who could live to be an old, old man before you die –'

She broke off as a hand appeared from behind her and grabbed the boy's arm, wrenching him away.

'Let go of this child! How dare you! I'm going to call the police!'

It was the teacher. The furious woman facing her suddenly was tall and thin, dressed in a denim skirt and Indian cotton top, with sensible flat shoes and a heavy dragging rucksack on her shoulder. Her face, lined and exhausted, was at this moment, red with anger.

'Go and wait with the others, Mick. Now!' She made no attempt to find out why he was crying.

Stephanie stared at her in shock. 'You don't understand. He was asking me –'

'Oh yes, I understand all right!' The woman was positively spitting at her. 'People like you can't get a real

272

man, so you try and seduce a child!' Her voice rose hysterically.

'What do you mean? I didn't! You're wrong!' Stephanie was aware suddenly of a crowd gathering round her. The gallery attendant was heading their way. The children were streaming back towards them. Other people were staring. Shaking their heads. Muttering.

'Look, he spoke to me first. He was looking at my sketches. I put my arms round him because he started to cry –'

The woman wasn't listening. She was shouting now. Calling for witnesses, demanding again that someone fetch the police.

And then as suddenly as it had started, it was all over. The attendant was there at their side. 'I saw it all,' he said firmly. He calmed the woman down. He explained what he had seen. He soothed and cajoled and pacified. In minutes she was walking away, Mick, subdued and defiant, trailing behind her, the other children already streaming ahead.

'You OK?' The attendant looked at Steph. 'Don't you worry about that. Too much responsibility, too little pay. No one to help her. Poor woman doesn't know if she's coming or going. All she can do is count them again and again and hope she hasn't lost any.' He paused. He had gentle brown eyes in a richly wrinkled black face and she saw him studying her with a shrewdness which disconcerted her. 'You're more upset than she was, you know that?'

Steph nodded, blinking back tears. 'It was that boy. His sister had died. He was confronting death for the first time and he was so afraid.'

273

'And he had no one to talk to?'

She shook her head. 'No one, I suspect. Just a broken-hearted mother who had enough grief to cope with herself.' She sniffed. 'He saw my drawing of the boy.' Stooping she picked up the sketch pad. 'And somehow he identified with it –' She paused, staring at the page. The child's mummy was there, in the centre of the blank sheet, neatly sketched in minute detail, perfect for an illustration. She fumbled at the pages, turning them over, searching frantically. 'I don't understand it. He's gone. The boy I drew has gone!'

'He steal it?' The attendant nodded after the departing figures. The rest of the crowd had melted away.

'No. No! Of course he didn't steal it. He wouldn't have. Couldn't have. There's no page missing. It is as though it was never here!' She closed the book and stared at him. 'I can't have imagined it. Can I?'

Shrugging, he looked round the gallery for a minute or two in thoughtful silence. 'Working here, day after day, I see a lot of strange things. I've seen figures walking between the glass cases when there was no public in here. I've seen eyes looking at me from inside some of those mummies, and the eyes followed me round the room. I've seen things inside the cases move. There were some ear rings. Beautiful. Gold. The kind of thing a pretty lady would love. One day they were in there –' he nodded towards a side case full of artefacts, 'the next they were there, where they should have been, with her.' He gestured towards the mummy of a young woman.

Stephanie stared at him, unsure whether to believe him. 'Doesn't anyone notice?'

274

'Apart from me?' He raised an eyebrow and cocked his head to one side. 'Sometimes. Then they blame whoever arranged the exhibits. Whoever got the labelling wrong.' He chuckled.

'And my drawing. How do you explain that?'

'Who knows? But nothing happens by accident. The lad in that glass case, the little kid, Mick. You. You all needed each other at that moment. You gave the boy life in that sketch. You gave Mick the hug he needed. And, who knows, maybe you needed one too!' He grinned at her.

'You're quite a philosopher, do you know that?'

He shrugged. 'I'd have to be, to work here.'

She watched him walk away, then she turned back to the glass case and stared down at the wide-eyed blank stare of the mummy. She couldn't get the memory of the thin, vulnerable bones of the child she had held so briefly in her arms out of her head. He had been outwardly all that she detested in children. Noisy. Aggressive. Challenging. Somehow out of control, and yet beneath that exterior he had been hurting so badly; pleading for reassurance. And he had come to her.

Slowly she slipped the sketchbook into her bag. One of the sketches would be right for the article. She had done enough. In the corner of the gallery the attendant was talking to a group of women. There were several French students clustered near her now. The school party had long gone.

She thought suddenly of Dan – his quiet pleading, his patience as he tried to explain how much he wanted a child, his anger when she refused even to discuss it.

Did he feel this strange need to bring security and love to a small vulnerable human being?

She turned towards the entrance, glancing towards the attendant again and she saw him smile and lift a hand. She hadn't changed her mind. It wasn't that easy. Too many strange things had happened in the space of the last hour even to comprehend them all. But maybe, just maybe, it would make her think again.

'Bye!' She didn't realise she had spoken out loud to the mummy in the sterile glass case till she saw some-one a few paces away glance up at her, startled. She shrugged apologetically.

The murmured farewell in her ear had been after all, surely, purely in her imagination.

Day Trip

This story is true. Well, more or less. But you must look away, gentle reader, if rude words offend you, for this story can only be told as it happened, with the real dialogue. Asterisks just will not do! It happened one day in autumn.

As Caroline pocketed her car keys and made her way onto the platform her heart sank. It was a small station; often she was the only person to board the train here, especially when she left for London mid-morning, but today the worst happened. There was another passenger waiting as the train drew in – James Campbell, the owner of the huge, immaculate house at the end of the winding lane where Caroline's cottage stood in its quarter acre of wild garden. There was no time to walk to the other end of the platform. The train was stopping. He was already opening a door, smiling at her with that cold superior smile of his, and bowing slightly to indicate she should enter the carriage ahead of him.

It is hard to incline one's head graciously while carrying a shoulder bag, a heavy tapestry portmanteau and an A1 black plastic portfolio, especially while dressed in a long flapping skirt which threatened to tangle with her sexy high-heeled boots, but she managed it. With a creditable attempt at dignity she walked to the only set of empty seats and sat down, facing what used in days of old to be called the engine. If he had any tact at all, any discretion, any sense of decency and good manners he would move to the other end of the carriage.

He didn't. He came and sat down opposite her.

She wasn't sure quite when her antagonism for this man had begun to develop. The day she moved into the cottage probably. Independence meant an enormous amount to her. This was her first real home and no one, but no one, was going to interfere in the way she decorated it. Or lived her life in it.

She had had an idyllic childhood in her parents' home. She would be the first to admit that she really had no grounds for complaint at all. No abuse. No deprivation. But she had not at any time been allowed to express her own personality in the decoration of her room. Her nursery, her bedroom, her teenage den – the same room, different incarnations – had all been decorated and furnished to her domineering mother's taste. Which was attractive. Stylish even. In anyone else's home she would have admired it. In her own it represented oppression of her individuality and her spirit. Her marriage had been to an interior designer. Perhaps inevitably, given her longing to create her own environment, it had been a disaster. In the house she shared with him she wasn't even allowed to choose the colour of her own toothbrush. The marriage lasted no time at all.

And then at last she was free. Her mother, her father and even, for heaven's sake, her ex-husband offered to help her house hunt. When she found the cottage all three felt she had made a mistake. Her mother thought it too twee for words, her father felt it was hopelessly impractical and a bad investment and Phil, her ex, had just one word for the thatch, the honeysuckle, the small leaded windows. Naf.

Undeterred (in fact, if truth were known, greatly encouraged), she embarked on an orgy of do-it-yourself. Decorating, embellishing, improving. Rejecting the share of tasteful furniture due to her as the marital home was divided she settled instead for a dollop of wonderful cash and began to haunt antique shops and car boot sales, country craft fairs and rural art galleries. That was when she discovered she could paint – and, to her astonishment, sell – the wild colourful amazing tangles of flowers which rampaged round her garden.

The first and, to be honest, only dampener on her exuberance outside her own family had been: James Campbell.

'I trust you intend to do something about those thistles, Mrs Evans.' His patrician profile had appeared over her gate one day as she was sitting, her face shaded by a broad-brimmed straw hat, sketching the offending plants. He had spotted her and them from his Range Rover and stopped especially to speak to her. No, hello; no, I hope you're settling in OK; no, welcome to the neighbourhood. Just instant criticism followed by a curt nod before he turned back to his barouche.

Seething, she planned to make a midnight visit to his own regimented acres at dead of night later in the summer. With pockets full of thistle down.

Their relationship from that moment on had steadily deteriorated, his only remarks on the rare occasions they met were patronising and critical and on one occasion were actually conveyed via a formal complaint about her flowering hedges to the Parish Council. Apparently her blackthorn and her holly, her roses and her honeysuckle were scratching the barouche as he drove past.

The train stopped at the next station and several more people boarded. To her relief James Campbell did not look up. He had immediately on sitting down opened his *Financial Times*. She was spared the horror of having to make polite conversation with him as she produced her own reading – a rather shabby copy of Mrs Leyel's *Herbal Delights*. His refusal to further acknowledge her presence was perhaps intended as a slight. If it was it sadly misfired. She was intensely relieved.

Some raucous laughter from the seats across the gangway caught her attention and she gave a quick glance across at their neighbours. Two young men had boarded the train at the last stop, dressed in combat trousers and tee-shirts with huge black boots, their hair cropped short. Perhaps squaddies from the local barracks? They were very young, teenagers even, fresh-faced, wide-eyed but, once the thick layer of acne had run its natural course, would both be quite good-looking.

She bent her head to Mrs Leyel once more, whilst straining to decipher their accents. Scottish. That much was easy. East coast probably rather than west as she felt her ears throb to the barrage of strangulated glottal stops. Not dangerous young men. Not hostile. Just loud.

The coffee trolley was approaching down the carriage, inching its way between anxious mothers with restless children, Jaeger dressed ladies going to town to lunch with old school friends, business men – not the dawn rising kind, the older more leisurely breed – students and tourists. And people like her. One offs. In her case, visiting a magazine with some newly commissioned illustrations. The trolley was doing good business – tea, coffee, Cokes, orange drinks, Kit-Kats and flapjacks. It stopped alongside them and James Campbell lowered his paper for a fraction of a second to shake his head curtly at the girl. Caroline too declined but with a smile. The two young men sat forward eagerly. The girl obviously instantly tuned to their speech and had no difficulty in interpreting an order for two cans of lager each, but firmly declined the suggestion that a third, to keep in reserve, might be even better. She pocketed their change, handed over the drinks and then to Caroline's delight wagged – actually wagged – her finger at the boys. 'Now, no nonsense, you two. Behave yourselves, you hear me?' she admonished loudly. 'And put the empties in the bin!' How did she do it? How did she escape with her life? She must have brothers, Caroline thought, to give her that ease of communication with them. Or was she just a natural leader of men? Far from being angry, they beamed at her and sat back to enjoy themselves as she trundled on her way.

281

Caroline realised suddenly that James Campbell had folded his paper in half. He was still reading, but the slightest glance enabled him now to see across it to their neighbours. And her. She frowned, trying to concentrate on the words on the page in front of her, but it was hard. The voices of the young men were growing louder and she discovered suddenly that her ear had grown accustomed to the lilt and staccato of their speech in spite of the impression that they were talking through mouthfuls of marbles. They were discussing a night on the town which they had both enjoyed. And they had, she suddenly realised, only a limited vocabulary when it came to description. The more baby-faced of the two tipped back his head and drained his can. He then stood up and obedient to instructions carefully tucked it into the litter bin behind his seat. He reseated himself and produced the second can with a flourish.

'Och it was a fucking guid night!' The expression of contented reminiscence reached her clearly. 'I like watching fuitball; I like clubbing.' He beamed across at his companion. 'But not as much as I like fucking and brawling.' He paused. 'But, oh fuck, I like brawling best!'

Caroline bit her lip tightly to keep her face straight. She had seen the expression on the face of the woman in the next row of seats. It was scandalised. Her eyebrows had hit her hairline. Beside her, two more travellers were staring hard at their feet. Caroline glanced up at James Campbell. The *Financial Times* was trembling slightly. She could see his knuckles white against the pink paper. She frowned. No doubt he would take it upon himself to throw them off the train at the next stop.

The boys' conversation had changed tack slightly, but not in any adjectival sense. 'It's fucking impossible to get back tae Edinburgh,' – so that is where they came from – 'and down tae fucking Colchester in that space of fucking time!' The second can was neatly disposed of in the bin. They were oblivious to the other passengers, intent now on travel plans. 'It's fucking scandalous. If you like fucking brawling, you should do something about it! Go and have a fucking brawl with the fucking train arrangers!'

The *Financial Times* slipped a little and just for a second Caroline caught a glimpse of James Campbell's face. It was very red. His eyes were narrowed, his mouth held in a tight-lipped grimace. Tears of laughter were streaming down his face. She stared, still trying to hold back her own mirth, and suddenly he looked up and caught her eye. His mouth twitched. He reached for the newspaper supplement which he had discarded on the seat next to him and held it out to her with a shaking hand. 'You'd better borrow this!' Already he had disappeared once more behind his own screen.

Caroline opened the paper hastily, aware that one of the boys was staring at her suddenly. But he wasn't angry. There was no cry of 'What are you looking at then?' On the contrary, his huge blue eyes were full of sympathy and understanding. 'Are you OK, hen?' he asked gently. 'Fucking hayfever!'

As the train drew into London Caroline refolded the paper and handed it back to its owner with a smile. 'Thank you.'

The boys had been first off the train, not a can, not a crisp packet to be seen, the seat where they had been sitting spotless. 'I don't think I could have coped with that without your help.' His face had returned to normal except that his eyes were no longer cold and critical. 'I hope you're not going to report them to their f –' she stuttered. She had almost said it. 'To their commanding officer!'

He shook his head. 'I haven't enjoyed a train journey so much in a long time. Did you see the faces of those women?'

They were making their way out onto the platform now and somehow he was carrying her portfolio as well as his briefcase. He glanced across at her and she realised suddenly that not only were his eyes not cold, they were a startlingly bright blue. 'You haven't got time for a coffee, I suppose? To help compose ourselves before we are launched into the metropolis?'

And, gentle reader, do you know, against her better judgement, she agreed!

Barney

Theo Dexter, the house agent, was a young man of about her own age, Kay thought, or a little older. Good-looking in a floppy, self-deprecating, Hugh Grant sort of way. When the key wouldn't turn he looked at her with an apologetic shrug.

It infuriated her. She stopped herself from grabbing it from him. 'No one seems to have been here for a long time.' She shoved back her hair from her face with barely concealed impatience.

'No one else wants to see the cottage.' He smiled.

She refused to be charmed. She needed somewhere to live. Now. Somewhere cheap. Very. The fact that this ruin was falling down was a plus. It suited her mood. And no one would come looking for her here.

'Please try again. Give it a good rattle.'

His cautious shake was followed by a hefty thump then, two hands on the key, a bit of bicep-flexing. She watched, more amused now than cross. The place was beginning to work its magic. Another struggle and she heard a grating noise from the lock. In a moment the door was pushed open. The interior smelled musty and damp, but not unpleasantly so. And it was very silent. They stood in the narrow hall for a moment, orientating themselves. Straight ahead there was a narrow staircase. To the right, a door opened on to a small living room; to the left, a kitchen with an ancient Rayburn, a dresser, and a scrubbed oak table.

'Perfect!'

Kay's enthusiasm shocked Theo into a response which was, she felt, for an estate agent, probably candid in the extreme. 'You've got to be kidding. Honestly, the place is a dump!'

She laughed. 'It's quiet. It's pretty. It's cheap. It's all I can afford.'

He grimaced. 'You'd better look upstairs before you commit yourself.'

She led the way, suddenly feeling ridiculously and uncharacteristically happy.

The stairs were steep and creaking, the banister loose. At the top there was a small landing lit by a window almost obscured on the outside by honeysuckle. On either side they found two identical bedrooms.

'Still perfect?'

Kay caught Theo looking at her and grinned, unaware that her sudden happiness had made her radiant. Her previously rather severe features had become beautiful in a way which fascinated him.

She looked away first. 'I suppose it's too much to hope that there is a bathroom?' Practicalities had a way of bringing one back down to earth.

He raised his eyebrows. 'Believe it or not, there is. At the back. The old boy probably kept coal in the bath.'

'Then I shall have a supply of fuel.' Turning, she stepped back on to the landing and stopped in surprise. A small brown dog was sitting at the top of the stairs.

'Hello.' She stooped and held out her hand.

'Who are you talking to?' Theo appeared in the doorway.

'The dog.' She glanced up.

'What dog?'

'That one.' She turned back. The dog had disappeared. 'He must have run back downstairs. We left the front door open.' The fresh air had certainly improved the feel of the place. The mustiness had gone and she could smell the roses and mock orange from the front garden.

The bathroom proved an almost pleasant surprise. Not modern certainly, but not too squalid either. If water and electricity could be coaxed back into the property the place was definitely viable.

They stopped off on the way back to have a sandwich in a thatched pub. Sitting at the table in the garden she glanced at her companion. 'You must think I'm mad to make an offer for a house like that.'

He returned her look with a quizzical smile. 'Mildly dotty, certainly. But I keep telling myself that the customer is always right.'

'I'm running away.'

'I assumed you weren't trying to hit the high spots.'

'A relationship on the rocks. There was quite a lot of heartbreak and a bit of publicity.'

He smiled again. She liked the way he did it, mostly with his eyes. 'That's tough. Well, I doubt if anyone will find you here.'

'I don't really think anyone will try. It's all over. But I need some space.'

'You'll get that. There's an acre of garden we never even looked at.'

She nodded. 'An acre of nettles and brambles if we're honest?' When they laughed together she knew she was already beginning to heal.

It was ridiculously easy to buy the place. She didn't bother with a survey and her first, unbelievably low offer was accepted by Alice Cross, the old lady to whom the cottage had been left. Expecting to have to haggle for it, Kay was stunned that the only condition of the sale was that she should love it the way 'old Harry' had loved it. And take care of Barney.

Barney, after due enquiry, turned out to be a dog. A small brown dog. She liked dogs so she agreed. The only problem was that since that first sighting there had been no sign of Barney anywhere. No one in the village seemed to know anything about him. Alice merely shrugged when asked and said he would turn up.

Kay moved in two months after she had first seen the cottage, complete with a bag of dog biscuits for Barney should he appear, and with some trepidation invited Theo for a drink to celebrate. He was, after all, the only person she knew in the area. He came and stayed for lunch. By the time he left she knew he was unattached and even nicer than she had remembered. And no longer infuriating.

288

Two days later he returned with a strimmer and a saw. The next weekend he brought wine, a couple of pasties and a bunch of roses.

On the Saturday after that they saw Barney again. She and Theo were standing just inside the front door. The dog was exactly where she had seen him before at the top of the stairs. By now the cottage was clean, sparsely but attractively furnished with the few things she had retrieved from her disintegrated past. She had gone round the place with a pot of white paint and had covered a multitude of sins with pictures and strategically placed pot-plants. It felt more like home than anywhere else she had ever lived.

'Barney?' Kay called. He wagged his tail and, turning, trotted out of sight.

'How on earth did he get in?' The door behind them was closed.

'It doesn't matter. He's here now.' Kay made for the stairs.

But they couldn't find him.

After ten minutes' fruitless search they gave up. 'I'll put down some water and biscuits for him. He's obviously found a way of sneaking in and out.' She was looking forward to befriending the little dog.

Their next visitor was equally unexpected. They were gardening as the gate clicked open. Alice was standing there watching them. She smiled and nodded as though approving of what she saw. 'Harry would have liked this. He hated it when he was too old to look after his garden.'

Then followed the guided tour. Everything was approved with evident delight. In the kitchen Alice noticed the bowls on the floor. 'You're an animal lover. That's good.'

'I'm afraid we haven't been very successful with Barney.' Kay thought it best to be honest.

Alice turned and looked at her. Her pale blue eyes watered slightly as the sunlight through the window caught her face. 'How many times have you seen him?'

'Well, only twice actually.'

Alice nodded. 'And you've both seen him? You and your young man here?'

Kay smiled. 'Yes, we've both seen him. This morning. Upstairs.'

Alice smiled. 'That's where he always sits. At the top of the stairs.'

'We've put food down for him.' Kay gestured at the dog biscuits.

Alice laughed. 'I don't suppose he's touched those.'

'No.'

Alice chuckled again. She laid her hand on Kay's arm. 'I'll tell you a story. Harry and I were sweethearts before the War. Then he went away. He didn't come back and I never got his letters. In the end I began courting someone else. I was married by the time he came home and moved in here, to his parents' old place.' She paused. 'I visited him here.' Kay saw the sudden twinkle in her eye and glanced at Theo. He was smiling.

'My Bill was a hard man,' she went on. 'Cruel when the drink got to him. Harry and I still loved each other so much. It was on my third visit that I first saw Barney.'

Kay frowned. 'What date are we talking about?'

'About 1947,' Alice chuckled. 'Barney had belonged to Harry's parents,' she went on. 'His father gave the puppy to Harry's ma on their first wedding anniversary. They were so in love.' She paused. 'She died when Harry was born. Told the dog to look after the house for her.'

There was a moment's stunned silence.

Kay's whisper was barely audible. 'You mean he's a ghost?'

Alice beamed at her. 'That's right. He won't be needing your biscuits, my dear. Just make him welcome. Love him. And let him look after you.' She glanced from one to the other. 'That goes for both of you. You must both belong here or you wouldn't both have seen him.'

That night Theo stayed. It seemed the right thing to do.

You've Got to Have a Dream

She didn't care!

She sat looking at the phone after she had put it down, stunned by the realisation. She really didn't care!

'I know you've been expecting it, Meg.'

He was more or less right. She had. She must have been. But not in that way. Not at that moment.

'It's the right time for the break, Meg, and if I accept the job and go to live in Bristol the office will pay for my move. You can keep the house. It's always been more yours than mine. You deserve that at least.'

Which was the nearest he would ever get to an apology, to an acknowledgement of the last two years of heartache. She did not bother to ask if Angela was going with him. It was presumably a foregone conclusion. She found she was smiling suddenly. Why had he not made these world-shaking statements this morning as they ducked and wove around the kitchen, grabbing coffee and cereal and toast. Why wait till both he and she were at work, miles from each other. Why? Because he was a coward, that's why!

'Bastard!' She said it almost affectionately.

Nicola glanced away from the screen on her desk, her fingers still clicking busily over the keyboard. 'Douglas?'

'Who else?'

'Need an ear? Or a shoulder?'

Meg laughed. 'Maybe an extra set of brains. He's off. Leaving me. So, where do I go from here?' In spite of her light tone there was suddenly a catch in her voice.

Nicola saved her document and spun her chair to face her friend.

'Cake shop. Come on. The office can take care of itself for an hour or two. That's what all these machines are for. They don't need people.' She switched on the answer phone. 'Let's go and brainstorm.'

As they grabbed their coats and turned the notice on the door to 'closed' Nicola stopped and looked closely at Meg's face. 'You don't still love him, do you? No lurking regrets?'

Meg shook her head. 'Only for all the time I've wasted hoping things would get better.'

It was over two years since they had set up their small flat share agency. Since its first months where the office had consisted of Meg's kitchen table, a second hand word processor and two box files they had expanded to the point where there was room to take on staff, something they had been planning over the last few days.

'Pity we haven't already got our new gofer. Then we

wouldn't have to shut.' Nicola led the way into the coffee shop three doors up from the office. 'Of course we could have an extension put in here!' she joked. 'We spend enough time drinking their coffee!' In fact her mobile and note book were already on the smoked-glass table in front of them as they sat down. 'Right. Fire away.' She reached for the note book. 'Bullet points!'

Meg laughed. 'Nicola, this is my life we're talking about. It doesn't have bullet points.'

'That's the first place you've gone wrong then. Everyone's life has bullet points. Or should have. There was some song my mother used to trill over the washing up when I was a kid. "You've got to have a dream or how are you going to have a dream come true!" So, what's your dream? Clearly not the wayward Douglas or you would be crying into your latte. Thanks, Allie.' The waitress had brought them two large coffees and two apricot Danish pastries without being asked. 'So.' Nicola turned back to Meg. 'Let's go back to basics. Number one. Do you like the job enough to go on wanting to do it forever?'

Meg smiled. 'I wonder why that's first.'

'Because it affects me. If you don't like it, I'll buy you out.'

There was a moment's stunned silence.

'Do you mean that?' Meg scanned Nicola's face.

The latter nodded. 'I love working with you. Don't get me wrong. This is not a takeover bid, but if you hate it or feel trapped by it or need a change for whatever reason or just some different scenery I'll use my grandmother's legacy and buy you out. That would give you enough bread to start again with something fresh.

Now. Next point.' She wrote 'No. 2' on her piece of paper. 'The corpse of the marriage. How much will you get? Half the house?'

'The whole house. So he says.'

'Get it in writing.' Once Nicola had slipped into practical mode she was formidable. 'It is the least he could do. I've never seen Douglas do a damn thing to that house, whereas you've turned it into a real home. Number three. Money.'

Meg shook her head. 'Not a lot. But having no children means it's less complicated.'

'What about the need for revenge?' Nicola's pen was hovering over the margin ready to write number four.

'That's a bullet point?'

'Oh yes.' Nicola stared thoughtfully down at her plate for a moment. 'Anger can fester. You may think you don't care now, but you might later. When you're lonely, feeling down, maybe you even start to miss him. Then you'll start to think about the slag who seduced your happily married husband.'

'He wouldn't go for a slag,' Meg found herself protesting, 'and if we'd been happy she wouldn't have managed to seduce him.' She shook her head.

'Don't you believe it. The thirty-somethings trawling the male workforce are sophisticated babies.' Nicola raised a cynical eyebrow. 'They want someone else's man; one who is mature and steady and knows how to look after a woman and who is preferably rich or soon to be rich. They weren't prepared to take a chance on a penniless youngster still in college, like you and I did. No, they waited. Waited for a man who's been perfectly trained by another woman. Like great black spiders.'

She scowled. 'Don't forget, I know what I'm talking about. This was before your time, but one of them hooked my old man when he was in hospital for God's sake! I only turned my back for a few hours and she had him convinced he'd die without her personal physio talents! By the time he was fully conscious after the op. she had got him to agree to move in with her. By the time he left hospital he thought he'd never walk again unless she was beside him. But we're not talking about me.' She cut a wedge of Danish and inserted it into her mouth.

The minute or two of silence which followed allowed Meg space to think for the first time since the morning's shattering phone call.

Even so, after Nicola's unexpected tirade she couldn't resist asking the question. 'Did you extract your revenge?'

Nicola smiled. 'Oh yes.'

'What was it?'

'I let her have him.'

'Wasn't that a rather hollow victory?'

'Nope. Their marriage lasted five months. Then when he begged to come back I said no.' There was a hardness in her voice Meg had never heard before. 'She took him for every penny he had had left after I finished with him.'

Meg glanced at Nicola's face and for a fleeting second she glimpsed the pain in the other woman's eyes. Nicola had loved her husband and to Meg's certain knowledge there had never been anyone to replace him.

'OK!' Nicola uncapped her pen again. 'No revenge then. So, on to the dream. The dream before real life and the saintly unseduceable Douglas made you compromise.' She had written a '4' in the margin.

'I wanted to sail single-handed round the world.' As soon as she had said it Meg stopped, completely stunned by her own words. Where had they come from? She opened her mouth to call them back, deny them, but instead she found herself saying, 'Not without stopping. Nothing like that. I would stop everywhere. Every island. Every country. Every port. Every deserted river mouth. And I would buy a camera and take a million photos and produce wonderful travel books to feed other people's dreams.'

Nicola stared at her, astonished. 'Can you sail?' she asked at last.

'No. Haven't a clue!' They gazed at each other for a full minute, and then dissolved into gales of laughter.

'I think point five had better be sailing lessons,' Nicola said quietly. 'Followed by six and seven, photography and navigation.'

It took her two and half years, still working in the daytime with Nicola, attending evening classes and courses and boat shows and photographic exhibitions. She lost weight, she grew her hair, she changed her wardrobe and she acquired a genuine, slightly-weathered tan, all unlooked-for but glorious side effects of her new found interests. Douglas had gone to Bristol, remarried, and then, as predicted returned to London without wife, house or much money. He met Meg for a drink – for old times' sake – and found her, to her extreme gratification, newly attractive. Too late. Meg had bought a boat with Nicola's buy-out money.

When she finally sailed, heading for southern climes,

she wasn't alone. Her navigation instructor was with her. Just to make sure she didn't take the wrong turning. She planned to allow him to disembark in the fullness of time but until that moment they were getting on far too well and having much too much fun to worry about the future.

And the boat? She had called it *No. 8*. 'Bullet Point' had not had quite the romantic ring she sought and seemed a bit warlike for her purposes, but locked in her document case with the charts and papers, was Nicola's original list. When she returned to England with some of her million photos and the manuscript for her first book Meg planned to frame it.

First-class Travel

As she rode the escalator up from the crowded District Line, Abi glanced furtively at her watch. Normally she didn't allow herself to do that. To see the hands moving round as she fought her way through the crowds was to invite stress. If she left her time-check until she arrived on the teeming concourse of Liverpool Street Station she could see which trains were there on the departure board, and she could make a spot judgement. Run or saunter, or go grab a coffee. The stress was thereby minimised.

Today had been particularly bad. The crowds seemed heavier than usual and she had had an especially exhausting afternoon in court. A child custody case – the worst kind. The 5.42 was still alongside Platform 11 and she had four minutes to get there. With every step her briefcase and large shoulder-bag grew heavier, but on this occasion it was worth the hurry. To get home as soon as possible, to have a cool bath and a long, lazy gin and tonic on the terrace at the back of the cottage was the sole thing on her mind at this moment.

The cottage had seemed a sensible buy when she and Don split up: two small homes in exchange for the beautiful Georgian townhouse that had been sacrificed on the altar of divorce. Initially, she had been pleased with her purchase. Idyllically pretty, with a thatched roof in a charming, riverside village. But it was lonely. There was no one to share her frozen meals with. No time to meet the neighbours. No energy to go out and seek for company, male or female. No possibility, given her long, long hours of work, of even a cat or a dog for company . . . She sighed.

The first-class allocation on these trains was a joke. It was to be found at the end of the first carriage, a small glassed off section, only seating a mere sixteen people, presumably all the business travellers – people like her whose tickets were paid for by their firms because they needed to work in that precious hour or two on the way to and from home. If she were travelling Intercity there would have been a table to work at, and above all she wouldn't have to wait till she got home for the G&T, but as it was even the token space and relative quiet provided in this small area was welcome.

She slid the door back and climbed into the one vacant place with murmured apologies to the other passengers upon whose toes she was treading. The train was hot and stuffy. The windows were dirty, misted with condensation, and closed. She leaned back wearily as the train pulled out of the station. What, she asked herself for the hundredth time that week, was it all for?

Her neighbour reached down into his own briefcase and brought out a laptop. Opposite her a mobile phone trilled importantly and was immediately silenced. She sighed and closed her eyes. If someone didn't open a window soon they would all suffocate anyway, and that would be the end of all their problems.

At Chelmsford half the train passengers disembarked. Those who remained spread themselves more comfortably and someone at last lowered a window. Abi did not open her eyes.

When she awoke, the train was standing at a small station, the doors blessedly open. Soon it would be dark. Nearly everyone had gone now. She was the only person left in the first-class ghetto.

In the distance, she could hear an announcement over the station loudspeaker. Someone blew a whistle. The doors were actually closing when three young men, heavily tattooed, jumped on the train. Of one accord they turned towards the first-class compartment and slid open the door.

'Hello, darling!' The first one greeted her with a leer. 'Not too proud for a bit of company, I hope!' They sat down in the set of seats next to hers across the gangway.

Her heart had sunk to her shoes. The first-class compartment, in theory a haven, was a challenge to people like these, and it had become, suddenly, a trap. She smiled non-committally and closed her eyes again, hoping that a calm demeanour would bore them into looking for someone else to bait. It didn't.

'Come on, darling. Want a drink?' A can of lager was waved under her nose.

She shrank back and shook her head. 'No thanks.'

'No thanks!' The mimicry was mocking, the atmosphere of threat and barely suppressed anger increasing every second. She found to her surprise that she was thinking very clearly. What were they going to try? She doubted if they would actually hurt her. Best not to think about that. Concentrate on her belongings instead. Her briefcase was pushed back on the rack. Legal briefs. Court papers. Confidential memos. She doubted if this bunch could even read, but nevertheless their theft would compromise the case. She had little jewellery on. Earrings. A slim gold bangle, hidden under the cuff of her blouse. A couple of rings – one Victorian, which had belonged to her grandmother's grandmother. That she would be devastated to lose. The rest, well, it could be replaced. Her shoulder-bag contained more papers. Some money. Credit cards. Mobile.

Mobile. She glanced at the bag, now lying beside her on the seat. Could she reach it and dial? The communication cord, so often glanced at, its position noted, just in case, was out of reach above the door, outside the compartment. No use at all.

Her chief tormentor had fallen back into his seat, amusing himself with draining his can of lager. Finishing it, he crumpled it up in one fist and hurled it suddenly and with enormous force at the window near her. She jumped back in her seat and he let fly a string of obscenities before reaching into the bag he had dumped on the seat beside him for a new can.

Abi glanced at the window. With it rapidly growing dark outside, it was hard to see where they were, but surely it could not be many minutes before they reached the next station. No sooner had the thought crossed her mind than her heart sank. Whatever they intended to do, it would be before they arrived so that they could make their escape. If only she had a rape alarm, or something with which to defend herself.

The third young man had risen slowly to his feet. His hair was longer than that of his friends and lay greasy on his collar. Clutching his can, he staggered across to stand immediately in front of her, his legs actually touching her knees. 'I think I'm going to throw up,' he announced casually.

'. . . In which case, I think it would be a good thing if you got off the train, young man. I doubt if any of you have first-class tickets – or any tickets at all. You leave the train at the next stop. Do you understand me? All of you?'

The sliding open of the compartment door had been sufficiently sudden, the deep voice sufficiently loud for the youth to spin round in surprise. His companions, who had begun to sing discordantly, fell silent.

Abi's rescuer was tall and broadshouldered, casually dressed, in his forties, Abi guessed, and he was undeniably black. She took a deep breath and waited for the torrent of racial abuse she thought was bound to follow. It didn't come. The stranger looked at each one in turn for several seconds as though memorising their faces, then, with a nod at Abi, he turned away without a word. She saw him resume his seat about half a dozen rows away. She did not dare look at her three persecutors.

She reached into her bag and produced her mobile. Aware that they were watching her, she pressed the 9 button three times and at last looked up at them directly. All three stood up.

As the train drew into the next station they jumped off and disappeared into the dark. Abi put away her phone. The only sound in the carriage now was the distant rattle of an empty lager can being kicked along the wet platform.

From her seat, Abi saw her rescuer glance up and register that they had gone. She caught his eye and smiled gratefully, wondering if she should go and thank him properly, but already he had looked down, immersed, she could see, in a pile of papers.

The last long haul before the final stop was blessedly peaceful. Abi reached her own briefcase down at last and withdrew a memo. The compartment still reeked of lager and the atmosphere of violence lingered, but she had left the door open and the sight of the distant, dark, slightly greying head bent so studiously over his own reading matter reassured her. She reached for a pen and began to make notes, trying to put the disturbance behind her.

'I must speak to the driver!' The woman's voice behind her made her jump. She turned round, scanning the compartment. It was empty. The door behind her, locked shut, led only, she knew, to the empty driver's cab and the rear of the train.

She frowned. She must have imagined it. Perhaps she had dreamed it, fallen asleep or been in that unreal hypnotic state when strange voices from time to time accost one loudly out of the ether. Rubbing her eyes she turned back to her papers.

'Please. Help me! I must speak to the driver!'

Abi jumped to her feet, her papers sliding from her lap in all directions. The voice had come from the seat behind her – quite loud, perfectly clear, the accent elegant, almost over-refined. There was no possibility she had imagined it. She turned round slowly, clutching the back of the seat as the train sped northwards on the last stage of its journey, scanning every inch of the compartment, under every seat, the luggage rack, even the litter bin.

'I don't mean to pry, but are you all right?' He had been watching her, and now he approached, a look of concern on his face. 'Did they steal something?'

'No, they didn't take anything. It was a woman.' Abi looked up at him, confused. 'Did you see a woman in here? Sitting behind me?'

He shook his head. 'I don't think so.' Stepping into the compartment, he sat down and leaned over, rounding up her papers from the floor. 'Yes, come to think of it, I believe a woman got on the train as those boys got off. I noticed her and thought it strange because she was wearing such an old-fashioned hat. But I didn't see where she went. I was reading. I didn't take much notice, I'm afraid, once they got off.'

Abi had watched them get off. She had seen no one get on. She shook her head. 'She's not here now. Look, you can see that the whole carriage is empty.' She gestured wildly down the length of it.

'She could have walked on through.'

'No.' She shook her head. 'No, this is the last carriage. The end of the train.'

Far away, at the front, they heard the two-tone hooter as they rattled through an empty station without stopping.

'Are you sure you weren't asleep?' He had the most

wonderful smile, she realised suddenly. Gentle. Understanding. Inviting confidences. Slowly she shook her head. 'I suppose I must have been.' She gave an awkward laugh. 'I'm sorry. I suppose those awful louts unnerved me so much I was hallucinating or something.' She paused. 'I haven't thanked you for saving me. I was so sure they were going to rob me at the very least.'

He laughed. 'Bravado, most of it. You showed no fear, so would probably have been OK. They're often cowards, that sort.'

'You handled them like an expert!'

He nodded. 'So I should. I was head of an inner city school for sixteen years. I expect I dimly reminded them of some sort of authority figure.'

Abi laughed. 'I should have guessed. Are you still a teacher?'

He shook his head. 'No. I've done my bit for British youth. I'm a straight academic now. Writing books on education.' He glanced at the window. 'Nearly there.' He handed her her papers. 'Will you be all right now?'

She nodded. 'Thank you again. I'm really grateful.' He smiled again as he rose to his feet and then he was gone, back to his own seat, where she could see him busy packing his briefcase.

When they disembarked from different doors she saw him striding ahead of her, out of the station and into the darkness.

For the rest of the week Abi was nervous coming home. She watched jumpily as the train began to empty, aware that in her bag at last was the rape alarm she had always promised herself she would buy. And she kept her eyes open for her rescuer, unable to keep the image of his smile out of her head. Their mutual station served dozens of small villages. He could have come from any one of them, but there was no sign of him again. Until Friday.

It was on the last leg of the journey that he knocked on the door of the compartment where she was once more sitting alone, and slid it back with a smile. 'May I join you for a moment?' He was formally dressed today in an immaculate grey suit and sober silk tie. 'I trust you're none the worse for your adventure on Monday?' He paused a second then, not giving her the chance to reply, went on, 'I've discovered something about the woman in the compartment and I wondered if you would like to hear about her.'

She looked up and met his eyes. 'You make her sound rather intriguing.'

'She is. Or rather was.' He paused. 'Something about her disappearance puzzled me, as I think it puzzled you. It nagged at my brain until I began to remember a story I'd heard, and yesterday afternoon I had some time to spare so I went to the newspaper library to check. I found her. Or at least, I think I did. The woman who spoke to you was a ghost.' His eyes held hers soberly, challenging her to laugh. She didn't. A cold draught tiptoed lightly across her shoulders.

'She was called Sarah Middleton. In the 1950s she was travelling on a train on this line when she was attacked. She managed to pull the communication cord but by the time they found her she was dead. When they interviewed the other passengers later someone who had been in the same compartment with her said

307

she had been very agitated. That the man she was with was very aggressive. When the passenger got off, she tried to alight as well, but the man pulled her back. Apparently she was screaming, ''I must speak to the driver''.'

Abi closed her eyes. She shivered. 'Why on earth didn't he help her?'

'He thought it was none of his business. He assumed the man was her husband. He even thought she might be drunk. Didn't want to interfere. And you weren't dreaming. Apparently, she has been seen several times by different people over the years, travelling this stretch of line.'

'Poor Sarah. Did they catch him?'

He shook his head.

'So her spirit can't rest.' She shuddered. 'That's a terrible story.'

The train was slowing. He glanced at his watch. 'I photocopied the newspaper stories. I haven't got them with me – I wasn't sure if I would see you again – but I could send them to you. Or perhaps I'll keep them on me in case I do bump into you again. I go up and down this way several times a week to visit the British Library. I live in Seaton.'

'So do I.' She hesitated, but only for a moment. 'You could always drop them in.'

They walked together to the car park and found their cars next to each other. Their houses, they discovered, were in adjacent roads. How they could have failed to meet or even see one another in the post office on Saturday mornings filled the conversation for the next five minutes.

'After all, you could hardly miss me.' Grant laughed. That was his name. Grant Stevenson. She glanced, suddenly a little shy, at his six-foot frame and the black face, unusual in this lonely part of East Anglia, and she laughed with him.

Before they parted, she had discovered that he was a widower with three children all in their twenties, that he was forty-five – twelve years older than she – that he had published three books, two on educational theory and one on local history – hence his memory of the story of poor Sarah Middleton – that she was invited to supper the following evening and that, undeniably, she found him astonishingly attractive.

Moving On

In the spring the garden came to life like a friend she had not seen for months. It smiled. It reached out and she reciprocated. It nestled round the cottage like a silken scarf and kept it safe. When Roy turned one Saturday morning from the window and delivered his ultimatum she felt as though her friend had been violated before her eyes.

'That's it. I'm not commuting any more. I've had enough. We're selling up and moving to London.'

The trouble was she had always felt guilty about his travelling. Each morning he was out of the house by 7.15 – in the glorious dawn at some times of year; but at others scraping the ice from the car and setting off up slippery ungritted country roads to stand on a platform in the cold north wind at the mercy of the railway system.

And she? What did she do? In spring and summer she drank coffee when he had gone, then slipped out into the balmy air with her forks and trowels and secateurs and breathed the sweet air and felt the warmth of the sun on the back of her hands. In winter, sometimes she sat by the Aga and read or listened to the radio with Sally-Su, all huge Siamese eyes and charm, on her knee. Sometimes she crept guiltily back to bed.

'There's no need for you to get up. No point in both of us suffering.' He said it with a smile. He meant it nicely, but she had always got up with him; climbed from the warm cocoon. Without acknowledging it perhaps she had, if she were honest, heard an edge to his voice, but she had never said anything.

'I'm amazed you've let me make that journey every day! You've just watched me go and never given it a thought!' His voice had grown harsh suddenly. So suddenly she couldn't believe it. 'Most wives would have got a proper job to help; most wives would have offered to move long ago!'

'Most wives?' Libby shook her head as though warding off a blow. He, after all, had chosen the cottage, insisted they buy it, convinced her that she didn't need a job and that she would love the country when, years ago, he had uprooted them from all their London friends, at the time as if on a mere whim.

But that was when they thought there would be children. Instead, a long while later there had been Ching-Miaou and then her daughter, Sally-Su.

Libby's guilt and her misery stopped her rational thought processes. She stood by while people tramped through the cottage and discussed cutting down the old apple tree to make room for a garage. She was there in body to look at new houses in narrow car-lined terraces, to glance up at the low-flying jets and nod and smile when told 'you'll soon find you don't notice them at all', and she stood dully with the measuring tape while Roy explained how she would enjoy choosing new curtains and carpets and sorting out the furniture to get rid of the dead wood. In spirit she was hiding in the garden at home. Hiding and crying.

Sally-Su was far stronger. She spoke her mind. Every intruder and every change brought forth complaints. When at last it was too late to stop her human beings making the supreme mistake and she was in her cat basket on the way to London in the car her wails became first vituperative then heart-rending, then sullen and finally despairingly lost.

It was some time before it dawned on Libby that it still took Roy the best part of an hour to reach the office. But now she did not get up with him. She stayed in bed, sometimes until mid morning, not even reading. Just cuddling the sulking fabric-shredding monster which had once been a loving cat. It was impossible to find a job. A middle-aged woman with no qualifications? In the country she could have found any amount of part-time work easily had she wanted it. Here they laughed at her. Laughed!

Roy's hours were longer now. He stayed at the office late and sometimes went in all day on Saturdays, so she saw him barely at all. Neighbours, guarding their privacy, did not do more than smile defensively and scuttle away. She was drowning.

Then, one morning – it was 4th of July, a date she thought later with a grim smile, that reeked of significance – she woke up.

Roy had not come home. A phone call at nine the night before had informed her that as the meeting was running late and there was an early start next morning he would camp down in the office. She had thought nothing of it. His microwave meal was still in the freezer anyway. She hated her London hob and split level oven. TV and bed were an unchallenging alternative to watching Roy eat.

The early night meant she woke to see the sun streaming in across the carpet. Somewhere a blackbird was singing. She lay, staring up at the ceiling and knew suddenly without a shadow of doubt that Roy was having an affair, had probably been having an affair even before they had moved.

Once she started looking it was so obvious. The long blonde hair on a jacket – oh please, that obvious? That clichéd? The two theatre ticket stubs in a pocket, a broken pearl ear ring in his jacket, the programme for an art exhibition he would never have gone to on his own in a million years. And then it all began to fall into place. His new interest in modern decor, the different trendy expressions in his speech, the quote the other day from an article in *Marie Claire*.

For a while she sat, her head in her hands, then she straightened. The sun was still there. It had reached her bare feet and she could feel the warmth caressing her skin.

She wasn't sure of the actual moment when she realised she was free. She ought to be distraught. She was hurt and insulted and angry but at the same time an imperceptible, almost subliminal lightness had begun to form around her heart.

313

There was a quiet chirrup from behind her. Sally-Su jumped onto the bed. The cat sat facing her, eyes inscrutable.

'You knew, didn't you?' Libby spoke out loud. 'You should have said. We needn't have moved. We could have refused. We needn't have made it easier for him.'

She stood up and padded downstairs, the cat, tail high, paws mincing, behind her.

'But we don't have to stay here. We can go home, back to our friends. It won't be the same house, of course, but it would just be you and me. And we'd find somewhere with a little garden which we could make beautiful.'

Almost without thinking she reached into the cupboard for a tin of sardines. 'I wonder if she really wants him. Was it just the chase, do you think? Take him away from his wife just for fun, then, when she's got him, get bored, move on to find the next married man. Or does she genuinely love him?'

She hooked her finger into the ring pull and levered off the lid. Sally-Su was sitting on the work top only inches away. She did not move. Every muscle was tense, her eyes sapphire blue, only the tiniest black slits showing the concentration of her mind.

Libby lifted out a sardine on a fork. 'Shall we share them?' She licked a drop of olive oil off her finger tip. 'Then I'm going to ring our solicitor to see what we need to do next. And then –' she dropped the sardine on a saucer – 'you and I are going to start to plan what we are going to do with our freedom.'

He had the grace to look abashed when she confronted him; but then the relief showed through all too soon. 'I'm so sorry, Libby. I wouldn't have hurt you for the world!'

But he had. He had hurt them both.

They put the house back on the market and this time Sally-Su showed no interest at all in who looked round. She did not like this London home and she did not care who walked around it. She lay curled on Libby's bed and ignored even the most heartfelt compliments from the strangers who came to stare. Had she known how much London house prices had escalated in the intervening months she would have sat up and pricked her ears. Even splitting the value of the place she and Libby would be able to afford something deep in the country which would meet with her approval.

Libby found it just eight miles away from where they used to live. The cottage would need a lot of work and so would the garden but it had the basics – an inglenook fireplace, a lot of charm and an old apple tree with gnarled branches perfect for climbing – from a cat's point of view – and from Libby's it was close to all their old friends. It was like coming home. Only one thing worried her. How was she going to support herself? That was a tricky one. His job had always more than paid for them both. In fact he had actively discouraged her from working, hated her occasional part time jobs – a matter of rather strange old-fashioned pride, or even possessiveness, she thought – which was why she had spent so much time and energy on the garden. It hadn't mattered then, the garden had been just about enough. But now suddenly her world had changed. 'You needn't think I'm going to support you so that you can swan around doing nothing all day in the country while I work myself into the ground up here! No solicitor would countenance that for a minute. You are perfectly capable of working. In fact you'll probably remarry.' He was rapidly working himself into a frenzy of self-righteous indignation at all the money he might have to give her.

There seemed no point in reminding him that her life of leisure had been his idea. And that in fact leisure had been the last thing on her mind and was the last thing on her mind now. Life suddenly was full of possibilities, limited only by the presence of one small cat.

And strangely it was the cat who got her the job. Sally-Su was ecstatic at the new house, inspecting it, her tail erect, commenting loudly on every feature, inspecting the furniture to make sure her favourite bits had arrived safely. ('You can have that, it's all scratched and smelly,' Roy had said about more than one item. From the selection he rejected Libby decided his new love did not like antique furniture. Good!) While she was thus occupied, the phone had rung and it turned out to be the local antique shop with whom Libby had left her number to enquire about a small table she had seen in the window. As she was talking Sally-Su came to stand near her, voicing her own opinion loudly. The shop owner heard her down the phone and laughed. The conversation became extended. He was a cat lover; he adored gardens; he was a widower; he could show her the new restaurant that had opened in the last few months; he needed someone to watch the shop while he was out buying more stock . . .

Sally-Su liked the sound of this new gentleman; he was obviously a cat person and from a cat's point of view things were shaping up rather nicely. Once she had inspected him she would decide whether he could stay in their lives. She smiled as only a cat can smile. Anyone would have thought she had arranged the whole thing.

'You've Got a Book to Write, Remember?'

'It's a lonely house.' Brian Foster glanced at his passenger. 'We only ever used it for holidays.'

Caro nodded. 'I know. I've read the particulars.'

Brian had arranged to collect her from the station following her telephoned enquiry about the ad in the *Sunday Times*.

> *Isolated cottage.*
> *Breathtaking views.*

'As I told you,' he went on, 'it's just too far to come often enough to justify keeping it.' He shrugged, squinting through the windscreen at the single-track road ahead. 'Are you planning to go back south tonight?' He glanced towards her. She was a striking woman. Tall. In her early forties at a guess, she was staring straight ahead, seemingly uninterested in Brian or his attempts at conversation.

He swung the car onto an even narrower road. 'I

wish the weather was brighter,' he said with a sigh. 'But I suppose it's better to see it at one of its less glamorous moments.' Two other prospective buyers had already seen it at its less glamorous moments and both had high-tailed it back to civilisation.

She put a hand out to the dashboard to steady herself as the old Land Rover lurched through a pothole. He grimaced. 'We – I – keep this car up here and fly to Inverness from London.'

'How long have you had the cottage?' She didn't look across at him as she spoke.

'Five years.'

'And there is vacant possession?'

'That's right. I'm staying up here long enough to sell it; then I'm off.' He tried to keep his voice light. She needn't know about the heartbreak, the anger, the misery the cottage had caused. 'You should be able to see it about now,' he added. He pointed. 'White blob on the shore of the loch down there.'

She sat forward and stared across the rain-soaked moor. 'What's that other building near it?'

'That's the broch.' He slowed the car as he approached a water-filled gully which crossed the road in full spate. 'Our local piece of heritage.'

'It's a ruin?'

'For a couple of thousand years. It's Iron Age they think.'

He did not speak again until they drew up outside the cottage. It was a charming place, Patricia had seen to that. Whitewashed with a neat fence to keep out the deer. Pointless that had been. They could jump fences twenty feet high as far as he could see and had made short work of her pretty garden. Now there was heather and bog myrtle and foxgloves in the flower beds, just as there was outside the fence. Nature's way of telling you that you were here on her terms, not yours.

They climbed out and stood for a moment, Brian staring out across the rain-pitted waters of the loch, Caro at the cottage. He heard her sigh softly and his heart sank as he pushed open the front door and ushered her inside.

The room was dark, smelling rich with peat smoke, simply furnished with a small sofa, a round table with four chairs, an empty bookcase. At the far end a sink and cooker and a small dresser formed the kitchen. He went over to the table and reached for some matches. 'As you see, no electricity, just calor gas and oil lamps. That does – did – us fine. All mod cons.' He forced himself to smile. 'Spring water and even plumbing. The bedrooms are here.' He strode towards a small lobby. Two rooms led off it, one with a double bed, the other with bunks. Both were cramped and dark and looked out onto the wet hillside behind the cottage.

'I'll take it.'

He stared at her. 'You can't be serious.'

'You do want to sell it?'

'Yes. Yes, of course.' He tried to restrain the wave of relief that swept over him.

'I'll take the furniture too. I think you said that was included if I wanted it?'

'It is. Oh, indeed it is.'

'And the Land Rover?' For the first time she gave him a real smile. 'I can't believe you want much for that.'

He shook his head ruefully. 'Indeed not. In fact I'll throw it in for nothing.'

'Good. Thank you. I can pay you in cash. When can I move in?'

He blinked. 'When you like, I suppose. As you see, we – I've – moved all our personal belongings out. I don't want any of the crockery or kitchen stuff –' Pretty kitchen stuff, so eagerly bought, so much hated now. 'As far as I'm concerned you can have it today. Don't you want to see anything else?' He was almost disappointed. Now that he knew she liked it he wanted to show her round properly, he wanted her to admire the details, he wanted above all for her to know how much he had loved this place. Once.

She shook her head. 'I'll see it all soon enough.' For a moment her voice softened. 'It's just what I wanted.'

Her needs were minimal. All her worldly belongings, the items she had allowed herself to keep after forty-four years of living and loving and suffering, filled a couple of large suitcases and a few cardboard boxes. The day she moved in nature decided to be kind. The sky was a soft downy blue, the water of the loch as iridescent as a dragonfly's back; autumn sunlight warmed the stone walls and shone obliquely across the deep window sills into the rooms. She wasn't a martyr. She had bought some warm woollen throws for the sofa and beds, some decent food and wine as well as the basic supplies and she had brought an ancient typewriter. It wasn't until she had signed on the dotted line that she had thought about her lap top. It was there in one of the boxes – fully charged, but for how long? The answer would be to invest one day in her own generator, if she stayed, but for the time being she would make do and appreciate the primitive life she so craved.

Abandoning her boxes she wandered down towards the loch. Out of sight, around the corner, the long narrow arm of water opened into the sea, but up here it was calm and transparent, moving gently to the touch of the lightest wind. There might not have been another person in the world.

Except there was. As she turned back towards the house she saw the figure out of the corner of her eye just for a second on the far side of the inlet.

She frowned, squinting against the shimmering reflections. No, there was no one there. No one at all. She had imagined it.

For the first thirty-seven years of her life Caro had been a normal person. She had gone to school, proceeded to university, come out with a respectable degree. She had been drawn to journalism, worked on regional papers, then a national before marrying a photographer and producing two talented children for whom she had given up steady work and gone freelance. Phil Spalding had been the kindest, nicest, best thing that had happened to her until his God had taken him away. He had become a parson – something she had tolerated with a certain amount of horrified humour. But that had not been enough for God. Phil had developed cancer and seven years ago he had died. She had tried to accept it; tried to live with it; tried to come to terms with such cruel and unnecessary waste, but she couldn't. Her life had fallen apart. The children had drawn away, involved in their own lives and friends, trying to be supportive but afraid of her anger and bitterness. There was nothing left. Until she had the dream. 'Pull yourself together, Caro,' Phil had said. He looked much as he had before the illness started to take its toll. Tall, good-looking; his eyes gentle but firm as he stood at the end of her bed. 'You are frightening everyone away and ruining their lives and your own. Be alone for a bit. Get to know yourself again. Get away from here.' He waved his arm around the room – their room. 'You've got a book to write, remember?' He smiled, that lovely quizzi-cal smile, and reached out to her. She sat up; wanting to touch him, to hold him close, to smell the lovely warmth of his skin, but he had gone and she fell back on her pillow and cried.

It was the turning point. She gave the kids most of the contents of the flat, sold it and gave them each a third of the money in trust, keeping the rest for herself. Her plan had been to travel and write that book – the book she had been going to write when she first met Phil. Then she had seen the ad in the paper and she had heard Phil's voice in her head as clearly as she had always heard it in the past. 'Go for it, Caro. You need to give yourself some space. Then start writing.'

Space! She looked round and laughed out loud. What had she done!

Two days later she saw the figure again. Just an out-line really, on the shore near the broch, standing watch-ing her as she pottered around. She narrowed her eyes against the glare off the water. It was the same man.

It took an hour to walk around the inlet. It was a cool misty day and she took deep lungfuls of the pure air as she walked. The broch consisted of two castle-like concentric circles of dark stone, about thirty feet high, with steps and passages within the thickness of the double walls. It was completely ruinous on one side, fairly intact on the other. In the centre a perfect circle of grass and weeds had grown lush, sheltered from the wind. She stood and stared round listening to the silence, the lap of water on the stones on the beach, the cry of curlew and sandpiper, the hiss of wind across the dried heather stems outside the walls. Suddenly she shivered. She turned round slowly, staring up at the blind, shadowed walls. Someone was watching her; she could feel it.

'Hello?' she called, her voice echoing off the stone. 'Is there anyone there?' There was no answer.

She did not stay long. As she picked her way back around the loch, scattering wagtails and gulls before her, a figure appeared on top of the ruined wall and watched her leave. She didn't turn round and never saw him.

'You'll be wanting to charge up your phone and your lap top while you're here?' Mrs Maclellan welcomed her into the post office shop with a smile. 'Mrs Foster always did that. I make a small charge for the electricity which I'm sure you won't mind.'

Caro's mouth dropped open. So that was how it was done! She had thought very little about her predecessors and was, she realised, completely incurious about them. Rich. Spoiled. A bit petulant. That was how she visualised Patricia Foster. Of no interest at all.

Slowly she fell into a routine. Once or twice a week

she drove to the village; sometimes she explored further afield and at last she had time for herself. Time to think. To remember. And to write. She bought back-up batteries for the lap top and smiled at the thought of Mrs Mac retiring on the proceeds of her battery charging service. And she continued to wave from time to time to her unknown neighbour across the loch. Because he was still there.

The first time she saw him close up was a shock. She had been sitting on the shore with her notebook, outlining her thoughts for a series of articles – the idea for the book had still not come – when she glanced up and saw him only a hundred yards away. Dressed in some sort of rough highland garb, his hair long and unkempt, he was watching her. He was younger than she had expected; quite good-looking. She raised her hand in greeting, but he ignored it, staring right through her. She shrugged and turned back to her notes. When she looked up again he had gone.

The next time, though, he looked straight at her and he smiled. She felt a shock of pleasure. The smile was warm; friendly. 'Hello!' It was the first time she had spoken to anyone for several days. He didn't reply. She wasn't sure if he had even heard her but just for a moment his gaze lingered appreciatively before he turned away.

'Who is the young man I see out by the broch?' she asked next time she was in the village.

Mrs Mac glanced up from Caro's purchases, frowning. 'There's no one lives up there. No one at all,' she said sharply. 'You keep away from there. It's a dangerous old place.'

Two days later when Caro saw him in the distance he raised his hand in greeting before turning away. She stared into the watery sunlight, trying to see which way he went. His presence was beginning to irritate and intrigue in equal measures and it was almost without conscious decision that she set off after him, intent on finding out where he came from.

The broch was shadowy, very still within the high dark stone walls. She stood in the centre looking up. 'Hello?' she called.

A pair of jackdaws flew up, crying in agitation as they circled before settling back into the silent shadows.

'Hello? Are you there?'

And suddenly there he was standing at one of the dark recesses in the broken wall. He raised his hand and beckoned.

She made her way across the grass to the archway in the grey stone. Under it a flight of broken steps led up inside the wall. She stood at the bottom looking up into the darkness then, cautiously, she began to climb. 'Where are you? I can't see.'

Groping her way slowly she rounded a bend in the stair and there he was, standing above her, framed by gaping stone. Seeing her appear he smiled, that warm gentle smile, and beckoned again.

She took another step towards him eager to be in sunshine again but as she reached the top he stepped back out of sight. Where he had been standing there was no wall. Nothing to support her at all. With a scream she found herself clawing at the stone as she began to fall.

* * *

The bespectacled face swam into focus for a moment, disappeared and then returned in more solid form. It smiled. 'So, we are awake at last. How are we feeling?' The hand on the pulse at her wrist was warm and solid. Reassuring.

Every bone and muscle in her body throbbed. 'What happened? Where am I?'

'You fell at the broch. You're in hospital, lass, thanks to Mrs Maclellan.'

Caro realised suddenly that the post mistress was sitting on the far side of her bed.

'How did you find me?' Slowly she was beginning to remember.

'Mrs Maclellan took a lift out with the post van to see you.' The doctor paused, wondering how to describe the woman's hunches; her second sight. 'She remembered what you had said about the laddie up at the broch and wanted to warn you about him. Luckily for you, they saw you fall, from the road.'

Caro closed her eyes. She felt sick and disorientated. 'What did you want to warn me about?'

The two beside her glanced at one another. The doctor shrugged. 'It's our belief that you saw a lad called Jamie Macpherson. He lived near the broch some while ago and fell in love, so the story goes, with a young woman he met up there. No one knows what happened but one day the boy disappeared. They found him where we found you, at the foot of the wall. He had a lassie's silk scarf in his hand.' He paused, scrutinising her face cautiously. 'Mrs Foster knew the story. She was quite obsessed about it. She would stay up here when her husband went back to London, making notes to write a book about it.'

Caro lay back against the pillow, her eyes closed.

'Poor lady. It seems she followed him to the broch one day and climbed the stair just as you did.'

Caro frowned. 'I don't understand. You said he was dead?'

He nodded. 'They should pull that old place down. It's too dangerous. The steps are broken. She fell. Just as you did. Only in her case, no one came.'

'She was killed?' Caro's eyes flew open.

He nodded gravely.

'Oh how awful. Poor woman. How sad. No wonder her husband wanted to leave.'

'Aye.'

'Did you follow Jamie out there?' Mrs Maclellan sat forward on her chair.

Caro shrugged. 'I followed someone. Young. Good-looking. Wearing a highland plaid.'

'That's him.' The woman nodded.

'And he's a ghost?'

'Aye.' She was matter-of-fact.

Caro shivered.

'I suppose you'll leave us now, once you've recovered.' Mrs Maclellan shook her head sadly.

Caro shrugged, trying to make sense of the jumble of words spinning in her head. 'I don't want to leave. I love it here.' She smiled weakly. 'I'm a writer too, like Mrs Foster.' Was that a voice she could hear in her head? 'Go for it, Caro. This is the book!' She looked up at them. 'Perhaps I should write the story for her? And for him?' She hesitated. 'I wonder, would that help them find peace, do you think?'

'Aye, I think that would be the right thing to do.' Mrs

Maclellan smiled at her. Was she the only one, she wondered, who could see the handsome clergyman standing next to the bed, nodding in approval.

Sands of Time

1

It had snowed in the night and a skim of white lay across the rough grass, clinging to the banks of rhododendrons, weighing down the leaves into graceful arabesques across the track.

Toby Hayward parked his car near the ruins of the ancient castle which rose from the uneven ground ahead of him. A tall man, in his early forties, he looked the archetypal Scotsman, with sandy hair, high colour and handsome regular features. Dressed in a shabby waxed jacket and old boots he stood for a moment trying to find his bearings. The place was deserted; it was too cold for visitors and the forecast that the weather was going to grow worse would deter any strangers from joining him in this very personal pilgrimage. The ruins were picturesque, huge and gaunt, the high broken walls, the gaping windows, the areas of

330

castellation silhouetted against the snow and the back-drop of stately ancient trees.

The imposing stable block that had once graced this great pile and which had been destroyed by fire in the latter half of the nineteenth century had long ago been pulled down. The castle itself had also been ravaged by fire, this time shortly after the end of the First World War. The ruins had not been rebuilt. Toby grimaced. Two devastating fires. Coincidence? Who would ever know now.

He fished in his pocket for the guidebook his mother had given him before he left London for Scotland a couple of weeks earlier. It traced the history of the castle and of the Carstairs family from the fourteenth century to its heyday under the ninth earl, the infamous Victorian traveller and occultist. On page twelve there was a reproduction of a portrait of the earl. Chewing his lip Toby stood staring down at it. The Roger Carstairs who gazed out at the world also had handsome regular features, offset by dark arrogant eyes. He was dressed in the sort of middle-eastern costume favoured by Lord Byron and T.E. Lawrence.

Turning the page Toby stared down at the entry about Lord Carstairs. It was the final paragraph that intrigued him.

'The ninth earl maintained his enigmatic repu-tation to the last. The date and manner of his death are unknown, but rumours abounded as to the full horror of what occurred. It was said that he had perfected a method of trans-porting himself from place to place and even from one time zone to another by magical or shamanic techniques which he had learned on his travels in Egypt, India and North America. The methods he used, so it is said, left him vulnerable to the demonic forces which one day overwhelmed him. Maybe the ninth earl did not in fact die at all. As you look around the ruins of the castle which was once his home, be aware that the eyes which scrutinise you from the shadows may not be those of a ghost. They may be those of a man in hell.'

Toby shuddered. What rubbish. Who wrote this stuff?

He moved on across the grass leaving transparent ice-sheened footprints in the snow, heading for the main entrance to the castle with its imposing flight of steps. These led up to the rounded arch which had once surrounded the huge oak door and he stood there for a moment looking into the gaping space which had once been the great hall. The echoing cry of a jackdaw broke the intense silence and he watched the black shadow of the bird sweep between windows open to wind and snow.

For four years now Toby had lived within ten miles of this old pile without being aware of its existence.

He wished he still didn't know.

He moved forward into the space which had once been the centre of the household's activity and looked up. Five fireplaces, one above the other, rose up within the floorless keep, each successively smaller. A huge pile of twigs filled the top one, the chosen dwelling place of the jackdaw family, sole occupants now of the building which had seen so much of Scotland's history. And, so it turned out, that of his own family. He shuddered. The cry of the jackdaw was echoed by the wild mew of a buzzard circling the surrounding hills.

Toby rammed the guidebook into his pocket and moved on. It was cold within the walls of the castle, shadowed from the sun which outside was fast melting the night's fall of snow. All around him he could hear the sound of water, from the river which ran in full spate round the bottom of the escarpment on which the castle stood, from the sea of rhododendrons and from the dripping icicles and the melting snow.

Slipping on the icy, worn stone steps, he ducked out of the keep and walked into the rectangular area which, according to the guidebook, had formed the north tower, an extra block of living quarters built in the sixteenth century, but which had then been torn down to form the base of the carriage house and stables constructed much later by the seventh earl. It was here that his grandson, Roger Carstairs, had kept his museum, the collection of artefacts which had been destroyed by the catastrophic fire started, so the story went, by a disaffected servant while Roger was away on his travels. Included in this collection, presumably, were all the things he had brought back from his trips to Egypt.

Toby sighed. Egypt. Where only a few brief weeks before he had first met Anna.

He had set out on the visit to Egypt with such optimism. True it was going to be a package tour from Luxor to Aswan, with a boat full of strangers, but that was OK. That was his job. A painter and travel writer, he was going to report the experience for a Sunday paper in full humorous detail – the ups, the downs, the good places, the spoiled places, the nice people, the sad people. He was going to go home with a sketch book full of wonderful ideas and as a bonus he would catch some winter sunshine.

He had met Anna Fox on the flight out. Or at least tried not to meet her. He was well aware that he was being boorish, but he had vowed, if he was stuck next to some gossiping idiot for the five hour flight, that he would not be sucked in. The fact that the woman next to him had been beautiful with her long dark hair and her hazel eyes and in the event, far from being a gossiping idiot, had in fact been extremely interesting, had not penetrated his thick skull. Not then. Not for sometime. Although he had at least become aware that, far from engrossing herself in some trashy airport paperback, she had spent the journey reading an old diary, a Victorian diary, which, from his occasional oblique glance across at where it lay on her lap, seemed very interesting indeed.

The scream of the buzzard was louder now. It was circling closer, scanning the ground. Toby ducked instinctively as the broad-winged shadow flicked over him and disappeared behind the high grey walls.

He moved forward thoughtfully, picking his way over the remains of the more recent walls, which were marked now by no more than a couple of courses of stone. How odd that only the earlier foundations remained. Of the comparatively new Georgian and Victorian grandeur there was nothing to be seen. He moved across what had once been the open courtyard, slipping on the uneven cobbles. It wasn't so strange to think of

Roger Carstairs living here. An urbane, sophisticated world traveller, he had been still, in his blood, the wild border Scot, descendant of caterans and murdering reivers, a man used to getting his way; a man used to taking what he wanted, whether it was an artefact – or a woman. There was one artefact he had failed to obtain, and it had belonged to the one woman whom he had failed to win. There was a paragraph about her in the guidebook. Fishing it out of his pocket, Toby glanced down at the page which opened in front of him. Roger had met the artist Louisa Shelley in Egypt. Their relationship had, according to the author of the guide-book, been nothing short of stormy. Toby grimaced. What an understatement. But then the author hadn't had the opportunity of reading Louisa's diary. The diary in which Anna had been so engrossed when he first met her.

Behind him, from the keep, a chorus of angry shrieks and a shower of twigs falling five storeys into the open undercroft beneath the keep signalled a quarrel amongst the avian residents of the castle. Toby glanced up as a ragged black feather drifted down. He bent and picked it up, then straightening abruptly he glanced round, the feather in his hand. He had heard someone laugh. He frowned uneasily. The deep throaty chuckle had seemed to come from immediately behind him. He turned to stare at the shadowed embrasures, the open doorways. There was no one there. The buzzard had headed away now towards the distant hills. The jack-daws had subsided into silence as they preened on the top of the wall in the sunlight. In the shadow of what remained of the tower it was intensely cold. Toby found himself listening carefully. Had some more visitors arrived while he was wandering around lost in thought? Shivering he rammed his hands deep into his pockets. Just for an instant he had imagined that someone, somewhere, had whispered his name.

God! The place was getting to him. The atmosphere was in some way thickening. He stretched out his hand as though he could touch the air around him. There was no one there. No one that he could see. And yet he had the feeling that he was being watched. Watched by whom?

He could guess.

It was his great-great grandfather.

His hand closed around the guidebook. To think that when he had set out on the trip to Egypt he hadn't believed in ghosts. He hadn't believed in a lot of things. But then he hadn't known of his descent from Lord Carstairs. He had vaguely heard of the man – who hadn't? His sinister reputation was the kind that reverberated down the years, leaving an unpleasant taste in the mouth. As it happened the earldom had died out with the death of the eleventh earl. As far as he knew there were no direct descendants left. Just his mother, Frances. And him.

He smiled grimly. What a cocktail of blood to inherit.

2

Serena Canfield was kneeling before a small ornate altar in the front room of her maisonette in West Hampstead. She was still very aware of the emptiness of her home.

It was several years now since her much loved partner and soulmate had died. The aching gap and the silence left by him had been only partially filled by a succession of tenants and Charley, the latest, had just returned to her parents' home. The ensuing peace had initially been supremely welcome, but lately, perhaps because her next door neighbours on one side were away, on the other side out at work all day, the quietness of the place had begun to worry her.

The last of her prayers completed, she sat back on her heels in silent meditation.

An attractive woman in her mid forties with short dark hair, it was Serena's huge green eyes which immediately caught the attention. She was a self-confessed modern-day priestess of Isis – something which at the beginning of their cruise up the Nile, had intrigued and amused her fellow passengers. She had been visiting Egypt as part of a spiritual journey which she had been following for many years now. The visit had been traumatic and in many ways frightening, but it had done nothing to lessen her faith. On the contrary, it had left her more certain than ever of the power of her chosen goddess.

Opening her eyes she surveyed her altar. There, between a statue of Isis and the stately, smug Bast cat with its single gold earring and its inscrutable gaze, stood a small old bottle. The pale encrusted glass reflected no light at all. Rather it seemed to absorb it. She reached out to touch it, hesitated, then almost defiantly she picked it up. The bottle seemed unnaturally cold. Un-easily she glanced round the room. It was full of shadows, the only light coming from the candles on the altar and a small table lamp in the opposite corner. Before she had started her prayers she had closed the curtains. By now it would be dark outside, the streets wet with sleet reflecting the car headlights as home-coming commuters turned down the road and competed for parking positions. She could hear an engine revving now as someone tried to back their car into an impossibly tight slot. A stray beam from the headlights as they manoeuvred penetrated the curtains and hit the wall near her. She caught her breath. Something had moved, caught in the beam. A figure, here in the room with her, or just a trick of her overwrought imagination? 'Blessed Isis, be here. Protect me. Show me what to do with this bottle of your tears.' Serena whispered the words out loud. She took a deep breath, trying to steady her nerves. Her hands holding the little bottle were shaking.

Why had she told Anna that she would take care of it? That her prayers could keep it safe; keep its powers contained. A bottle that in its three thousand years of history had caused nothing but grief and pain. What was it Anna had said, back in Egypt? Generations of people through thousands of years had died fighting for possession of this tiny artefact with its legendary contents. So, why, in the name of all the gods was Serena looking after it?

Outside, her neighbour killed the car engine. The headlights were extinguished and after a moment she heard a door bang. She took comfort from the fact that next door the lights were coming on and that who-ever had come home was turning on the TV, pouring a drink, going to look in the fridge, all the everyday things that reassured. Suddenly she did not feel so alone.

Climbing to her feet she carried the bottle over to the lamp. Strangely she had never examined it closely before. The glass was etched and blistered by time; small cement-like patches of hardened sand had set around the base of the sealed stopper. She stared at it, frowning. So small and yet so powerful. It was her fault that it was here. Anna had wanted to get rid of it in Egypt; to give it back to the goddess to whom it belonged. It was Serena, fool that she was, who had retrieved it and its burden of legends, its curses, its attendant ghostly guardians. When Anna tried again to dispose of it, everything had gone wrong. It wouldn't stay lost. It had returned. She gave another shudder. Had Hatsek and Anhotep, the priestly ghosts from ancient Egypt, travelled with it to London? Were they here now, in her small house, watching over the bottle in her hand? She froze suddenly, her fingers tightening involuntarily around it. A strange scent was drifting round her. She sniffed cautiously, her eyes straining into the corners of the room. There was no incense on her altar today. Just candles. But this was not beeswax she could smell. She swallowed nervously. This was subtle. Exotic. Redolent of the desert wind. It was the smell of *kyphi*, the incense of the gods.

She took a step back, terrified, scanning the room. There was no one there. No ghostly figures in the shadows. It was her imagination.

She looked at the bottle in her hand then quickly went to drop it back on the altar. Blowing out the candles she made for the hall, heading for the phone in her small galley kitchen at the back of the house.

Slamming the kitchen door she leant against it as she dialled Anna's number.

'Anna? I'm sorry. I am going to bring it back.'

On the altar in the darkness in the front room a small plug of sand, dislodged when she had put the bottle down, scattered its grains around the statuette of Isis. Beneath the plug a hairline crack in the ancient glass was exposed to the air for the first time. For a while nothing happened. Then an infinitesimal smear of moisture bloomed on the surface of the glass.

In the dark two wispy figures coalesced, smoke-like, hovering above the altar. For a moment they hung there unseen. When new headlights strobed the darkness from the road outside they had dissipated back into the shadows.

3

Anna was sitting at the table in her living room writing letters when Serena arrived the next morning. The two women gave one another a hug then Anna ushered Serena inside. Anna's grey-green hazel eyes were shadowed and tired, her complexion pale, her long dark hair tied back with a blue scarf.

'Anna, you have to make a decision about what to do with this.' Serena's voice was tense. 'I don't think we can keep it, and, I'm sorry, but it's begun to scare me.'

Anna showed her into her living room and watched as Serena put a small bubble-wrapped parcel down on the table. 'What's happened?'

Serena hesitated as they sat down, one on either side of the table, the parcel between them. 'I have seen shadows. I'm not sure. Nothing has happened that I can put my finger on. I've just become uncomfortable about having it in the house. I think –' She glanced up to hold Anna's gaze. 'I think the priests are still guarding it. I think I've seen them.'

'Here? In London?' Anna looked shocked.

The two women had been friends since their first meeting in Egypt on that fateful cruise. Together they had read Louisa Shelley's diary, together they had learned to fear the forces that surrounded the bottle which had once been Louisa Shelley's and which now, in spite of her attempts to rid herself of it, belonged, it seemed inexorably, to Anna.

'I know I offered to look after it when the Egyptian authorities returned it to you. I know I said I could cope. But I'm not sure I can.' Serena hesitated. 'We have to make a decision. Something has to be done. And done fast! I don't think we can destroy it. I think to do so would unleash untold terrors. That is what Lord Carstairs thought; didn't he? He knew more about it than anyone and he wanted to possess it so badly because he believed it contained incredible power. I don't know what kind of power, but I think we should assume that he was right. Listen, Anna, I've been thinking. I'm prepared to go back to Egypt, if that is what you would like. I'll take the bottle back to Philae and leave it there in the Temple of Isis. The goddess can have it back.'

'I can't ask you to do that, Serena.' Anna stared at her aghast. 'You've already done so much to help me.

Oh God, I wish I knew what to do for the best. It's too dangerous for you to take it back! It's too dangerous for us to keep it here.'

'Well, we have to do something.' There was another short silence. 'This is all my fault, Anna. If I had let you leave the bottle where you wanted to, in the temple, so much would have been different.' Serena hesitated again. 'What do you think should happen to it?'

Anna stood up. Walking over to the mantelpiece she picked up the small leather-covered diary which was sitting beside the clock. They both stared at it. 'I don't know. Oh God, Serena, I don't know how to make a decision like this. I have no idea what to do. I just want to get rid of it. I never want to see it again.'

'If we can't decide, perhaps we need another opinion,' Serena put in quietly. 'What do you think Toby would suggest?'

'He would say get rid of it. One way or another.'

Serena nodded. 'Why did you send him away? He helped you so much, Anna.'

'I know.' Anna sighed.

'And he is in love with you.'

'Yes.' Anna bit her lip. 'I think he is.' She took a deep breath. 'I got too close to the story, Serena. Too close to Louisa. She sacrificed everything to keep the bottle from falling into Lord Carstairs' clutches.'

'But Toby isn't Carstairs. For goodness' sake!'

'I know.'

She had thought about Toby often over the past weeks, wondering where he was, asking herself why she had sent him away. It wasn't his fault he was Roger Carstairs' descendant; it was just a supreme irony. And she was missing him more than she would have admitted even to herself.

'Why don't you ring him?' Serena was watching her face. 'Ask him to come over. See what he thinks we should do.'

'You're right.' Anna nodded. Suddenly more than anything else in the world, she wanted to talk to Toby.

'He's gone home, Anna.' Frances Hayward was enormously pleased to hear from her. She had not forgiven herself for scaring off the woman whom she had dared hope might be potential girlfriend material for her only son. 'To Scotland.'

The stunned silence which followed that revelation betrayed clearly the fact that Anna had not considered the possibility that he might not be in London, if she had even remembered at all that he did not live there permanently. 'I'll give you his phone number.' Frances wished heartily that she could produce her son with a click of the fingers. Suddenly the Scottish borders seemed very far away.

Serena had seen Anna's shoulders slump with dejection and waited as she scribbled a number and ended the call. She shook her head looking back at the small bottle, still in its bubble wrap, on the table. 'I'm sorry. I thought it could just sit in my front room indefinitely. But it was beginning to get to me. It really was.' She glanced up at Anna again with a rueful shrug. 'I probably imagined the priests.' She looked away quickly. 'But even so I'm scared. Ring him. I don't think we can make this decision alone. I think we need help.'

Toby was standing in front of his easel in the long low conservatory built on the back of the stone farmhouse he now called home. He had moved after his wife had died and it had taken him a long time to put past unhappinesses behind him and settle in. But slowly, between trips abroad, the routine of writing and painting and hacking his way through the jungle of what might one day be called a garden had brought about a feeling if not of permanence, then at least of ease with himself in this place.

The portrait was coming on even better than he had ever dared hope. At first it had seemed a crazy idea. The illustration in the guidebook was so small and fuzzy; the detail hard to make out. A reproduction of a long lost portrait from an obscure collection in America. Perhaps it was the empty canvas that had inspired him. It had been standing there for months, ignored in favour of watercolour paper. But suddenly, after his visit to Carstairs Castle, the idea had come to him out of nowhere. He had clamped the canvas in place and set to work conjuring those strong saturnine features into paint. He stood now staring at the eyes of his illustrious ancestor. Dark, compelling, powerful. He had no idea what colour they had been in real life. He couldn't tell from the illustration. In the event the eyes he had painted were, though he hadn't yet realised it, his own.

He looked up suddenly, the brush suspended in mid air. The light was going. Striding over to the windows he gazed out across the garden towards the hills. The sky was the colour of Welsh slate. Huge drops of icy rain were beginning to plop one by one onto the leaves of the magnolia grandiflora which added such presence to the house. He sighed. Time to stop work.

He stood back and surveyed the portrait again as he reached for a paint rag. The face was almost alarmingly life-like. He frowned. He was not over modest about his own capabilities but he was not a fool about them either. He could recognise something exceptional when he saw it and this was exceptional. His best piece of work ever.

Go on. You don't need more light.

The voice in his head was peremptory.

Toby gave a wry smile. He was not usually that dedicated either. Any excuse to stop; grab a cup of coffee, read the paper.

The portrait is nearly finished. Why delay?

Why indeed. He picked up his palette again.

The eyes were holding his own with so powerful a gaze that he found for a moment he couldn't look away. It was like staring into a mirror. He scowled uncomfortably, aware that behind him the rain was beginning to hit the windows with unusual violence, rattling against the glass, resounding on the roof panels above his head. The wind had begun to roar in the boughs of the Scots pine at the end of the garden, a sure sign that a vicious storm was building in the north. Toby stepped back away from the easel.

No. Go on. Finish it!

The conservatory was growing darker by the minute. Turning towards the table spread with paints and pencils he reached for the lamp and turned it on. It was not a light he could paint by but it flooded the studio area with a warm glow. Putting down palette and brush he sighed. No more painting today.

Now! Finish it now!

'Don't be silly. I can't finish it now. It's too dark.' To his surprise he had spoken out loud against the noise of the storm. Appalled, he stared round. The voice, the voice that was egging him on, had come from inside his own head. Or had it? He glanced at the picture. It was barely visible outside the range of the lamplight. He moved closer to it. It was finished, or as near as dammit. All it needed was one or two more touches of the brush. He reached for one and leaned closer, adding a small twinkle to the eyes, a quirk to the corner of the mouth. Then he stood back again, satisfied.

Yes! It's done.

He was going mad. The sudden conviction that the voice had come from the portrait was the craziest thing that he had come up with yet. Lord Carstairs, traveller, visionary, occultist, magician, speaking through a portrait painted by the man who had inherited his blood-line?

Oh God! Toby could feel the fear crawling up his back. What had he done?

He didn't react for several seconds when the phone rang, echoing round the conservatory, the bell an eerie counterpoint to the drumming of the rain. When at last he picked it up he was still standing facing the portrait as though afraid to take his eyes off it for a single second.

'Toby?' It was Anna. 'Toby, are you there?'

Her voice was warm, friendly, the hesitant suspicion with which she had sent him away, gone. 'Serena and

I want your advice. About the bottle. Serena has brought it back. It made her uncomfortable.' She didn't have to explain the reason why to Toby. He had been there on the cruise. He had seen what happened.

'Please, Toby. You couldn't possibly come back, could you?' Anna paused. 'We –' She hesitated. 'I need you.'

Behind Toby the rain drummed even more loudly. He was smiling. Part of him had been steeling itself against the fact that he might never see her again; that the warmth and affection – he didn't dare call it love – which had begun to burgeon between them had shrivelled and died before it had had a chance to develop. And now here she was asking, begging him to go back.

'Of course I'll come.' He turned back to the portrait with a broad grin. 'I'll come as soon as I can. Don't do anything until I get there.'

As he put down the phone he was aware of a strange overwhelming sense of triumph.

5

'He'll be here tomorrow.' Anna looked at Serena with a shrug.

'I bet he was glad to hear from you.' Serena smiled.

'I think he was. Yes.' Anna gave a deep sigh. 'But what do we do in the meantime?' She was staring at the small bubble-wrapped package on the table. I don't want it here overnight any more than you do. Not if I'm here on my own.'

Serena grimaced. 'You've got a garden, haven't you? Why don't we put it out there. A London garden in

March. That should cool the ardour of any passing ghosts!'

'And you could bless it. To keep it safe overnight.'

'Of course I will.'

'And stay here with me?'

Serena laughed out loud. 'I saw that coming.'

'Please. I have such faith in you, Serena. You know what to do. You've studied all these esoteric subjects. You know how to deal with the paranormal.'

'So why have I brought it back to you, Anna?' Serena spoke very softly. 'Because I was afraid I didn't know what to do any more.'

The two women sat for a moment staring at the package. Then Anna stood up again. 'Come on. I know where we'll put it. Just till Toby comes.'

Outside the back door the cold hit them. Pulling on coats as they went they walked out into the walled garden and stood on the path. Serena gazed round in delight. 'It's beautiful! Did you do all this?'

Anna nodded. 'My pride and joy. That's why I started taking photographs – to keep a record of it all. And that's why my ex let me keep the house.'

'Bloody hell! That's generous!'

'No. It was the price of guilt.' Anna led the way down the path through a rustic arch and into a small hidden area walled with budding clematis and roses. In the corner was a little pond. At its centre an ornate iron confection which in summer was obviously a fountain sat on a small island of sparkling granite. 'I'll put it there. Surrounded by water.' She was holding the parcel gingerly with her fingertips. Kneeling on the rim of the pond she leaned forward and dropped it onto

348

the island. 'There. Will that contain it, do you think?'

There was a pause as both women looked round. A stray breeze rustled through the weeping cherry near them, stirring the hanging branches into a moving curtain of delicate pink flowers. A cat's paw of ripples sped across the water's surface and was gone.

Serena nodded with more certainty than she felt. 'They say witches can't cross water. I'm not sure about Egyptian ghosts. Or djinn. It's worth a try.'

'Weave a spell for me. Just to make sure.'

Serena gave her deep throaty laugh. 'I can't imagine what you really think of my so-called powers, Anna. I don't do spells. I'm not a magician. I have studied Egyptian spirituality, that's all.'

'It's enough.' Anna caught her arm and squeezed it. 'Go on. It's only got to last the night.'

She stood and watched as Serena prayed and added her own fervent p.s. to the message then they turned and walked back towards the house. Neither woman looked back.

The storm struck about midnight. Anna lay in bed staring up at the ceiling listening to the rain, wondering if Serena in the room across the landing was doing the same. Switching on the lamp by her bed she sat up, shivering. She climbed out of bed and padded across to the window. Pushing back the curtain she peered out. The garden lay in total darkness; rain streamed down the window panes and spattered the paving of the terrace below. Climbing back into bed she lay back on her pillows and closed her eyes with a shiver. The lamp was still on; she made no move to turn it off.

*   *   *

349

On the stone island the bubble-wrapped parcel lay glistening in the darkness. All around it the sound of water filled the silence. The rain on the stone pathways; the rain on the leaves; the rain in the pond, splashing the lilies, dripping from the small fountain head, filling the basin higher and higher. Slowly the rain was seeping into the wrapping. Inside it another plug of ancient sand began to dissolve. The guardian priests leaned closer. In the darkness the wraithlike shapes were all but invisible. Their anger was growing stronger.

In her dream Anna could see the sun setting across the desert; she could smell the hot air wafting from vast distances; it was scented with *kyphi*; she could feel the heat of the desert beneath her feet. In her bedroom a drift of sand appeared on the carpet and blew gently to and fro as though shifted by the desert wind. Toby. She wanted Toby. In her dream she was searching for him, knowing only he could save her, knowing that somewhere he was waiting for her. Restlessly she turned over, her hair spreading across the pillow. Even in her sleep she was afraid.

6

Toby drove down overnight through the storm to his mother's house in Battersea, had a couple of hours' sleep, a quick shave, a cup of coffee and was at Anna's door by ten. She opened it so quickly he guessed she had been watching for him through the curtains.

They stood for a moment staring at one another,

awkwardly, then Toby stepped forward. He gave her a peck on the cheek. 'Hi. Good to see you again.' He longed to take her in his arms.

'And you.'

'I'm glad you phoned. It felt very far away from the action, up there in Scotland. I was wondering how you were and what was happening.'

'I've been trying to get back to normality.' She found she was staring into his eyes as though mesmerised by his gaze. She hadn't realised how much she had missed his presence near her. 'It seems I can't quite manage it without your advice.' She smiled at him and, reaching out, took his hand. 'It's so good to see you.' There was a moment's constrained silence and then it was over; they were both smiling and reaching out towards one another and Anna was blinking away tears of relief and happiness.

As Toby hugged her he was overwhelmed with contentment. 'Oh God, I've missed you so much. I was afraid –'

'So was I. I was a fool to let you go. I've thought about you every second.' She clung to him. 'Oh Toby, it's been so awful without you, and it's taken this to bring me to my senses. This terrible fear. I can't tell you how dreadful it was last night after Serena brought the bottle back.'

When they had convened over the coffee pot in the kitchen that morning, the two women had both been exhausted; both had woken in the night; they did not have to compare notes to know that they had both suffered from nightmares.

The bubble-wrapped parcel had been retrieved

cautiously and fearfully from its island and superficially dried with a dish cloth. It was once more on the table when Toby followed Anna inside. Serena was already sitting in front of it and when the other two joined her all three sat looking down at the bottle in its wrapping in silence for a few seconds.

Toby could feel a strange knot of excitement in his throat. He wanted to grab the small parcel. To make sure it was safe. He glanced up from one face to the other. 'So? What has been happening and what are the options so far?' His gaze returned to Anna and he smiled at her. But he could feel the fear in the room. It was like an electric tension in the air.

'Serena has offered to take it back to Egypt – to Philae – and leave it there buried in the sand, or perhaps to try throwing it in the Nile again.' Anna shivered. 'Or perhaps one of us could throw it into the Thames. That might work. It might just disappear for ever in the mud. Or, I had another idea this morning. I could take it to the British Museum. This is twenty-first-century London; the age of reason and science. Let the experts decide what should happen to it. Maybe a glass case is the best place for it. Maybe they would even open it and see what is inside –'

Her suggestion was greeted by a moment of total silence as they considered what she had said. Toby gazed down at the parcel thoughtfully; rationally. The opposition when it came seemed to explode from inside his own head.

No!

He put his hand to his forehead uncertainly.

Keep it, you fool!

Use it!

His lips hadn't moved; he was sure he hadn't spoken and yet both women were staring at him incredulously.

'Toby?' Anna's face was white.

His mouth had gone dry. For a moment he didn't dare speak. The voice, which had boomed out so suddenly, had come from him and yet for a moment he had not even been aware of what had happened. He put his hands out in front of him as though to reassure himself that the table was still there. 'Did you hear someone say to keep it?' he whispered.

Anna frowned uncertainly. It was Serena who nodded.

'So, who was it?'

Serena raised an eyebrow. 'It was a voice, Toby. A voice from the past.' Sometimes she wished she didn't hear these things so clearly. She had spent so long training, so much time reading, learning the old prayers which people mocked as pastiche, so many hours meditating to develop her skills, but sometimes, more and more often lately, she had found herself wishing she hadn't. Wishing she didn't hear, didn't see, things that most people never even suspected were there.

'Toby?' Anna reached out towards him and put her hand over his. 'Are you all right?' The room was suddenly very cold.

He nodded. He swallowed hard, clutching at her fingers. 'Sorry. I'm not sure where that came from. Put it down to the sleepless night. And take no notice. I think all your options are good ones. Have we decided the bottle shouldn't be destroyed?'

'Absolutely.' Serena frowned. 'According to the diary

the hieroglyphic inscription which came with it was clear about its power. If it was released something awful would happen. We don't know what, but surely it is not worth taking a risk. The people who made this bottle, the priests who put the tears of Isis inside it, have thought it worth fighting over for thousands of years. Lord Carstairs thought it was worth killing for. It isn't just a skin lotion!'

'No.' Toby frowned. He was watching the bottle as if any moment he expected it to move. Abruptly he stood up and strode over to the window, seeking fresh air. Lifting the curtain he peered out into the street, deep in thought, then, taking a breath, he swung back to face them. He had to get a grip on himself. 'Are we still being sucked in by all this? I know in Egypt it was hard not to be – we were part of it all there: Louisa's story; the ghosts; the curses. It all went with the landscape. But not here. Not now, not in London.'

'Last night,' Anna said softly, 'I dreamed about Egypt. I thought I could smell the incense again, feel the heat of the desert. But it was here in this house. There was sand drifting across my bedroom floor. I could see it all so clearly. And I knew, in my dream, that when you came back it would all be normal again.'

'Nothing is going to be normal as long as this thing is in the house!' Toby came and sat down again. He reached out towards the bottle then he withdrew his hand, suddenly afraid to touch it. He glanced up and met Serena's steady gaze. Had she too realised that the voice in his head had had nothing to do with the ghosts of ancient Egypt? It had rung with the patrician tones of Victorian England.

Which was crazy. He had known for only a matter of weeks that he was descended from Carstairs and yet he was allowing it to play on his mind so much – to influence him to such an extent – that he was vocalising the man's thoughts; a man who had been dead for at least a century! An image of the Carstairs Castle guide-book swam suddenly into his head. The paragraph which had caught his attention in the castle ruins, the paragraph which had, if he was honest, terrified him to such an extent that he couldn't get it out of his head: 'Maybe the ninth earl did not in fact die at all. As you look around the ruins of the castle which was once his home, be aware that the eyes which scrutinise you from the shadows may not be those of a ghost. They may be those of a man in hell.' He put his head in his hands for a moment then he looked up. He took a deep breath. 'So, Anna, which suggestion do you prefer?'

She looked suddenly defeated and unhappy again. Her expressive large eyes were blank. For a moment she didn't react to his question; when she did it was to shrug helplessly. 'I think on average I like Serena's idea. I think it should go back to Egypt, if she is willing to take it.'

No!

The voice in Toby's head exploded with rage once more.

Stupid, foolish women.
They don't understand. They will never understand!
Don't let them touch it!
Take it! Take it back to Scotland! We can use it there!
Pick it up!
I will tell you what to do with it!

'I must take it back to Scotland.'

Toby heard himself repeat the words, zombie-like.

'That is what I'll do. Take it to Scotland.'

'Scotland?' Anna seemed puzzled. 'Why Scotland?'

'Toby –' Serena reached out towards him and touched his hand. 'Are you all right?' She turned to Anna. 'Listen, he's exhausted. Why don't you go and put on some coffee.'

Anna hesitated. Then she nodded. Standing up she moved towards the kitchen. 'I don't see why it would help to take it to Scotland.'

In Scotland I can use it. Pick it up, man. Waste no more time with these women!

'Toby!' Serena's voice was filtering through into his consciousness. 'Toby, listen to me. Don't let him use you. Think about something else!' She had pushed back her chair and reaching out she took Toby's hands as they lay on the table. She grasped them tightly. 'Repeat after me. Come on! Repeat after me: Mary had a little lamb! Its fleece was white as snow!' Her voice was insistent, cutting through the other, drowning it out.

The temperature in the room had plummeted.

'Mary had a little lamb –' Somehow he managed to frame the words.

'Good. Again!'

'Mary had a little lamb –'

He was forcing the phrase out, his lips stiff, his mouth dry.

Anna had stopped in the kitchen doorway. She had turned and was watching, white faced. 'What is happening? What is the matter with him?' It was scarcely a whisper.

'He's being used, Anna. Someone is speaking through him.' Serena was still holding Toby's wrists, pinning them to the table.

'Who?' Her mouth had gone dry.

'I think it is Lord Carstairs.' Serena glanced up at her. 'Who else would be interested in what happened to the bottle?'

Anna gasped. 'No, that can't be true. It can't be. Why? How?'

The man her great-great grandmother's diaries had described as a nightmare, a visitor from hell, a tormented and tormenting soul, was speaking through the man whom she thought she loved. The man she had come to trust; the man who had saved her from her own personal demons, was now fighting some terrifying battle of his own.

Running to his side she put her hands on his shoulders. 'Toby? Speak to me! Please –' Her voice slid up in panic. 'Speak to me.'

He turned towards her and it was then she saw it. The face that was not his, the eyes that for a fraction of a second were not his eyes. 'Toby!' Her cry cut through his anguished struggle. The nursery rhyme stuttered into silence as he saw her expression. He read it all in her eyes. Wrenching his hands away from Serena's firm grip he stood up and, pushing Anna aside, he turned to look into the mirror which hung over the fireplace. The face he saw looking back at him was not his own. It was that of a stranger! A handsome, arrogant, dominating stranger! The stranger whose portrait he had painted with such skill and care in his conservatory in Scotland. With a cry of horror he stepped back,

357

his hands tearing at his features, desperate for reassurance that they still belonged to him, then he turned blindly and made for the door, racing up the staircase. He headed for the bathroom. His reaction in a crisis had always been to stick his head under a cold tap.

There was a mirror over the basin. For a moment he stood in front of it with his eyes shut, then, finally plucking up the courage, he opened them and leaned forward, scrutinising his face with care, searching fearfully for some sign of the intruder. The face of his ancestor. What he saw was reassuringly familiar again. Turning on the tap he scooped a handful of cold water over his face, then he studied his image carefully once more, noting the drops of water clinging to his sandy eyebrows, dripping from his nose, running down the planes of his cheeks. Same old face. Fortyish, handsome-ish, rugged-ish. Sandy hair. Nice smile. Or so he thought. Hoped. Up to now. With a sigh he reached for the towel. He was tired and he was stressed. He probably needed a caffeine fix, that was all. The illusion that there had been another man inside his head, the illusion that the eyes that had stared back at him from the mirror downstairs only moments before had not been his, had lasted only a few terrifying seconds, but that moment of vivid imagination had shaken him badly. He groaned.

'Toby?' A face appeared over his shoulder in the glass and he grimaced. The suddenness of its arrival had made his heart thud uncomfortably.

'Serena?' He turned towards the woman standing in the bathroom doorway.

'Are you all right?'

He nodded. 'I felt a bit odd, that's all. Is Anna OK?'

Serena shook her head. 'She's gone, Toby.'

'Gone?'

Looking down at the towel in his hands as though he didn't know it was there, he rammed it back onto the rail and took a step towards her. 'What do you mean gone?'

'After you ran out of the room she stood up, grabbed the bottle and fled out of the front door. She couldn't cope with Carstairs. I don't know where she is.'

Fool!

Find her!

Don't let her dispose of the bottle!

'Fight it, Toby!' Serena reached out to him.

He couldn't.

He laughed.

The stupid woman was standing in his way.

With a violent push he shoved past her and ran for the stairs. In seconds he was out in the street, looking for Anna.

7

Anna had grabbed her coat and shoulder bag. She was shaking with fear and horror when she stuffed the bottle, still in its bubble wrap, into the bottom of the bag.

'Anna!' Serena had followed her into the hallway. 'Where are you going?'

'I don't know. I just have to get away. You saw what happened! Why did I ask him to come? I should have known it would be a mistake. I'm such a fool.'

'Let me have it. I'll take it back to Egypt. Today. I'll go straight to the airport.'

'No.' Anna shook her head. 'No, Serena, I have to deal with this myself.'

She was gone, running down the steps and ducking across the street before Serena had time to move. At the end of the road she paused and looked back. Serena hadn't waited. She had stepped back inside and the door was closed.

Suddenly Toby had become the enemy; whatever happened, whatever she did, for Louisa's sake, she would not let him get his hands on the bottle.

The cab dropped her off in Great Russell Street. She stood for several minutes in the forecourt of the British Museum staring up at the huge pillared façade. She wasn't entirely sure why she had come. It was just one idea; one thing that she could do with the bottle. If she walked around the galleries, looked for other glass artefacts from Egypt, perhaps a solution would present itself. She had not reached any definite decision. She did not necessarily intend to show it to anyone. She didn't actually have to do anything at all. Slowly she walked towards the main entrance and began to climb the steps.

The Egyptian galleries were teeming with visitors; children; school parties. She stood, looking round. If someone came up to her. If someone said, can I see your Egyptian bottle, if someone said, may we have it, maybe she would have agreed. Handed it over. Sighed with relief that here it would be safe from Lord Carstairs. But no one knew. There were no Egyptologists patrolling the galleries. They were somewhere behind closed doors, out of sight, poring over ancient artefacts with scalpels and microscopes and computers or whatever it was they used. The attendants were not interested in her. She stopped in front of a mummy case and looked down at it. Somewhere at the end of the gallery a boy let out a shout and small feet pattered as a group of children out of control and bored ducked in and out of the exhibits. She didn't notice. She was gazing down at the painted wooden face with its wide staring eyes. All she had to do was speak to someone. Ask to see an expert. Hand it over. Get rid of it. Leave the decision to someone else.

Turning her back on the glass case she looked round wildly. There must be someone she could speak to.

And there was. She was walking towards Anna down the centre of the gallery. A woman in her fifties, her greying hair neatly styled, spectacles swinging from a chain around her neck, her matching blue skirt and sweater contrasting with the scarlet plastic clipboard file she was clasping to her chest. An identity tag and set of keys confirmed her as member of staff. An Egyptologist. An expert. She would know what to do.

Clutching her shoulder bag tightly, Anna stepped forward and stood facing her, waiting as the woman moved towards her, her eyes fixed on the floor as she walked, her expression distant, preoccupied, her thoughts clearly far away. As she approached Anna, who was standing squarely in her path, she diverted slightly to miss her. Anna stepped sideways in step with her and at last the woman looked up.

'I'm sorry.' Anna smiled uncertainly.

361

The woman gave an apologetic shrug and attempted to walk on. Only Anna's hand on her arm stayed her. She frowned.

'Please.' Anna's hand closed on her sleeve. 'Please. I must talk to you.'

The woman stepped back. She was clearly only dragging herself away from her own preoccupations with difficulty. She scanned Anna with pale blue intelligent eyes, obviously trying to place her, to put a name to the face.

'It's about a bottle. A small Egyptian bottle. I need help. It contains the tears of Isis. It's haunted. It's dangerous –' Anna was grappling with the flap of her bag.

The woman took another step away. She frowned warily. 'Egyptian you say?' She was clearly under the impression that Anna was slightly unhinged. 'I'm sorry. I'm not the person you should be talking to.'

'No! You will know about it. You will know what to do.' Anna's certainty that this woman would take charge, would remove all the responsibility from her, was absolute. 'Please, let me show you quickly. It will only take a minute. It's so important.'

'I'm sorry.' The woman was beginning to look agitated. 'I am truly sorry. I don't work in this department.' She was glancing round for an attendant.

Anna stopped dead, staring at her. 'But you must. I was so sure.'

Her stark shock and misery were so obvious that the woman almost felt sorry for her.

'You're not an Egyptologist?' Anna was incredulous.

'No.'

'But I was certain.'

The woman shrugged again. She was edging away steadily. 'Abyssinian bas-relief,' she said apologetically. 'I was just socialising in Ancient Egypt. May I suggest you go back to the central enquiry desk?' And turning away, she was gone.

Anna swallowed hard. The crowds seemed thicker than ever. More children streamed past her to surround the mummy cases, each with his or her small clipboard; more noise echoed beneath the high ceilings. She was beginning to feel disorientated and dizzy.

'Are you all right?' The man beside her had been watching her for several minutes.

She focused on him with difficulty. 'Yes, I'm fine.'

'Are you sure?' He frowned at her through the top of his bifocals. 'Shall I call the attendant?'

'No!' Suddenly she was hugging her bag more closely to her. 'No, I'm all right. I'm leaving.' Had his hand been hovering? Had he been after her purse? He might have stolen the bottle! Suddenly almost overwhelmed with a hysterical desire to laugh she dodged away, leaving him standing watching her in puzzled confusion as she pushed her way back towards the exit.

Outside the ice cold wind brought her to her senses. The wet London street, the hot-chestnut man selling his wares by the museum gates, the suitcases of tacky souvenirs, so many of them new-minted ancient Egyptian – it was all too much. Stepping out into the road she raised her hand to hail a black cab, climbed in and settled back into the seat with a sigh of relief.

It had just turned the corner into Bloomsbury Street taking her safely out of sight when Toby appeared, walking fast, heading across the forecourt and up the steps into the museum.

8

Toby was standing almost where Anna had encountered her Abyssinian specialist when Carstairs abandoned him with a curse. Sweating with fear Toby stared round. He had no idea how he had got to the museum. He remembered nothing of the journey; he had no idea how he had found his way to the ancient Egyptian galleries. All he knew was that he was shaking violently and he wanted to be out of there as soon as possible. Obviously Anna was not there, otherwise Carstairs would have stayed with him. Why else had Carstairs brought him here? He rubbed his face with the palms of his hands, trying to get a grip on himself. What was happening to him? What was he to do? Where should he go?

It took him a while to thread his way back to the main entrance. Once outside he too searched for a cab, quickly feeling better in the damp cold air.

In less than an hour he was sitting across the table from his mother, shaking his head. 'It was my imagination. It must have been. But the voice was so loud. So real. And Serena and Anna heard it too.' He rounded on her. 'Why in God's name did you have to tell me we were related to Lord Carstairs?'

'I thought that you would be interested, Toby.' Frances sighed. She was a tall handsome woman with wild grey hair. The resemblance between mother and

364

son was obvious. 'Personally, I thought it was rather glamorous. I never mentioned it in the past because you weren't interested in family stuff, but once Anna had showed me that diary –' She paused. 'I do see it is awkward for you as far as Anna is concerned. I am so sorry. He does seem to have given her ancestor a very hard time.'

Toby groaned. This whole sorry mess was all his mother's fault.

Here he was, independent, if not entirely back on an even keel after the succession of best-forgotten traumas that had rocked his life, and Frances had managed to bowl him a killer ball – in Anna's presence – which had slipped under his guard without his even seeing it coming. He smiled tiredly at the explosion of mixed metaphors and clichés running through his brain. He knew he was being unfair but just at the moment it was hard to be anything else.

And perhaps Anna was right. She usually was. She was a good judge of character. After all, she had not cared for him much at the beginning of their relationship. If it was a relationship. It certainly wouldn't be now. He sighed. She was so beautiful, Anna. So vulnerable. Her ex-husband had somehow isolated her, kept her prisoner in a glass palace so that when she finally broke free of the marriage she was like an exquisite butterfly, unspoiled, naïve. But not nearly so naïve as he was!

He groaned again. 'It is the understatement of the year to say he gave Louisa a hard time!' He scowled. 'And this morning, for a few minutes –' He shuddered. 'He seemed to be giving me one as well. Do you believe in possession? In life after death? Is it even remotely possible that what I've told you really happened, or have I gone stark staring mad?'

Frances raised an eyebrow. 'I don't think you're mad. I don't know what to think. I don't know what I believe. I confess I did go and see a medium once – hasn't everyone? And what she told me was convincing – not guesswork at all. But in this case, I think maybe you're right. I don't mean I think you are mad, but I think it may be a hefty dose of over-imagination. Egypt seems to have had a pretty powerful effect on you all.' She paused. Toby's anguish was obvious. She bit her lip. 'It's hardly surprising when you consider the potent mix of Louisa's diary, and the legends and myths and ghosts, and on top of all that the death of that poor young man you were travelling with. All that with the magic of the Nile itself.' Climbing to her feet she put a hand on his shoulder, then went over to switch on the kettle. 'I'm sure Anna is fine. She's no fool. She'll look after herself.' She paused. 'Maybe you shouldn't have come down to London. Perhaps after all it would do no harm for you two to be apart for a bit while you both take stock. What did Serena think about all this? Where did she go after Anna left?'

'Home, I presume.' He shrugged. 'I've no idea what she thinks, though I can guess. Oh God, I wish I knew where Anna went. And what she intended doing with that damn bottle.'

'You don't care what she does with the bottle, Toby,' his mother said firmly as she made a pot of tea. 'Do you?' She glanced up and scrutinised his face sharply.

He shook his head. 'Not a fig. No.'

'Good. Then leave it at that. She knows where we are. She knows she can always contact you here, and I am sure she will when she is ready.'

'But I frightened her –'

'No, from what you have told me you all frightened each other. Don't go convincing yourself you are a channel of some kind or a spirit medium or even, heaven forbid, the reincarnation of Lord Carstairs! You had never heard of the man a few weeks ago. You have not suddenly turned into a villainous Victorian occultist with swirling black moustaches and a silk lined cloak.'

'He didn't have moustaches!' Toby grimaced wryly.

'Well, whatever! From the diary he appears to have been extremely handsome.' She smacked the cup of tea down in front of him, spilling a little into the saucer. 'He did seem to have some strange habits, but then a lot of those Victorians were extremely odd. Keep focusing on the solid clergymen in our family, Toby. None of them kept pet cobras which obeyed their every whim like he did. Much more healthy to have a labrador! Don't let him become an obsession.' She frowned. 'Did you go to Carstairs Castle?'

'Of course I did. You gave me the guidebook, remember!' The guidebook which had spelt out the enigma of Lord Carstairs' final disappearance.

They stared at each other. Toby felt a strange chill strike between his shoulder blades. The hairs on his arms were standing on end. 'It happened there. He was waiting for someone to come along. A patsy. A descendant!'

'No. No, Toby. That's fantasy!'

'Is it?' He stared down at his cup without touching it. 'I've painted a portrait of him. That's how I know he didn't have moustaches. I know exactly what he looked like. It's the best thing I've ever painted.' He glanced up at her with a grimace. 'That's when it happened. Oh God, what have I done?'

'Toby. This is nonsense.'

'No. It isn't. It's happened.' He stood up. 'Christ! It's like being told I might have got cancer! There might be something hiding inside me. Lying in wait. Something I can't control.'

'Toby! Stop it!' Frances was terrified.

'What am I going to do?'

'You're going to pull yourself together. Look at all the problems you've come through before, Toby. You're going to remember that you are a strong, determined fighter. Roger Carstairs is dead. He has to be. Any other idea is a complete nonsense. I doubt if he is even a ghost. Even if he had some kind of weird pseudo consciousness it would be no more than that of a wraith; nothing you couldn't override. I doubt if he even has that. I don't think he exists at all in any form.' She was trying to convince herself. 'I don't think he's anything more than a waking nightmare. Your nightmare.' She stood up, agitated. 'For goodness' sake, Toby. Don't lose this chance. Anna trusts you –'

'Not any more she doesn't.' The interruption was very bitter.

'She will, Toby. She knows you. She knows you are strong. Look how you took care of her in Egypt. When she was so ill at the end you brought her home. You looked after her. You brought her here.'

368

'I did, didn't I?' He sighed. 'If only I could guess where she was. Where she would have gone.'

And suddenly he knew.

She would have gone back to her Aunt Phyllis in Suffolk. Of course. It was so obvious. It was Phyllis who had given her the bottle when she was a child, Phyllis who had given her the diary, Phyllis who had suggested she go to Egypt, and it was to Phyllis's house that they had driven – both of them, together – to talk about the horrors and adventures of the trip they had just shared. Phyllis was her mentor and her home was Anna's natural sanctuary. The first place she would head for.

9

Serena was once again sitting cross-legged in front of the small altar in her front room, deep in meditation. Reaching out into the darkness, questing back into Egypt, towards the scented misty distances, she was seeking answers; advice; help for her friends. She could see the still, deep waters of the Nile, she entered the temple, walking across the sand blown courtyard, she could smell the *kyphi*, hear the sound of distant music, see the shadowed shapes of temple attendants at the periphery of her vision.

Help me; help Anna. What should we do with the bottle containing thy tears?

Her prayer wove across the distances, drifting, seeking answer.

Shall I bring it back to Egypt?

She was there. She could see. She could hear,

but there was no answer. The bottle was not hers to take back. It had gone and she did not know where it was.

Pressing her palms together she lowered her head in acknowledgment of the goddess, crossed her arms across her breast, hands on shoulders in the time-old Egyptian pose, and opened her eyes. The room had grown dark while she was praying. Standing up with a groan at the stiffness in her knees she blew out the candles, extinguished her incense and went to switch on the light.

Outside the street was dark. It was still pouring with rain. Serena shivered and, drawing the curtains, bent to switch on the electric fire. The central heating had gone off for the night while she had been praying and now the house was chilly. Glancing at her watch she wondered if it was too late to ring Anna – to see if she had come home yet.

The phone rang on and on in Anna's empty house in Notting Hill. Glancing at the notepad beside her on the kitchen worktop Serena saw the second number she had jotted down. Toby's number – or rather Toby's mother's. Toby, who had pushed past her, his face a mask of anger, his head filled with the thoughts of an angry, vicious stranger. Serena hesitated, shivering.

Frances Hayward was awake. Unable to sleep, she was huddled in the kitchen over a cup of cocoa and the newspaper when Serena rang. 'I have no idea where he is. Where they are. Toby went off after her several hours ago; he thought she would have gone to see her great-aunt Phyllis. Do you know where she lives? I don't drive so I couldn't follow him and I don't know

Phyllis's phone number or address. I think it's Suffolk somewhere. I never thought to ask. He went off in such a hurry.' Frances was glad to have someone to talk to. 'I am so worried about them. This whole thing seems to have blown up into something so strange.'

'Lord Carstairs seems to have been a terrifying man.' At home in her kitchen Serena shook her head. 'Just the idea of him is frightening enough. If he has indeed established some sort of link with Toby then we should be worried. We had enough problems with the Egyptian bottle without Carstairs sticking his oar in.' Her voice was dry. 'We needed Toby on our side.'

'He is on your side. He loves Anna.'

'I know.' Serena's wistful smile was betrayed in her voice. 'But unfortunately Carstairs doesn't. He has no reason to. And he is strong. I don't know if Toby could fight him. That first time, it took him by surprise. It took us all by surprise. I don't know how Toby would cope if Carstairs tried to speak through him again.'

'So you do believe all this?' Frances sighed. 'I was so hoping it was Toby's imagination.'

'It's not his imagination, Mrs Hayward. I'm afraid Lord Carstairs is all too real. In his way.' Serena shook her head.

There was a short pause. 'He said you told him how to drown Carstairs out,' Frances said hopefully.

'But will he do it?' Serena shivered. She was thinking that it was Carstairs, not Toby, who had pushed her out of his way.

Frances was silent for a moment. When she spoke again her voice was full of doubt. 'I'm sure he will do his best, Serena. He loves Anna. He really does. He

371

would never knowingly do anything to put her in danger. He would do anything to protect her.'

'If he can.' Serena sighed. 'If you hear from them, will you tell me? I'll give you my mobile number. Please, call me anytime. I mean it.'

There was nothing more she could do. Turning out the lights she climbed up to her bedroom and laid the mobile on her bedside table. Downstairs the smell of incense from her ceremony began to dissipate. Soon it would be gone.

Frances walked slowly through her house deep in thought. If she could find out Phyllis's address she could ask Serena to go there. Serena had sounded sensible and caring; she was knowledgeable and she had somehow managed to cut through Toby's torment, teaching him her nursery rhyme mantra.

Out of the blue the name came back to her.

Lavenham.

That was it. And surely it wasn't a big place? She reached for the phone.

Phyllis Shelley's number was listed.

Serena wasn't asleep. She answered the phone on the second ring; she was in the car and on the road within half an hour.

10

Leaving London just as the rush hour was starting, it had taken Toby three hours to drive to Lavenham. Pulling up his car in the darkness of Phyllis's deserted street in the picture-book small town he sat for a moment, his head resting on his hands on the rim of the steering wheel. Faint light showed through the tightly closed curtains of Phyllis's oak-beamed cottage. Now he was there he was wondering why he had come. Supposing Anna wasn't there? What would he say to the old lady? And if she was there, what was he going to do then? What was Lord Carstairs going to do? He shuddered. Suddenly he felt very sick.

A twitching curtain indicated Phyllis Shelley had heard the car draw up outside. With a deep sigh he reached down to release his seat belt and climbed out.

She showed him into her sitting room where an apple log fire smouldered reassuringly in the hearth, supervised by a large sleepy cat. It was apparent at once that Anna was not there. A quick phone call established she was not at home either – or if she was, she was not answering her phone.

Phyllis, smartly dressed in a blue cardigan and matching skirt, her grey wiry hair neatly cropped, looked far less than her eighty-eight years. After one glance at Toby's pale face and drawn expression, she wouldn't let him explain the reason for his visit until he had consumed a glass of whisky, some tomato soup and a cheese sandwich in the chair beside the fire. Only then was he allowed to speak, but by then he was fairly certain her calm scrutiny had winkled out most of his innermost secrets without him having had to utter a word. She asked him nevertheless. 'So, what has gone wrong, Toby?' She had a quiet voice with a thread of steel in it. 'You love each other. Can you not work things out between you?'

He gazed down at the glowing ashes. 'Not in this case.' He bit his lip ruefully. 'It appears Lord Carstairs has come between us.'

She raised a haughty eyebrow. 'And how, pray, has he managed to do that?'

He gave a wry smile. 'Just how unfair do you think it is possible for fate to be? It appears that I am his great-great grandson!'

He looked up in time to see a twitch of humour for a fleeting second in her eyes. 'That doesn't sound like fate, Toby. That is The Fates. Did you never believe in them?'

He shook his head morosely. 'You don't even seem surprised!'

She smiled – openly this time. 'I won't spout the cliché about how when you reach my age you cease to be surprised about anything. It does however happen to be true. There is obviously some deeper destiny working its way out here.' She paused thoughtfully. 'What does surprise me is that Anna should have let it come between you.'

'I told you why. It's not destiny, Phyllis. It's Carstairs.' He told her what had happened.

It was several minutes before she said any more. Seeing her so deep in thought he was content to sit back in his chair staring at the flames, somehow purged of his fear by having told her. His moment of peace was short-lived.

'How strong are you, Toby?'

He shrugged. 'It depends.'

'Let's imagine the worst. Suppose Lord Carstairs is an unquiet spirit of some sort. Maybe he is a common or garden ghost.' She gave a small snort of derision. 'Or maybe he sold his soul to the devil or maybe he is one of the undead.' She paused thoughtfully with a sideways glance at her guest. 'Supposing he is still determined to own the ampulla. Supposing he believes he can use it for some sinister purpose. Supposing the fact that you are his great-great grandson has somehow allowed him to make a connection with you so that he thinks he can use you in some way.'

'Use me as a medium?' It was what his mother had implied. Toby shuddered. Discussing the subject so dispassionately somehow made the nightmare worse.

Phyllis nodded uncertainly. 'Something of the sort.' She hesitated, then went on, feeling her way with care as she spoke. 'It seems to me that in this case he would be dependent on you as the host acting for him. He would need your mouth to speak; he would need your hands to gather in his precious ampulla and he would need you to use it for whatever purpose he has in mind.'

'So, if I refuse to comply he would be helpless.' Toby nodded, slightly comforted.

'Exactly.'

'But –?' He was watching her face.

'There are no buts, Toby, if you are strong.' She gave a gentle smile. 'And this has only happened once, has it not? You don't know that you will ever hear of or from him again; you don't know that what happened was any more than a momentary hallucination. But I don't think we should underestimate him.' She paused, then went on thoughtfully. 'And I don't think that now is perhaps the right moment for you and Anna to test your resolve.'

'That's what my mother said.'

'Well, she's right. Are you sure Anna is on her way here?'

He shook his head. 'I thought this the most likely place she would come.' He stood up. 'I couldn't think of anywhere else. But I know so little about her, Phyllis. I don't know who her friends are; her relations. I am in so many ways still a stranger, and –' He hesitated. 'I am not sure how long I can stand the suspense of all this. It's like having a time bomb inside me!'

'He's not inside you, Toby! Don't imagine that.' She looked very stern. 'It is your body. Your brain. He cannot use them unless you let him.'

'What if I can't help it?' He was staring down at the fire.

'That sounds very defeatist. You can't afford to be weak. Not for an instant.'

'It would be easier if I knew when he was going to strike.'

'If he is going to strike.' She sighed. 'If anything else happens, Toby, it is because he still wants the bottle. My guess is he would wait until it is nearby. He would wait for Anna. And you're right. I think she might come here.'

'Then I must go.' Turning to face her, he sighed. 'I can't risk being here when she arrives.'

'You'll have to face her one day. I have a feeling Carstairs could wait longer than you would be able to.'

'You're not suggesting I stay? Face him out?'

'I'm not sure what I'm suggesting, my dear.' She looked round helplessly. 'I'm not an expert in all this. I don't know what we should do. Perhaps we should ask your friend, Serena. She seems to have been the only one with any idea of how to deal with this situation.' She raised a quizzical eyebrow. 'It is fairly specialised.'

In spite of himself Toby chuckled. 'You can say that again. As was her solution. A recitation of "Mary had a little lamb"!'

'Simple but effective,' Phyllis replied drily. 'You are lucky there was someone there who took what happened seriously. I suspect a great many people would have laughed it all off anyway and said you were all hallucinating!'

'Those people were not with us in Egypt!' Toby commented grimly. 'You know, I would almost be relieved to think I was suffering from schizophrenia – under the circumstances it would be preferable to the other possibility.' He shuddered.

'You don't mean that, my dear.' She shook her head. 'Now, may I suggest that you stay the night. It's far too late to drive back to London and I doubt if Anna will come tonight. Then tomorrow we will try and establish where she is and what if anything she has done with her scent bottle. And then, and only then, can we decide what you should do next.'

11

Toby!

Toby, wake up you fool. She is here!

The figure standing beside Toby's bed was tall, insubstantial in the near darkness of the room. Outside the half drawn curtains the sky was bright with stars. It was very cold. Toby had turned off the electric fire before he climbed into the high old-fashioned bed and pulled the eiderdown up over his head, and now, in the warm cocoon of mattress and blankets and sheets he turned over with a groan and settled more deeply into sleep.

Toby! The bottle contains power beyond your wildest dreams. With the help of the goddess Isis you could achieve anything, be anyone. You could rule the world. Listen carefully, Toby. I will tell you what you need to do.

Outside the window a car had driven up. Briefly the lights reflected on the wall by the door, then they were gone. As the clouds had cleared the temperature had started dropping. Soon there would be ice. The engine fell silent; the lights were switched off. A door opened and slammed and footsteps echoed up the path beneath his window. He did not hear them; nor the rattle of the knocker on the oak panel; he was not aware of the light going on, on the landing outside his bedroom, or of Phyllis, wrapped in a red chenille dressing gown, tiptoeing lightly down the stairs, opening the door, drawing Anna inside and with a glance up towards his bedroom door, leading her into the sitting room. There, with new logs thrown onto the glowing embers the two women sat down to talk quietly and urgently by the light of one small lamp.

'I saw Toby's car.' Anna shook her head. 'I nearly didn't come in. But I didn't know what else to do. Where to go. I sat in a coffee place for ages, then I drove round for hours before I decided to come here. What did he say? Where is he?'

'He's upstairs. Asleep. He explained what happened, Anna.'

'What am I to do?'

'Have you still got it?'

Anna nodded, glancing towards the shoulder bag she had thrown down on the sofa next to her.

In his dream Toby watched her reach over and fumble in the bag, produce the small bubble-wrapped parcel and hold it in her hand, staring down at it.

'I am afraid to keep it; afraid to destroy it. Supposing that unleashes something? Someone? I need to hide it, Phyl. Hide it somewhere Toby and Carstairs can't find it.'

The sleeping Toby gave a grim smile. How stupid did she think he was? He was watching her. He would know what she did with it. He knew her every thought. And every thought of the guardian priests who hovered so anxiously over her. He frowned. In his sleep he paused to wonder why the priests were so anxious. So angry. They were afraid.

Phyllis was thinking deeply. 'I don't believe we should hide it in the house. In fact, maybe you shouldn't hide it at all. I will. It might be better if you didn't know where it was.'

'Phyl, I don't want you to put yourself in danger.'

'Danger!' The old woman was indignant. She ran her fingers through her hair, leaving it standing on end. 'I gave it to you in the first place. I gave you the diary. I sent you to Egypt. Anna, my dear, I got you into all of this and it's up to me to get you out.' She held out her hand. 'Give it to me.'

Anna handed over the bottle with a shiver. For a

moment both women stared round the room, sensing the drifting cold. They saw nothing.

'Right. Now I want you to go up to your usual bedroom. I have put Toby in the green room at the top of the stairs. Get a good night's sleep and in the morning it will all be taken care of.'

No. Don't let her do it.

You must get it now.

That woman has inner strength. She can defy us. Anna is weak because she loves you. A cynical laugh. *She can't quite bring herself to think you would hurt her. More fool her. You would hurt her, wouldn't you, Toby? You would do anything I ask you. You will get up and go downstairs now, Toby. You will take that bottle from the women and you will give it to me!*

Under the eiderdown Toby was growing more and more restless. Twisting his head from side to side he threw off the covers and turning he thumped the pillow with his fist.

Get up, Toby!

The figure moved closer, coming to stand immediately beside the bed. With another groan Toby obeyed, his eyes still closed.

That's right. Now move to the door and open it. Come downstairs. Now.

As the door into the sitting room opened Anna and Phyllis looked up startled. Toby was standing there, dressed in the ancient striped pyjamas which Phyllis had produced from the airing cupboard, his hair on end, his feet bare. His eyes were tightly closed. He stepped into the room and held out his hand.

I need that bottle.

Phyllis put it behind her back.

'Toby?' Anna was staring at him. 'Toby, wake up! Do you hear me, wake up!'

Toby had stopped just inside the doorway. For a moment he remained unmoving then slowly he opened his eyes.

'Anna?' He stared at her in astonishment. 'When did you get here? I must have fallen asleep. What time is it?'

'It's late.'

'It must be.' He moved towards the fire, rubbing his face slowly with his hands. 'I'm sorry. I'm still half asleep. I can't think clearly. Thank God you're here. I was so worried about you.' He put out a hand towards her. 'I had such a terrible dream.' He hesitated. He couldn't bear to be standing so close to her and not touch her. Gently he put his finger on her shoulder, then cautiously, carefully, he drew her into his arms.

For a moment she resisted, stiff against his embrace, then she relaxed. 'Toby. Are you all right? I've been so frightened.' She was nestling against him.

'There's no need, my love. No need at all. You're safe now. Quite safe.'

All you need to do is give me the bottle. His grip tightened slightly. *Where is it?*

'Toby?' Anna pulled away from him sharply. 'Toby? What did you say?'

Toby frowned. Had he spoken out loud? Please God it wasn't happening again. 'I'm sorry. I didn't mean to say that. I don't care where the bottle is –' He ran his hand across his forehead, pushing back his hair. He

381

stared round frantically. 'I love you, Anna. I would never try and take it unless you let me.' He shook his head. 'It's just that I can't seem to see straight.' He shut his eyes again as a twinge of pain hit him.

You will give me the bottle.

'Phyllis?' Anna was terrified. 'It's happening again. That is not his voice. His lips didn't move.'

'I can see.' Phyllis backed towards the fire.

'Oh God, it's not Toby. Something has happened to him. He's not there. Carstairs has taken him over.' Anna's voice cracked into a sob. 'Toby, can you hear me? Toby, please. Fight him!'

'Anna, my dear. Move away.' Phyllis kept her own voice calm with an effort. 'Have you got your car keys?'

Anna nodded. 'They are there, in my coat pocket.'

'Get them. Get ready to run.'

Toby had moved a couple of steps closer to Phyllis. He seemed to be working on automatic pilot. His face was blank.

Ah, Miss Shelley. So it is you who has it. Give it to me. I don't want to hurt you. This is nothing to do with you. The bottle is mine by right.

Behind him Anna had pulled on her coat. She drew the keys out of her pocket with a shaking hand.

'You're going to have to take it off me, Toby. Or should I address you as my lord?' Phyllis moved a step closer to the fire. She was almost standing in the hearth. 'It is my lord, isn't it? Toby is not there. You have pushed Toby aside. You have walked in and taken his body because you are too weak to achieve anything on your own!'

You don't think it an achievement to take his body?

The voice was mildly amused.

Behind her back Phyllis transferred the small parcel to her right hand. Moving so fast Anna almost failed to see what was happening, the old woman tossed it swiftly towards her, at the same time diving towards the poker which had been lying on the hearth.

Anna did not wait to see what happened. She was into the hall in a moment, bottle in hand, pulling open the front door and diving towards her car. With a frantically revving engine and a shriek of tyres the car sped away from the hedge and disappeared up the road.

Behind her Phyllis was staring at the body of the man lying at her feet, blood pouring down his face into the carpet.

12

Where do I go?

Changing gear Anna pulled onto the main road.

What shall I do?

She gritted her teeth, desperately trying to steady her breathing.

Drive carefully. The roads are icy. Don't be a fool. Calm down. He can't reach you here.

The bottle was lying in the foot well on the passenger side where she had thrown it. She couldn't see it in the dark, but she could hear the bubble wrap rustling as the car swung round the corners.

What had happened to Phyl? Was she all right? What would he have done when he realised he had been

383

thwarted? Oh please God, take care of her. Don't let him hurt her.

She drove on. She didn't know where she was going, all she knew was that she had to get rid of the bottle. Once and for all. Water. She had to find some water and throw the bottle into it. That would be the best thing to do. See it sink without trace. Deep water. Bottomless water which would suck it down for ever. Weight it down with something. Make sure it could never float to the surface again.

Her brain was working frantically as she threw the car down the narrow winding roads. She needed to go east, towards the sea. Which way? Her mind had gone blank suddenly. All she could think was:

Bring it back. Bring it back. Bring it back now!

The voice in her head was not hers.

'No!'

She clamped her hands on the wheel until her knuckles went white. She was speaking out loud now. 'Never! You can't have it! Toby, fight him. Please fight him. Oh Toby!' She shook her head angrily as her eyes filled with tears. How could this be happening? She had loved Toby, she realised it now. Really loved him. She had thought he was the one who would make her happy at last. And Carstairs, bloody, vicious, awful, DEAD, Lord Carstairs was taking him away from her.

But Toby wasn't here. That voice had been in her own head. Not Toby's. Oh dear God, what was she going to do?

She was heading towards the A14 now and almost without realising she had done it she swung the car onto the eastbound carriageway, heading towards the

384

coast. She put her foot flat to the floor and felt the car gather speed alarmingly as she tried to put distance between herself and the source of the mocking voice in her head. Before her the road stretched away empty, leading towards the sea.

In the back seat a shadowy form had begun to materialise, invisible against the black upholstery. She didn't hear the quiet chuckle above the sound of the screaming engine.

13

'Are you OK?' Phyllis bent anxiously over Toby's recumbent form. He groaned, somehow forcing his eyes open to see the old woman in the red dressing gown standing over him, the poker still in her hand.

'What happened?' He put his hand to his forehead and brought it away, sticky with blood.

'I'm afraid I hit you with the poker. Or at least, I didn't hit *you*, I hit Lord Carstairs.'

Toby blinked. Somehow he forced himself into a sitting position. 'How did I get downstairs?'

'You walked, my dear.' Phyllis lowered the poker, satisfied that the rightful owner was once more in charge of his body. 'You were sleep walking. Your eyes were closed. You woke up but then somehow he seemed to overwhelm you again. I had to hit you. You were trying to get the bottle from Anna.'

'Anna?' He looked round. 'Oh God! I remember now. Did I hurt her? Where is she?'

'She's gone. She's all right, but if I had any doubts

before about what you said had happened to you, I have none now. It was awful. Frightening. It was not you I hit.' She shook her head ruefully. 'But even so, I might have killed you. I don't know my own strength. I'm so sorry.'

'So Anna got away?'

She nodded. 'And I don't know where she's gone so there is no point in asking me.' She frowned. 'Do you think I ought to call the doctor. Perhaps you need a CT scan or something.'

He laughed – then winced. 'I doubt that. I've got a tough head. I might need a psychiatrist, but not a doctor.' Levering himself onto his feet he groped for a chair. 'Did I threaten her? I can't believe this is happening to me. I love her.'

'So do I, Toby.' She shook her head sadly. 'And I don't know what to do. She's safe for the moment. That's the main thing.'

'I hope to God she gets rid of that damn bottle. Permanently.'

'She's afraid to. She's afraid that will unleash some awful curse upon the world.'

'I'm far more afraid that it will release some awful curse upon her. Oh, God! I wish I could speak to her.' He paused. 'Mobile! Has she got a mobile?'

Phyllis shrugged. 'I have no idea.'

'How stupid! I should have her number. I should have asked her. Who would know?'

She shook her head.

'There must be someone! Her father? She told me about her father.'

'With whom she doesn't get on. No, Toby, let it be.

Anna is safe now, wherever she is. For the time being it is better if she is as far away from you as possible.'

The Orwell Bridge. She was heading towards the Orwell Bridge, that soaring arc of white concrete flying high above the river which divided Essex from Suffolk. Anna smiled. At last, as her fear abated, a plan was taking shape in her mind. The river was deep in the centre; it must be. Deep, and its bed must be mud. Thick black mud which would contain whatever was in the bottle absolutely and completely for ever. It was there she would throw it to its final resting place.

The decision made, she pushed the car harder, concentrating on the road rolling out in front of her, unaware of the restless anger building in the seat behind.

A woman's body. At first the idea had been exciting; titillating even. A curiosity. Something to be enjoyed; played with. But now he was not so sure. She was beautiful – in some ways not unlike her great-great grandmother, the woman who had so teased and angered and enticed him. But she had a different energy. She was stronger; isolated there inside her head. The love she had harboured for Toby had been reined in, fenced off, and in the fencing, he was not sure that there were any gaps so that he could slip inside her head as he had done so easily with his own great-great grandson. He had spent too long in the dark. His strength and his focus had waned. But that would change. His frustration was growing, and with it his substance.

On the back seat of the car the shadows deepened.

387

They were taking on a shape. If Anna glanced in the mirror she would see it now. She didn't. Her eyes were fixed on the empty road. Several lorries hurtled by on the opposite carriageway, heading for the Midlands. She didn't see them. She was feeling sleepy. The exhaustion of the last days; the wakeful nights and nightmares, the lack of sleep, were catching up with her.

Carstairs was concentrating on Anna's thoughts. He sensed her tiredness; it made her vulnerable. Weak. Soon she would be defenceless. He was only marginally aware that they were travelling at some speed; that he was seated in some sort of horseless carriage which was travelling faster than he would have believed possible. It was not until her eyelids drooped and the car began to veer across the empty road that he realised the danger.

At the last moment, her eyes flew open and her hands wrenched the wheel straight as a vicious shot of adrenaline knifed through her stomach. Carstairs felt the fear; he saw the danger through her eyes. He heard the small parcel roll around in the front of the car. He smiled.

'Shit!' Anna banged the steering wheel with the flat of her hand. 'Be careful, you idiot!' She was talking to herself again. Clutching the wheel tightly she concentrated on the road and now at last she glanced up into the driving mirror. The back of the car was in darkness, her passenger only shadows. She noticed nothing unusual as she drove on.

Ahead she saw a lay-by signposted. She swung the wheel and pulled in. Drawing to a halt she locked the doors and sat with her head back against the head rest, breathing deeply. She was shaking all over. A short nap.

She must have a short nap. She couldn't keep her eyes open.

On the floor beside her a tiny drop of moisture seeped slowly through the bubble wrap, spread across the shiny bumpy plastic and was absorbed by the carpet of the car. Inside the wrapping, in the warm darkness, the crack in the glass bloomed with another thin line of liquid. The life force of the ages was beginning to run out. The priests, hovering over the lay-by, were losing their power.

Anna's eyes closed. This time she didn't open them again. She felt safe now that she had stopped. Her breathing slowed. Behind her the shadowy figure leaned forward. Anna didn't feel the light brush of his finger through her hair.

As the level of her sleep deepened she began to dream. Her bedroom was dark, her nightgown light as a feather, her feet bare. She was standing at the window, looking out into her small back garden. It was lit by brilliant moonlight and in the distance she could see the arched glitter of her small fountain, playing quietly into the pond, where bright concentric ripples spread out into the darkness at its rim. On the lawn she could see two wispy figures, one dressed in shadowed white, one in the skin of an animal. Hatsek and Anhotep. The priests of Sekhmet and of Isis, the would-be guardians of the little bottle, the men who had followed it through aeons of time. Their power was waning. They could feel it and they were angry. They turned as though sensing her watching them and she felt the strength of their impotent fury as a knife blade in her heart. With a gasp she staggered backwards, away from the window.

Hands gripped her shoulders. *Don't be afraid. They can't hurt you. Not any more.*

She gave a small cry of surprise and fear as the hands tightened, stopping her from turning round to face him. She felt warm breath on the nape of her neck. *You are safe here, my dear. Quite safe. I won't let them come near you.*

'How can you stop them?' She could feel him behind her. He was taller than her and very strong. Now she could feel warm lips on her neck. She tried to struggle free but she couldn't move.

Surely you would rather speak to me than with them.

His hands slid forward to her breasts, caressing her, feeling for the buttons on the front of the nightgown, one by one slipping them free of their embroidered loops. The garment, feather-light silk, was slipping off her shoulders and she could do nothing to stop it.

'Please. Who are you?'

There was a quiet laugh. *Don't you know?*

He was turning her to face him and she found herself looking up into his eyes. The dark, handsome face looking down into hers was that of a stranger. He bent to press his lips against hers and she felt desire knife through her body. Behind her in the garden the moon vanished behind a curtain of cloud. The two wispy figures on the lawn faded.

She was behaving like a harlot, unable to control herself, pressing her body against his, feeling every line of muscle in his tall frame, hungrily reaching for his lips as his hands roamed her hot eager body . . .

In the distance a loaded container lorry heading for the coast thundered towards her. As it raced past the lay-by her car shook and rocked. Anna awoke with a start in time to see the tail lights retreating into the distance. She blinked hard, pushing herself up in the seat. The buttons of her blouse were undone, her skin was on fire. It was almost as if . . .

She groped for the dream but it was gone.

With a yawn she stretched. Then she reached for the ignition. She didn't hear the quiet exultant laugh from the back seat.

14

Passing Ipswich Anna drove on, ahead of her the Orwell Bridge and beyond it the road to Felixstowe. When she drew up at last at the side of the road it was on the apex of the bridge. Exhausted, she sat for a moment, staring out of the windscreen at the empty road ahead. From the car she couldn't see the river, only the expanse of road stretching away ahead; the central reservation; the parapets on either side. They didn't look high. She should be able to see over. Taking a deep breath she bent and fumbled for the parcel. It had rolled under the passenger seat and for a moment she couldn't find it. Swearing under her breath, she leant across the handbrake and the gear lever, her fingers groping frantically in the darkness, encountering nothing more than empty space beneath the seat.

Behind her, the shadow that was Lord Carstairs stirred. She did not notice.

'Damn! Where is it?' She leaned further across the seat. And then her fingers closed around the bubble wrap. It rustled under her touch and for a fraction of a second she drew back. Had Carstairs somehow conjured a snake to guard the bottle as he had on their boat on the Nile? Was it possible that now, here on the Orwell Bridge, there was a cobra, coiled around the bottle to prevent her from throwing it into the water? There was no snake. Almost as she thought it her fingers encountered the small parcel again. It was wedged in the far corner beneath some integral part of the seat. Gently she waggled it free, her fingers slipping on the wet paper, and then she had it. She didn't pause to wonder why it was damp; wonder where those few drops of moisture had come from. She didn't hear the anguished wailing from the shadows around her in the dark above the car or suspect that the guardian priests were nearing the end of their strength. Sitting up triumphantly she opened the car door and stepped out into the road. An icy wind whipped past her as she walked around the front of the car, stepped over the low metal traffic barrier and leaned against the parapet, looking down. The water was a long way below, just visible in the darkness.

Don't do it.

The voice at her elbow made her cry out in fear.

Don't dare to commit such sacrilege. You will take this bottle back to Scotland. To my house. There you and I will make use of it as I planned all along.

Anna stared round, terrified. The wind was tearing at her hair, her coat, bringing tears to her eyes. There was no one there. No one in sight. A lorry rattled past in the fast lane, with horn blaring, then she was alone again on the deserted bridge. The voice had not come from inside her head. It was real. External. Coming from the dark recesses of the night.

'Who is it? What do you want with me?' But of course she knew. Clutching the bottle she peered round desperately, trying to see him. 'Where are you? You bastard! How did you get here?' Terrified she turned to face the road. There were no cars or lorries in sight, no pedestrians. The road was completely empty again.

My great-great grandson proved weak and ineffectual. The voice echoed in her head. She couldn't see where it was coming from. *He wanted to protect you. How stupidly gallant of him, and how convenient that you should have given him the slip so effectively! And,* there was a short pause, *that we should get on so well.*

How could he be speaking to her, close to her, in her ear, and yet she couldn't see him? She turned round again, her eyes darting from left to right, frantically trying to see shadows where there were none, trying to see a figure where there was no one to see. Below the bridge the black was deeper, more opaque above the clear reflective darkness of the river. The night was suddenly very silent. 'Go away!' Her voice came out as a broken whisper. 'Go away, leave me alone.'

Scotland, Miss Shelley! If you please.

'Where are you? I can't see you.'

You don't need to see me.

'I do. I am not getting into the car with a passenger I can't see.'

There was a quiet laugh, nothing but a whisper in the silence. *You brought me here, Miss Shelley.*

'If I did, it was without knowing it.' Dear God, he had been there in the car behind her as she drove. As she stopped in the lay-by. As she dreamed. She gave a small cry of horror. 'I may have brought you here, but I am not taking you any further. This is where it stops. This is where everything stops.' She raised the bottle in her hand, moving towards the parapet. 'This ends now.'

But someone had grabbed her wrist, wrestling with her, holding her arm with iron fingers. She could feel them grinding her bones, she could feel him next to her, smell the sudden waxy perfume of the pomade he wore in his hair, she could feel the enormous strength of the man overwhelming her.

But she couldn't see him. There was no one there. She was alone on the bridge in the dark wrestling with an invisible figure. The man from her dream. He was the man in her dream. It was all coming back to her now. The smell of his pomade was filling her nostrils. It had been Lord Carstairs tearing off her nightdress, caressing her breasts. His breath on her neck. His whisper in her ear. Her face grew hot. She had wanted him so badly. She wanted him now.

Desperately she tried to wrench herself free. But he was dragging her away from the edge. Somehow he was pulling her back towards the car. 'You bastard!' she sobbed, struggling violently. 'Let me go. This isn't happening. How can it be. Let me go!'

He was stronger than she was by a long way. She couldn't fight him. Somehow he thrust her back through the open door of the car and it closed behind her with a slam.

Scotland! The voice was in the car with her. She sat behind the wheel panting. Tears were running down her face. Throwing the bottle down on the seat beside her she stared round the car, turning to scan the back seat. It was empty.

'Where are you?'

There was no answer.

'Are you there?' She was trembling; her own voice was a whisper.

Silence.

Was he still there? She didn't know. She could hear nothing. Smell nothing. The car was empty. Still.

'Right.' She put her shaking hand to the ignition key. 'Well, in case you hadn't realised, I am not a bloody taxi! I am not taking you to Scotland.' But where was she going to take him? She didn't know.

Pulling away from the kerb she was startled by the sudden blast of a car horn behind her. The first car she had seen in ages tore past in the fast lane, leaving her gasping with shock. She had stamped on the brakes and for a moment waited, her eyes closed, trying to pull herself together, until at last she managed to look up and slowly engage gear once more.

Her mind was whirling, trying to think, trying to be calm, trying to decide what to do.

I am still here, Miss Shelley!

She jumped. He spoke softly, his breath warm on her ear. It was easy to hear him above the scream of the engine.

Remember we are going to Scotland! Please don't imagine you can fool me. I shall know if we cease going north.

North. She was trying to picture the map. She was heading over the river and into Suffolk. By no stretch of the imagination was she on her way to Scotland; as far as she could remember she was going east. Still towards the sea.

The car was picking up speed again. Her brain was beginning to work, sorting out her options.

A chuckle came from the seat behind her.

I can read your thoughts, my dear. A talent I always had with women. We will turn off the turnpike at the first opportunity. Once we get there, then we can resume our so pleasant dalliance. But not until then, I fear.

Anna felt the heat coming to her cheeks. 'I don't think so.' She took a deep breath and gritted her teeth. 'I am going to need petrol soon. So, my lord, I trust you understand enough about modern transport to believe me when I say we are going nowhere without it.' Her eyes flicked to the dashboard. The needle was indeed dancing on the red. The tank was emptying fast.

There was no answer from the back.

She drove on. Ahead, the turning to Woodbridge led off the road.

Here. We will leave the turnpike here.

She gave a cry of fear as a cold hand closed over hers. She had no choice. The car veered off the A14 and turned north.

She was past Woodbridge on the A12 when at last, in answer to her prayer, she saw a service station ahead.

Drawing up at the pumps she sat for a moment taking deep breaths. The bottle lay beside her on the seat. There was no comment from behind. Presumably her remark about petrol had somehow been understood.

She had no handbag with her. How was she going to pay for the petrol? In spite of herself she smiled. Was her unwelcome passenger going to present her with ghostly gold sovereigns to complete the transaction? Half-heartedly she leaned forward to open the glove pocket. Of course. She always left a ten pound note there, tucked into the *A-Z* for just such an emergency. And there too was her forgotten mobile phone.

She was still desperately trying to picture the map in her head. It was years since she had driven this way, but when she was married she and Felix had come up here sometimes after visiting Phyllis, heading for the coast. Exploring. Suddenly she had an idea. Aldeburgh. Somehow she must guard her thoughts. Fend him off. Keep him out of her head. She would head for Aldeburgh. There she could bring the car right up to the sea's edge; to the wild shingle coast. And she knew exactly how she was going to convince him that that was the perfect place for them to go.

Leaving the bottle on the seat she climbed out of the car. Ten pounds' worth was not going to get her far, but with luck it would get her to the sea. Her hands were still shaking as she unscrewed the petrol cap and reached for the nozzle. She glanced into the back of the car. It was in shadow, but there would be nothing to see anyway. Was that, she wondered, why he was seeking all this power? Was that what he wanted, to find the means to bring him back to life?

In the shop she paid her ten pounds and then ducked into the ladies. Shutting the door she stood for a moment with her back against it, her eyes closed. Had he followed her? Was he in there with her? Oh God, if she went to the loo would he be watching? She stretched out a hand in front of her. It encountered nothing. How had he done it? On the bridge, he had gripped her wrist. He had felt like flesh and blood. He had been strong. She had sensed him, smelt him.

'So, are you there?' She whispered the words out loud. 'Are you so little the gentleman that you would follow a lady in here?'

There was no answer.

Had he left her then? Was he still in the car? Or was he outside the door waiting? She swallowed hard. Then she reached cautiously into her pocket for the mobile. 'Please. Answer. Serena?'

Serena's phone was switched off. The phone service picked up the call. Sobbing with frustration Anna left her number in a whisper. 'I am heading towards Aldeburgh. I'm going to throw it in the sea! Serena, tell them Carstairs is with me. He isn't in Toby any more. Help me. Please!'

15

When Serena had arrived in Lavenham at last it was after midnight and Toby was once more asleep. Phyllis led her into her kitchen where it was warm. 'Don't be too horrified when you see him. I hit him over the head with the poker and he's got a terrible lump.' She chuckled. 'It did the trick though. Carstairs vanished!'

Serena smiled. 'I didn't think of that. You're obviously a woman of action!' She surveyed her elderly hostess admiringly as she explained who she was. Phyllis was obviously not only a very brave woman, she was also far more alert than her visitor, who after the long drive was exhausted. 'So, what do we do? Should we wake Toby?'

They decided, on the principle of letting sleeping dogs lie, that they wouldn't wake him yet. He too had been exhausted and he had a headache and they would achieve nothing by dragging him downstairs. After all, Anna and the bottle weren't there and he could be no danger – or help – to her. Not now. Not tonight. Not until they knew where she was.

They didn't have to wait long. Serena, asleep on the sofa in the sitting room by the fire, heard Toby as he stumbled downstairs. Climbing to her feet she went to meet him in the hall. 'I heard about your run in with the poker.' She eyed his bruise.

He nodded ruefully, his hand to his head. 'I came down to get a drink of water. I've got a filthy headache.' He followed her into the kitchen. 'But you will be glad to hear it did the trick. Carstairs is gone.'

'Are you sure?' Phyllis appeared behind them. She had heard him come downstairs.

She waved her guests into chairs at the kitchen table, gave Toby a glass of water then set about making them all a pot of coffee. The cat, Jolly, was sitting in front of the Aga licking its paws.

'I'm sure. I don't know how, but I can sense it.' Toby's face was grey with fatigue and the huge bruise on his forehead was swollen. Outside it was still dark.

Serena ran her fingers through her hair. 'You don't think he followed Anna? After all, she has the bottle.'

'Dear God!' Toby stared at her in horror. 'That never occurred to me. I thought it was me he was using. Because we were related.'

'It was you,' Serena said thoughtfully. 'But if the bottle has gone maybe he is not interested in you anymore. You can't help him while you are here; you can't help him unless you are with her.'

'I wish I knew where she is. Do you think she's gone home?' Toby stood up and went over to the window. Lifting the curtain he peered out. There was still no sign of it getting light.

'Not if she's running away.' Phyllis was sitting staring at the coffee pot. 'She'll have gone somewhere none of us will find her. As far as she is concerned Toby is the enemy.' She glanced at him. 'I'm sorry, my dear. But it's true.'

'And always will be?' Toby groaned in despair.

Phyllis glanced at Serena helplessly. 'I do so hope not.'

Serena shrugged. 'I'm out of my depth. I've only studied ancient Egypt. I've never had to cope with a Victorian occultist. I don't know where to start.'

'Mary had a little lamb,' Toby said softly. 'That worked.'

For a moment they were all silent.

Outside, in Serena's car, her phone had finished charging. It lay forgotten, nursing its secrets in silence.

16

Anna tore open the back door of the car and looked in. 'Where are you?' Her anger had temporarily conquered her fear.

There was no reply.

Biting her lip she slammed the door and went round to the driver's side. Pulling that door open in turn she stared down at the bubble-wrapped package lying on the passenger seat. She didn't notice the infinitesimal patch of damp beneath it on the dark leather.

What would happen if she dumped it here? She could throw it into the bins she could see at the side of the garage building. Drive off and leave it. Or she could take it to a bottle bank. Toss it in amongst a thousand wine bottles to be ground to dust and recycled into some innocuous item which would find its way onto a supermarket shelf somewhere.

Don't be foolish. Do you realise what would happen if it was broken?

Somehow he had picked up on that thought.

The power that would be released would devastate the world! We want that power, you and I. Oh, Miss Shelley, we could do so much with that power!

'What? What do you want to do with all this power?' Smothering a sob of frustration, Anna fired the question into the dark. 'What is it with you men? Why do you all want to dominate the world?'

A mere woman would not understand such matters, Miss Shelley. The tone was mocking.

'And another thing, I wish you'd stop calling me Miss Shelley. That is not my name!' Anna snapped back at him. 'My name, if you wish to be so formal, is Anna Fox.'

A car had driven up and parked opposite her on the far side of the pump. She saw the driver stare at her, startled, as he reached for the nozzle.

Very well, I will call you Anna. And please, do not try

running away from me. I can move at the speed of thought.
Get in, my dear. We have to go north! I have everything we
need at Carstairs Castle. My laboratory is waiting.

'I doubt it!' Anna retorted. She climbed in reluctantly,
tossing her mobile onto the other seat to lie beside the
bottle, and reached for the seat belt. With the car light
off her neighbour couldn't see who she was talking to
and talking to her passenger seemed to be the right
thing to do. 'If I remember rightly Carstairs Castle is a
ruin. I think the whole place has been razed to the
ground.' She put the key in the ignition and turned it,
waiting for his reaction to that piece of news. None
came. She smiled to herself quietly. 'As it happens I do
know the place to go. I've thought of the perfect place
of power.' She glanced over her shoulder towards the
empty seat. Would he suspect her plan? See through
her? 'Trust me, my lord. Let me show you.'

She waited.

Silence.

She could feel the small hairs on the back of her neck
stirring.

'OK. Let's go.' It couldn't be that easy. Surely he was
not going to believe he had won her over? Was he really
that conceited? Carefully she engaged gear and pulled
back out onto the A12 once more. Somehow she had
to veil her thoughts. She couldn't let him know that
she had reached a decision. That she was going to fling
the bottle into the sea, to let it sink or float or grind to
pieces amongst the shingle. Mary had a little lamb. She
held her breath, listening. Oh God, it was worse when
he was quiet. She didn't know if he was still there. She
could imagine him sitting on the seat – was he relaxed,

legs crossed, watching the passing scenery or was he leaning forward, his hand on the back of the seat just behind her neck? She jerked forward slightly, feeling the tiptoe of fear again. Mary had a little lamb. Concentrate on anything but where she was going. What she was going to do.

As she approached the turning towards Aldeburgh she slowed the car, her hands gripping the wheel, holding her breath. The road she took ran due east.

This is the wrong way. We need to go north!

She smiled grimly, almost relieved that the silence had been broken. So he was still there. Still awake. Still with his built-in compass. 'I told you, I am going to a place of power I know. A wonderful place. You will like it.' She was visualising the white-domed silhouette of Sizewell nuclear power station.

You are deceiving me! Turn round!

'I am not deceiving you. I told you, we are going somewhere just right for your purposes.'

You do not know what my purposes are, madam! Turn round!

'I can't.' She gripped the steering wheel even more tightly. 'I have to go on. It's the perfect place. You'll see.'

Stop now!

'I told you, I can't. I have to go on.' She pushed her foot to the floor. 'It's important we get there before sunrise.'

Ahead a thin strip of cloud had begun to lighten, tinged with palest red. Above them, the sky was still dark, studded with stars. The road sparkled with dusted frost. Gritting her teeth she pushed the car on down the straight narrow road, heading inexorably towards the sea.

I told you to stop!

'Not yet. Not till we get there. It's not far.'

I do not trust you. Shelley women are dissemblers. They tease. They lie!

'Not me.'

The needle on the speedometer was moving steadily to the right.

'You must trust me. I know what I'm doing. Wait, it's not far now.' Mary had a little lamb.

Stop. I insist. You plan to destroy the bottle. I will not allow it!

'I am taking you to a place of power. It is called a power station.' She was gabbling frantically. 'You must believe me. It is the right place to go. There the power of the bottle will be magnified. It will be ten times greater. More even than you dream of.'

Stop now. Turn round.

'I can't. This is a narrow road. I'm not allowed to turn. We're nearly there.'

Anna. Please obey me. Do not make me angry.

And suddenly she felt the touch of his fingers on her neck. Ice cold. Strong.

She leaned forward, hanging on to the wheel. 'Don't touch me! Keep your hands off me. If we crash the bottle will be broken.'

The bottle is wrapped. It will not break. Come, Anna. Slow down, my dear.

Suddenly the fingers were caressing. Not cold this time, but warm, enticing. The hands she had felt in her dream.

'We need to be there by sunrise.' She gripped the steering wheel ever more tightly, forcing herself to concentrate on the road. It was growing lighter by the minute.

Don't think about what she was going to do. Don't let him read her thoughts. Keep that bland, deadly silhouette there in her head. And recite. That was what Serena had said to do. Recite. Block him out. Mary had a little lamb. Its fleece was white as snow. And everywhere that Mary went the lamb was sure to go . . .

17

Serena and Toby had wandered through into the sitting room while their hostess, abandoning the idea of going back to bed, went upstairs to get dressed. Toby stood looking down at the cold hearth. 'Shall I light a fire?'

Serena nodded. 'Why not?'

He picked up the poker from the carpet where Phyllis had let it fall hours before. Examining it he grimaced. 'I can't believe I survived being hit by this.'

Serena smiled wearily. 'The Carstairs family obviously have tough heads. And the Shelleys are pretty feisty. Try not to worry. She'll be OK.'

'If I just thought she could contact us. Ring me. Anything.' The phone in Anna's flat just now had rung on endlessly.

'She's not going to ring you, Toby.' Serena watched as he picked some logs out of the basket. 'If she calls anyone it will be Phyllis. Or perhaps me.' She felt automatically in her pocket for her mobile and frowned. 'Of course. I left it on charge in the car. Perhaps I'd better fetch it.'

Toby felt the draught of cold air as she pulled open the front door. He stooped, crumpling up a newspaper he had found lying on the chair, piling the logs carefully over it with handfuls of kindling, building them into a pyramid. In the distance he heard Serena's car door bang. There was a box of matches on the huge black beam which served as a mantelpiece. He picked it up and shook it. Reaching for a match he was striking it as he heard Serena come back in, closing the door behind her.

The paper caught. Then the dry twigs, crackling up with a satisfying roar. He sat back, staring down at the fire, feeling the sudden warmth on his face. Then he looked up puzzled. Serena had not reappeared. Instead he heard the creak of floorboards above his head. She had gone upstairs.

Serena tapped lightly on Phyllis's door and went in. 'She's called in. Listen.' She dialled up Anna's message and held it to the old lady's ear.

'Oh God!' Phyllis stared at her. 'We were right. He went with her. What do we do?'

'Shall I tell Toby?' Serena bit her lip. 'He's out of his mind with worry, but he is so vulnerable to Carstairs. Oh, Phyllis, I don't know what to do for the best.'

'Ring her back. That's what she's asked you to do. Call her. Now. Quickly.' She handed the phone back to Serena and watched anxiously as Serena keyed in the number.

18

The phone rang as Anna turned the car into the high street and threaded her way towards the sea. She grabbed it. 'Serena? Is that you? I'm here. In Aldeburgh –' The phone hissed and crackled and went dead. She stared at it in disbelief, then she threw it down. She could see the sea wall ahead of her. She was driving slowly now, manoeuvring as close as she could to the beach.

Carefully she drew the car to a halt.

'We're here. The place of power.' From the beach he would be able to see the power station in the distance. Surely he would realise that it was different; something strange he would never have seen before; would sense its sinister aura. Just so long as he gave her time to reach the sea.

'We're there. Let me show you. It's the most amazing place.' As she groped for the door handle she found herself smiling wryly. Maybe he was not so clever after all. And she had to keep it that way. Cajole him. Go along with him. Fool him. She was wondering how high the tide was. She would only need a few seconds to reach the sea. Not long.

In her mind's eye she conjured again the picture of the power station, so close along the coast. Its great white dome would be easily visible from the edge of the sea.

As she climbed out into the bitter dawn, the bottle was in her hand. 'OK. Come on. I'll show you where we're going. More powerful than anything you ever dreamed of.' It was windy here. Her hair whipped round her face. She paused, half expecting the rear door of the car to open. It didn't. There was no sound. Nodding grimly she turned towards the sea wall, and searching for a gap set off into the teeth of the wind down across the pebbled beach.

The tide was nearly high; it hurtled in against the pebbles with a rattle of falling stones and shingle and she stood for a moment staring at it, dazed by the noise. In front of her the sky had begun to turn red. Along the coast the dome reflected the hint of blood.

It was bitterly cold. She stared round, to see if Carstairs was following her. There was no sign of him. Her fingers tightened round the bottle.

Stray shreds of mist were drifting in off the sea.

Suddenly she began to run down towards the tide line, the pebbles shifting and lurching beneath her feet. She was there. He couldn't stop her now.

In her hand one of the last drops of moisture worked its way through the wrapping in her hand to dampen her fingers in the wind. Above her head a cloud seemed to coalesce and waver. She sensed its presence. Stopping she whirled round in time to see two figures, white, wispy in the dawn light. They towered over her, arms outstretched towards her. She could feel their anguish – and their anger. 'Oh God, the priests! They know what I'm going to do!' Clutching the bottle to her she backed away, terrified. They were coming towards her. They were growing in strength. Their mutual enmity forgotten, they were intent on one thing – the small bottle in Anna's hand and the final few drops of its precious contents. In a moment they would envelop her.

'No!' Her scream rang out into the roar of the sea and was echoed by the cry of a gull. A small trickle of moisture ran up her arm. It was warm. Healing. Blessed.

Hold on to it. Don't let them have it!

Carstairs' voice was strong.

Save it, Anna. Keep it for us!

Inside the bottle the last drop of liquid seeped past the cork. And was blown away in the wind. As their final echoing shrieks of despair dissipated into silence the two figures began to fade. The last traces of mist vanished over the sea.

Anna took a deep breath. She was only yards from the water. They couldn't stop her. No one could stop her now.

'Can you feel it? The power?' she cried. 'Over there. Along the coast? And here. Even better, here in the sea! This is where the bottle belongs! This is where it is going! To follow the priests into oblivion!' Running down across the last strip of pebbles she headed for the waves.

No! Stop!

Suddenly he seemed to realise what she had in mind. She felt a blow on her shoulder. She spun round as fingers grasped her wrist. The bottle was being wrestled from her hand. The bubble wrap tore free and she saw it bowling away along the shingle as the bottle slipped from her grasp and fell amongst the stones. Without a second's thought she swooped on it and falling to her knees she picked up a large smooth stone. She had forgotten the danger. She had forgotten to be afraid. Her only thought was to prevent Roger Carstairs snatching the bottle from her. At all costs she had to stop him from getting it. Lifting her arm she brought the stone down on the bottle with all her strength.

No!

His scream of anguish was appalling as the glass splintered, and suddenly the whole world seemed to stand still. The wind dropped. The sea grew silent. She knelt there on the stones staring down at the small patch of broken glass. Amongst the splinters, a few damp grains of sand sifted, ran down into the shingle and disappeared.

Anna cringed, waiting.

Nothing happened. No explosion. No Egyptian goddess. No archangels. No high priests. As the last touch of moisture evaporated into the air the power was gone. On the horizon the sky was blazing, but it was a silent sunrise.

Then slowly she became aware of the sound of the sea again. And the wind. A gust blew past her and the final grains of Egyptian sand disappeared. The crunched slivers of glass settled in amongst the stones and vanished. In a few moments the rising tide would come and obliterate the spot. She climbed to her feet and watched as the sea crashed in up the beach, swirling, clean. Purifying.

A gull flew up the beach past her, its eerie cry echoing in the wind.

It seems you win, Anna.

He was still there.

'The priests have gone.' She was defiant; triumphant.

Indeed they have. The breath of Isis sustained them. They were always beyond my command.

'You thought something would happen, didn't you?

410

You thought the whole world would blow up!' Shaking as much from cold as fear, she was staring down at the line of waves breaking on the shore at her feet. She had already lost sight of the place where the bottle had broken.

Indeed I did. As did you. Which makes you a brave woman. A worthy descendant of my Louisa. There was a pause. *But a foolish one. Did you think to thwart me so easily? I will find the power I need. One day.*

She turned. There was still no sign of him. The beach was empty. 'What is it you want power for? You still haven't told me.'

Nor will I! But when I have it the whole world will hear once again of Roger Carstairs!

She shuddered.

And so will you, Anna. So will you. But in the meantime, maybe after all you are the right woman for my great-great grandson. You could make a man of him.

Anna was staring out to sea, her hands wedged into her pockets.

On the horizon a crimson segment of sun was beginning to show.

'Do you remember the Egyptian dawn?' she whispered. 'The birth of the Sun God, Ra?'

But the tears of Isis had vanished; there was no place any longer for Egyptian magic in this cold land on the edge of the world. In seconds the rising sun was swallowed by a line of black cloud. The crimson path of light in the sea was extinguished; the water turned grey. Sizewell power station vanished in the drifting mist.

There was a quiet chuckle. She turned. It sounded so

close. So real. Then she felt him. His hands were on her shoulders. His lips on hers.

So. The god has gone too. For now. Goodbye. Good luck, my dear. She could feel his breath on her cheek. Smell the sweet pomade. *We could have been so good together. It is a shame we weren't born in the same century, Mrs Fox. A great shame. But I will return for you one day. Make no mistake about that.* The voice was fading to a whisper. *Until then, farewell.*

And the voice was gone.

Only the sound of the shift and suck of the tide on the beach and the cry of gulls broke the cold silence of the dawn.

19

When Toby and Phyllis and Serena arrived it had been full daylight for a while. Anna was sitting on the sea wall, her hands in her pockets, her coat collar turned up around her neck. The tide was at its height, gentler now, lapping at the seaweed and shells which marked its highest point. Soon it would start its retreat and draw back across the beach, leaving it sparkling and clean.

Anna looked up as they approached. She smiled wearily. 'It's all over. The bottle has gone.'

They stopped in their tracks. 'Are you sure?' It was Toby who voiced the thought they all shared.

She nodded. 'I smashed it.'

'And what happened?'

'Nothing! The tears of Isis had evaporated. All there was left inside were a few grains of sand.'

'And Carstairs?' Toby scanned her face anxiously.

She frowned. 'Carstairs has gone too.' Stiffly she rose to her feet. 'He left you a message before he went.'

Toby frowned. He braced himself visibly. 'What was it?'

'He seemed to think you and I had a future together.' She reached out and took his hand. 'He gave us his blessing; he said he thought a Shelley woman could make a man of you!'

'What?' For a moment his face was a picture of indignation. Then it relaxed and he reached out towards her and drew her into his arms. 'She might at that,' he said softly. 'She just might, if she could ever grow to trust me again.'

She smiled. 'I trust you, Toby.'

As they kissed in the ice cold wind Serena and Phyllis exchanged glances.

'Yes!' Phyllis raised her thumb in triumph.

Nestling into Toby's arms Anna clung to him tightly. The rest of Lord Carstairs' final message she would keep to herself.

The Storyteller

I am a storyteller.
I sit by the fire
With the night at my back
And wait for you to come.

I am a storyteller.
One by one you draw near
And sit down in the shadows
Silently
To wait
For the weaving of words.

I am a storyteller.
I paint pictures in your head
Which dance and spin and live
And change the world into mirrored glass.

I am a storyteller.
I conjure the sea
And juggle the stars.
I deal the cards
I cut the pack.
And captive, with a shiver,
You glance over your shoulder
Into the night.

I am a storyteller.
I hold the strings in my hand.
I command your tears and I let you laugh
And you hold your breath as I weave my
    tale.

I am a storyteller.
Silent. Alone, I watch others play.
From the shadows
I peer into warm lighted windows
Unnoticed. Outside. On my own.

I am a storyteller.
I hold the reins.
I knit with emotion
At the foot of the blade.
Splashed by your blood
I tell them your history.
Then I turn back again
Into anonymity and silence.

I am a storyteller.
You must listen with care.
I can banish your boredom
And teach you to listen.
But when I finish
I will no longer be there.

I am a storyteller.
When the fire flames die
At last I am quiet.
You go back to your houses;
To the lights and the noise.
And I fade back
Into the dark.

Hiding from the Light

Barbara Erskine

The *Sunday Times* bestseller.

**Across the peninsula the mist rolled in, its icy
fingers curling up the cliffs. Inside their houses
people stirred in their sleep and children cried in
the dark.**

The parish of Manningtree and Mistley has a dark history.
In 1644 Cromwell's Witchfinder General tortured scores
of women there, including Liza, the herbalist, whose
cottage still stands, and Sarah, the daughter of the manor.
And the spirits of his victims still haunt the old shop in the
High Street, they say.

Emma Dickson gave up her high-flying career to live
in Liza's cottage but now, as Halloween approaches, she
is being driven half-mad by visions of the terrible past.
In despair, Emma turns to the young rector for help but
he, too, is in the grip of something inexplicable and
dangerous . . .

As past and present entwine, Erskine draws us into a story
of good against evil that races towards a heart-stopping
climax.'   *Woman and Home*

0 00 651208 9

Kingdom of Shadows

Barbara Erskine

Clare Royland is rich and beautiful – but unhappy. She wants for nothing materially, but as her marriage is increasingly overshadowed by husband Paul's own financial cares, loneliness encroaches. A growing obsession with an ancestress from the distant past fuels this isolation. Haunted by inexplicable dreams that terrify – but also powerfully compel – Clare is forced through fear and fascination to look inwards to the past. What she sees, horrifies …

In 1306, Isobel, Countess of Buchan, is persecuted for her part in crowning Robert the Bruce, her lover.

Duncairn, Isobel's home and Clare's beloved heritage, becomes a battleground for passions that span the centuries. As Paul's worries draw him further towards recklessness, Clare must fight to save Duncairn. She must find the strength to save herself from the manipulations of Paul. And from the powers of Isobel …

'Her forte is mood, atmosphere and the toe-curling frisson'   *Sunday Times*

ISBN: 0 00 717 3628

HAZARDS

access to geography

HAZARDS

Malcolm Skinner

Hodder & Stoughton

A MEMBER OF THE HODDER HEADLINE GROUP

Orders: please contact Bookpoint Ltd, 130 Milton Park, Abingdon, Oxon OX14 4SB. Telephone: (44) 01235 827720. Fax: (44) 01235 400454. Lines are open from 9.00–6.00, Monday to Saturday, with a 24 hour message answering service. You can also order through our website www.hodderheadline.co.uk.

British Library Cataloguing in Publication Data
A catalogue record for this title is available from the British Library

ISBN 0 340 84636 4

First Published 2003
Impression number 10 9 8 7 6 5 4 3 2 1
Year   2009 2008 2007 2006 2005 2004 2003

Cover photo: the ruins of the Espiritu Santo church in Antigua Guatemala, destroyed in the 1976 earthquake but never rebuilt (by Michael Hill)

Produced by Gray Publishing, Tunbridge Wells, Kent
Printed in Great Britain for Hodder & Stoughton Educational, a division of Hodder Headline Plc, 338 Euston Road, London NW1 3BH by Bath Press Ltd.

To Judith and Katharine for all their practical help and advice.
To all my fellow companions, both students and colleagues,
in Alpine Europe 1988–1995.

Great things are done when men and mountains meet.
This is not done by jostling in the street. (William Blake)

Contents

Acknowledgements

The publishers would like to thank the following individuals, institutions and companies for permission to reproduce copyright illustrations in this book:

© Crown Copyright (N Britton) for use of *Emergency Management and Civil Defense in New Zealand* (1998) used on page 11; Federal Emergency Management Agency (FEMA) for use of *The FEMA Disaster Life Cycle* used on page 120; Leicester City Council for an extract from *Leicester Link* (May 2001) used on page 97; NDMC-UNL (The US Drought Monitor is a partnership between the National Drought Mitigation Center, United States Department of Agriculture, and National Oceanic and Atmospheric Administration) for use of *The US Seasonal Drought Outlook* (February 2003) used on page 58.

Every effort has been made to trace and acknowledge ownership of copyright. The publishers will be glad to make suitable arrangements with any copyright holders whom it has not been possible to contact.

1 An Introduction to Hazards

In 1989, the international community agreed on a far-reaching and innovative strategy to counter the threat of natural disasters. The United Nations General Assembly proclaimed the 1990s the International Decade for Natural Disaster Reduction (IDNDR), and established a multisectoral framework of action. The aim of this plan was to carry out the IDNDR's objective to 'reduce the loss of life, property damage and socio-economic disruption caused by natural, technological and environmental disasters'. We are by now used to seeing images of disasters brought by newspapers and television. Our awareness of these events has been increased by global communications and the dramatic images of flooding, cyclones, tornadoes and earthquakes that are brought into our homes. The impact of a **hazard** brings about the **disaster** with its disruption to human systems, including death and injury, property and communication system damage, and the disruption of economic activities. Natural or environmental hazards therefore pose a risk to human populations. That risk is increased because we build precarious shanty towns on unstable tropical slopes, urbanize flood plains and volcanic zones, live in areas with active faults and on coasts that are susceptible to hurricanes and flaunt anti-seismic building codes. The problem is also exacerbated by the failure to recognise a potential hazard and to act accordingly. Natural hazards, and their effects upon people, tend to have the following common characteristics:

- their origins are clear and the effects that they produce are distinctive, such as earthquakes causing buildings to collapse
- most natural hazards only allow a short warning time before the event (some hardly at all)
- exposure to the risk is involuntary although this applies mainly to the inhabitants of LEDCs. In MEDCS, most of the people who occupy hazardous areas are often well aware of the risks, which they choose to minimise or even ignore
- most losses to life and damage to property occur shortly after the event although the effects of natural hazards can be felt in communities long after that time (disease, disruption to communications and economic activities)
- the scale and intensity of the event requires an emergency response.

IDNDR have recognised that cities are particularly vulnerable to hazards. Figure 1 shows a selection of recent disasters connected with natural hazards that have affected urban areas and, taken collectively, represent the range of social, health, economic, environmental, cultural and historical effects that disasters can bring. Spectacular disasters affecting megacities are often featured in the news as such vast urban areas attract attention because of their size, having large concentrations of people, industry, communication networks and often being the centres of national government. Huge disasters, though, are only the tip of the iceberg as IDNDR maintain that the evidence shows the cumulative damage from thousands of lesser disasters may be even greater than that of a spectacular single disaster featured in the news. Figure 1 shows the location of recent disasters resulting from earthquakes, volcanic eruptions, mudflows, floods and cyclones.

In the second half of the twentieth century it would appear that the world has become a much more hazardous place. Table 1 shows the total number of reported disasters in the three decades since 1960, together with statistics on selected categories. There is, though, no evidence that volcanic eruptions and earthquakes are occurring more often than they did in the past. If the physical environment is not becoming more hazardous, then it must be that more people are being placed at risk from potentially hazardous events. There could be several reasons for this:

- population growth
- urbanisation
- pressure to develop marginal land

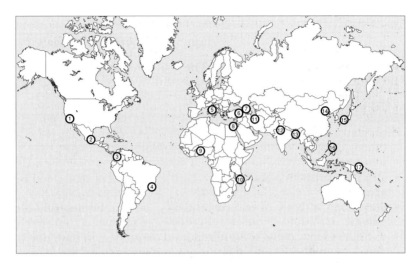

① **Los Angeles (pop. 12.4 million), USA**
The 1994 Northridge earthquake was the strongest to shake the region in two decades, killing only 57 but causing over $30 billion of economic losses.

② **Mexico City (pop. 15.7 million), Mexico**
A 1985 earthquake killed over 10 000 people, left tens of thousands homeless, destroyed nearly 34 000 buildings and affected 65 000 others.

③ **Armero (pop. 25 000), Colombia**
1985 volcanic eruption and mudflow rapidly buried the town and killed 21 800 – most of its inhabitants.

④ **Rio de Janeiro (pop. 9.9 million), Brazil**
1988 floods affected nearly 20% of Rio inhabitants. Nearby cities of Petropolis and Acre also were stricken. Economic losses were just under $1 billion. Greatest damage was to squatter settlements on unstable slopes.

⑤ **Naples (pop. 1 200 000), Potenza (100 000), Salerno (200 000), Avellino (60 000), Italy**
The 1980 earthquake in Southern Italy killed more than 3000 people in these and nearby cities. Dozens of historic urban centres were hit; about 75% of buildings around the epicentre were destroyed. The Pugliese aqueduct (largest freshwater distribution network in Europe) was blocked.

⑥ **Erzincan (pop. 300,000), Turkey**
The 1992 Erzincan earthquake affected 230 000, killed 547, and damaged or destroyed over 18000 buildings.

⑦ **Spitak (pop. 50 000), Gumri (220 000) and Vanadzor (180 000), Armenia**
The 1988 Spitak earthquake killed over 25 000. New constructions (rapidly and shoddily built) were the first to collapse. Lack of water, sewage, electricity or gas caused 120 000 people to evacuate.

⑧ **Cairo (pop. 9.7 million), Egypt**
5,000 buildings were destroyed and nearly 12 000 were damaged, including historical monuments and many schools. The earthquake was perceived as "unexpected." [1992]

⑨ **Cotonou (pop. 650 000), Benin**
In the 1988 and 1991 floods, economic life stopped for a week. Floods are recurrent – 56% of houses are flooded regularly.

⑩ **Nocala City (pop. 1.4 million), Mozambique**
The 1994 cyclone Nadia destroyed 75% of homes and cut power and transport lines.

⑪ **Manji (25 000), Zanjan (25 400) and Rudbar (95 000), Iran**
The 1990 Manjil earthquake destroyed three towns. It killed 40 000 people and left 500 000 homeless. (Rural areas affected include 1600 villages.)

⑫ **Uttarkashi (pop. 240 000), India**
The 1991 earthquake triggered severe landslides which killed 2000 people. About 90% of the houses in Uttarkashi collapsed.

⑬ **Cittagong (pop. 2.4 million) and Cox's Bazaar (40 000), Bangladesh**
A 1991 cyclone killed 140 000 in these cities and nearby islands.

⑭ **Tangshan (pop. 1.8 million), China**
The 1976 Tangshan earthquake killed 148 000 people and injured 81 000 in Tangshan City. 95% of houses and 80% of industrial buildings collapsed or were seriously damaged.

⑮ **Kobe (pop. 1.5 million), Japan**
A 1995 Hanshin-Awaji earthquake killed 6300 people (75% crushed/suffocated, 10% burned) and caused over $100 billion in losses.

⑯ **Ormoc City (pop. 45 000), Philippines**
A 1991 mudflow following Tropical Storm Thelma killed 5000 people and left nearly 46 000 homeless. Damage was $27.7 million.

⑰ **Rabaul (pop. 30 000), Papua New Guinea**
In 1994, the Rabaul volcano erupted. Inhabitants evacuated the area rapidly, but 40% of buildings, transport and communications were damaged by ash and lava.

Figure 1 Selected recent major disasters in urban areas

Table 1 Reported disasters per decade, 1960–89

	1960s	1970s	1980s
All reported disasters	528	1128	2228
Earthquakes	89	139	392
Volcanic activity	13	25	55
Floods	142	356	603
Landslides	23	50	81

- economic growth creating more built environment that could be damaged
- increasing inability of governments to cope with even small-scale events
- it could be that an increase in reported disasters is, in part, due to the development of communications and mass media coverage.

It is also apparent that poor people are much more vulnerable to hazards compared to those who live in MEDCs. On the other side of the coin, though, the built environment within richer countries will suffer more damage simply because there is more of it, as well as the fact that greater monetary investment is involved. The cyclone that struck Bangladesh in 1991 was responsible for an estimated 131 000 deaths and a monetary cost of $1.7 billion, whereas a hurricane of similar strength that hit Florida in 1992 (Hurricane Andrew) killed only 60 people but was estimated to have caused damage totalling at least $20 billion.

This book will recognise the impact that natural hazards can have upon people and the built environment, but it will also examine several other hazard phenomena that have an enormous impact upon human populations. Some features of the natural environment can be altered to such an extent that they pose a threat to people, such as atmospheric pollution in urban areas and the resultant smog. We also tend to forget that there are elements in the natural environment that may cause people harm, but not with the often-spectacular impact of earthquakes, volcanoes and hurricanes. Transmittable diseases, such as malaria, typhoid, Ebola and AIDS, are part of the natural environment and can have a catastrophic impact upon populations in certain parts of the world. It is also true to say that some hazards are completely contained within the human environment as they are initiated by people and impact upon others. A good example of such a human hazard is burglary, something faced by many of those who live within the world's urban areas. In this book the main consideration will be natural hazards but it will also examine the origins, impact and management of smog, transmittable disease, burglary in urban areas and nuclear waste.

1 Origins of Hazards

Some hazards are entirely natural in origin, such as earthquakes and volcanic activity and, in the case of these two phenomena, origin refers to the large-scale tectonic processes that bring them about. Other hazards in the physical world may not be entirely natural and are referred to by some as '*Quasi-natural hazards*' or '*modified physical hazards*'. The role of humans in the formation of smog has been mentioned above, but there is also some evidence that recent increases in atmospheric extremes, such as cyclones and severe storms, are the result of the global warming impacts of human interference in the atmosphere. This is particularly true in the case of river flooding. Many flooding disasters are due, in part, to an extreme rainfall event, but the situation is made worse in many cases by the amount of deforestation that has taken place leading to much more rapid run-off. As hazards have often been described as extreme geophysical events, it should be noted that 'extreme' also refers to the origins of the particular hazard. In the case of water, for example, 'extreme' signifies a substantial departure in both a positive and negative manner from what could be considered a mean or a trend. If precipitation is way above average and run-off and discharge are high, then a flood event could result; if values of precipitation are low over a certain period, then a drought disaster will be visited on a region.

Many hazard events are also the response to other hazards. Earthquakes, for example, can be responsible for landslides, fires, tsunamis (giant waves), flooding (through dam burst) and human-based hazards such as crime with looting and robbery. In the human sphere itself, it is often difficult to explain the exact cause of the hazard. We know, for example, what brings about a burglary, but what motivates the person(s) to commit that crime is not always easy to ascertain and does not easily fall into the remit of geography.

2 Distribution

This refers to the spatial distribution made by the hazard event. Earthquakes and volcanoes, for example, are generally associated with tectonic plate boundaries although events do take place outside of these areas. Tropical cyclones (hurricanes/typhoons) occur between 5 and 25 degrees north and south of the equator. The impacts also vary in size of area that they can affect. Landslides and other forms of mass movement, for example, are very localised in the area they can affect, whereas volcanic activity can spread dust on a global scale and bring about short-term climatic change.

3 Frequency/Magnitude (Scale)

Frequency refers to the distribution of the hazard event through time (its temporal distribution), whereas magnitude assesses the size of the impact. Frequency can be expressed as the number of events of a given magnitude that occur over a period of time. It is not an easy thing to measure as data tend to be relatively recent and therefore it is difficult to predict events that have a long-term return period. Some hazards, such as landslides and avalanches, may occur only once in a specific area but others occur in the same area from time to time. There is evidence, for example, that strain builds up gradually within the rocks of a faulted area and then is abruptly released resulting in an earthquake. Some hazards are distinctly seasonal, for example tropical cyclones. The frequency of burglary is predicted by insurance companies when setting premiums for areas, although the data are undoubtedly flawed as not all burglaries are reported and therefore logged.

Magnitude is measured in many different ways: some physical processes have magnitude scales, for example the **Richter** scale for earthquakes or the **Saffir-Simpson** scale for tropical cyclones; some scales incorporate the possible effects upon people and the built environment, for example the **Mercalli** scale for earthquakes; other observers use death tolls or the cost of damage through insurance figures. The evidence can be taken from a number of different sources, but it is important to recognise the reliability (or not) of that evidence. The Richter scale may indicate the force of the earthquake, but it does not give its overall effect upon people and the built environment. As we have seen, hazard events in MEDCs are likely to cause low loss of life but with high damage costs, whereas the reverse is often true in LEDCs.

The repetition of hazard events can also be considered in terms of frequency distributions. At the most basic level, the magnitude–frequency principle leads us to expect many small insignificant events and, in the long term, increasingly fewer events as magnitude rises (Figure 2a). Knowing something about the frequency of river flow reaching a certain level, for example, is important in planning flood protection. Estimating the probability of a river reaching a certain level involves calculating a **recurrence interval**. When a flood event on a river is described as a 100-year flood, what is really meant by this statement? This actually implies that the chances of the river reaching that level in any 1 year are about one in 100 or 1%. This does not mean, however, that the event occurs at regular 100-year intervals, nor even that it occurs in every 100-year period. It is possible to plot graphically the probability of a flood event and its magnitude and this becomes a very useful tool for river management purposes. Figure 2(b) shows the historic records of a river's flow levels plotted as a histogram and from this it is possible to envisage the relative amounts of time for which flows of different magnitudes occur. This can be translated into a probability curve (Figure 2c), which enables the probability of a flood event of a certain magnitude over a given time interval to be calculated. The shape of the distribution in Figure 2(c) resembles a typical normal distribution curve, although there is a longer tail to the left, indicating the low probability of an extreme event.

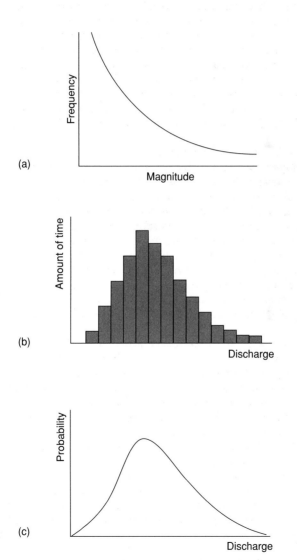

Figure 2 (a) Frequency of hazard events; (b) historic record of a river's flow; (c) probability curve for data in (b)

4 Effects of Hazard Events

The effects of a hazard event are the impact that it has upon the physical and human environments. Some commentaries differentiate hazard impact on the human environment into, first, the effect upon people and, secondly, the impact upon the built environment (buildings, roads and other communication systems, dams, power and water supply systems, etc.). It is also possible to differentiate between **primary** and **secondary** effects. The initial effect of an earthquake is therefore the ground shaking followed by the secondary effects of soil liquefaction, landslides/avalanches, tsunamis, and the effects on people and the built environment such as collapsing buildings, fires, flooding, etc. Secondary effects can be present for a long time, as problems do not stop when the hazard event is over. An earthquake may be over in a few seconds, volcanoes stop erupting and floods recede, but the knock-on effects may be with the population for years. Communication systems could be out of order for a long time, the ability to produce food crops may take some time to restore and the economy of a region may be so damaged that the legacy of the hazard event will be around for years. On Caribbean islands, for example, a hurricane can so damage the plantation system that the population will have to struggle for a long time with the aftermath of the event, something that can represent an immense strain on the fragile economy of LEDCs.

5 Risk and Vulnerability

Risk is the exposure of people to a hazardous event, presenting a potential threat to themselves, their possessions and the built environment in which they live. People, though, consciously put themselves at risk from hazards and the question has to be why do they do it? Possible reasons include the following:

- **hazard events are unpredictable**: we cannot predict the frequency, magnitude or spatial scale of a hazard event
- **lack of alternatives**: due to social, political, economic and cultural factors people cannot simply uproot themselves from one place and move to another, giving up their homes, land and employment
- **changing the levels of risk**: places that were once relatively safe may have become through time far more of a risk. Deforestation, for example, could result in more flooding and an increased risk from landslides; coastal settlements could be in danger from rising sea levels as a result of global warming
- **cost/benefit**: there are many hazardous areas that offer advantages that in people's minds outweigh the risk that they are taking. Many people live on river flood plains because of the fertile soil and

other considerations, yet flooding is recorded as being the world's most commonly reported hazard event. Californian cities have a high risk from hazards, particularly earthquakes, but people see the many advantages of living there as greater than the potential risk

- **perception**: many people accept that hazards are natural events that are part of the process of living. Some communities go as far as to say that hazards represent 'God's will' and losses in such an event are inevitable (see later detail on hazard perception).

This raises the question, is the risk the same for all people in an area? In other words, are some people more vulnerable than others? It has already been noted that a similar-sized hazard event can have varying impacts in different parts of the world. People's wealth and the level of technology that they can apply do affect the degree to which the hazard event will impact upon them. Richer people and countries can protect themselves from hazards by building sea defences, constructing earthquake-resistant buildings, providing better emergency services, etc. They can also be better prepared by being made more aware of the risk through education. There is no doubt then that poorer people are more vulnerable, and this is best seen in many cities in LEDCs. As they have grown this has meant that more and more people have been forced to live in hazardous areas, such as very steep hillsides that are prone to landslides, and in the lowest lying parts where they are at risk from floods.

6 The Perception of Hazards

People react to the threat of hazards in different ways because of the way in which individuals receive and process information. Perception is influenced by many factors such as socio-economic status, education, occupation/employment status, religion, cultural/ethnic background, family and marital status, past experience, values, personality and expectations. Perception of a hazard will ultimately determine the course of action taken by individuals in order to modify the event or the responses they expect from governments and other organisations. There is often a great difference in the perception of a hazard between residents of MEDCs and LEDCs. In wealthier countries there is the sense that the better that you are prepared, the more able you will be able to withstand the impact of the hazard and perhaps even prevent the disaster event from taking place. This is usually based upon government and community action, and is backed by capital that will fund technologically based solutions. The sense of helplessness in the face of many hazards tends to increase with the level of poverty and the deprivation of people. Even in MEDCs there are groups of disadvantaged people who tend to look upon hazards as part of their way of life as they are seen to be unavoidable, just as the bulk of the populations of LEDCs see the impacts of hazards as being part of the condition of poverty. The way that people perceive hazards can therefore be classified into:

- **Fatalism (acceptance)**: hazards are generally natural events that are part of living. Some communities would go as far as to say that they are 'God's will'. Action is therefore usually direct and concerned with safety. Losses are accepted as inevitable and people remain where they are.
- **Adaptation**: people see that they can prepare for, and therefore survive, the hazard event(s) by prediction, prevention and/or protection, depending upon the economic and technological circumstances of the area in question.
- **Fear**: the perception of the hazard is such that people feel so vulnerable to the event that they are no longer able to face living in the area and move away to regions perceived to be unaffected by the hazard.

7 Management of Hazards

People respond to hazards and the threats they can pose to life, possessions and property by seeking ways to reduce the risk. Responses can come from individuals, the local community with people working together, or from national governments. Some hazards are also being tackled on an international scale, as can be seen with the setting up of the International Decade for Natural Disaster Reduction (IDNDR) by the United Nations in 1989.

The traditional approach presents hazards as natural problems that people must battle with in order to survive. All societies learn to live within the natural environment and it is the extreme nature of many hazard events that causes the problem. At the same time, people are not passive in the face of hazards as they can use defences against them. The more sophisticated a society's technology, the more able it is to combat hazards. A good example of this would be the way in which buildings can now be designed to withstand seismic shocks during earthquakes by incorporating certain features such as shock absorbers, cross-bracings and counterweights.

A key feature of the modern approach is that hazards are best combated by efficient management. Modern management techniques, with their gathering of information, careful analysis and deliberate planning, aim to make the most efficient use of the money available to confront hazards. One of the modern processes in confronting hazard events is **integrated risk management**, which is a system that incorporates identification of the hazard, analysis of the risks, establishing priorities, treating the risk and implementing a risk reduction plan, developing public awareness and a communication strategy, and monitoring and reviewing the whole process. A good example of such a management scheme was developed by the New Zealand government and is shown in Figure 3.

How people respond to a hazard will depend upon the nature of the hazard, past experience, economic ability to take action, technological resources, hazard perceptions of the decision-makers, and the area's social and political framework. People and organisations therefore try to manage hazards in the following ways:

- **Prediction**: for some hazards it is possible to give warnings that will enable action to be taken in order to reduce the impact. Improved **monitoring**, information and communications technology have meant that predicting hazards and issuing warnings have become more important in recent years. Dealing with tropical cyclones

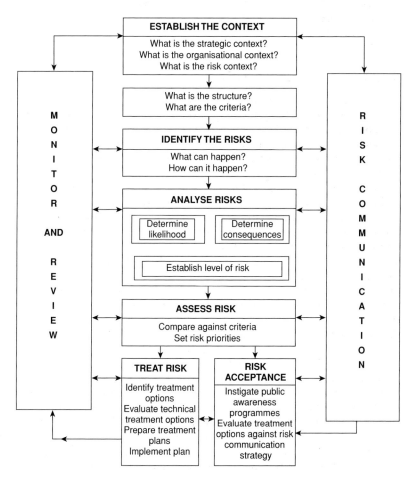

Figure 3 The process of risk management

through such agencies at the National Hurricane Centre in Florida is a good example of how prediction depends upon monitoring and warning through the use of information from satellites, and land, sea and air-based recordings.

- **Prevention**: the ideal situation would be to prevent the occurrence of the hazard event. For most hazards this is entirely unrealistic, and the best that can be achieved is some form of modification, often to the environment, through controls such as the building of sea walls to prevent storm surges inundating coastal areas.
- **Protection**: the aim is to protect people, their possessions and the built environment from the impact of the hazard. This also covers attempts to modify losses with insurance (particularly in MEDCs) and aid (usually in LEDCs). In MEDCs, areas affected by hazard events are able to draw upon central government funds. One way in which people can react is to change their attitudes and behaviour towards hazards and so reduce their vulnerability. **Community preparedness** involves prearranged measures that aim to reduce the loss of life and property damage through public education and awareness programmes, evacuation procedures, and provision of emergency medical, food and shelter supplies. In south-eastern Australia, for example, a community education programme has been established to combat the wildfire hazard. This programme, known as Community Fireguard, has been set up to assist people to develop their own wildfire survival strategies. (Some details of this programme can be found in the section devoted to wildfires.)

All attempts at management must be evaluated in terms of their success in prediction, prevention and protection. Successful schemes include the use of dynamite to divert lava flows on Mt Etna, and pouring sea water on lava fronts in Iceland. On the other hand, the Japanese felt that they were well prepared for earthquakes and yet in Kobe (1995) over 100 000 buildings were destroyed (with three times that number damaged) and the death toll reached over 6000 with 35 000 injuries (the reaction and response of local and national government to the Kobe earthquake will be covered in Chapter 7).

8 Hazards and the Media

It is through the media that most of us come into contact with the range of hazards that will be covered in this book. Television tends to be by far the most powerful medium; having the ability to show us the reality of hazard events or to perpetuate myths about them. Television can also motivate public solidarity in the face of the suffering that disasters bring. The problem with TV news coverage is that it is selective, the results that we see on our screens often bear little relation to the distribution of important events around the world. Events far away may only receive limited coverage. Media reports on recent major earthquakes, such as those in India and Armenia, showed the major structural collapses and the impact upon people, but coverage was brief and was soon replaced on news bulletins by more important domestic news. The media, however, can be responsible for making people aware of a tragedy, something that will initiate and sustain a public response. It is true to say, though, that in some cases prolonged exposure or a number of events happening close together might promote 'donor fatigue' amongst the public.

Many have commented, though, in adverse terms about the role of the media in disaster coverage and its tendency towards **voyeurism**. Television often presents high-impact images of landscapes strewn with debris and faces of desperation and grief, the intrusion of the camera into moments of intensely private human suffering. It also gives us the gripping drama of daring rescue teams working against the clock to save trapped and buried survivors. Some journalists have even gone as far as to suggest that coverage of recent disasters could be called 'sexy', although there are others who view recent trends with distaste, referring to such material as '**disaster pornography**'.

Communication, however, is an important part of disaster prevention and management. Many channels such as signals, leaflets, speaker cars, public events, newspapers, radio, television and, increasingly, the internet are used before and during a hazard event. Mass media have certain characteristics that make them advantageous for hazard communication. They provide easy access to large numbers of people and some methods constitute a very robust system that will remain working even in cases of partial breakdown. On the other hand, sources dealing with the media know that it can be a difficult channel through which to operate, as people affected by a hazardous event have no direct control over the content and form of information transmitted. Sources who want communication with the public have to deal with journalists who do not form a 'passive information channel', but act as gatekeepers, interpreters and commentators. The media can therefore support or obstruct the disaster management of many agencies and relief organisations.

Summary

- A hazard is an event that threatens life, possessions and the built environment.
- There are different categories of hazards: natural (environmental), technological and human.
- Disasters are extreme events and are the realisation of particular hazards.
- Natural hazards pose a risk to populations and that risk can be increased by human actions such as building on unstable slopes.
- Risk is the exposure of populations to a hazardous event.

- Cities, particularly those in LEDCs, are particularly vulnerable to hazards.
- More people are being placed at risk from hazardous events as many choose to live in potentially hazardous areas.
- The nature of losses from hazard events varies at a global scale, with the highest loss of life in LEDCs and the highest economic losses in MEDCs.
- Hazards can be studied through their origins, spatial distributions, frequency and magnitude (scale).
- The effects of hazard events can be classified as either primary or secondary. Several secondary effects can last for a long time after the event.
- People's wealth and the level of technology that they can apply do affect the degree to which the hazard will impact upon them.
- People perceive hazards in three main ways: fatalism (acceptance), adaptation and fear.
- Attempts to manage the hazard fall into three categories: prediction, prevention and protection.
- The choice of response is governed by the nature of the hazard, past experience, economic and technological resources, social and political conditions, and perception.

Exercises

1. Explain why natural hazards should not be called 'Acts of God'.
2. Why are poor people more vulnerable to a hazardous event?
3. Look at the following lists of effects resulting from a hazardous event:
   - Immediate: deaths, injuries, damage to built environment, loss of possessions.
   - Secondary and longer-term: disease epidemics, disruption of economic activity and loss of employment, disruption of social activity, fall in area's income, fear and worry among the population.

   What factors will affect how severe the above impacts will be on people, and how long they may last?
4. What factors do you think will influence a person's perception of a hazard?
5. Why are urban areas, particularly large ones, considered to be very vulnerable to hazardous events? The information presented in Figure 1 will help you with your answer.

2 Tectonic and Other Geomorphological Hazards

1 Earthquakes

Causes and distribution

As the crust of the Earth is mobile, there tends to be a slow build up of stress within the rocks. When this pressure is suddenly released, parts of the surface experience an intense shaking motion that lasts only for a few seconds. This is an earthquake. Within the crust, the point at which this pressure release occurs is known as the **focus**, and the point immediately above that on the surface is known as the **epicentre**. The depth of focus is very important, and is one of the factors determining the amount of surface damage resulting from the event. Three broad categories are recognised:

- **shallow focus**: 0–70 km deep – which tend to cause the greatest damage and account for 75% of all earthquakes
- **intermediate focus**: 70–300 km deep
- **deep focus**: 300–700 km down.

Seismic waves radiate from the focus rather like the effect of throwing a stone into water. There are three types of seismic wave, each travelling at different speeds. The primary (P) waves travel fastest and are compressional, vibrating in the direction in which they are travelling. Secondary (S) waves travel at half the speed of P waves and shear rock by vibrating at right angles to their direction of travel. Longitudinal (L) waves travel the slowest and near to the surface. Some of them shake the ground at right angles to the direction of wave movement whilst others have a more rolling motion that produces vertical ground movement. P and S waves travel through the

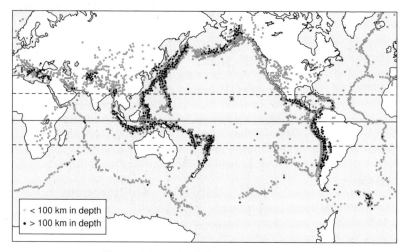

Figure 4 Location of recent earthquakes

interior of the earth and are recorded on a **seismograph**. By studying earthquakes, and the seismic waves they generate, it was possible to build up the picture of the interior of the Earth. The vast majority of earthquakes occur along plate boundaries (Figure 4), the most powerful being associated with destructive margins. At conservative margins, the boundary is marked by a **fault**, movement along which produces an earthquake. The best known of these is the San Andreas fault in California where the fault line represents the boundary between the North American and Pacific plates. In reality, the San Andreas system consists of a broad and complex zone in which there are a number of fractures of the earth. Some earthquakes occur away from plate boundaries and are associated with the reactivation of old fault lines, such as the event that occurred on September 2002 in the Midlands area of England. (The effects of this earthquake will be dealt with later in this chapter.) It has also been suggested that human activity could be the cause of some minor earthquakes by the building of large reservoirs where water puts pressure on the surface rocks or by the subsidence of deep mine workings.

Magnitude and frequency

The magnitude of earthquakes is measured on two scales. The Richter scale (Figure 5) is a logarithmic scale in which an event measured at 7 has a ten-fold increase in the amplitude of measured seismic waves over an event measured at 6 on the scale. The energy release is also proportionate to the magnitude, so that for each unit increase in the scale, the energy release increases approximately 30 times. The largest event ever recorded was measured at 8.9 on the scale (off north-eastern Japan in 1933 and in Prince William Sound, Alaska in 1964). The earthquake in the English Midlands in 2002 at 4.8 on the scale was large for the British Isles, but small when compared to major earthquakes such as 1999 Turkish earthquake that measured 7.4 and which killed over 14 000 people, injured 25 000 and completely destroyed over 20 000 buildings.

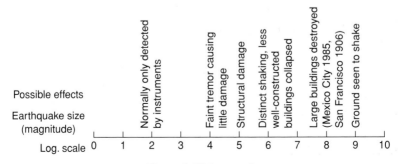

Figure 5 Richter scale

The Mercalli scale measures the intensity of the event and its impact. This is a 12-point scale that runs from Level I (detected by seismometers but only felt by a very few people – approximately equivalent of 2 on the Richter scale) to Level XII (total destruction with waves on the ground as it is actually seen to shake – approximately 8.5 Richter).

Seismic records enable earthquake frequency to be observed, although such records only date back to the middle of the nineteenth century (1848) when an instrument capable of detecting seismic waves was developed.

The effects of earthquakes

The initial effect of an earthquake is ground shaking, the severity of which will depend upon the magnitude of the earthquake, the distance from the epicentre and the local geological conditions. In Mexico City, for example, the earthquake of 1985 produced seismic waves that devastated the city as they were amplified several times by the ancient lake sediments upon which the city is built. Secondary effects include the following:

- **soil liquefaction**: soils with a high water content lose their mechanical strength when violently shaken, and start to behave as a fluid
- **landslides/avalanches**: slope failure occurs as a result of ground shaking
- **tsunamis**: giant sea waves generated by both volcanic action and earthquake activity. Most tsunamis, though, are the result of undersea earthquakes involving movement of the sea bed
- **effects on people and the built environment**: collapsing buildings; destruction of road systems, railways, bridges and other forms of communication; destruction of service provision such as gas, water and electricity; fires resulting from ruptured gas mains and fallen electricity lines; flooding; food shortages; disease; disruption of the local economy either subsistence or commercial. Some of the effects are short term; others occur over a longer period, the length of time depending very much on the ability of the area to recover.

CASE STUDY I: THE EFFECTS OF AN EARTHQUAKE IN AN MEDC

THE NORTHRIDGE EARTHQUAKE, LOS ANGELES, 4.31 A.M. 17 JANUARY 1994

There have been five earthquakes in the Los Angeles area since 1933 that measured at least 5.8 on the Richter scale (see Figure 6). They were:

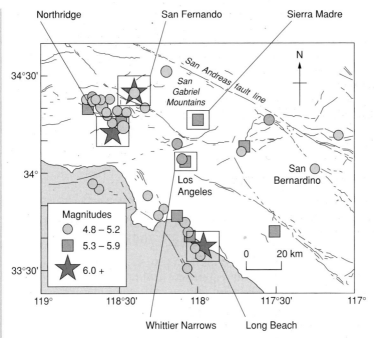

Figure 6 Recent earthquakes in the Los Angeles
basin (since 1932)

- 1933 Long Beach 6.4 Richter; 120 people died
- 1971 San Fernando 6.6 Richter; 65 people died
- 1987 Whittier Narrows 5.9 Richter; eight people died
- 1991 Sierra Madre 5.8 Richter; two people died
- 1997 Northridge 6.7 Richter; 57 people died.

The Northridge earthquake occurred in the early hours of a
Monday morning and was the result of movement along a thrust
fault, whose presence was not known to geologists. The focus of
the earthquake was at a depth of 18.4 km. The low death toll has
been attributed to the fact that the earthquake occurred in the
early morning, if it had occurred later then far more people
would have been away from their homes, many on the roads of
the area. The main effects of the Northridge earthquake were:

- 57 people killed and over 1500 seriously injured
- 12 500 structures suffered moderate to serious damage
- 11 major roads were seriously damaged and had to close;
  roads were damaged up to 32 km from the epicentre
- over 11 000 landslides were triggered
- 20 000 people were immediately made homeless

- nearly 600 aftershocks were recorded in the days following, resulting in damage to already weakened buildings
- several days after the event, 9000 premises had no electricity; 20 000 had no gas; 48 500 had little or no water
- the damage bill came to over $30 billion
- around 700 000 applications were made to federal and state assistance programmes for financial help.

CASE STUDY 2: THE EFFECTS OF AN EARTHQUAKE IN AN LEDC

THE GUJARAT EARTHQUAKE, NORTH-WEST INDIA, 8.46 A.M. 26 JANUARY 2001

One of the most powerful earthquakes to strike the Indian sub-continent in the last 100 years was centred near the small town of Bhuj. This earthquake, with a focus at 17 km below the surface, was measured at 7.9 on the Richter scale, the shock waves from the event being felt over the border in Pakistan, where several people were killed, and across the sub-continent in Bangladesh and Nepal (see Figure 7). The death toll was high as many buildings were simply not able to withstand the tremors, even in an area that was known to be a seismically active zone. One resident complained that '*ours was not a well-designed building, it was built 12 years ago but it just fell to pieces as all the beams and pillars buckled instantly*'. A month after the event, the Indian government gave the following details on the effects of the earthquake:

- the death toll was put at just under 20 000 although some experts have estimated that at least 30 000 people died in the earthquake
- over 160 000 people were seriously injured
- over 1 million people were made homeless
- around 345 000 dwellings were destroyed, ranging from blocks of flats to simple mud-constructed houses, and over 800 000 buildings suffered some form of damage
- small towns, such as Bhuj, Bhachau and Anjar, had at least 90% of their dwellings destroyed and some villages were totally devastated
- in Bhuj all four hospitals were destroyed, which made it difficult to deal with the many injured survivors as emergency medical facilities had to be brought into the region from other parts of India and from outside of the country.

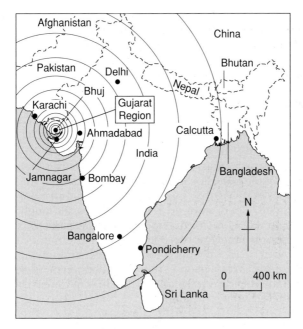

Figure 7 The Gujarat earthquake 2001

The earthquake also destroyed much of the heritage of the area including princely forts, palaces, temples and monuments, many of them hundreds of years old. Communications were seriously disrupted and many power lines were brought down. One of the most disturbing aspects of the aftermath of the event was that there was widespread looting of damaged property, something that the authorities struggled to bring under control. In the days following the earthquake there were several hundred aftershocks, one measuring over 5 on the Richter scale, and these caused considerable damage, as they did in the Northridge event, to already weakened buildings.

The Indian authorities feared widespread epidemics following the event, but prompt action meant that expected outbreaks of typhoid and cholera did not occur although there was evidence of widespread diarrhoea and gastroenteritis. In an area still heavily dependent on agriculture, the loss of 20 000 cattle had an enormous impact. The overall cost of the earthquake has been estimated at $4.5 billion and it has also been suggested that over 1 million people have been in receipt of some form of aid as a result of the event.

CASE STUDY 3: AN EARTHQUAKE IN THE BRITISH ISLES

THE DUDLEY EARTHQUAKE, ENGLISH MIDLANDS, 12.45 A.M. 23 SEPTEMBER 2002

The focus of this earthquake was just to the west of Dudley (West Midlands) at a depth of 9.6 km, and it is believed to have resulted from movement on an old fault line known as the Malvern Lineament (Figure 8). By world standards, it was a very light event, but in British terms it was extremely large as it measured 4.8 on the Richter scale. For most people who observed the event all that happened was that buildings trembled and doors and windows rattled. There were no serious injuries, although some people were treated for cuts due to breaking glass and for shock. The most serious damage reported was falling chimney stacks and tiles, which also dropped on to cars, and an amount of broken glass. Many people reported that pictures fell off walls and that crockery was smashed and, in a few areas, tarmac surfaces suffered some cracking.

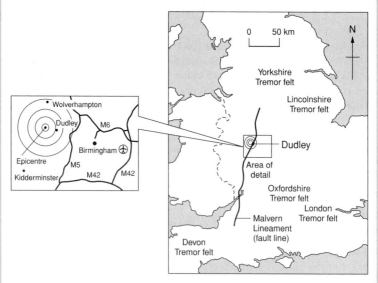

Figure 8 The Dudley earthquake 2002

Management of the earthquake hazard

Prediction. The prediction of earthquakes is very difficult. Regions at risk can be identified through plate tectonics, but attempts to predict a few hours before the event are questionable. Such attempts are based upon monitoring groundwater levels, release of radon gas and unusual animal behaviour. Fault lines, such as the San Andreas, can be monitored and the local magnetic fields measured. Areas can also be mapped on the basis of geological information and studies made into ground stability in order to predict the impact of an earthquake and to produce a hazard zone map that can be acted upon by local and even national planners.

Close studies of fault lines can sometimes indicate the point along the fault where the next earthquake could be due. A study of the pattern of the events along the San Andreas fault between 1969 and 1998 indicated the existence of a '**seismic gap**' in the area of Loma Prieta (i.e. the area had not had any real seismic activity for the past 20 years). This area suffered an earthquake in October 1989, which measured 7.1 on the Richter scale and was the worst to hit the San Francisco region since 1906. In total, 63 people died as a result of the event with over 3700 seriously injured. Because of the seismic survey this event was not entirely unexpected, but like all earthquakes it was not possible to predict it precisely. Such a system, however, would not work for events such as the one at Northridge, as this took place on an unknown fault line.

Prevention. Trying to prevent an earthquake is thought by almost all to be impossible. This, however, has not stopped studies into the feasibility of schemes to keep plates sliding past each other, rather than 'sticking' and then releasing, which is the main cause of earthquakes. Suggestions so far as to lubricating this movement have focused on water and oil. Some people have even gone as far as to suggest nuclear explosions at depth!

Protection. Since earthquakes strike suddenly, violently and without warning, it is essential that everyone from civil authorities to individuals are prepared. In the USA, the Federal Emergency Management Agency's Programme has the following objectives:

- to promote understanding of earthquakes and their effects
- to work to better identify earthquake risk
- to improve earthquake-resistant design and construction techniques
- to encourage the use of earthquake-safe policies and planning practices.

Protection therefore means preparing for the event by modifying the human and built environments in order to decrease vulnerability. It also includes attempts to modify the loss by insurance and aid. Some of the ways include the following:

- **Hazard-resistant structures**; buildings can be designed to be aseismic, in that they can be earthquake resistant. There are three main ways in which this can be achieved:

  (a) by putting a large concrete weight on top of the building that will move, with the aid of a computer program, in the opposite direction to the force of the earthquake in order to counteract stress
  (b) putting large rubber shock absorbers in the foundations that will allow some movement of the building
  (c) by adding cross-bracing to the structure to hold it together better when it shakes.

  Older buildings and structures, such as elevated motorways, can be **retrofitted** with such devices to make them more earthquake-proof. A comparison between the 1989 Loma Prieta earthquake (7.1 Richter) and the 1988 event in Armenia (6.9 Richter) shows the effects of different types of buildings. The greater earthquake-proof buildings of California resulted in 63 deaths, whereas in Armenia over 25 000 people died, many inside buildings that collapsed as a result of soft foundations and no earthquake proofing features. In the town of Leninakan, for example, over 90% of more modern 9–12-storey pre-cast concrete frame buildings were destroyed.

- **Education**: for many areas this is the main way that loss of life can be minimised. Instructions are issued by the authorities in how to prepare for such events by securing homes, appliances and heavy furniture, and assembling 'earthquake kits', Children can have earthquake drills at school, as can people in offices and factories. Government offices and many companies in Japan observe Disaster Prevention Day (1 September), which marks the anniversary of the Tokyo (Kwanto Plain) earthquake in 1923. Following the Loma Prieta event (1989), the American Red Cross issued a list of supplies that people should keep at hand in case of an earthquake. These include water (at least 3 days supply for all persons in the house and pets!); a whole range of foodstuffs (particularly canned and high-energy foods); clothing and bedding; first aid kit; tools and supplies (to include radio, torch batteries, can opener, matches, toilet paper, small fire extinguisher, pliers, aluminium foil). Figure 9 shows the instructions issued by the Metropolitan Government of Tokyo advising people what to do if an earthquake should occur in that city.

- **Fire prevention**: 'smart meters' have been developed that can cut off the gas if an earthquake of sufficient magnitude occurs. In Tokyo, the gas company has a network that transmits seismic information to a computer, which then informs employees where to switch off major pipelines so reducing the number of fires.

- **Emergency services**: need careful organisation and planning. Heavy lifting gear needs to be available and many people should be

---

Tokyo Metropolitan Government

What to do if a big earthquake hits

The worst shake is over in about a minute, so keep calm and quickly do the following:

(1) Turn off all stoves and heaters. Put out fires that may break out. Do not become flustered by the sight of flames, and act quickly to put out the fire.

(2) Get under a table or desk to protect yourself.

(3) Do not run outdoors where you are liable to be hit by falling objects.

(4) Open the door for an emergency exit. Door frames are liable to spring in a big quake and hold the door so tight they cannot be opened.

(5) Keep away from narrow alleys, concrete block walls and embankments, and take temporary refuge in an open area.

(6) For evacuation from department stores or theatres, do not panic and do as directed by the attendant in charge.

(7) When driving in the streets, move the car to the left and stop. Driving will be banned in restricted areas.

(8) Evacuate to a designated safety evacuation area when a big fire or other danger approaches.

(9) Walk to emergency evacuation area. Take the minimum of personal belongings.

(10) Do not be moved by rumours. Listen for the latest news over the radio.

Figure 9 Tokyo earthquake drill

given first aid training, as it could be some time after the event that trained medical personnel arrive. Much of the preparation in California involves the establishment of computer programs that will identify which areas the emergency services should be sent to first.

- **Land-use planning**: the most hazardous areas in the event of an earthquake can be identified and then regulated in terms of land use. Certain types of buildings should be put in areas of low risk, such as schools and hospitals. It is also important to have sufficient open space, as this forms a safe area away from fires and aftershock damage to buildings.

- **Insurance**: in MEDCs, people are urged to take out insurance to cover their losses, the only problem being that for individuals, this is very expensive. In the Kobe earthquake in Japan in 1995, for example, only 7% of the people were covered by earthquake insurance.

- **Aid**: most aid to LEDCs has generally been to help in the few days after the event, providing medical services, tents, water purification equipment, search and rescue equipment, etc. Aid over the longer term is much more problematical; it is something that is needed for the reconstruction of the built environment and redevelopment of the economy.

2 Volcanic Activity

Causes and distribution

Most volcanic activity is associated with plate tectonic processes and is mainly located along plate margins (Figure 10). Areas that have such activity are typically found:

- along mid-ocean ridges where plates are diverging. The best example is the mid-Atlantic ridge where Iceland represents a large area formed from volcanic activity
- associated with rift valleys. The East African Rift valley has a number of volcanoes along it, including Mt Kenya, Mt Kilimanjaro and Mt Nyiragongo (see later)
- on or near subduction zones. The line of volcanoes, the 'Ring of Fire', which surrounds the Pacific Ocean is associated with plate subduction. This tends to be the most violent of all activity
- over hot spots, such as those that occur in the middle of the Pacific Ocean and give rise to the Hawaiian Islands.

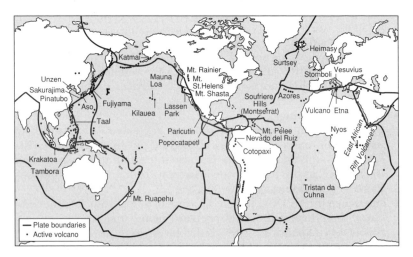

Figure 10 The world's active volcanoes

The magnitude and frequency of events

There have been attempts to classify volcanic activity by noting the physical differences in eruptions and by using a table that runs from 0 (non-explosive) to 8 (very large). The impact of the hazard event is usually measured in terms of loss of life or the cost of damage to the built environment. To determine the frequency of eruption of any volcano, its previous history of eruption can be interpreted by vulcanologists/geologists using the deposits associated with the volcano itself and those within the wider region that it can affect.

The effects of volcanic activity

A volcanic event can produce a number of effects, the impact of which can range from the area immediately around the volcano to the entire planet. The effects can be categorised into primary and secondary:

- **primary**: these include **tephra** (solid material of varying grain size, i.e. volcanic bombs to ash, ejected into the atmosphere); **pyroclastic flows** (very hot [800°C], gas charged, high-velocity flows – mixture of gases and tephra); **lava flows**; **volcanic gases** (including carbon dioxide, carbon monoxide, hydrogen sulphide, sulphur dioxide, chlorine – emissions of carbon dioxide from Lake Nyos (Cameroun) in 1986 killed 1700 people)
- **secondary: lahars**, volcanic mud flows such as the ones that devastated the Colombian town of Armero after the eruption of Nevado del Ruiz in November 1985); **flooding** (melting of glaciers and ice caps such as the Grimsvoton glacial burst on Iceland in November 1996); **tsunamis** (giant sea waves – see later chapter); **volcanic landslides; climate change** (the ejection of vast amounts of volcanic debris into the atmosphere can reduce global temperatures and is believed to have been an agent in past climatic change).

Volcanic effects become hazardous when they impact upon humans and the built environment, killing and injuring people, burying and collapsing buildings, destroying the infrastructure and bringing agricultural activities to a halt.

CASE STUDY 4: THE EFFECTS OF A VOLCANIC ERUPTION

THE ERUPTION OF NYIRAGONGO, CONGO, JANUARY 2002

Associated with the southern section of the East African Rift Valley, the Congolese volcano, Nyiragongo erupted in January 2002. Although it was known to be an active volcano there was very little warning given to the dense populations that live on its lower slopes, particularly in the area of Goma in the Congo and Gisenyi, over the border in Rwanda. Some of the effects of the eruption were:

- lava flows that destroyed at least one-third of Goma, a town with over 200 000 inhabitants
- the commercial centre of Goma was destroyed along with the airport
- the death toll reached 147
- it was estimated that over 350 000 people fled the area, which caused an enormous problem in providing food and shelter, particularly in the small country of Rwanda
- sulphurous lava entered Lake Kivu and poisoned the water that was the major source of drinking water in the region
- the rise in the temperature of Lake Kivu allowed toxic gases to rise from the lake bed
- several earthquakes accompanied the eruption, one measuring over 5 on the Richter scale
- thousands of people required medical attention, first from the effects of smoke and fumes from the lava that caused eye irritation and respiratory problems, and secondly from such complaints as dysentery linked to the drinking of contaminated water
- there was a vast amount of looting from abandoned homes and commercial properties
- the long-term problem was that the economic base of the area had been very seriously damaged.

Figure 11 Goma residents clamber over lava that covers the area

Management of the volcanic hazard

Prediction. It is easy to locate volcanoes, but it is very difficult to predict exactly when activity will take place, in particular, the timing of a major eruption. The Colombian volcano, Nevado del Ruiz, came to life in late 1984 with small-scale activity but vulcanologists, although they knew the danger a major eruption would pose to the surrounding area, were unable to predict when a major event would take place. The volcano continued with small-scale activity for several months and people were obviously not prepared to evacuate their homes on that basis. When the final violent eruption came, on 13 November 1985, almost all of the population had remained in this area and devastating lahars, resulting from melting ice and snow, swept down the valleys killing over 20 000 people.

A study of the previous eruption history of any volcano is important, along with an understanding of the type of activity produced. At the present time, research is being conducted to see if it is possible to give a fairly accurate timing for an eruption, using the shock waves that are produced as magma moves towards the surface, expanding cracks and breaking through other areas of rock. There was some success in predicting the recent eruption (2000) of Popacatapetl in Mexico, but it remains to be seen if such techniques can be applied to all volcanoes.

Protection. With volcanic activity, protection means preparing for the event. Monitoring a volcano will possibly give a time when the area under threat should be evacuated. This includes observations of land swelling, seismic activity, changes in groundwater levels, changes in the chemical composition of groundwater, emission of gases, magnetic field studies and the shock wave analysis referred to above. The governments of several countries in volcanic areas have made risk assessments and from them produced a series of alert levels in order to warn the public. In New Zealand, the government has produced a five-stage table that includes the following:

1   Signs of volcanic activity. No significant volcanic threat
2   Indications of intrusive processes. Local eruption threat
3   Increasing intrusive trends indicting a real possibility of a hazardous eruption
4   Large-scale eruption now seems imminent
5   Destruction within the Permanent Danger Zone (as identified). Significant risk over a wider area.

Geological studies of the nature and extent of deposits from former eruptions and associated ashfalls, lahars and floods may also provide evidence for hazard assessment. Figure 12 shows the hazard assessment made in the environs of Mt Rainier (Cascade Range – USA), one of the most studied volcanoes in North America.

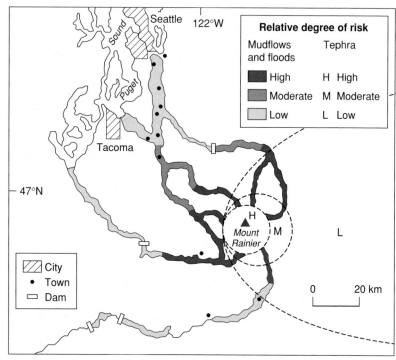

Figure 12 Risk assessment of Mount Rainier (Cascade Range)

Once the lava has started to flow, it is possible, in certain circumstances, to divert it away from the built environment. On Mt Etna in Sicily, both the digging of trenches and the setting off of explosives on the lava have been successful, whilst in 1973 the inhabitants of Haeimaey (Iceland) were able to divert a lava flow by pouring sea water on the front so it would quickly solidify. Where the direction of risk is known, it is possible to erect barriers that will protect settlements from lava flows and lahars, as has been done in parts of the Hawaiian Islands.

Following risk assessments, it is possible to identify areas at greatest risk and, as with earthquakes, land use planning can be applied to avoid building in such places.

Many devastated areas in LEDCs require aid for considerable periods of time as volcanic events can be prolonged and very damaging to the local economy. Such aid is needed for monitoring, evacuation, emergency shelters and food, long-term resettlement of the population, and the restoration of the area's economic base and infrastructure.

**CASE STUDY 5: AID TO AN ISLAND AFTER
A VOLCANIC ERUPTION**

**MONTSERRAT (WEST INDIES) SOUFRIERE HILLS
1995–7**

During and after the eruption of this volcano, the British government had to provide, or assist in, the following, as Montserrat is a dependent territory of the UK:

- evacuation of 7000 of the island's population to neighbouring islands such as Antigua, or resettlement in the UK, and financial help with that resettlement
- resettle some of the population from the volcanic south to the 'safer' north
- set up temporary shelters in the north
- re-establish air and sea links with the island
- build new permanent housing
- move the capital from Plymouth (now destroyed) to Salem
- provide farming areas for those resettled in the north
- more investment in monitoring via the Montserrat Volcanic Observatory trying to find any predictive patterns in the volcano's activity that will enable risks to people to be quantified.

The total amount that the British government could eventually spend on mitigating the effects of the eruption and a 3-year development plan for the island will be over £100 million.

3 Mass Movement on Slopes

Under the influence of gravity, materials are often seen to move rapidly downhill and this constitutes an important hazard, particularly in mountain areas. Hazards of this type are caused by large volume combinations of rock, soil, water, ice and snow moving under the influence of gravity and, usually, water. There are many terms used to describe these movements and some authors use many categories for them, but at its simplest they can be classified as either **landslides** (rock and soil) or **avalanches** (ice and snow mainly). It is also possible to recognise **rockfalls**. Mass movement hazards are on the increase (see Table 1) as population and land pressure force people to inhabit potentially unstable slopes. Movements of this type are usually triggered by torrential rainfall or by seismic activity such as earthquakes.

Landslides

Landslides are the result of slope failure that involves the downhill transfer of material by one of three main mechanisms, namely, fall, slide and flow (there are also toppling and spreading). It is difficult to classify landslides, as many of them are very complex in nature, however, the one proposed by Varnes in 1978 has been accepted. Varnes classified landslides by speed and type of movement/material involved (see below):

Type of movement	Material involved
Falling	Rock
Toppling	Debris
Sliding or slumping	Earth
Lateral spreading	
Flow	

The **rate of movement** scale for landslides is:

- 3.0 m per second – extremely rapid
- 0.3 m per minute – very rapid
- 1.5 m per day – rapid
- 1.5 m per month – moderate
- 1.5 m per year – slow
- 0.06 m per year – very slow.

Many of the phenomena occurring within this classification, though, operate far too slowly for them to be able to present a hazard to people.

Landslides can be small events such as a localised cliff collapse or they can involve the large-scale catastrophic movement of whole sections of mountainside. Slopes are part of the evolution of the landscape and they will respond to a natural set of factors such as rock type, vegetation and climate, eventually achieving a state of balance or equilibrium. If conditions change, either naturally or through the intervention of man, this state of affairs is also likely to change to produce an unstable slope that responds by altering its profile in order to achieve a new equilibrium. Such environmental changes that can bring about landslides include torrential rainfall during a hurricane, and the vibrations resulting from earthquakes or volcanic eruptions. Some of the factors that contribute to slope instability are shown in Figure 13.

Southern Italy has areas that are highly susceptible to landslides. There are several factors that have contributed to this including the mountainous nature of much of the terrain, weak sedimentary rocks, summer drought followed by torrential downpours and extensive deforestation that has reduced the forest cover from around 90% to less than 30%. There is also widespread poverty in the region that has made many people more vulnerable to hazards. On 6 May 1998, there was a series of devastating mudflows that affected the area east of Naples and Mt Vesuvius. Several villages and towns were hit, but the

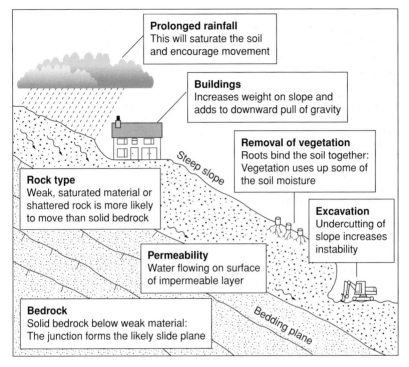

Figure 13 Factors that promote landslides

main centre to be affected was the town of **Sarno**, where a wall of mud, at least 2 m high, swept through the middle of the urban area. These slides, which killed over 100 people, followed days of very heavy rainfall on slopes that had seen continuous tree removal in the years preceding the event, one authority on the area describing the main cause as '*wild urbanisation in high-risk zones*'.

Other large-scale disasters that occurred in the second half of the twentieth century included:

Piave valley, northern Italy 1963. A huge slide of rock into the Vaiont reservoir created a wave of water that overtopped the dam and surged into the valley below inundating settlements, including the town of Longarone. There were over 2000 deaths.

Ormoc City, Philippines 1991. Torrential rainfall from tropical storm Thelma resulted in devastating mudslides that affected many shanty towns on steep slopes. The mudslides killed 5000 people, leaving 46 000 homeless.

Northern Venezuela 1999. Very heavy rainfall (the wettest for 100 years that included 900 mm in 2 days), coupled with deforestation to make way for shanty towns, led to devastating landslides and mudflows. Around 30 000 people were killed and over 400 000 made homeless as a result.

Las Colinas, El Salvador 2001. Over 1000 people were killed by a landslide that occurred as a result of an earthquake that measured 7.6 on the Richter scale. The slope in question was situated above a middle-class neighbourhood but it had been partly deforested and cut away by developers. One resident who survived, said '*it was a disaster waiting to happen. The developers kept digging further and further into the base of the mountain despite everything we said*'.

Avalanches

An avalanche is a sudden and rapid movement of snow (sometimes with ice and rocks) down a slope. Slopes have to be at least 25 degrees or the snow will not slide downhill. Heavy snowfall on previous layers of snow and ice is one cause of an avalanche because as layers of snow build up it is possible for a weak layer to develop with the thawing and refreezing of the snow. Avalanches can also result from rapid thawing, which destabilises the snow fields. In mountain areas there are certain times when avalanches are likely to be more frequent, for example in the French Alps three-quarters of all the avalanches recorded occur between January and March.

Most avalanches occur well away from people and the built environment, and therefore these events do not constitute a hazard. As settlement has expanded in mountain regions, though, particularly with the growth of tourism and winter sports, people are becoming increasingly vulnerable to the avalanche hazard. The winter of 1998–9 saw heavy snowfall in Alpine Europe, which resulted in two serious avalanches. On the **9 February 1999**, after nearly 2 m of snow had fallen in a few days, a large avalanche hit the small resort of Le Tour near **Chamonix** in France and killed 12 people. Two weeks later (**23 February**) a much bigger avalanche devastated the Austrian town of **Galtur** where 38 people lost their lives. Although avalanches were not unknown in the Galtur area, scientists did not believe that one could travel so far in the direction of the town. This led to new investigations that showed the extent to which avalanches can gain in volume as they move downhill and move a greater distance as a consequence.

Managing the hazards

Landslides. There are a variety of **engineering techniques** that can make a slope more stable. These include drainage, terracing (or benching), retaining walls, stabilising the base of the slope and stabilisation by anchoring (anchors driven into the rock strata). **Forecasting, warning and evacuation** are possible techniques as many movements do give warnings before the event such as bulging walls, cracks, tilted poles and fences, and minor slumps, therefore education of the public is essential. **Hazard mapping** can be applied, with the possibility of restricting growth on certain potentially vulnerable slopes. In already developed areas, this poses a great problem as the indication of a possible hazard may reduce land values.

Avalanches. One way to reduce the avalanche threat is to create a series of smaller avalanches through **controlled explosions** and therefore reduce the risk of a major event as the snow pack is much reduced. This is a very expensive method of control. In areas where there is extensive tourism and winter sports, **risk management** involves mapping avalanche paths and attempting to control human activities. At times of high risk, ski areas and even roads may be closed and skiers directed to safer slopes; major ski resorts will issue daily bulletins on the avalanche risk. Keeping the snow on the mountainside or trying to deflect it once it has moved is the purpose of **engineering** solutions. **Fences** will trap snow on the upper slopes, **deflection structures** can be built to protect houses and pylons, and **avalanche sheds** have been constructed to protect transport routes. Such engineering techniques may be successful but many complain about the expense and the unsightly nature of the constructions. Some areas have tried **afforestation** as a means of slowing down the slides of snow but this form of protection takes years to mature.

Summary

- Earthquakes and volcanic activity are mainly associated with tectonic plate boundaries although events do occur away from them in other areas.
- Earthquake magnitude is measured by the Richter scale. The Mercalli scale puts a more human dimension into the measurements.
- The effects of earthquakes and volcanic activity can be divided into primary and secondary categories.
- Some of the secondary effects can last for many years after the event.
- People are more vulnerable to the events in LEDCs as against MEDCs.
- Financial costs of such disasters are much higher in MEDCs.
- Prediction and warning of earthquakes is difficult to achieve, therefore people have to be better prepared to live with the hazard.
- The exact timing of serious volcanic eruptions is, again, difficult to determine, so responses have to concentrate on monitoring, warning and evacuation.
- As people have increasingly developed slopes, particularly in LEDCs, landslides are more common and people are increasingly more vulnerable.

- The growth of tourism and winter sports has put more people at risk from avalanches.
- Both landslides and avalanches can be managed by a range of engineering techniques, but these are expensive and often unsightly.

Exercises

1. Describe the global distribution of either earthquakes or volcanoes.
2. For **either** earthquakes **or** volcanoes, name **two** pieces of evidence that can be used to show the scale of the hazard event. Comment on the reliability of such evidence.
3. **Either**
   (a) For either earthquakes or volcanoes, describe methods by which the hazard can be predicted and managed. Discuss the effectiveness of such methods.
   or
   (b) 'Geological activity is responsible for hazards that produce some extreme impacts in terms of loss of life and damage to property. If the consequences of such hazards are to be reduced, then appropriate management is necessary.'
   With reference to either earthquakes or volcanoes, discuss the above statement.
4. Why do the impacts of earthquake and volcanic hazards vary so much between LEDCs and MEDCs?
5. Why have people become increasingly vulnerable to the hazards that result from mass movements on slopes?

3 Atmospheric and Climatic Hazards

1 Tropical Cyclones (Hurricanes)

Origins and formation

Tropical cyclones are violent storms between 200 and 700 km in diameter and represent the end product of a range of weather systems that can develop in the tropics. They begin with an area of low pressure into which warm air is drawn in a spiralling manner. Small-scale disturbances enlarge into tropical storms with rotating wind systems, which may grow into a much more intense and rapidly rotating system, the cyclone. Why tropical storms should be triggered into becoming cyclones is not entirely clear, but there are several conditions that need to be present in order to generate such disturbances:

- an oceanic location with sea temperatures over 26°C (continuous source of heat to maintain rising air currents)
- a depth of ocean of at least 70 m (sufficient warm water and a large supply of moisture to provide latent heat, released by condensation, to drive the system)
- a location at least 5 degrees north and south of the equator in order that the Coriolis effect can bring about the maximum rotation of air (the Coriolis effect is weak at the Equator and will not allow a circular motion to develop)
- low-level convergence of air in the lower atmosphere circulation system
- rapid outflow of air in the upper atmospheric circulation.

The tropical cyclone exists whilst there is a supply of latent heat and moisture to provide energy and low frictional drag on the ocean surface. Once the system reaches maturity, a central eye develops. This is an area 10–50 km in diameter in which there are calm conditions, clear skies, higher temperatures and descending air. Figure 14 shows the general structure of a typical mature tropical cyclone. Once the system reaches land or the colder waters towards the poles, it will decline as the source of heat/moisture is removed.

Distribution

Tropical cyclones occur between latitudes 5 and 20 north and south of the equator, as nearer to the equator the weaker the spin (Figure 15). Once generated they tend to move westwards to be at their most destructive in:

- the Caribbean Sea/Gulf of Mexico area (known as **hurricanes**) – hurricanes season August–October (the area has 11% of all tropical cyclones)
- the western side of Central America (east Pacific) – hurricane season June–October (17%)

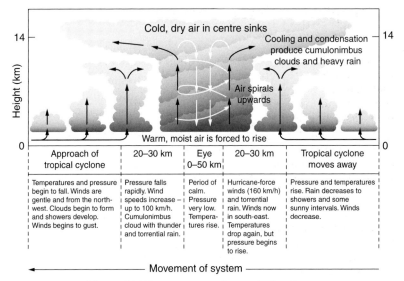

Figure 14 The structure of a tropical cyclone

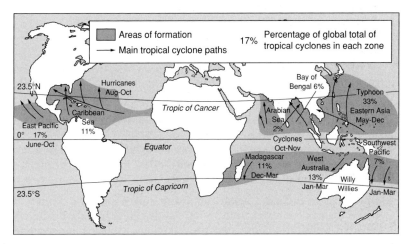

Figure 15 The global pattern of tropical cyclones

- the Arabian Sea/Bay of Bengal area (known as **cyclones**) – cyclone season October–November (8%)
- off South-east Asia (known as **typhoons**) – typhoon season May–December (main area with one-third of all cyclones)
- off Madagascar in South-east Africa – cyclone season December–March (11%)

- northern Australia (known as **willy-willies**) and the south-western Pacific – season January–March (20%).

Magnitude and frequency

Tropical cyclones are measured on the **Saffir-Simpson scale**, which consists of five levels based upon central pressure, wind speed, storm surge and damage potential. Scale 5, for example, has central pressure at 920 mb or below, wind speed at 69 metres per second or greater (250 kilometres per hour), storm surge at 5.5 m or greater and a damage potential that refers to '*complete failure of many buildings with major damage to lower floors of all structures lower than 3 m above sea level. Evacuation of all residential buildings on low ground within 16–24 km of the coast is likely*'. The average lifespan of a tropical cyclone is 7–14 days. Every year about 70–75 tropical storms develop in the world, of which around 50 will intensify to become tropical cyclones.

The effects of a tropical cyclone

People's vulnerability to this hazard depends upon a whole range of factors, both physical and human. The main physical factors that can determine the impact of a cyclone include:

- intensity of the cyclone (Saffir-Simpson scale 1–5)
- speed of movement, i.e. length of time over area
- distance from the sea
- physical geography of the coastal region, i.e. width of coastal plain/size of delta; location of any mountain ranges relative to the coast.

The human factors are concerned with how well a community has made preparations to resist the effects of a cyclone and these are considered later under the heading 'Hazard management'. There are several ways that tropical cyclones represent a hazard to people and the built environment:

- **winds** often exceed 150 km per hour and have been known to reach over 300 km per hour. Such winds can bring about the collapse of buildings, cause structural damage to roads and bridges, bring down transmission lines and devastate agricultural areas. High winds can hurl large pieces of debris around, which often cause a number of deaths
- **heavy rainfall**, often over 100 mm per day, causes severe flooding and landslides (very common in Hong Kong). High relief can exaggerate heavy rainfall and totals in excess of 500–700 mm per day have been recorded in some areas
- **storm surges**, resulting from the piling up of water by wind-driven waves and the ocean heaving up under reduced pressure, flood low-lying coastal areas and often extend far inland if there is an

extensive area of flat land such as the Ganges delta. Storm surges cause the bulk of deaths that result from tropical cyclones. A 1970 cyclone that affected Bangladesh, which covers the Ganges delta, produced a storm surge of 6 m that killed over 300 000 people. Coastal areas affected by this flooding often take a long time to recover agriculturally as the soil becomes contaminated with salt.

CASE STUDY 6: THE EFFECTS OF A HURRICANE ON AN LEDC

HURRICANE MITCH, CENTRAL AMERICA, NOVEMBER 1998

Hurricane Mitch began as a tropical storm around 22 October in the southern Caribbean Sea. In its early days, it moved slowly westwards on an unpredictable track, typical of so many such disturbances in the region. Wind speeds increased, though and, as the system deepened through the last days of the month, it became classified as a hurricane, building into one of the most severe to hit this part of the world, a Category 5 (Saffir-Simpson). After following its predicted westward track, it suddenly turned southwards to hit the north Honduras coast, moving through that country, and then Nicaragua before departing through El Salvador and Guatemala (see Figure 16). What made Hurricane Mitch so devastating was not the winds (although they did reach 300 km per hour), but the fact that the system was so slow moving and produced torrential rain. It has been estimated in some places that the hurricane produced over 1000 mm of rainfall in 5 days, as much as the region receives in an average year. This led to severe flooding as rivers burst their banks, and there was even the case of an over-filled crater lake in a dormant volcano (Casita in Nicaragua) bursting through its side. The rain fell in areas where the soil consisted of weathered ash and lava that had not been well managed by farmers removing vegetation to create arable land. As a consequence, disastrous mudslides accompanied the floods, sweeping away, and burying, people, homes and farmland. The main effects of Hurricane Mitch were therefore:

- the death toll is believed to have been between 15 000 and 20 000
- many settlements were completely wiped out, including some towns, particularly on the northern coast of Honduras
- transport links were obliterated. In Nicaragua, 50 main bridges were destroyed, along with countless minor ones,

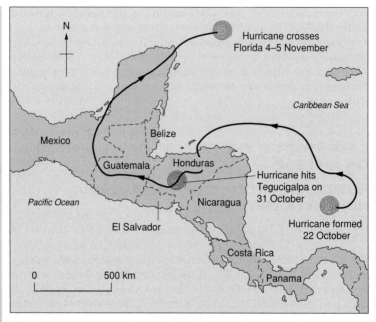

Figure 16 The track of Hurricane Mitch

including all those on the roads leading to the capital, Managua

- vast numbers were made homeless, In Honduras, it was estimated that 20% of the population lost their homes
- the centre of the capital city of Honduras, Tegucigalpa, was turned into a vast lake as the Rio Choluteca overflowed
- the crater lake in the dormant volcano, Casita, burst through the crater walls sending a 6 m high wall of mud and water onto the villages that surround it, killing 1500 people
- 70% of the Honduran economic output was lost, mainly in agriculture, where the coffee and banana plantations were severely affected. Even where crops could be harvested, the lack of communications meant that produce could not be marketed. Agricultural losses for 1998 and 1999 were put at $1.5 billion
- Honduras and Nicaragua, the two countries most affected, were already amongst the poorest in the Americas, each with a GDP, at that time, of under $700 per capita
- land worked by many farmers had been covered by a deep layer of mud, which baked hard after the hurricane had passed

- food supplies were destroyed leading to serious shortages and food prices increased rapidly
- crime vastly increased as abandoned homes and businesses were looted
- power transmission systems were destroyed and fuel sources became depleted (immediately after the disaster, the Honduran Air Force had only fuel for 5 days, important in a country where most of the roads had been left impassable)
- the limited, and mainly agricultural, export base in Nicaragua and Honduras, was severely cut, having implications for servicing large foreign debt commitments
- large amounts of aid had to be supplied.

Hazard management

Prediction. The prediction of tropical cyclones depends upon the state of monitoring and warning systems. Weather bureaux, such as the National Hurricane Centre in Florida (USA), are able to access data from geostationary satellites and from both land and sea-based recording centres. The USA also maintains a round-the-clock surveillance of tropical storms that have the potential to become hurricanes by the use of weather aircraft. Such information is compared with computer models so that a path can be predicted and people warned to evacuate an area. It is essential that such warnings are correct, as there is a high economic cost associated with evacuation and, as with all false alarms, people might become complacent and refuse future advice. It has been estimated in the USA that to evacuate coastal areas, the cost is roughly $1 million per kilometre of coastline due to losses in business, tourism and the provision of protection. As cyclones tend to follow an erratic path, it is not always possible to give more than 12–18 hours warning and in most LEDCs, where communications are poor, this is insufficient for a proper evacuation. Some areas, however, have established warning systems that do give the people a chance to take some precautions. Examples include areas of central America (e.g. Belize) and along the shores of the Bay of Bengal (India/Bangladesh). In 1997, a tropical cyclone warning in the Cox's Bazaar area of Bangladesh allowed for the evacuation of over 300 000 people. As a result, the death toll in the disaster was kept below 100. This shows that real progress is being made within some LEDCs in educating the people and in warning systems.

    Prevention. Like other natural hazards, tropical cyclones cannot really be prevented, but there has been research into the effect of cloud seeding in order to cause more precipitation. The theory is that if the cyclone could be forced to release more water over the sea, then this would result in a weakening of the system as it approached land.

There was some concern expressed over the effects of this on the global energy system, and as a result, research has not continued.

Protection. Protection, as with all natural hazards, means being prepared. Predicting the landfall of a tropical cyclone will enable evacuation to take place together with the emergency services being put on full alert. If evacuation does take place, then protection units, such as the National Guard in the USA, have to be called in to prevent homes and commercial properties from being looted. People are also made aware of how to strengthen their homes and commercial properties in order to withstand the high winds. **Cyclone/hurricane drills** can be practised along the lines of those that are carried out in earthquake-prone areas. In Florida, for example, there is 'Project Safeside', a hurricane awareness programme that is composed of precautionary drills for use in schools and the Emergency Operations centre of the state. Where storm surges are a problem, **land-use planning** can identify the areas at greatest risk and certain types of development can be limited in such areas. In LEDCs, in those parts prone to tropical cyclones, concrete storm shelters have been constructed and countries are actively seeking international aid in order to build more. In Bangladesh, for example, fewer than 500 have been built although it has been estimated that over 10 000 are needed. **Sea walls, breakwaters** and **flood barriers** can be built and houses put on stilts. The sea wall that was built to protect Galveston (Texas) from further flooding, after the storm surge of 1900 that killed over 6000 people, was so expensive that it is unlikely to be repeated elsewhere. In the USA, local authorities are required to address this problem by limiting expenditure on developments in high-risk areas and directing population away from them, as well as having sound plans to reduce evacuation times and for post-disaster redevelopment. In LEDCs, however, the need for land usually outweighs such considerations. Some structures can be **retrofitted** (adjusting the building to make it resistant to winds) to ensure greater safety during an event. In Dominica (West Indies), in 1994, some homes were retrofitted as part of a joint exercises carried out by the Organisation of American States and the government of Dominica. The value of the project was shown in the following year when all the retrofitted buildings withstood the impact of Hurricane Marilyn.

As with other natural phenomena, people in MEDCs are urged to take out insurance, whereas in LEDCs it is important that following a cyclone event aid is available, both in the short and long term, as damage to the economic base of the affected area is likely to last for a number of years.

The ability of people to resist natural hazards, such as cyclones, very much depends upon a range of political and economic factors. LEDCs suffer more because land-use planning, warning systems, defences, infrastructure and emergency services are inadequate, and this usually results in a higher death toll. MEDCs will have some planning systems in place, sophisticated warning arrangements, better defences and infrastructure, and emergency services that are much more comprehensive and better prepared. Countries such as the USA therefore suffer much lower deaths from individual hurricanes but they have to bear a much greater monetary loss because of the damage to the built environment. It is true to say, however, that the loss of a house in a MEDC will probably be covered by insurance, but the simpler dwelling of the inhabitant of a LEDC may very well be a greater loss, taking into account the time invested in it and the years of irreplaceable and uninsured savings that it represents. The cyclone that hit Bangladesh in 1991 was responsible for an estimated 131 000 deaths and a monetary cost of $1.7 billion, whereas a hurricane of similar strength that hit Florida in 1992 (Hurricane Andrew) killed only 60 people but caused damage estimated at £20 billion.

2 Mid-latitude Storms

Origin and distribution

Temperate storms affect large areas of the world outside of the tropics but become only a real hazard when they affect densely populated areas such as Europe. Storms are associated with mid-latitude depressions that develop under the jet streams and along the polar front, which forms on the junction of cold polar air and warmer tropical air. Hurricanes, as we have seen, depend on convection over a warm sea but temperate depressions are more dependent on inter-actions between contrasting air masses. These depressions track westward across the temperate latitudes bringing wet and windy conditions to western continental areas, conditions that occasionally become extreme. Such storms are more common in winter because the extremely low temperatures of the polar winter increase the con-trast in air mass temperatures at the polar front.

Effects of mid-latitude storms

Mid-latitude storms can cause widespread and costly damage. There are a number of reasons for this:

- There are a large number of them. It is not unknown for several storms a month to cross Europe during the winter period.
- Depressions cover a much wider area than do hurricanes.
- There is a high concentration of wealth in the areas that they cross. Such storms affect densely populated wealthy industrial countries where there is a great deal of built environment that may be damaged.

The variety of effects produced by the depression. These include the strong winds that often blow at over 100 km per hour in exposed areas; the heavy rainfall associated with the passage of the frontal systems (warm front, cold front, occluded front); river flooding produced by the heavy rainfall that often falls on ground saturated from the previous depression; coastal flooding and wave damage resulting from the strong winds blowing over sea areas for long distances (large fetch); heavy snowfalls that replace the heavy rainfall in some winter storms; mini-tornadoes that sometimes develop in the updraughts associated with the passage of a front (the effects of such an event at Selsey, on the south coast of England, in January 1998, are recorded in the next section on tornadoes).

CASE STUDY 7: THE EFFECTS OF A WINTER STORM ON THE UK

SUNDAY, 5 JANUARY 1998

Figure 17 shows the effects of a storm that swept through England in 1998 as seen by a national newspaper. As a deep depression moved through the country, strong winds and heavy

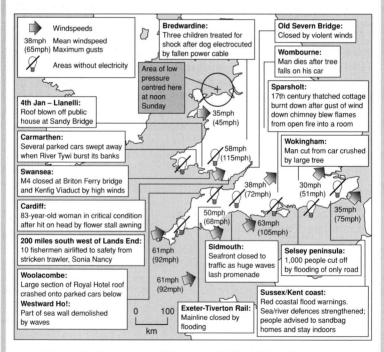

Figure 17 The storm of 5 January 1998 and its effects across southern Britain

rainfall developed on its southern flank and brought widespread damage to much of southern England and Wales. Winds were reported as gusting up to 180 km per hour and as a result of the heavy rainfall, there was widespread flooding. The major effects were therefore:

- large waves battered coastal areas, particularly in the south and west, causing widespread damage to property and to sea walls and other coastal defences
- coastal flooding also resulted from the large waves and high sea levels
- large number of trees were brought down, some causing fatalities and damage to property
- roofs blown off houses and commercial property
- widespread disruption to power supplies as cables were brought down. It was estimated that over 100 000 homes were left without power at some time during the event
- several rivers burst their banks as a result of heavy rainfall, flooding many houses and washing away a number of vehicles, e.g. the Arun in Sussex and the Tywi in west Wales
- ships were in trouble because of huge seas and many ferry services were cancelled, particularly those across the English Channel
- widespread disruption to transport, as railway lines and roads were flooded and high winds made motorway driving and the crossing of certain bridges dangerous. Speed restrictions were put in place on several motorways in south-east England
- as the system moved north-east it brought heavy snowfall to Northern Ireland and parts of Scotland. In the Scottish Highlands, the snowfall was so heavy that avalanche warnings were issued for the area around Glencoe.

Severe storms have been a part of the climate of north-western Europe since people began recording such events. The storm and flood of **January 1362** was known as the 'Great Drowning' and is considered by many to have been the greatest natural catastrophe to hit the area in the past 1000 years. Vast tracts of Denmark and northern Germany were inundated and roughly half the population drowned (estimates have put this somewhere between 30 000 and 100 000). In England, the winds were so severe that several church towers were demolished in London and other parts of the south. The 'Great Storm' of **November 1703** is believed to have caused over 8000 deaths as well as sinking a substantial portion of Britain's naval and merchant fleets. Apart from the storm of January 1998 recorded above, other recent major events have been:

- **October 1987 'the Great Storm'**: a severe storm crossing southern England killing 19 people and bringing down an estimated 15 million trees. Wind speeds gusted to over 160 km per hour causing much structural damage and insurance claims totalled well over £1 billion.
- **January–February 1990**: eight storms were recorded as having crossed western Europe in the 5 weeks from 25 January to the end of February. The storm of 25 January again affected southern England, causing greater damage and death toll (47) than the storm of 1987.
- **December 1999**: storms swept across Britain and France causing widespread damage, particularly in France where 33 people were killed and 100 000 trees uprooted in the Paris region alone. One-quarter of all French homes were without electricity for a limited period and there was major disruption to the country's telephone and transport systems.

Managing the hazard

As with tropical cyclones, the major part of management concerns **prediction** and **warnings**. The population of western Europe has access to sophisticated weather forecasts but even the UK Meteorological Office was unable to give sufficient warning of the 'Great Storm' of 1987. Warnings can put the relevant government departments, local authorities, commercial companies and individuals into a state of readiness. Emergency services can be alerted and put on stand-by, flood defences can be prepared and vulnerable structures protected.

In the longer term, it should be possible to improve land-use planning in order to discourage housing in high-risk areas, such as river flood plains, and to tighten building regulations within those areas. Planners should be looking for improved **design** for high-rise buildings and bridges and, in the case of governments and local authorities, a greater **investment** in protective structures such as flood barriers. One suggestion is that insurance premiums should in future be related to wind and flood hazard potential in order to discourage poor siting of the built environment.

3 Tornadoes

The origins of tornadoes

A tornado (probably from the Spanish word for a thunderstorm, '*tronada*') is the most violent of atmospheric storms consisting of a rotating column of air extending downwards from a cumulonimbus (thunderstorm) cloud. They are short lived, small in size and capable of doing enormous damage, as their energy is concentrated into a small area. Tornadoes form through the interaction of warm and cold air, and always over land. As the warm air becomes unstable through the day because of heating from the ground, small centres of low pressure develop into which air is drawn and as it moves upwards, forms cumulonimbus clouds leading to a thunderstorm. The converging air is deflected by the Coriolis force and spins in and upward through the storm creating a vortex. The spin within the vortex is aided by an atmospheric feature known as wind shear, where air is moving at different directions and speed with height. **Supercell** thunderstorms are the best for tornado formation, as they have one very strong upward movement, together with strong downdraughts. Towards the rear of the storm and in the downdraughts, a funnel of air may appear that lowers and touches the ground initiating the tornado. As the thunderstorm moves across an area, the tornado will move with it.

Distribution and frequency

Tornadoes result from the interaction of contrasting air so they tend to be found in the middle latitudes but they can also develop in the powerful updraughts initiated within hurricanes. The USA has over three-quarters of all recorded tornadoes and also the most violent of them. The main reason for this is that in central areas warm air from the south over the Gulf of Mexico often meets colder air from the Arctic north and the conditions are right for tornado formation. Thus, they are most common in a belt running southwards from Nebraska through the central plains down to Texas, and tornadoes are so common here at certain times of the year that the region has been dubbed 'Tornado Alley'. In most years, there are over 30 tornadoes recorded in the British Isles, but these are small, low-intensity affairs, although they can cause quite significant local damage. The tornado season in the USA is during the spring and summer and they can occur at any time of day, although most happen in the late afternoon and early evening due to the build up of heat. Most British tornadoes occur between September and January when air mass contrasts are most marked.

Magnitude

Tornadoes are measured and classified by the Fujita Intensity Scale (Table 2), which rates the intensity of a tornado by the damage that it causes. There is also a scale devised by the Tornado and Storm Research Organisation (TORRO) which is similar to the Fujita scale, but which classifies tornadoes into 11 categories.

The effects of a tornado

The main damage caused by a tornado is due to the high wind speeds

Table 2 Fujita scale

F-Scale	Winds	Character of damage	Relative frequency
F0 (weak)	40–72 mph	LIGHT DAMAGE: Some damage to chimneys, TV antennae, roof shingles displaced. Small branches broken on trees.	28%
FI (weak)	73–112 mph	MODERATE DAMAGE: Roof decking removed, carports overturned, some trees uprooted, automobiles overturned. Unanchored homes sliding.	40%
F2 (strong)	113–157 mph	CONSIDERABLE DAMAGE: Roofs blown off homes leaving strong walls standing. Sheds and other outbuildings demolished, unanchored mobile homes overturned, block structure walls collapsed, roofs peeled back. Small wood missiles observed.	23%
F3 (strong)	158–206 mph	SEVERE DAMAGE: Exterior walls and roofs blown off homes. Metal buildings collapsed or are severely damaged. Forests are flattened. Most block structures collapsed.	6%
F4 (violent)	207–260 mph	DEVASTATING DAMAGE: Few walls, if any, standing in well-built homes. Pile of debris on foundation, large steel and concrete missiles thrown far distances.	2%
F5 (violent)	261–318 mph	(RARE) INCREDIBLE DAMAGE: Homes on slabs levelled with debris removed. Schools, motels and other marginally engineered buildings have considerable damage with exterior walls and roofs gone. Top storeys demolished.	less than 1%

that can reach over 500 km per hour. The lifting force of the funnel can be considerable, easily moving large lorries and even railway carriages. Pressure differentials between the outside an inside of a building (which can be over 150 mb) have a very explosive effect as the sides and roof of the structure fly outwards. As a result there is much flying debris, which itself does an enormous amount of damage. The effects of the tornado tend to be very localised as it moves across country. The area of devastation will be only a few hundred metres wide and buildings just outside of this narrow zone might get away with only minor structural damage.

CASE STUDY 8: A 'TWISTER' IN TORNADO ALLEY OKLAHOMA CITY, 3 MAY 1999

On 3 May 1999, 61 tornadoes affected Oklahoma and southern Kansas resulting in 44 fatalities, nearly 1000 injured people and a bill for damage of $1.3 billion. At 7.25 p.m., an F5 tornado (Figure 18) struck the southern suburbs of Oklahoma City and then proceeded to cut a 500 m-wide swathe through the largely residential areas of Moore, Norman and Del City. The tornado was responsible for 41 deaths in Oklahoma City with at least 500 people being seriously injured. At its maximum, it has been estimated that the winds within the system reached over 400 km per hour, so powerful that they ripped up railway tracks, shredded trees, and tossed cars and trucks around as if they were small logs. Power lines were also brought down, cutting off electricity over a

Figure 18 Tornado damage in the suburbs of Oklahoma City

wide area of the state. At least 2000 homes were either completely destroyed or so badly damaged that they were uninhabitable, leading to somewhere around 10 000 people being made homeless. As with similar disasters, the authorities reported that in the aftermath they had do deal with several cases of people caught looting damaged property.

CASE STUDY 9: A TORNADO IN THE UNITED KINGDOM

SELSEY, HAMPSHIRE (SOUTHERN ENGLAND), 7 JANUARY 1998

The Selsey tornado (Figure 19) struck at 11.45 p.m., caused by a cold air stream flowing over relatively warm air in contact with the warm sea, which at 11°C was 2 degrees higher than the norm for January. The tornado that resulted, in world terms, was light, being classified as a T3 on the TORRO scale, but only a F1 (weak) on the Fujita scale. At its maximum, it has been estimated that winds in the system reached over 150 km per hour, the whole event having been preceded by a violent hail shower. The event became well publicised because Selsey was the home of the well-known TV astronomer, Patrick Moore, and as his house lay in the path of the tornado it was not surprising that his property suffered damage, particularly to two of his three mini-observatories. The tornado removed the gable ends from a number of buildings, stripped tiles from roofs, blew over outbuildings (garages/sheds/greenhouses), destroyed garden fences and uprooted several trees. The resulting flying debris, broke many windows and damaged cars. There were no fatalities, however, and injuries were minor, although some people were quite seriously affected by shock. The cost of the damage was estimated at £2 million.

Managing the hazard

With such a violent, and sometimes quite sudden, event, prediction is vital. Using radar and satellite technology, it has been possible to give general warnings to areas that tornadoes are on the way. It is not really possible, though, to predict the exact path of a storm as a vortex may not always reach the ground, or it may touch down only briefly, and when it does touch down its subsequent path can be very irregular. Only the USA, though, has a formal tornado forecasting and

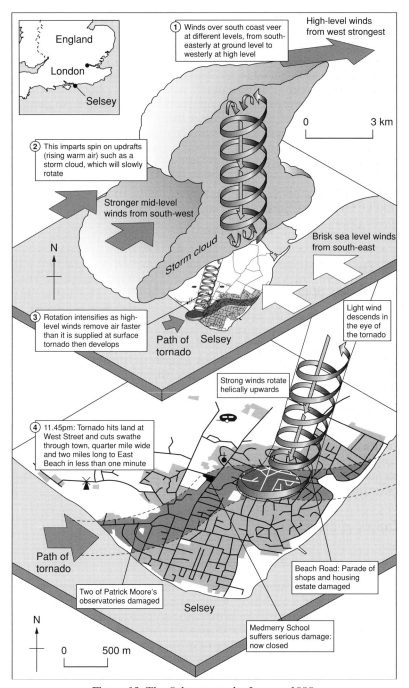

England

London

Selsey

(1) Winds over south coast veer at different levels, from south-easterly at ground level to westerly at high level

High-level winds from west strongest

0   3 km

(2) This imparts spin on updrafts (rising warm air) such as a storm cloud, which will slowly rotate

Stronger mid-level winds from south-west

N

Storm cloud

Brisk sea level winds from south-east

(3) Rotation intensifies as high-level winds remove air faster than it is supplied at surface tornado then develops

Path of tornado   Selsey

Light wind descends in the eye of the tornado

Strong winds rotate helically upwards

(4) 11.45pm: Tornado hits land at West Street and cuts swathe through town, quarter mile wide and two miles long to East Beach in less than one minute

Path of tornado

Two of Patrick Moore's observatories damaged

Beach Road: Parade of shops and housing estate damaged

Selsey

Medmerry School suffers serious damage: now closed

N

0   500 m

Figure 19 The Selsey tornado, January 1998

warning system. Scientists are trying to understand more and more about tornadoes in order to improve the warning systems. The feature film *Twister* took research into the phenomena as one of its themes, the two leading characters spending most of the film trying to get their instruments into the heart of a big storm (and of course, in true Hollywood style, eventually succeeding!). Because of this uncertainty over warnings it is important to be prepared, so people need to be aware of the threat and how best to avoid it. There is advice given by authorities as to the best places to be in the house when a tornado strikes or what to do if caught out in the open. In 'Tornado Alley', many houses are built with underground shelters so that families can protect themselves if it is likely that a tornado is going to pass over them. It is also possible for local authorities to insist upon solid construction of buildings that will have a greater resistance to the event.

4 Drought

A definition of drought

Drought is a temporary feature, usually short term, although it is possible for the phenomena to run into a period of years. It is a period of abnormally dry weather that persists long enough to produce a serious hydrological imbalance. The severity of the drought depends upon the degree of moisture deficiency, the duration and the size of the affected area. Unlike other hazards, drought develops slowly, which makes it very difficult to define when it has started and even when it has ended! It is not the same as **aridity**, which is a very dry permanent condition, nor is it the same as **desertification** that is associated with human activity and results from large-scale and long-term land degradation in the drier parts of the world. Drought is therefore characterised by a moisture deficiency below the normal levels for the environment concerned.

Causes of drought

As drought is the result of a variation from normal conditions, there are several ways in which this could occur, including:

*   **Variations in the movement of the ITCZ**: as the ITCZ moves north and south through Africa, it carries a band of rain with it. If the ITCZ does not move as far north and south as usual, areas of Africa will not receive their normal summer rain and it is possible that this could occur for a number of years. The **Sahel** region of northern Africa has suffered in this way, the area being affected by tropical continental air associated with the sub-tropical high pressure systems rather than the ITCZ bringing seasonal rains.

- **El Niño**: El Niño (the warming up of sea-surface temperatures in the eastern Pacific and its effect upon atmospheric circulation) can bring major changes to rainfall patterns. When this effect occurs, some areas bordering the Pacific Ocean receive far less rainfall than normal, and this is known to have caused droughts in Indonesia and Australia. Its effects, though, are often much wider, and droughts in the USA, Canada, eastern Brazil and South Africa have been attributed to this periodic change.
- **Changes in the track of mid-latitude depressions**: in temperate regions, depressions bring certain areas a large amount of their total rainfall. If anticyclonic conditions persist for some time, depressions will track north and south of their usual areas resulting in drought. The UK was affected by droughts in 1976 and the period of the late 1980s through to 1992, all due to the presence of 'blocking anticyclones', which kept depressions, with their rain-bearing fronts, out of the British Isles.

Distribution

Drought can occur virtually anywhere on the planet as its causes are widespread and as a consequence the hazard is not confined to any geographical location. It is true to say, though, that those areas where rainfall tends to be unreliable are those that suffer most from drought. The main areas therefore include parts of Australia, the Sahel area of Africa (south of the Sahara) and the Great Plains area of the USA.

The effects of drought

Moisture deficiency in a drought will cause soil and groundwater sources to decline, which will ultimately lead to a reduction of the sources of water that produce streamflow. Rivers, therefore, eventually decrease in volume and dry up, as happened in the British Isles in recent droughts. The deficit in soil moisture will eventually not meet the needs of particular plants and agricultural crops, which brings a severe situation to those areas that depend upon farming. Drought therefore has important implications for national food production and economies that export crops. In LEDCs it can intensify food-supply problems, resulting in severe hardship for individuals and crippling problems for the governments of such countries. **Famine** is one result of drought, although there are a number of factors that are responsible such as politics, civil war, local economic conditions and other aspects of the environment as well as drought. On the Great Plains of the USA, the Dust Bowl effect of the 1930s affected 50 million acres of land, rendering farmers helpless and thousands abandoned their properties and moved westwards to California looking for a new life. In the 1950s, the Great Plains again suffered from severe water shortages when several years went by with rainfall well below normal and crop yields plummeted as a result.

In MEDCs, drought has serious implications for water-resource systems. It seems in the UK that after only a few weeks in summer without rainfall, we are told to stop washing our cars, cease watering the lawns and take other water conservation steps.

In the natural environment drought can lead to dust storms, wildfires, pests and diseases. It can also lead to such a reduction in vegetation that, when the rains come again, there is little left to intercept the water, so that flooding results.

CASE STUDY 10: DROUGHT IN AN LEDC
SOUTHERN ETHIOPIA AND SOMALIA, 2000

Ethiopia's worst drought of the twentieth century occurred in 1984–5 when dramatic pictures of starving refugees were brought to the television screens of richer western countries. Fifteen years later, in 2000, the ITCZ did not reach far enough north and the rains failed leading to another severe drought, which had the following effects on people's traditional means of survival:

- it was estimated that the drought affected 43% of the population of the area
- the drought led to unusual movements of people and livestock as herders moved in search of water and fresh pasture. Migrations tend to be a fact of life among such people, but not on such a scale
- milk, one of the main components of the people's diets (particularly women and children), became less accessible
- food prices began to rise within the region
- as a result of migrations, too much pressure was put upon those areas that had water and decent pasture
- the lack of food and water took a heavy toll on herders with dramatic livestock losses as thousands of cows, sheep, camels and goats died
- the death of livestock led to a deterioration in people's nutritional status
- thousands of families abandoned their lands and headed for the cities and many internally displaced persons (IDP) camps had to be set up. One camp, on the outskirts of the town of Denan, contained at least 13 000 people
- large amounts of foreign aid were required for these camps as the rate of malnutrition was estimated at over 50%.

CASE STUDY 11: DROUGHT IN THE UNITED KINGDOM

THE UK DROUGHT, 1988–92

In the UK, there tends to be a winter maximum of rainfall that usually refills reservoirs and underground stores of water. During the winters of 1988–1991 there was much less rainfall than the average expected. In parts of the south-east of England, for example, in the winter of 1991–2 the monthly rainfall was well below average (November's rainfall was only 84% of average, December's only 28%, January's 28% and February's was 52%). During this time, the weather was dominated by anticyclones, which blocked frontal rainfall moving in from the Atlantic. Summers also tended to be drier and warmer during this period, leading to higher rates of **evapotranspiration** from the surface, soil and vegetation. The drought in south-east England was worsened by the **level of water extraction** from underground sources, therefore the water table continued to fall. Rain, when it fell, often came in short heavy downpours that fell on hard ground, which meant that it tended to run-off rather than infiltrating the soil and topping up underground stores.

The lower water table caused many rivers, streams and marshes to dry up and it has been estimated that river levels in the south and east of England reached their lowest since the end of the eighteenth century. One well-known example was the River Darent in Kent, which almost completely dried up, although extraction by Thames Water was partly responsible. This also meant that wildlife associated with rivers, streams and marshes was put under severe pressure. Water supplies were also put under great pressure in south and eastern England, leading to hosepipe bans, the closing of car washes and in some cases rationing, with standpipes in the streets as water supplies became unreliable. Agricultural yields were down in some areas, as farmers could not get enough water onto their fields. Not all of the UK was affected by drought, though, as frontal systems still affected the west (rainfall in Wales, for example, was over four times heavier than south-east England).

Like many droughts, this one ended with the heavy rains of the autumn of 1992, which was followed by equally heavy winter rainfall (1992–3). This very quickly replenished underground sources, and rivers and streams that had been affected by the drought began to flow again.

Dealing with drought

Drought cannot be prevented, therefore dealing with it mainly involves water storage and community preparedness, which includes attempting to predict the hazard. Some ways of drought management are:

- **Prediction**: the monitoring of both short- and long-term weather developments and the use of models has enabled some countries to set up warning systems, particularly with regard to the El Niño phenomenon. Satellite monitoring can also allow scientists to spot early stages of ecosystem degradation. In the USA, for example, the Climate Prediction Centre issues information on drought to cover continental USA and Hawaii on a 3-month basis. Figure 20 shows an example of such information.
- **Engineering**: building dams and storage reservoirs, improving water transfer systems, constructing desalinisation and water recycling plants.
- **Preparation**: in MEDCs, people are urged to adopt water conservation measures or governments may legislate to enforce such policies. In LEDCs, community preparedness is far more complex as it is tied up with the environment, the social and political systems, traditional coping and famine avoidance strategies. In reality, responses are more likely to come from the individual rather than the community as a whole or through the government. **Land**

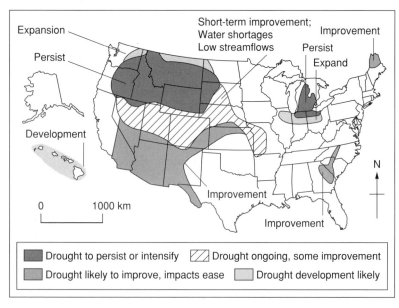

Figure 20 USA drought prediction for late 2002–early 2003

management is one way that the impact of drought can be reduced but this is difficult in LEDCs, as land degradation is tied up with wider economic and political factors. In MEDCs, such as the USA and Australia, **dry farming techniques**, which conserve moisture, are often used to enable farmers to survive a drought period.

- **Aid**: large-scale drought, and its impacts in LEDCs, often results in the supply of aid, usually from the international community, either through national governments, agencies of the United Nations or through charities such as OXFAM, the Red Cross and Comic Relief. Short-term aid is likely to be in the form of food, medicines, etc., but longer-term aid is vital in order that farming communities can re-establish themselves. Such aid could be in the form of help to build new irrigation schemes, advice on land management and the provision of education for farmers.

5 Smog

What is smog?

Urban areas generate huge volumes of pollution and as many of the particles are hygroscopic (attract water), water vapour can condense around them when relative humidity is less than 100%. The major atmospheric pollutants of urban areas are:

- **suspended particle matter (particulates)**: this is the solid matter in the urban atmosphere and derives mainly from power stations, industry and vehicle exhausts (particularly from burning diesel fuel). Such particles are usually less than 25 microns in diameter and are responsible for fog/smog, respiratory problems, soiling of buildings and are believed to contain carcinogens. Other particles in the atmosphere include cement dust, tobacco smoke, ash, coal dust and pollen. Coastal cities will also have a vast number of sea salt particles. As most pollution particles have a diameter of less than 10 microns, they are known as **PM10s**
- **sulphur dioxide**: produces haze and acid rain, and causes respiratory problems
- **oxides of nitrogen**: produce accelerated weathering of buildings, photochemical reactions, respiratory problems, acid rain and haze
- **carbon monoxide**: associated with heart problems, headaches and fatigue
- **photochemical oxidants (ozone and peroxyacetyl nitrate [PAN])**: associated with smog, damage to vegetation, and a range of discomforts to people including headaches, eye irritation, coughs and chest pains.

Air pollution varies with the time of year and air pressure conditions. Concentration of pollutants may increase five to six times in winter because of temperature inversions trapping them over the city

(Figure 21). Temperature inversions are associated with clear skies and calm to near-calm conditions, both of which are typically found under an anticyclone. Light winds therefore allow the pollutants to remain in the area and not be dispersed, and because anticyclonic conditions are stable poor air quality may persist for many days. Fog developing under these conditions mixes with the pollutants and a smog is formed. This was a very common occurrence in the cities of Europe in the nineteenth century, brought about by the high incidence of coal burning, particularly on domestic fires. Britain suffered particularly badly, many of the smogs being so thick and coloured that the term 'pea-soup' was applied to them. In December 1952, a smog in London lasted for several days and was responsible, so it was claimed, for over 4000 deaths (although modern research has indicated that this figure could have been much higher). It was this event that persuaded the British government of the time that action needed to be taken in the form of legislation in order to control coal burning.

More recently, there has been an increase in **photochemical smog**. The action of sunlight on the nitrogen oxides and hydrocarbons that are emitted in fossil fuel exhaust gases leads to the production of ozone. Los Angeles has had a serious problem with photochemical smog (see Chapter 6) because of its high density of vehicles, frequent sunshine and the topography that traps the high concentration of photo-oxidant gases at low level. High levels of ozone can have serious consequences as people suffer from eye irritation, respiratory complaints and headaches. European cities have seen a growth in photochemical smog in the second half of the twentieth century, particularly when anticyclonic conditions prevail that can trap the pollutants at low levels. Athens is often quoted as the worst sufferer in Europe, but conditions can be equally as bad in British cities, particularly London. London also suffers from high levels of nitrogen dioxide at certain times, which is the result of emissions from vehicle exhausts.

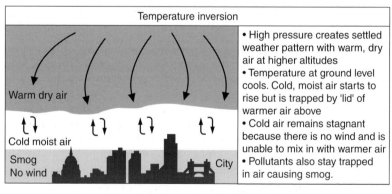

Figure 21 Inversion of temperature

Figure 22 is a copy of a newspaper article from December 1991 showing how smog in London is linked to health problems. Photochemical smog is more common in summer than the winter because of the concentration of sunshine.

Pollution reduction policies for urban areas

There are a number of ways in which governments and other organisations have tried to reduce atmospheric pollution in cities:

- **Clean Air Acts**: after the London smog of 1952, the government decided that legislation was needed to prevent the amount of smoke entering the atmosphere. The Act of 1956 first introduced smoke-free zones into the UK's urban areas, which slowly began to clean up the air. This early act has been reinforced by later legislation passed by the UK parliament. In the 1990s, for example, very tough regulations were imposed on levels of airborne pollution, particularly on the level of PM10s in the atmosphere. Local councils in the UK are now required to monitor pollution in their areas and establish **Air Quality Management Areas** where levels are likely to be exceeded and some have planted more vegetation in order to capture particulates on leaves.
- **Vehicle control in inner urban areas**: a number of cities have looked at ways of controlling pollution by trying to reduce the number of vehicles that come into central urban areas. In Athens, for example, the city declared an area of about 1 square mile in the centre to be **traffic free**. Many British towns and cities have **pedestrianised** sections of their CBDs. In London, attempts to

Health warning as smog covers London

LONDON returned to the days of the pea-soup fog this weekend as pollution from car exhausts combined with freezing temperatures to produce smog that exceeded levels in many of the world's dirties cities.

Britain's leading lung experts called for tighter controls on city-centre traffic, as doctors linked air pollution to a rise in hospital admissions for acute asthma attacks.

Specialists advised that babies, the elderly and anyone with respiratory problems should not go into busy car-filled streets. Even the healthiest were urged to avoid vigorous exercise such as jogging and cycling in cities, because of the danger of pushing pollutants more deeply into their lungs and increasing the risk of chest infection.

High levels of nitrogen dioxide from car exhaust fumes were recorded in cities throughout the country yesterday as motorists ignored warnings of fog and black ice and took to their cars for Christmas shopping.

Figure 22   Pea-soup fog returns to London
(*Daily Telegraph*, 15 December 1991)

control vehicle numbers have been made by bringing in a **conges-tion charge** (in effect, a road toll), which means that vehicle owners will have to pay if they wish to drive into the centre. In Mexico City, the city council passed **driving restriction** legislation, known as 'Hoy no Circula' (Don't Drive Today) that bans all vehicles from being driven in the city on 1 day each week (Monday–Friday). When ozone readings are very high, the ban extends to two week-days and one weekend day.

- **More public transport**: attempts have been made to persuade more people to use public transport rather than using their cars in the city. Such schemes have included Manchester's development of a **tram system (Metrolink)** , the imposition of **bus-only lanes** into city centres, the growth of **park-and-ride schemes** and the encourage-ment of **car-sharing** arrangements.
- **Zoning of industry**: industry has been placed, wherever possible, downwind and legislation has forced companies to build **higher factory chimneys** in an attempt to emit pollutants above the inver-sion layer.
- **Vehicle emissions legislation**: motor vehicle manufacturers have been forced to develop better fuel-burning engines and introduce **catalytic converters**, which remove some of the particulates from exhaust fumes. The switch to **lead-free petrol** has also brought about cleaner air.

6 Wildfires

The nature of wildfires

Wildfire is a natural process in many ecosystems and can be a necess-ary and even beneficial process in some of them. It is also true to say that fire can be a very destructive process in the natural world, one which has both natural and human causes. Fires can be major events, occurring on a large scale and causing widespread destruction and killing much wildlife. Surface fires sweep rapidly over the ground, consuming plant litter, grasses and herbs, and scorching trees, and it is possible for ground temperatures to rise to over 1000°C. At higher levels there are crown fires that spread through the canopy of the trees. The nature of a fire will depend upon the types of plants involved, strength of the winds, topography of the area in question and the behaviour of the fire itself. Once vegetation has dried out, the nature of a fire will depend largely upon the wind, as the largest fires occur in dry windy weather with low humidity. Wind drives the fire forwards and burning embers that ignite more vegetation are more easily spread in windy weather. The key factors therefore in any fire are the climate and the nature of the plants involved.

Causes and spread of fire

For a natural fire to occur and to spread, two things are needed:

- **An ignition source**: in the case of natural fires lightning is by far and away the main cause. Climate will affect the frequency of electrical storms, particularly ones in which there is no rainfall. Increasingly, fires are the result of human intervention, particularly those that occur in and around settlements. Such fires are started by carelessly discarded cigarettes, children playing with matches, agricultural fires (controlled burning) that get out of hand and camp fires. In some cases, there is evidence that devastating fires of this type have been deliberately started by arsonists. In the USA and Australia, greater access to wild areas by tourists has increased the danger of fires through some of the ways listed above.
- **Fuel**: the fuel has to be of sufficient quantity and dry enough to burn. Climate affects the frequency and duration of droughts, during which the vegetation and litter has an opportunity to accumulate and dry out. Climate also affects the type of vegetation that will grow in an area and the rate at which litter can be produced.

Distribution

Wildfires are essentially a rural hazard and can occur in most environments, although with the continued expansion of human habitation, wildfires now occur within the boundaries of even substantial settlements in California, Australia and the countries of southern Europe. Natural fires occur in areas where there is a combination of dry vegetation and lightning strikes. Clearly, areas with a dry season are susceptible to fires as are those regions of the world that have a semi-arid climate. Such regions include sections of Australia, California and other parts of the USA and Canada (Florida, for example), and southern Europe (particularly southern France, Italy, Greece, Turkey and the Mediterranean Islands such as Sicily, Cyprus, Corsica and Sardinia). Fires and natural ecosystems are often closely linked, particularly Mediterranean climatic regions and the savanna grasslands. Fire can clear vegetation and aid new seed germination, stimulating the growth of certain plants, and it can rid an area of insects and some parasites. Some species are therefore pyrophytic in that they can withstand fire through some mechanism such as resistant bark, e.g. the baobab tree. In Australia, plants such as banksia need fire for their woody fruit to open and thus regenerate.

Fire has not been a real hazard of tropical rainforest areas due to the humid climate, but recent burning for forest clearance has sometimes got out of hand, resulting in widespread fires that burned out of control for long periods. This has happened in both the Amazon Basin (Brazil) and South-east Asia (Indonesia) in recent years.

The effects of wildfires

Wildfires can have many effects:

- **Loss of life**: although many fires are events from which people can get out of the way, some fires move so fast that people can be trapped, although this is not usual. Californian fires of 1991 killed over 20 people and 13 firefighters were lost in fires that affected Colorado (USA) when their escape routes were blocked, but in devastating fires in Florida in July 1998 there was no loss of life (see Case Study 13).
- **Loss of property**: at one time, only a few rural communities were at risk from this hazard, but with urban expansion, the fringes of major cities are now susceptible to fires, particularly Los Angeles and Sydney (Australia). The cost of damage and the fighting of huge fires can sometimes run into hundreds of millions of dollars. Huge fires of this type can sometimes leave thousands of people homeless.
- **Evacuation**: during the course of a fire, widespread evacuation of people has to be considered. Such people may not be allowed to return home for several days, therefore accommodation and food will have to be found during that time.
- **Loss of crops, timber and livestock**: forest fires have a huge impact in timber producing areas with the loss of trees that will take many years to replace. It has been estimated that the USA spends an average of over $10 million per day in fighting such fires.
- **Release of toxic gases and particulate pollution**: fires in Indonesia in 1997 (see Case Study 12) left a huge haze covering a large area of South-east Asia. Many thousands of people had to be treated for breathing difficulties and it has been suggested that it was also responsible for two major accidents. First, when two ships collided off Singapore and, secondly, for the crash of an Airbus aircraft, which resulted in the death of 234 people.
- **Increased flood risk**: in certain environments, where rain comes in heavy bursts, the loss of so much vegetation, and the consequent decrease in interception, can lead to flooding after rainfall.
- **Damage to soil structure and nutrient content**: with the intense heat generated at ground level, wildfires can destroy many soil nutrients and lead to an alteration to the soil's structure.
- **Loss of wildlife**: In Indonesia, the fires of 1997 destroyed the Wein River Orang-Utan Sanctuary on Kalimantan. There are now serious concerns about the numbers, and the ultimate survival, of these rare animals.

CASE STUDY 12: WILDFIRE IN AN EQUATORIAL ENVIRONMENT

INDONESIA (SOUTH-EAST ASIA), SEPTEMBER 1997–APRIL 1998

Even though this part of Asia has an equatorial climate, extensive forest fires are not unusual. Large fires occurred in 1982–3, 1987, 1991 and 1994 and probably, at times, affected a similar sized area to the fires of 1997–8. The fires of 1998 extended over the islands of Sumatra and Borneo (Figure 23), but also affected the atmosphere of an area stretching over 3000 km from east to west, covering an area equivalent to the size of western Europe. There is no doubt that the El Niño effect, that produced a drought, created the conditions for the fires but these were considerably aggravated by lax enforcement of forest management policies in Indonesia. The government blamed small farmers and shifting cultivators for forest clearance, but there can be no doubt that large logging companies and the owners of plantations should shoulder more of the blame.

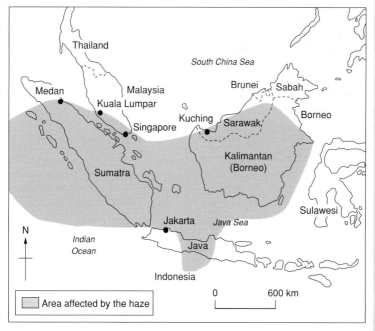

Figure 23 The extent of the haze produced by the Indonesian fires of 1997–8

The main effects of the fires were:

- over 300 000 hectares of forest were affected
- as temperatures reached over 600°C at ground level, it is possible that many areas were scorched beyond recovery
- unique areas of vegetation were lost, such as limestone forests
- huge loss of rare wildlife, particularly the orang-utan
- the pollution from the fires produced a haze that caused
  extensive breathing difficulties and is believed to have been
  responsible for the collision in the dark of a bulk carrier and
  cargo ship in the Straits of Malacca (29 crewmen were killed),
  and the crash of a Garuda Airbus A300 on approach to Medan
  airport on Sumatra in which 234 people died
- over 50 000 people had to be treated in hospital as a result of
  inhaling smoke, the pollution reaching over four times the
  level considered to be 'hazardous'
- the smoke spread across international boundaries affecting
  people not only in Indonesia, but in Malaysia, Singapore,
  Brunei and Thailand
- large-scale loss of income in the tourist industry as many
  people cancelled holidays to the region.

Dealing with fires

There are several ways of dealing with this hazard and coping with the
effects. **Dealing with the event as it happens** involves expensive fire-
fighting, which can also be extremely dangerous. Spraying with water
and chemicals from the ground and the air is costly, along with beating out the flames and bulldozing large breaks in the vegetation to
halt the fire's spread.

Managing the hazard can be done in three major ways. The first
way is to **manage the vegetation** by controlled burning to get rid of
much of the litter and by creating firebreaks in the vegetation in
advance rather than during the fire. Secondly, the **built environment
can be managed** by increasing the gap between houses and vegetation, and by incorporating more fire-resistant methods in construction (such as fitting spark arresters to chimneys and using more
brick and stone rather than wood). **Warning systems** can also be put
in place by establishing lookout towers and even flying patrols. In
areas where there is tourist pressure, notice boards, warning tourists
of the fire hazard, can be placed at strategic locations. **Education** is
extremely important, giving people information on home safety and
how to avoid starting a fire. In Victoria (Australia), in February 1983,
there was a series of disastrous fires that claimed 47 lives, destroyed
over 2000 homes and cost around $200 million. As a result, a com-
munity education programme was established known as '**Community**

Fireguard', whose purpose was to assist people in developing their own fire survival strategies. To relay the message, the authorities avoided the 'top-down' approach that they had been using in favour of focusing on identifying the most vulnerable areas in fire-prone communities and then generating local interest to make residents aware of how they could be responsible for their own safety. From this, the residents developed their own fire survival techniques such as local warning systems, ensuring that buffer zones were maintained, conducting brush and street cleanups, running equipment training sessions and preparing emergency plans.

In MEDCs people are urged to carry fire insurance, although this can be fairly expensive in some areas of MEDCs.

CASE STUDY 13: DEALING WITH A FIRE IN THE USA

FLORIDA, JUNE–JULY 1998

In these 2 months of 1998 over 2000 separate fires broke out in the part of Florida that is inland of Daytona Beach and east of Orlando (Figure 24). At its height, the hazard forced over 120 000 people to flee from their homes, 200 of which were

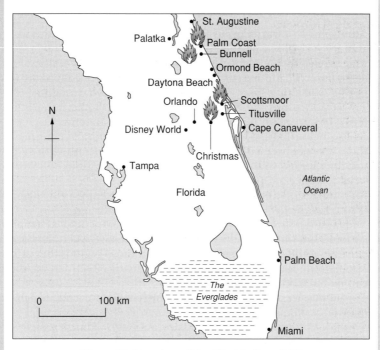

Figure 24 Location of the Florida fires 1998

eventually destroyed, the fires being described as the worst to affect Florida in the twentieth century. The fires affected an area of nearly 500 square miles and resulted in around 70 injuries (mainly firefighters) but no deaths. They were mainly the result of lightning strikes in wooded areas left tinder dry after a particularly dry spring. The fires were tackled in the following ways:

- over 5000 firefighters were involved, many being brought in from all over the USA
- the cost of fighting the fires came to over $100 million (the damage caused by the fires was assessed at $175 million)
- 120 000 people were evacuated, at some time, from their homes
- the Red Cross set up 40 emergency shelters in schools with thousands of people having to stay overnight
- 1500 members of the National Guard were called up to help with traffic control and provide security from looting
- bulldozers were used to create firebreaks in certain places
- planes and helicopters were used to spray water and fire-retardant chemicals.

Summary

- Atmospheric hazards occur in every climatic region in the world and are variable in both scale and duration.
- The spread of populations has made people more vulnerable to these hazards, and human activity has made a significant contribution in worsening some of them, such as fires and drought.
- Tropical cyclones are the most significant atmospheric hazard in terms of impact on people and the built environment.
- As the name implies, tropical cyclones are generally confined to those areas between 5 and 20 degrees north and south of the equator; they are not found near the Equator as the Coriolis effect is too weak to generate spin in the air.
- The impact of tropical cyclones differs according to the stage in the economic development of the countries affected.
- Mid-latitude storms are not as dangerous to people as tropical cyclones but they inflict large amounts of damage when they occur because of the concentration of wealth in those regions they affect.
- Mid-latitude depressions produce a variety of effects, all of which can be hazardous to people.
- Tornadoes are short lived, but extremely violent events, which do enormous damage in limited areas.
- Tornadoes can affect the British Isles, although damage is on a very much smaller scale than that which results from tornadoes in the USA.

- Drought usually takes some time to occur and people are often not aware that they need to do something about the hazard until it is too late.
- Drought impacts are often long term and vary with a range of social, economic and political factors.
- Smog is a man-made hazard resulting from the burning of fossil fuels and it affects urban areas where it can be damaging to people's health.
- There are a number of strategies for reducing the smog hazard, most of which involve limiting the use of, or the impact of, cars and fossil fuel-burning power stations.
- Wildfires are caused both naturally (lightning) and by people.
- Wildfires do not normally cause many deaths but have a huge impact on the built and natural environments.

Exercises

1. (a) Describe the factors that contribute to the development of tropical cyclones (hurricanes).
   (b) The nature of tropical cyclone (hurricane) damage varies considerably. Describe the **physical** factors that may be responsible for such variations.
2. Using a variety of examples, explain why, in different countries, human responses to tropical cyclones (hurricanes) are not the same.
3. (a) Some natural environments are more likely than others to experience fire as a hazard. Briefly identify such environments and describe their global situation.
   (b) Describe the conditions that lead to major fires in one of the natural environments identified in part (a).
4. Why should the late afternoon be the most likely time for tornadoes to develop?
5. What are the causes, consequences and potential solutions to:
   Either
   (i) poor air quality in urban areas
   or
   (ii) drought in the United Kingdom.

4 Water Hazards

1 River Flooding

River flooding is the most frequent of all natural hazards, reported flooding events accounting for between one-third and one-quarter of all reported disasters (Table 1), and it claims more lives, injures more people, and causes a wider economic and social impact than any other type of hazard event. River valleys are attractive places for people to live, offering water for a variety of uses (industrial, residential and for irrigation), valuable agricultural land, a means of transport, a source of energy and waste disposal, a place of recreation and a source of food through fishing, and it is this that has increasingly exposed more people to the risk of flooding as we develop such areas. Flooding is a natural part of any river system, and of the hydrological cycle, so floodwaters also bring benefits (such as maintaining soil fertility by depositing fresh layers of alluvium) as well as causing problems. Most floods are the result of rainwater moving quickly over the surface of the land (overland flow) or through the soil (throughflow), to produce a rapid rise in the discharge of a river that can be plotted as a flood hydrograph (Figure 25).

The causes of river flooding

There are several causes of river flooding:

- **Excessive rainfall**: resulting from such atmospheric processes as the monsoons, tropical cyclones, and a series of mid-latitude depressions, all of which bring periods of prolonged rainfall to the areas they affect. Much of the flooding in the United Kingdom is the result of a series of depressions dropping considerable quantities of water on already saturated ground resulting in rapid overland flow. Such floods, therefore, have become a regular winter occurrence along some of the rivers of the UK.
- **Intense rainfall events**: these produce flash floods, events that affect only small areas, but which are extremely powerful and often very damaging. An example of a flash flood that had devastating effects in a Pyrenean valley is given as a later case study.
- **Rapid snowmelt (often with rainfall)**: occur in late spring and early summer.
- **Volcanic action resulting in rapid snowmelt**: such as the Grimsvoton Jokulhaup (Icelandic for glacial burst) in November 1996.
- **Landslides**: such as that which fell into the Vaiont Reservoir and flooded the Piave valley in 1963 (referred to in the section on landslides in Chapter 2).
- **Collapse of dammed glacial meltwater lakes.**
- **Dam failures.**

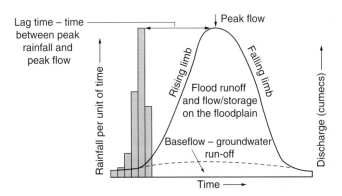

Figure 25 Flood hydrograph

The conditions that produce a flood are variable through time and space and there are many factors that combine to produce a flood, such as meteorological conditions, geology, vegetation, soil, relief and the influence of man. The nature and intensity of flooding can be affected by man in several ways:

- **The removal of natural vegetation**: causing interception to decrease allowing rainfall to finds its way into the river channel more quickly. This can also happen as a result of fire removing natural vegetation.
- **Urbanisation**: when catchment areas are concreted and covered in tarmac this leads to less infiltration and more run-off. Water is also transferred more rapidly into and through drains.
- **Poor agricultural practices**: such as incorrect ploughing, too much soil compaction and poorly considered drainage.

The frequency and magnitude of floods

Flooding is a hazard that shows the relationship between magnitude and frequency in that there will be a high frequency of low-magnitude events with a low frequency of high-magnitude events. Low-magnitude events therefore occur far more frequently than high-magnitude events. Figures vary for each river system and are a very important ingredient in assessing risk to river valleys and in the planning of flood control schemes. Planners are able to assess the possible height of a one in 10 year flood, one in a 100 year flood, one in a 1000 year flood, etc., and act according to the risk they want to cover and the money available.

Britain is increasingly faced with the hazard of river flooding. Problems have been compounded by intensive agriculture (wetland drainage, fields left bare longer, overstocking) and by the large amount of house building that has taken place on flood plains (over 2 million dwellings in the 1970s and 1980s). The Environment Agency is also warning that climate change has made flooding almost inevitable at certain times of the year in several parts of the country. In the period 2000–2002, 25 people died in Britain as a result of flooding and the Agency now reckon that at least 5 million people already live in flood-risk areas. From December 1997 through to June 2000, there were 30 recorded floods (including coastal) in England and Wales, the location of which is shown in Figure 26, along with information on some of the worst of them. As a result, the Environment Agency stated that '*Climate change has made Britain a 'hot-spot' for flooding, in which the risks to lives and property will increase ten-fold over the next century*'. They also warned the country, '*that the flood risk is now a daily part of life in England and Wales. Looking at recent history, reports of flooding are now on average nearly twice as frequent as they were 100 years ago*'.

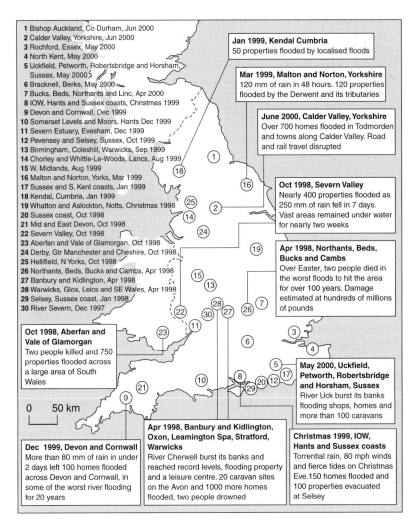

Figure 26 England and Wales major floods, December 1997–June 2002

The effects of flooding

Flooding has many social and economic impacts:

- **Deaths/injuries**: many people are drowned in flood events, the impact of which is far greater in LEDCs, where large populations live in river valleys and on flood plains and deltas, and have inadequate warning systems available to them. Several million Chinese died in the twentieth century as a result of flooding on the largest rivers of the country such as the Hoang-Ho and the Yangtze-Kiang.

- **Inundation by water of houses, industrial and commercial properties**: in the case of private housing this will mean expensive renovation but may reduce the potential market value of the property and increase the insurance premiums. Contents may also need replacing, as will the stock of shops and factories. The heartbreak and stress suffered by people whose homes are flooded, resulting in the loss and damage of personal effects, cannot be measured, but it is a serious problem for those involved.
- **Agricultural production lost and livestock drowned**: fields covered in water may take many months to recover, which will be devastating to a subsistence economy such as that found on the Ganges delta (Bangladesh). Vulnerability is highest amongst the poorest people in society due to lower levels of preparation and economic resilience.
- **Pollution/disease**: flood waters are often contaminated by untreated sewage, which leads to contaminated drinking water and the spread of diseases such as cholera and dysentery, particularly in LEDCs. Floods in tropical areas often encourage the spread of insects such as those that carry malaria and yellow fever.
- **Flooding of car parks, caravan parks and sporting venues**: loss of motor vehicles and caravans will result in large insurance losses.
- **Disruption to transport**: river valleys are major routeways for road and rail communication, and many bridges across rivers become impassable in time of flooding.
- **Increased insurance premiums**: insurance companies are increasingly looking at the viability of providing insurance cover in the UK to those houses in areas where river flooding is now a regular occurrence. The Association of British Insurers (ABI) has been putting pressure on the government to improve flood defences for several years. In 2002, the ABI raised the possibility that, in future, hundreds of thousands of homeowners in flood-prone areas would not receive insurance cover resulting in virtually unsaleable properties.

CASE STUDY 14: THE CAUSE AND EFFECTS OF A FLASH FLOOD

THE FLOOD AT BIESCAS IN THE SPANISH PYRENEES, 7 AUGUST 1996

The weather in the Pyrenees had been wet prior to 7 August. On that day, a cold front passed through the area, forcing very warm moist air to rise in advance of its passage. The height and steepness of the Pyrenees made this uplift much more vigorous, resulting in very active storms with torrential downpours All this water fell on ground that was already saturated from previous storms. The flash flood in question occurred in a valley with steep sides, which was another factor in increasing the discharge as the rainwater ran off very rapidly. In this part of the Pyrenees, a large amount of coniferous forest has been removed as tourism has increased (for roads, parking places, hotels, restaurants, ski runs, etc.), and this, too, increased the run-off. In 2 hours it has been estimated that over 50 mm of rain fell in the upper catchments of the valleys leading down to Biescas.

The main result was a flash flood that ran down the valley of the Barranco del Aso, which runs into the Rio Gallego just below Biescas. A small bridge acted as a barrier to the rocks, boulders and tree debris that was swept down the valley by the flood waters and caused the water to pond back. When the bridge finally gave way, there was a resulting surge in the flood. A wall of water, mud, rocks and trees, at least 2 m high, swept down the valley and through the Virgen de las Nieves campsite at its foot. Cars, caravans and tents were swept at least 1 km down the valley along with many people. The final death toll was 85, with over 200 people injured, and this could have been much worse but for the fact that at the time of the flood, at 8 p.m., many of the camp residents were off-site having dinner in Biescas. It has been estimated that this was a one in a 1000 year event.

Flood management

The approach to flood management has taken various forms:

- **Flood abatement measures**: these focus upon the stores and processes operating within the drainage basin and attempt to slow the movement of rainwater through the system. Such measures include **reafforestation, revegetation of river banks and flood plains** and **educating farmers** in methods that will reduce overland flow, such as continuous cropping and contour ploughing.
- **Storing water**: through building **dams** with storage reservoirs in order to hold back flood waters. **Flood barriers** can be constructed that will temporarily hold back the water, such as those constructed on the waterways of the Dutch polders.
- **Channel and bank modifications**: improving the channel, or **channelisation**, can create a way in which water can be removed faster. Changes may involve; channel straightening, artificial levees, widening and dredging, relief channels through meanders and concreting the channel. **Levees** have been built on many rivers, but if they fail the results can be disastrous, as the flood event will be made worse. Setting levees back from the river will provide a wider water storage area. Changing the channel shape and then **concret-**

ing it will increase the velocity of water, moving it more quickly through the channel. This method is commonly used in urban areas (see Chapter 6 on Los Angeles), but as a solution it has attracted criticism because of the appearance of the schemes and their lack of amenity value. Figure 27 shows a proposal for a scheme to be carried out on a small river within the Severn–Trent Water Authority. Within a short distance, the Authority has proposed to build levees set back from the river, construct relief channels (to be used only in time of floods), straighten the channel by filling in meanders, and a programme of dredging and clearing vegetation from the channel.

- **Forecasting and warning:** this involves the collection of meteorological and discharge data and the use of computer modelling, all of which enables flood warnings to be issued to the emergency services, local authorities and the general public. This involves **community preparedness** in being able to respond to such warnings.
- **Emergency action**: temporary flood defences can be erected such as **sandbags** or more sophisticated barriers. Along the River Severn, for example, **interlocking steel barriers** have recently been made available that will be used in Shrewsbury and Bewdley at a time of flood, as the residents of those towns have balked at having to look all year at huge and permanent defences. If the flood cannot be

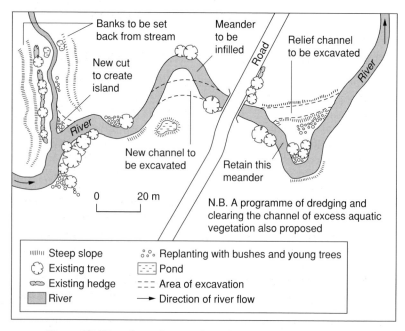

Figure 27 Plans for a river engineering project (Severn–Trent Water Authority)

prevented, then plans for evacuation must be in place well before the event if they are to be successful (see the case study below).

- **Planning controls**: central and local government can insist upon restrictions on building in flood-risk areas. Specific **building codes** can insist upon hazard-resistant designs such as waterproof basements and ground floors, sealed windows and even houses raised on stilts. In flood plain areas that are developed, authorities have attempted to relocate certain land uses away from high-risk areas. Detailed **flood-hazard mapping** has been carried out, although many are against publishing such information as it could reduce the value of their property.

Modern approaches to flood control favour natural options, as far as possible, and focus on the conservation benefit. Traditional engineering solutions have brought about the loss of rare wetland environments and the disturbance of bank and bed habitats during construction. Ecologically acceptable channel designs are now being attempted, and these may include: retention of wetlands habitats in key locations for temporary water storage (sometimes by pumping); re-introduction of meandering channels; use of floodplains as temporary flood storage; replanning land use next to rivers, for example, recreation and parking.

CASE STUDY 15: SMOOTH EVACUATION DURING FLOODS

SOUTHERN NETHERLANDS, FEBRUARY 1995

In February 1995, a large flood struck the southern part of the Netherlands leading to the evacuation of 250 000 people, the largest evacuation seen in the country since the World War II. Each emergency situation requiring evacuation is unique, but in all of them the risk of panic and chaos exists. The element in this Dutch case, which stands out as a model for others, was its emergency plan that stressed coordination among municipal services, and placed a high emphasis on communication strategy. That the evacuation went very smoothly (75% of people evacuated before the deadline) was put down to the following factors:

- **Early planning**: the city of Nijmegen developed a plan for itself and the surrounding region straight after the disastrous floods of 1993.
- **Specific planning to evacuate**: the authorities acted on their evacuation plans as soon as it was seen that the floods could become serious.
- **Integrated communication strategy**: steps were taken to ensure that officials in charge of disseminating information

were part of the decision-making management team. Good planning ensured that the press and public were informed on a regular basis about the threat posed by flooding and when an evacuation was necessary.

- **Cultural homogeneity**: virtually all inhabitants spoke the same language avoiding potential linguistic misunderstandings.
- **Slowly rising waters**: the water took many days to rise, giving people time to act without being completely rushed, as large parts of the Rhine Valley in Germany were flooded before the waters reached the Netherlands. This meant that most of the inhabitants (over 90%) had time to arrange their own accommodation without relying upon temporary public shelter.

CASE STUDY 16: THE INTRODUCTION OF A FLOOD CONTROL SCHEME

THE JUBILEE RIVER (RIVER THAMES BASIN) FLOOD ALLEVIATION SCHEME AND THE WINTER FLOODS OF JANUARY 2003

On average, floods have occurred in the Maidenhead, Eton and Windsor areas once every 5–7 years. In 1947, 2000 homes were inundated in a flood that was estimated to have a 1:56 chance of happening in any year. If such a flood happened again without a flood scheme then, because of developments within the Thames flood plain, at least 5500 houses would be affected this time involving 125 000 people. There would also be significant disruption to businesses, roads, railways and vital services such as electricity, gas and telephones. In the 1990s, the Environment Agency began the construction of a £100 million flood relief scheme for the area involving the construction of a 11.6 km channel (50 m wide and 4.5 m deep) to be known as the Jubilee River. This is designed to take excess water in time of flood and divert it past the threatened area, and was operational from September 2001.

In the later months of 2002, rainfall was heavy in the Thames Basin (see Figure 28) and widespread flooding occurred. From Figure 28 it is possible to see that the flooding did not affect the Maidenhead, Eton and Windsor areas but was extensive downstream of the Jubilee River in an area that is heavily built-up. Residents complained that it was the flood scheme that had made things worse for them, a claim denied by the Environment Agency. Some of the **attitudes** to this flooding are summarised below:

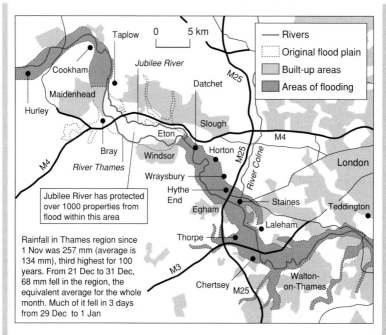

Taplow
0   5 km
Jubilee River
Cookham
Datchet
M25
Maidenhead
Hurley
Slough
Eton
M4
Bray
Horton
M25
London
Windsor
River Colne
Wraysbury
Hythe
End
Egham
Staines
Teddington
Laleham
Thorpe
Walton-
on-Thames
Chertsey
M25
M3
M4
River Thames

— Rivers
Original flood plain
Built-up areas
Areas of flooding

Jubilee River has protected
over 1000 properties from
flood within this area

Rainfall in Thames region since
1 Nov was 257 mm (average is
134 mm), third highest for 100
years. From 21 Dec to 31 Dec,
68 mm fell in the region, the
equivalent average for the whole
month. Much of it fell in 3 days
from 29 Dec to 1 Jan

Figure 28 The Thames Valley floods, January 2003

- **Residents of the Wraysbury/Chertsey area**. They claimed that
  the scheme had caused the Thames to rise faster and higher
  than any time since 1947, although rainfall and other conditions were nothing like as bad when saturated ground and a
  sudden thaw added hugely to water levels: '*In successfully pre-
  venting flooding upstream, the problem has been simply moved to our
  doorsteps*'. They are concerned that if this becomes a regular
  problem, then the value of their properties would plummet,
  mortgages would be impossible to obtain and insurers would
  refuse cover.
- **Windsor and Maidenhead Council**. Delighted with the
  scheme: '*The Jubilee River was developed to stop Maidenhead and
  Windsor flooding. It has been a great success*'.
- **Environment Agency**. The Agency claims that the channel
  worked according to plan and the flooding in the area in
  question was caused by water from local rivers entering the
  Thames below Windsor: '*The Jubilee River does not create any more
  water than would be in the river at any other point up or downstream.
  The Thames flow downstream of the channel has been no greater than
  it would be if there was no scheme at all*'.

2 Coastal Hazards

Large areas of coastline are very attractive for a wide range of human activities. In England, for example, at least one quarter of the coast has been developed for housing, industry, agriculture and leisure activities. The coastline, however, is under attack both from erosion and from the possibility of low-lying stretches, particularly estuaries, being flooded. Both mass movements and flooding have been considered in previous sections of this book, but here we shall look at these hazards in a coastal context.

The causes and effects

The processes that are involved in coastal retreat are **marine erosion** (waves attacking vulnerable coastlines) and sub-aerial processes leading to **mass movements** (rock falls, landslides, mudflows and slumping – see Chapter 2). **Longshore drift** may also contribute, moving material away from a coastline and leaving an area exposed to the various forms of marine erosion. Coastal erosion is a significant problem as it results in cliff face slumping, the loss of coastal land that may have been developed for human activities, the erosion of beaches and flooding.

Coastal flooding results from waves generated by storm systems accompanying the passage of a **tropical cyclone (hurricane)** or a **mid-latitude depression** (Chapter 3).

Areas of low atmospheric pressure also generate a storm surge where the surface of the sea is lifted as a result of the lower pressure upon it. Coastal flooding will also occur when a **tsunami** is generated (see next section). The risk of flooding is increasing on coastlines that are sinking, such as for much of southern England, and in river estuaries where there is a possible combination of river flooding and storm effects, including surges. The potential global (eustatic) rise in sea level as a result of global warming poses a threat to many coastlines, one which could become very severe in the next 100–200 years.

Coastal areas contain a variety of landforms that are increasingly under pressure from natural processes and human activities. In the past, the response to this has been a range of protection and management strategies, but in some cases the solutions themselves have created additional problems.

CASE STUDY 17: THE EFFECTS OF A COASTAL LANDSLIP

THE COLLAPSE OF HOLBECK HALL, SCARBOROUGH, 4 JUNE 1993

Holbeck Hall, one of coastal Yorkshire's premier hotels, was built on top of the cliffs behind the South Bay at Scarborough at the

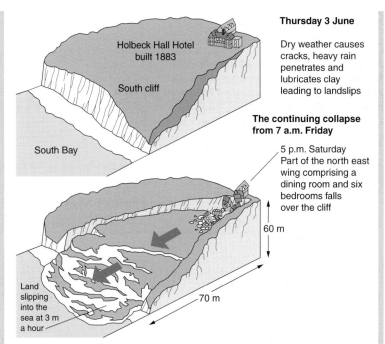

Holbeck Hall Hotel
built 1883

South cliff

South Bay

Land
slipping
into the
sea at 3 m
a hour

70 m

60 m

Thursday 3 June

Dry weather causes
cracks, heavy rain
penetrates and
lubricates clay
leading to landslips

**The continuing collapse
from 7 a.m. Friday**

5 p.m. Saturday
Part of the north east
wing comprising a
dining room and six
bedrooms falls
over the cliff

Figure 29 The collapse of Holbeck Hall, Scarborough

end of the nineteenth century. Although the cliffs here consist
largely of clay, the hotel was not considered to be in any danger,
being situated at least 60–70 m away from the edge. All this
changed in the early summer of 1993 when a period of dry
weather cracked much of the clay on the cliff tops. This dry
period was followed by heavy rainfall that penetrated the cracks
and began to lubricate the clay along certain lines of slippage.
The first warning came early on the morning of 4 June when
cracks began to appear in the lawns and rose garden towards the
edge of the cliff. Throughout the day, more cracks appeared and
sections of the garden began to slide down towards the beach. By
late afternoon, the area of slides had reached the hotel buildings
resulting in the collapse of the terraces and the conservatory. In
the early evening the collapse had affected the main part of the
hotel and a large section of it fell into the slide and began to
move towards the beach (Figure 29). As a result of this, the rest
of the hotel had to be demolished by contractors. The owners of
the hotel then sued the local authority for being '*in breach of its
duty of care to maintain the supporting land and the undercliff it owned
between the hotel grounds and the sea*'.

Coastal management

Coastal management has several aims:

- providing a defence against flooding
- providing protection against coastal erosion
- stabilising beaches affected by longshore drift
- stabilising and protecting sand dunes and salt marshes, which may be the 'natural' defences of a coastal area.

There are several ways in which this can be carried out.

The 'hard' engineering approach: This involves the building of some type of sea defence, each with a specific purpose (Figure 30):

- **Sea walls (sometimes recurved), embankments (dykes), flood barriers**: sea walls aim to absorb wave energy and the recurved structure will throw waves backwards. They must have a continuous facing because any slight gap will be exploited by hydraulic action. Sea walls need drain outlets so that too much water does not accumulate behind them. Embankments are usually made of earth or clay, and are normally less expensive to construct than sea walls.

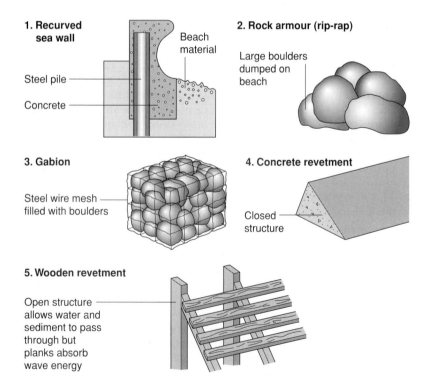

Figure 30 Coastal defence hard engineering solutions

Flood barriers, which protect against estuarine flooding, can be the most expensive of all hard engineering solutions. The largest coastal scheme of this kind is the one that protects the deltas of the Rhine, Meuse and Scheldt, known as the Dutch Delta Plan. This cost over £2 billion and is constructed to protect against a 1:500 event.

- **Rock armour (rip-rap)**: large boulders dumped in front of a cliff or sea wall that will take the full force of the waves.
- **Gabion**: the same idea as a rip-rap, but with a steel wire mesh container surrounding smaller boulders.
- **Revetment**: a concrete or wooden structure placed across the beach in order to take the full force of wave energy.
- **Groynes**: wooden breakwaters built almost at right angles to waves (usually 5–10 degrees from the perpendicular to prevent scouring on the downdrift side of the groyne). Groynes are essentially built to control longshore drift but will also break down the waves as they hit the coast. By halting the bulk of longshore drift in an area, there may be serious effects further down the coast as the groynes will cut off the supply of most beach material and this could leave the coast very exposed to erosion.
- **Cliff fixing**: often done by driving steel bars into the cliff face, both to stabilise it and to absorb some wave power.
- **Offshore reefs**: reefs make the waves break offshore, thus reducing the impact on the base of the cliffs.

Hard engineering solutions have several disadvantages. They can be expensive to build and to maintain (to repair a sea wall can cost up to £5000 per metre); defence in one place can have serious consequences for another; they cannot keep pace with rising sea level; they are sometimes an eyesore, spoiling the landscape.

The 'soft' engineering approach: uses natural systems for coastal defence such as beaches, sand dunes and salt marshes, which can absorb and adjust to wave and tidal energy. Soft coastal defence involves manipulating and maintaining these systems, without changing their fundamental structures. **Beach nourishment** is the attempt to replace material that has been lost through longshore drift. It is not unknown for local authorities to move material from one end of the beach to the other before the start of the tourist season.

Managed retreat: this involves abandoning the current line of sea defences and then developing the exposed land in some way in order to reduce wave power, e.g. through salt marsh development. In this way the scale of hard sea defences can be reduced. In some areas there have been proposals to ban new developments on coastal areas, such as in California, where it is already a requirement along certain stretches of coastline that building must take place at an agreed distance away from the shore.

Do nothing!: in recent years a school of thought has grown up that asks if coastal areas should be protected at all considering the tens of

We must surrender our land to the sea, say MPs

HUGE tracts of Britain's coastal and farm land, especially along the east and south coast, should be surrendered to the sea as part of a "peace accommodation" with nature, MPs said yesterday.

They set out a stark vision of a dramatically different coastal and riverside landscape complete with flood plains and regularly waterlogged farmlands as mankind showed more "humility" in the face of the sea.

Describing the millions spent of flood prevention and coastal defences as an unsustainable and "deluded" waste of money, the agriculture select committee said it was time to give up the fight along much of East Anglia and the south-east coast.

The report called for "managed realignment" of the coastline with "suitable compensation" arrangements for farmers and land-owners who lost property as a result. It said the current coastal defence policy "cannot be sustained in the long term if it continues to be founded on the practice of substantial human intervention in natural processes of flooding and erosion".

Instead planners should be "making room for the sea at the coast and for rivers in flood plains".

Farmers and land-owners attacked the report. The National Farmers' Union said its members "must not be left at the sea's mercy".

"The select committee is seriously oversimplifying the issues surrounding the use of low-lying farmland which is the basis for a large and important industry".

Extract (a)
Daily Telegraph,
August 1998

Too costly to let sea reclaim land

COASTAL land which should be given up to the advancing sea is being preserved at great cost by the Government – because it is too expensive to compensate the owners, the conference was told.

Dr David Carter of Plymouth University, who has drawn up shoreline management plans for the Ministry of Agriculture, said there were many places where "managed retreat" was the most cost-effective option to crumbling sea defences.

But local authorities and others involved in the new strategic plans for the coast were not taking the managed retreat option because of the lack of compensation.

A celebrated case is Medmerry Beach, near Selsea, West Sussex, where a single beach is trying to move inland.

If it succeeds, the sea will flood half a mile of shoreline, including the largest caravan park in Europe, home to 10,000 people in summer.

The Environment Agency is currently spending £500,000 a year keeping the beach in place.

Dr Carter said Medmerry was a test case. "If one thinks forward 20 years it is going to be impossible to restrain this beach when it doesn't want to be there." Rising sea levels and bigger waves, the result of climate change, were bound

to overwhelm this and many other low-lying areas such as the Essex coast and the Ribble Estuary over the next few decades.

Dr Carter said that new legislation was needed for the state to compensate private landowners.

He is working with English Nature on a project studying the possibility of creating new wildlife habitat on areas of managed retreat over the next few years around the Solent, Dungeness, the North Kent marshes and North Norfolk.

Extract (b)
Daily Telegraph,
January 2001

Figure 31   Views on managed retreat

millions of pounds that are spent annually in the UK in protecting the coast from erosion. Some people are now suggesting that it would be cheaper to let nature take its course and pay compensation to those affected. Both policies, 'Do Nothing' and 'Managed Retreat', have polarised opinion. Figure 31 shows two newspaper reports detailing why such policies should be carried out, and why in practice, it is often difficult to implement them. Extract (a) (August 1998) reports on the findings of the House of Commons Select Committee on Agriculture, which suggested that large tracts of land should simply be 'surrendered to the sea', as it was a waste of money in trying to protect them. Extract (b) (January 2001) indicates, that in some places, implementing such schemes could prove to be very expensive.

CASE STUDY 18: COASTAL MANAGEMENT IN THE UNITED KINGDOM

COASTAL MANAGEMENT ON THE ISLE OF WIGHT

Coastal defence options

The Isle of Wight Council, like all the others on the coast of the UK, has four defence options open to it:

- **Hold the line**. Retain the existing line of defence through maintenance of existing defences or by constructing new defences where existing structures no longer provide sufficient protection (Figure 32a).
- **Retreat the line**. Actively manage the rate and process by which the coast retreats, i.e. managed retreat (Figure 32b).
- **Do nothing but monitor**. Chosen for stretches of coastline where it is not technically, economically or environmentally viable to undertake defence works. The value of the built environment along the affected part does not exceed the cost of installing coastal defences.
- **Advance the line**. Build new defences seaward of the existing line.

Some examples of recent schemes within the Isle of Wight are (Figure 32c):

1. **Monk's Bay**. Cliff failure resulting from a combination of high-energy destructive waves and high rainfall associated with the severe storms of the winter of 1990–1 gave additional impetus for upgrading coastal defences here. The scheme involved constructing an offshore breakwater, six rock groynes, beach nourishment using 17 000 m^3 of sand and gravel, and a rock revetment to reinforce the existing sea wall

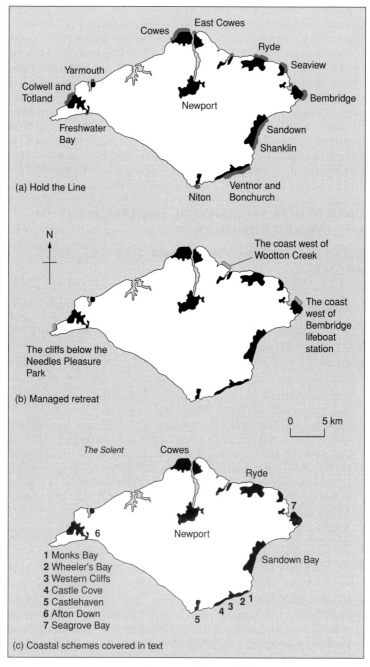

Figure 32 Isle of Wight sea defences

using 25 000 tonnes of Swedish granite. Re-profiling the slope and installing land drainage was also carried out in order to check the active mass movement of the cliffs on the western side of the bay. The collective value of the property far exceeded the £1.4 million cost of the scheme. This was completed in 1992, but sedimentation of the rock groynes is a problem that has developed.

2. **Wheeler's Bay**. The ageing sea walls were in danger of collapse, which would have reactivated ancient landslides making properties on the cliff behind unsaleable. Over 15 000 tonnes of Norwegian granite was placed seaward of the existing defences to form a rock revetement and the coastal slopes were regraded to make a shallower profile before installing land drainage. This scheme was completed in 2000 at a cost of £1.6 million and has led to a recovery in property values.

3. **Western Cliffs (Ventnor)**. High-energy waves have been removing chalk blocks, which protected an ancient landslide complex upon which houses have been constructed. The danger was that the landslide could be reactivated if sufficient of the chalk was removed. A rock revetement of 700 m length was constructed at the base of the cliffs using limestone blocks from the Mendip Hills (Somerset) weighing 6–8 tonnes each. There was also the construction of a series of rock groynes at 100 m intervals at the base of the cliffs.

4. **Castle Cove**. The existing wooden revetement sea defences were being left progressively ineffective as the clay cliff retreated. Property, valued in excess of £10 million, was becoming increasingly at risk as coastal processes activated ancient landslides. The scheme stabilised the environmentally sensitive cliffs by removing the top soil, stabilising the slopes, with thousands of tonnes of chalk, and installing land drainage before replacing the top soil. The cliff has been protected by a rock revetement of Somerset limestone, a concrete walkway and a gabion wall. Completed in 1996, the scheme cost £2.3 million.

5. **Castlehaven**. Landslides have removed part of a road here and are threatening property worth over £20 million. A scheme to stabilise the cliffs and protect them from active coastal processes has been proposed but the council is unable to obtain grant aid from DEFRA as there were objections from nature conservationists about the impact of land drainage on soft cliff habitats that support many nationally rare insects and plants. A public enquiry will have to be held to see if the scheme is environmentally acceptable.

6. **East of Freshwater (Afton Down)**. Where the A3055 passes over a chalk ridge, it is now within 10 m of the cliff edge. Sea defences to prevent any more cliff erosion would be economically unacceptable and therefore the council have devised a

scheme that stabilises the cliff top by anchoring the top of the cliff face on the landward side of the road at a cost of £750 000.

7. **Seagrove Bay**. The crumbling sea walls (maintained by residents) and unstable slopes forced the council to intervene as part of its policy of 'hold the line' in order to protect property. A scheme costing around £1 million, and completed in 2000, included a new concrete sea wall, with 200 m of rock revetement placed in front of it to dissipate the energy of the waves. Rock groynes were also constructed as a further layer of protection. Mass movement on the soft clay cliffs has been significantly reduced by installing land drainage.

3 Tsunamis

Cause and effect

Tsunamis (Japanese for 'harbour wave') are giant sea waves generated by shallow-focus underwater earthquakes (the most common cause), volcanic eruptions, underwater debris slides and large landslides into the sea. Tsunamis have a very long wavelength (sometimes over 100 km) and a low wave height (under 1 m) in the open ocean, and they travel quickly at speeds of over 700 km per hour (some tsunamis take less than a day to cross the Pacific Ocean) but, when reaching the shallow water bordering land, increase rapidly in height. Quite often, the first warning given to coastal populations is the wave trough in front of the tsunami that results in a reduction in sea level, known as a drawdown. Behind this comes the tsunami itself, which can reach to heights in excess of 25 m. The event usually consists of a number of waves, the largest not necessarily being the first.

When a tsunami reaches the land, its effects will depend upon:

- the height of the waves and the distance they have travelled
- the length of the event
- the extent to which warnings could be given
- coastal physical geography, both offshore and in the coastal area
- coastal land use and population density.

The wave will wash boats and wooden coastal structures inland, and the backwash may carry them out to sea. People are drowned or injured by the event as both the water itself and the debris that it contains are hazards. Buildings, roads, bridges, harbour structures and even soil are washed away, most tsunamis having an effect at least 500–600 m inland, depending upon the coastal geography. Tsunamis generated by the explosion of the volcano, Krakatoa, in 1883, have been estimated to have drowned over 35 000 people and produced waves that travelled around the world, the highest being over 40 m.

Distribution

Around 90% of all tsunamis are generated within the Pacific Basin, associated with the tectonic activity taking place around its edges. Most are generated at convergent plate boundaries where subduction is taking place, particularly off the Japan–Taiwan island arc (25% of all events), South America and the Aleutian Islands area. As already noted, tsunamis generated on one side of the Pacific can easily reach the other side in less than a day; the one generated by the Chilean earthquake of 1960 took only 22 hours to cross to Japan. The geological record also indicates that huge tsunamis have affected areas such as the Mediterranean Basin (e.g. the Santorini eruption around 1450 BC) and the North Sea area (see case study of the Storegga slide later in this chapter).

Hazard management

Prediction and warning. The monitoring of earthquake and volcanic activity should enable warnings to be given to vulnerable populations so that an **evacuation** can take place. A centre has been established on Hawaii (Pacific Warning System) that will give warnings to the countries situated around the Pacific Rim. This station is linked to several seismic and tidal observation stations throughout the Pacific and also to satellite information provided through a NOAA programme (National Oceanic and Atmospheric Administration). Giving warnings is not easy, though, as not all earthquakes generate tsunamis and false warnings can cost a lot of money to those areas where evacuation has been suggested. This may also lead people to ignore future predictions after false warnings. As most deaths from tsunamis occur within a few hundred kilometres of the source, local systems are often better in warning populations. In Japan there is the system set up by the Japanese Meteorological Agency that operates seismic detectors, uses computers to calculate the size of any potential tsunami and issues warnings via television and radio. Many of the LEDCs that surround the Pacific, though, have no real access to information of this kind or any way of warning their vulnerable populations.

Land-use planning. By removing vulnerable structures from waterfront locations, it is hoped that the effect of tsunamis can be reduced. Some cities in the USA have turned their waterfronts into public parks and other such open areas and moved businesses back away from the greatest points of danger (e.g. Crescent City, California). Trees can be planted in order to absorb the wave energy.

Hard engineering and building design. In those countries that can afford it, offshore breakwaters can be constructed, particularly to protect valuable coastal buildings such as power stations. Buildings themselves can be constructed with open ground floors to allow the passage of water.

CASE STUDY 19: 'ONE OF THE LARGEST TSUNAMIS OF THE TWENTIETH CENTURY'

NORTHERN PAPUA NEW GUINEA, 17 JULY 1998

Northern Papua New Guinea has a history of seismic activity where the Philippine Plate is subducting underneath the Indo-Australian plate. On the 17 July 1998, an earthquake was triggered some 12 miles off the northern coast with its focus around 33 km under the surface. This earthquake measured 7.1 on the Richter scale and was followed an hour later by a violent aftershock. This generated at least three tsunami waves, the highest of which was over 10 m high when it hit the coast. The small fishing and subsistence agriculture settlements of the coast together with roads and bridges were largely swept away, and trees were shredded and ripped out as the tsunami reached over 200 m inland. There was absolutely no warning, as the interval between the earthquake and the arrival of the tsunami was too short for any evacuation to take place, and it took almost all people completely by surprise. This meant that the death toll was high, probably in excess of 5000, although the final figure will never be

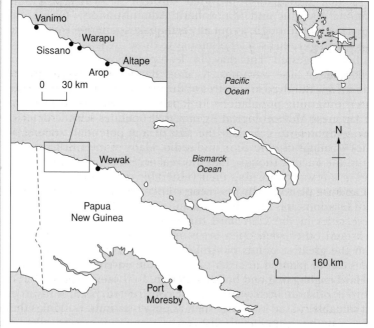

Figure 33 Area devastated by the tsunami of July 1998

totally known, with many people injured. The settlements of
Arop, Warapu, Sissano and Altape (Figure 33) were almost completely flattened with over 6000 people left homeless with a lack
of food and vulnerable to disease. The United States Geological
Survey described this event as '*one of the most devastating tsunamis
of the twentieth century*'.

The response to the event was slow as communications within
the area were destroyed and no information was received in the
capital, Port Moresby, until the following day. International aid
did not begin to arrive until 2 days after the tsunami had struck
and even then it was extremely difficult for rescue workers to
reach the affected region in numbers. The main problem was
trying to make sure that the survivors received food and medical
aid as the chances of disease in a tropical climate with so many
dead bodies lying around was very great. Many of the survivors
had also fled into the rain forests behind the coast, and search
and rescue operations had to be mounted to find them and
bring them into temporary accommodation.

CASE STUDY 20: EVIDENCE OF AN ANCIENT TSUNAMI

THE STOREGGA SLIDE, OFF THE COAST OF NORWAY AROUND 7250 BP

Investigations of layers found within coastal sediments in eastern
Scotland, the Faeroe Islands and western Norway indicated that
they were marine and must have been deposited by some high-
wave event. These deposits are now thought to have been laid
down by a tsunami that reached a height of over 6 m in Scotland
and probably higher in other locations (in Norway, it has been
estimated that the drawdown was 8 m with a wave height of over
16 m). The origin of the waves is believed to be from a huge sub-
marine slide of debris that occurred off the coast of Norway over
7000 years ago. This whole area, known as the Storegga slides,
appears to have been activated at least three times and the event
recorded in the deposits in Scotland was the second. This second
slide probably involved over 1000 km² of debris flowing down
the continental slopes at a speed in excess of 100 km per hour,
sufficient to generate a huge tsunami. It has been suggested that
this enormous slide produced waves that travelled across the
North Atlantic, causing severe flooding along the coastlines of
Iceland, Greenland and Spitsbergen.

Summary

- River flooding is the most frequently reported of all natural hazards.
- River valleys are attractive places to live, for a variety of reasons, but this increasingly exposes more people to the risk of flooding.
- There are several basic causes of river flooding, all of them being affected by the influence of man.
- The United Kingdom is faced with an increase in the incidence of the flood hazard.
- Although there are various forms of approach to flood management, modern approaches favour natural options, as far as possible, and focus on conservation.
- Large areas of coastline are very attractive for a wide range of human activities, however, the coast is under attack from both erosion and from the possibility of being flooded.
- Traditional approaches to coastal management involve both 'hard' and 'soft' engineering solutions.
- Increasingly, coastal management involves a managed retreat or, in some cases, doing absolutely nothing, as solutions to coastal problems become more expensive than the value of what is being protected.
- Some of the protection and management strategies, although they are solutions in one place, have caused problems in others.
- Tsunamis are waves generated by shallow focused earthquakes, volcanic activity and debris slides (both underwater and into the sea).
- Around 90% of all tsunamis are generated within the Pacific Ocean basin.
- The focus of tsunami management has been upon prediction and warning with some land-use planning in vulnerable areas.

Exercises

1. With reference to a located example, explain the physical causes of river flooding.
2. Why are both river and coastal flooding an increasing hazard in the United Kingdom?
3. With reference to a named drainage basin:
   (i)   outline one scheme to control river flow
   (ii) comment on the effectiveness of that scheme.
4. A number of strategies exist to combat the problem of rapid coastal erosion. Describe three of these strategies and explain why they were chosen for a particular named location.
5. (a) Why are tsunamis such a difficult hazard to predict?
   (b) What are the problems with the tsunami warning systems in operation at the present time?

5 Hazards Generated Within the Human Environment

1 Burglary in Urban Areas

Distribution and frequency

In the United Kingdom, the incidence of burglary tends to be higher in inner-city areas rather than in the outer suburbs. Insurance company premiums reflect this by being highest in urban districts with low-numbered post codes, i.e. the inner areas. In the West Midlands, for example, the figures for reported burglary offences (1999) were:

- 12.4 per 1000 households for the Halesowen/Stourbridge/Lye/Cradley/Kingswinford division (outer suburbs)
- 36.9 per 1000 households for the Birmingham Central division.

On the urban fringe, there is the opportunity offered by large, detached houses that are often screened from view and would-be burglars can benefit from the less developed social network. In the inner areas, younger, less experienced criminals are likely to offend nearer to their home territory because of familiarity. Information about potential targets is readily available in the immediate vicinity but decreases rapidly with distance, i.e. there is a strong distance-decay effect.

Information with regard to burglary in terms of distribution and frequency is often incomplete. Several sources can be used:

- **Police records**: not all crimes are reported, for various reasons, e.g. fear of retaliation; loss too small to bother about; goods uninsured; not willing to lose no claims bonus and receive higher premium after claim; desire to sort it out without recourse to authority (burglar known to victim); lack of confidence in police to solve the crime.
- **Insurance company records**: not all people are insured as premiums are often highest in inner-city areas (reflecting risk), and so not affordable. Some addresses might find it difficult to obtain insurance because of the history of crime there.
- **British Crime Survey**: the BCS, run by the Home Office, measures the amount of crime in England and Wales by asking people about crimes they have experienced. It therefore includes crimes that are not reported to police but critics say that it still seriously underestimates the true figures. It helps to identify those most at risk, and this is used in the planning of crime prevention programmes.
- **The media**: just gives a snapshot of the whole picture as only certain crimes are reported.

In terms of frequency of the crime, there have been several studies that suggest holiday times (particularly summer) and Christmas are periods when the incidence of burglary tends to rise.

The nature of the hazard (effects)

Burglary as a threat to people is more than someone simply removing goods from a property. The hazard itself can take several forms:

- removal of goods from property
- damage to property caused when trying to gain entry
- invasion of privacy
- psychological damage (fear of crime) may be so severe that people almost barricade themselves in their property or move away. Some people have been known to die in fires because the fire authorities could not reach them as their homes were so tightly secured that they were unable to escape in time. There was a reported case of this in Dover (Kent) in May 2000, where two elderly people were overcome by fumes having been trapped by a fire in their bunga-

low. The police reported that they had three locks on each door into the dwelling and another three locks on each internal door. Figure 34 shows the fear of crime as expressed by residents of Newcastle upon Tyne. As expected, more residents feel unsafe in the poorer inner-city areas such as Scotswood, Benwell and Elswick than in the more affluent areas of Jesmond and Dene.

Management

When setting premiums, insurance companies are to some extent predicting the frequency of burglary in an area (usually based on a post code, but in some areas premiums can be different from street to street). It is often difficult to distinguish between prevention and protection when dealing with burglary. Authorities often refer to crime prevention in leaflets and advertising, and then include within it advice to householders as to how they can protect their property. Prevention, at its roots, deals with looking at the reason why people commit the crime and see if those reasons can be addressed. In the UK, for example, a large amount of burglary is said to be drug related and therefore authorities have promoted schemes to get people off

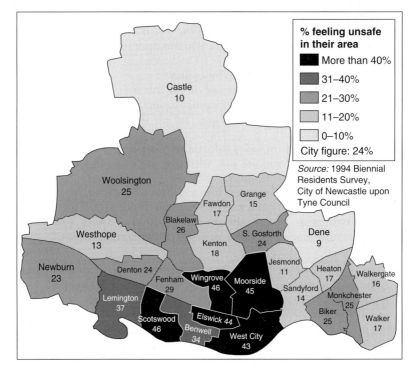

Figure 34 Fear of crime of the residents of Newcastle upon Tyne (1994)

drugs, which ought, in the long term, to lead to a reduction of burglary incidents. Unemployment has also been cited as being responsible, and governments partly have an eye on crime figures when bringing in policies to get people back into work. Many youth policies are aimed in getting younger people off the streets and into work or leisure programmes in the hope that crime will be reduced.

In trying to protect property from the burglar, people can either work individually or collectively. **Individually**, they can protect their homes with a range of devices (alarms, walls, fences, window locks, security lighting, guard dogs, etc.) and by taking out adequate insurance to cover their losses. **Collectively**, they can organise within their local area a Neighbourhood Watch Scheme. In some areas groups of worried residents have formed themselves into groups that patrol housing areas at night, although such vigilante action has been known to lead to violence and is disapproved of by the police.

At an **organisational level**, various initiatives have been set up by the police and local and national government. Such initiatives have included:

- placing of CCTV cameras
- free or low-cost security devices made available
- community policing
- TV and newspaper campaigns
- the setting up of burglary reduction schemes by local authorities (see Figure 35 for details of the scheme operated by Leicester City Council)
- larger penalties imposed by the courts
- information through leaflets and on the internet. The Metropolitan Police [London] has several documents, such as '*Burglary Prevention*', '*Security Alarms*', '*Windows*', '*Doors*' on an internet site (the document for '*Burglary*' is at www.met.police.uk/crimeprevention/burglary.htm and includes information on how a burglar's mind works, how to tell you are out, where to put valuables and what to do when you are on holiday)
- defensible space, where new housing developments have an input from several sources in terms of its design and layout. The aim is to deter a burglar by not offering easy entry or quick exit. Such designs now feature in many new inner-city developments.

The great danger with all initiatives is that records may show the scheme to be working in reducing burglary in one particular part of an urban area. The overall level of burglary in the city, however, may not have fallen, as crime has simply been displaced from a 'hard' area for burglars to succeed, to a 'softer' one.

There are organisations, such as Victim Support, that offer help to those affected by crime, such help being both practical (how to deal with insurance companies, emergency repairs, loss of official documents, how to obtain compensation) and supportive (counselling and advice).

Leicester
City Council Leicester City Council

How do I... ... make my home more secure?

THE THREAT of becoming a victim of crime – especially domestic burglary – is a worry to many people.

Recognising that there are proven steps that can be taken to reduce the risk of burglary, the city council – in partnership with Leicestershire Constabulary – operates a number of burglary reduction and community safety schemes across Leicester.

The schemes aim to reduce domestic burglary, improve community safety and address the growing fear of crime. They offer practical advice and home security improvements to households that have been victims of burglary or that are considered to be vulnerable to crime.

Each community safety scheme operates in its own qualifying area and offers a service that is generally free of charge for people meeting eligibility criteria.

The schemes are funded through the government's Single Regeneration Budget and Home Office money specially earmarked for burglary reduction initiatives.

All city council-run community safety schemes are managed by the housing department's renewal and grants team, with security surveys and the fitting of new security equipment being carried out by the team's area maintenance officers.

Security improvements available include the fitting of five-lever mortice locks to front and back doors, along with window locks, door chains, spyholes, kick plates and other equipment as recommended.

The following community safety schemes are currently running in the city:

- The Belgrave Burglary Reduction Project
- The CRASH project in greater Humberstone
- The Hinckley Road Burglary Reduction Initiative
- The Banish Project in Highfields and St Matthews
- The Braunstone Project
- The North West Leicester Burglary Reduction Project for Beaumont Leys, Mowmacre, Abbey Rise, Stocking Farm and Anstey Heights
- The Asfordby Street Project for Leicester University students living in Clarendon Park and Highfields.

Figure 35 Burglary reduction scheme, Leicester City Council

A variety of approaches to the prevention of burglary have been tried in the UK in recent years. Some of the schemes are detailed below:

- **Kingsmead Estate, Hackney**: injunctions were made against specific individuals and repossession orders against persistent offenders, followed up by a programme of activities for young people. Crime rates on the estate dropped sharply. Burglaries were down from 340 in 1992 to 50 in 1993.
- **Mozart Estate, Westminster**: removal of overhead walkways and other design changes on the estate brought a slight reduction in burglaries. Reports on the situation, though, commented on the need for economic and social regeneration before any major inroads into the problem could be made.
- **Possil Park Estate, Glasgow**: community security business was established to protect properties from vandalism and theft. The city council's evaluation concluded that the scheme had saved £250 000 in reduced costs of vandalism and theft in 1 year.
- **Southmead, Bristol**: activity schemes for younger people were established and operated mainly during the school summer holiday. It has been estimated that there was a reduction in domestic burglary of 64% during the period of the scheme.
- **Hull**: put more police on the beat. In 1999, the Humberside police were denied a Home Office grant to put more police officers on the beat. The city council agreed to put up £1 million to fund an extra 174 officers, allowing more highly visible foot patrols in inner areas. In 2000, it was estimated that crime in central Hull was down by 14% with particular drops in burglaries and stolen cars.
- **Leicester**: set up a scheme that gives advice and practical help to households with regard to burglary and other crimes (see Figure 35). Advice is given on home security together with a list of the projects to which people can apply for help. The city council also operates a non-profit-making service offering home security equipment at low prices. Help for the funding comes from central government through the Single Regeneration Budget (money targeted at inner-cities) and also from the Home Office, with money specifically earmarked for burglary reduction initiatives.

2 Transmittable Disease

A transmittable disease is one that is capable of being transmitted from one person to another. This can be done in several ways:

- inhalation of droplets
- ingestion of contaminated food or water
- skin penetration by insect bite or contaminated needles
- exchange of body fluids.

When the number of people with a disease is significantly measurable at a national or regional level, it is said to be an **epidemic**. If the disease exists on an international level then it is said to have reached the **pandemic** stage. Geographers are concerned with many transmittable diseases because they do not spread evenly throughout the world and thus resources to cope with the management of them vary from region to region. Understanding the geography of a disease helps to make sense of the social, cultural and economic impact it is likely to have across the planet and within different countries. Some of the major transmittable diseases that affect the world are:

- **Trypanosomiasis (sleeping sickness)**: a fatal disease in which the early symptoms are banal – headache, fever and vomiting with victims tending to doze off during the day. In the final stages the victims suffer bouts of insanity before falling into a coma, the whole process taking up to 3 years. Sleeping sickness is caused by a blood parasite spread by the tsetse fly.
- **Malaria**: caused by an infectious parasitic protozoan, which first settles in the liver and then multiplies to attack the red blood cells. Malaria is an acute, chronic infection that may be fatal if left untreated. If treatment is inadequate or inappropriate, then the infection may occur over many years. Infant mortality rates from malaria are particularly high in many LEDCs (between 1.5 and 2 million children die from malaria and its consequences each year in sub-Saharan Africa). The disease is spread by the female anopheles mosquito, which carries the protozoan from one infected person to a new victim.
- **Cholera**: a disease caused by infection with various strains of the bacillus *Vibrio cholerae*, transmitted in contaminated water and characterised by violent diarrhoea and vomiting. Death rates were once high, but have now been reduced through treatment to prevent dehydration and loss of body salts, together with the use of antibiotics.
- **Tuberculosis (TB)**: an infectious disease, caused by the bacillus *Mycobacterium tuberculosi*, which was formerly known as 'consumption'. It is a disease that attacks the lungs and from which over 3 million people die in the world every year. Antibiotics, however, are successful in treating 95% of all cases. TB is spread through droplet infection or from untreated milk from infected animals.
- **Ebola**: this disease was first recognised in 1976 in Zaire by the Ebola river and is caused by a virus that attacks and breaks down body tissue so that blood pours from every orifice. Death occurs within a matter of days among 90% of those that it infects. The virus is spread in several ways, either by eating infected monkey meat, or through contact with blood, faeces and body fluids of infected people.
- **Pneumonic plague**: a lung infection that can be fatal and is spread

from rats to humans via fleas. Once a lung infection is established, the coughing of victims makes the disease airborne. There was a serious outbreak of pneumonic plague in India in 1994.

Acquired Immune Deficiency Syndrome (AIDS)

AIDS is caused by the **human immunodeficiency virus (HIV)**. HIV is a slow retrovirus, which means that not only does it take years to show symptoms but it also invades the white cells by literally writing the structure of itself backwards (retro) into them and reproducing itself inside. These cells produce the antibodies that are the body's main defence against disease and without them the body becomes the target of everyday infections and cell changes that cause cancers. That is what is meant when people are said to be suffering from AIDS. There is some controversy over the origins of HIV. Some people believe that it is man made, produced by some chemical weapons laboratory, but the generally accepted view is that it evolved in sub-Saharan Africa, crossing over from the chimpanzee population, possibly in the 1930s. This could have been from eating infected meat or the bite from a pet. Some scientists have suggested that the virus had been present in the human population of central Africa for a long time, but only on a very local scale. Developments in the twentieth century, such as international travel, blood transfusions and intravenous drug use, brought it onto a world stage and produced a growing pandemic. In Europe and North America, the time-lag between infection with HIV and the development of AIDS is about 10 years, but progression is far more rapid in LEDCs, where 50% of victims are dead within 3 years. At the present time there is no cure for the disease.

The spread of AIDS

The virus has a short life outside of the body, which makes the main methods of transmission as follows:

- the exchange of body fluids during sexual intercourse
- through contaminated needles by intravenous drug users (IDU)
- via contaminated blood transfusions
- from mother to child during pregnancy.

Evidence shows that the disease seemed to start in small high-risk groups such as gay men, drug users and prostitutes, and then spread into the population as a whole. This meant that in the early stages in MEDCs, AIDS was regarded by many as a 'Gay Plague', therefore the heterosexual community took little notice of it and education about 'safe sex' was disregarded. In LEDCs, especially in Africa, the transfer of the virus was commonly through heterosexual sex, but this information was not generally known in most of the developed world. Three distinct patterns of distribution therefore developed:

- **Pattern 1** covers countries that began to see a spread in the late 1970s, first amongst homosexual, bisexual and drug-using communities and then later into the general population. This includes North America, western Europe, Australia and some parts of Latin America.
- **Pattern 2** includes those countries where the spread has been essentially through heterosexual contact. This covers the bulk of sub-Saharan Africa.
- **Pattern 3** covers those countries where the spread was later (in the 1980s) and brought in by travellers and, sometimes, imported blood for transfusions. This includes eastern Europe (including the former USSR), Asia, the Middle East and North Africa.

By 2002, it was estimated that there were over 40 million people worldwide living with HIV or full-blown AIDS. Over 70% of these people (28.5 million) were living in the countries of sub-Saharan Africa. North America had 900 000 people with the condition and western Europe 520 000. It has been estimated that 8.6% of the adult population of sub-Saharan Africa is HIV positive. There are nine countries with over 10% of the adult population infected and they are Botswana, Kenya, Malawi, Mozambique, Namibia, Rwanda, South Africa, Zambia and Zimbabwe. The United Nations (World Health Organisation) has estimated that by 2020, 70 million people will have died from AIDS. Figures published in November 2002 by the UN showed that for the first time women accounted for almost half the people living with AIDS, infected by HIV or dying from the disease. This was particularly so in sub-Saharan Africa where 60% of all those infected were women. In the same survey, it was estimated that over 33 000 people in the UK were infected with HIV, about 15 000 having died from the disease since the early 1980s

Evidence for frequency and scale

Evidence of frequency and scale can be obtained from medical records (from doctors and hospitals), national government health department records, the World Health Organization (WHO) and the media. Figures, however, can never be totally accurate for the following reasons:

- medical records are confidential to the patient
- many people with HIV are not aware that they are infected
- the social stigma of AIDS means that many sufferers do not report the illness until it is well into its latter stages
- AIDS is not always given as the cause of death because the sufferer may have died from an opportunist disease that invaded the body

- it has been suggested that the disease has been overestimated in parts of Africa in order to obtain money from wealthy governments and aid organisations.

The effects

The United Nations has estimated that only one in ten sufferers know that they have the virus in the early days of infection. Most people die because of the breakdown of their immune system allowing other infections to invade the body. Just as important in terms of the effects are the attitudes of other people to the disease, as sufferers may experience prejudice in terms of their employment and social life. This may even extend to the immediate family; there have been cases where children have been ostracised because one of their parents had the disease.

Life expectancy in much of sub-Saharan Africa will soon fall to levels not seen since the nineteenth century (Table 3). Some authorities are predicting that by 2010 people in many southern African countries will not generally be expected to live beyond their thirties. Populations of some of those countries will have started to shrink and in others population growth rates will have slowed to zero. AIDS has also reversed the decline in infant mortality that was seen across southern Africa in the 1980s and early 1990s, with rates in some countries now standing close to double what they would have been without the pandemic. In Africa, the effects on families have included loss of income-earning opportunities, the diversion of effort and income into care and medicine, and the withdrawal of children from school.

Table 3 Life expectancy projected for 2010 in selected African countries

	Life expectancy (age in years)	
	Without AIDS	**With AIDS**
Angola	41.3	35
Botswana	74.4	26.7
Lesotho	67.2	36.5
Malawi	59.4	36.9
Mozambique	42.5	27.1
Namibia	68.8	33.8
Rwanda	54.7	38.7
South Africa	68.5	36.5
Swaziland	74.6	33
Zambia	58.6	34.4
Zimbabwe	71.4	34.6

Source: Census Bureau (USA)

There has been a huge effect upon farming, with AIDS threatening food growing and income-earning potential in areas facing food shortages (Figure 36). Some countries have been faced with large numbers of orphans as a result of AIDS, which has put a great strain on local resources.

Management of the disease

There are various ways in which people and organisations deal with a disease such as AIDS:

- **Trying to find a cure**: at present, the hope of finding a vaccine seems remote, although research is continuing, in particular trying to find groups that might possibly possess some degree of natural immunity through their white cells.
- **Prolonging life through drugs**: there are drugs on the market that do represent a way of prolonging life, particularly in MEDCs. AZT (zidovudine), is one such drug, but it is expensive, a typical course costing $10 000 a year per individual. Even Nevirapine, a slightly cheaper retroviral drug, is beyond the reach of the governments of LEDCs, although a recent test case in the South African courts may mean that such drugs could be supplied considerably cheaper in future.
- **Plotting the course**: by plotting the course of an outbreak, it may be possible to predict the future spread of HIV and identify areas where resources should be concentrated.

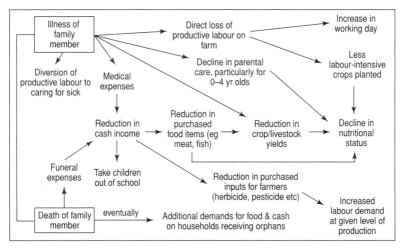

Figure 36 The implication for families affected by AIDS in Central and East Africa

- **Blood screening**: blood for transfusions in MEDCs is screened for antibodies to HIV, giving negligible risks of infection, although this was not always the case. Blood plasma products, such as Factor VIII, are also subject to special treatment.
- **Education and advertising**: many countries hope to prevent the spread of the disease by targeting vulnerable groups such as homosexuals and intravenous drug users. Raising the profile of the disease in schools through sex education has been a major feature in the programme of the UK government. Other campaigns in the UK have included free needles for drug users, free condoms and warnings to tourists about their behaviour in foreign countries.
- **Caring for victims and families**: looking after victims and their families has become the responsibility of many agencies. Several charities are involved in the UK, including the Terrence Higgins Trust and London Lighthouse.

CASE STUDY 21: BOTSWANA (SOUTHERN AFRICA)

The AIDS pandemic has had a huge impact in Botswana. In a total population of 1.6 million, it has been estimated that 39% of the county's adults are infected with HIV, with rates over 50% in the north-east of the country and amongst expectant mothers in urban areas. The virus has run rampant despite various measures to control it, the government is trying to manage the spread of the disease by focusing on prevention. In 2002, Botswana became the first African country to provide free condoms but the government also made anti-retroviral drugs available as part of its programme. It is able to do this because it has the most lucrative diamond mines in the world and, as a result, has a per capita income seven times the average for sub-Saharan Africa.

Life expectancy in the country has dipped below 40 for the first time since 1950 and in 2002 stood at just under 34 years. It would have been expected to rise to 74 years and 5 months by 2010 if there had been no AIDS pandemic, but the current projected figure for that year is only 26 years and 7 months.

There is also a serious effect upon the economy of the country because Botswana's wealth is increasingly unsustainable as AIDS is destroying the workforce. According to reports, the economy of the country will be one-third smaller by 2021 than it would have been without AIDS, and government expenditure will have to increase by 20%.

CASE STUDY 22: THAILAND (SOUTH-EAST ASIA)

In the late years of the twentieth century, Thailand had the most serious AIDS problem in Asia. The first case in the country was diagnosed in 1984 and from that point there was a rapid growth in infection rates, particularly amongst vulnerable groups such as intravenous drug users and commercial sex workers. Commercial sex workers were extremely vulnerable, infection rates reaching 30% by the early 1990s.

HIV spread rapidly to the heterosexual and non-intravenous drug using population as a result of low condom use and a high rate of premarital and extramarital male sexual contact with commercial sex workers. By 1995, over 5000 HIV-infected babies were being born each year. It was also clear that the pattern of infection seen in North America and Europe would not be repeated in Thailand, as it would not be limited to a few isolated risk groups. In 1999, it was estimated that 950 000 of the population were infected with HIV, of whom 110 000 had actually contracted AIDS. In that year, 66 000 people died from AIDS-related conditions, a pattern that was likely to be repeated in the early years of the twenty-first century.

As the scale of the problem became clear, the Thai government responded in a positive way. They already had a '100% Condom Programme', launched in 1991, but then they established a National AIDS Committee that came up with a hard-hitting campaign on TV, radio and poster sites. The awareness of commercial sex workers was targeted, with a supply of 60 million free condoms a year to help the programme. One of the results was that condom usage amongst men visiting commercial sex workers rose to over 90%. The success of the programme is such that HIV infection rates in Thailand now appear to be in decline. This success very much stands out against the record of other countries in South-east Asia, therefore in 1999, the United Nations and the Red Cross established a joint HIV/AIDS regional collaboration centre in Bangkok.

3 Nuclear Waste

What is nuclear waste?

Nuclear or radioactive waste is produced from the following sources:

- the generation of electricity using nuclear power
- the production of nuclear weapons
- industrial activities

- medical research and practice
- scientific research.

Nuclear waste can be categorised as follows:

Low-level waste. This includes materials that are only slightly contaminated such as gloves, overalls, laboratory equipment, and can be handled and transported fairly easily. Over 85% of nuclear waste falls into this category.

Intermediate-level waste. This is more radioactive and needs special handling. It derives from the metal casings holding used nuclear fuel rods, fuel debris and the various sludges resulting from the treatment of nuclear fuel. A total of 13–14% of all nuclear waste falls into this category.

High-level waste. Less than 0.1% of all nuclear waste falls into this category, but it is the most hazardous and arises from the reprocessing of nuclear fuel.

The hazard of nuclear waste

Nuclear waste is radioactive and the emission of alpha, beta and gamma rays are dangerous to body tissues, causing a range of cancers, leukaemia in particular. Some radioactive substances have a long half-life and therefore remain lethal to people for a very long time, plutonium-239, one of the most toxic, having a half-life of 24 000 years. Nuclear waste therefore represents a hazard when being:

- transported
- stored
- reprocessed.

The disposal of nuclear waste

The disposal of nuclear waste is one of the most sensitive of environmental issues. Nobody, whether for or against the creation of nuclear waste through nuclear energy or other means, wants to see this waste dumped in their proverbial backyard. The **dumping of waste at sea** officially stopped in 1983, when a moratorium was agreed by the members of the London Dumping Convention (a UN body that controls disposals of wastes at sea), but the USSR and the Russian Federation continued to dump beyond that point in time. Since then, radioactive waste has been dealt with in the following ways:

Burial. Much of the solid low-level waste can be disposed of by burial in shallow trenches. In the UK, solid waste of this kind is disposed of at a site at Drigg (Cumbria – 2 miles away from Sellafield, which is the main centre in the UK for the handling of nuclear waste). This site is owned and operated by BNFL (British Nuclear Fuels Ltd) through a company known as Nirex. This organisation was set up in the early 1980s by the nuclear industry, with the agreement of the UK government, to examine safe, environmental and economic aspects of deep geological disposal of radioactive waste. The waste is compressed and packed into 200-litre steel drums, which are placed in concrete-lined trenches and eventually covered over by a thick layer of clay and then landscaped. The same principal is to be applied to intermediate waste, but in this case the depository must be much deeper underground. BNFL, at the present time, encapsulates this waste in cement inside stainless steel drums and stores the material within its site at Sellafield. Nirex is actively looking for a site that can be used for deep storage and will address the following criteria and issues when making its final selection:

- **geology**: the site must be geologically stable and must not allow water to move through the site and carry away radioactivity
- **transport**: how the waste material is to be brought to the site
- **local economy**: how will the local economy of the area be boosted by having such an employment-creating site present? (an important a factor in an area of high unemployment and with few other job opportunities)
- **tourism**: if the area is one which has a thriving tourist industry, will people be put off from coming knowing that there is a nuclear waste facility in the area?
- **local opposition**: the strength of local groups against such a facility being created in their area
- **time**: the waste will have to remain in the site for a long period of time, therefore the question of long-term viability and security of the chosen site become issues.

In the USA, the government has proposed that all nuclear waste should be sent for storage at one site on the edge of the Mojave desert in Nevada. This site, known as Yucca Flats, will become the central used nuclear fuel repository for the USA from 2010. At the present time, nuclear waste is stored in over 130 locations in 39 states. The waste at Yucca Flats will be stored over 2 km into the mountain, in huge caverns that will be aluminium and fibre-glass lined, the whole area being stabilised with thousands of metal bolts driven into the solid rock.

Reprocessing. The main method involves chopping up the spent nuclear fuel from a reactor, then dissolving it in nitric acid. The process was designed to separate out plutonium from the other radioactive products in waste fuel. This was then to be used in the production of nuclear weapons and for use in the now-abandoned fast breeder reactors. The main plant at Sellafield is known as THORP (Thermal Oxide Reprocessing Plant) and handles material from both the UK and overseas (Japan, Germany, Switzerland, Sweden and the Netherlands). The other commercially operating reprocessing plant in Europe is at La Hague in France. Reprocessing is recognised as the largest source of radioactive pollution in the UK, the Sellafield plant releasing low-level liquid wastes into the sea via a pipeline, and it is also responsible for releasing some radioactive gases into the atmosphere. Greenpeace regard Sellafield as a *'nuclear dustbin'*, and have actively campaigned for its closure.

Storage. High-level liquid waste is converted into a powder and then mixed with molten glass in a vitrification plant. The end product, enclosed in stainless steel containers, is stored on site (in the UK, at Sellafield) in vaults where the radioactivity is contained. This is possible as vitrification substantially reduces the volume of the original waste.

CASE STUDY 23: ISSUES/PROBLEMS AT THE STORAGE AND REPROCESSING SITE AT SELLAFIELD (CUMBRIA)

Sellafield is by far and away the UK's major nuclear site for the storage and reprocessing of nuclear waste. As already stated, there are certain facilities (such as the THORP plant) that Greenpeace and other organisations would like to see closed. Issues and problems that remain include:

- All other countries (apart from France) have stopped nuclear waste reprocessing, as storage is now a cheaper option. Because uranium prices have fallen, most international experts agree that it now makes much less sense to reprocess thereby avoiding some of the dangers involved.
- Shipping plutonium and liquid nuclear waste across the world has obvious dangers from storm, collision and terrorist attack. Also, shipping nuclear waste by road and rail across the UK is potentially dangerous.
- Pollution of the North Atlantic/Arctic Ocean has increased. Sellafield has been the target of criticism from the Canadian and Scandinavian governments, particularly because of the increase of the radioactive isotopes caesium-137 and iodine-129 in the sea.
- The Irish government has for a long time campaigned against Sellafield, claiming a substantial rise in radioactivity in the waters of the Irish Sea and on the beaches that surround it. Monitoring of marine life in the 1990s found there to have been a 40% increase in contamination in lobsters. In February 1998, over 150 wild pigeons in the vicinity of the plant were culled after being found with higher than expected levels of radioactivity.
- Sites proposed by Nirex for nuclear waste burial, may be compromised by water passing through the rock surrounding the underground facilities.

Summary

- The incidence of urban burglary tends to be greater in the inner areas of cities rather than the suburbs.
- The records of the distribution and frequency of burglary and some transmittable diseases are incomplete for a variety of reasons.
- Burglary does not pose just a simple hazard of property removal, as people also suffer from the psychological impact.
- Management of the burglary hazard can take place at different levels, individual, collective and through official organisations.
- In many cases when burglary figures appear to be declining, it could be that the crime has simply been displaced to a 'softer' area.
- Transmittable diseases do not spread evenly throughout the world, thus the resources to manage them vary between areas.
- The AIDS virus has a short life span outside of the body, and can only be passed on in a few distinctive ways.
- There are three very distinct patterns for the spread of AIDS across the world.
- There is no cure for AIDS at present, so that is why money is put into education and other ways of trying to make sure that people do not pass on the virus.
- The problem of nuclear waste will be with us for a long time because of the long half-life of many radioactive elements.
- At the present time, the choice for that we have for nuclear waste is either storage or reprocessing.
- There has been a certain amount of controversy over nuclear waste reprocessing as it produces a substantial amount of pollution.

Exercises

1. Describe the nature and distribution of the hazard of burglary in urban areas.
2. For burglary in urban areas, name **two** sources of evidence that can be used to show the scale and frequency of the hazard. Comment on the reliability of evidence obtained from those sources.
3. For a named transmittable disease, describe some of the attempts that have been made to prevent and/or manage the hazard.
4. For a named transmittable disease, discuss how the success of attempts at prevention and/or management depends upon the perception and understanding of the hazard.
5. The disposal of nuclear waste has become an international issue in recent years. Discuss the reasons why this has happened.

6 Multi-hazard Urban Environments

1 Los Angeles

Los Angeles was established as a Spanish settlement in 1781 on an original site on the coastal lowlands of California. The settlement was physically isolated in its basin, as rising abruptly inland are the San Gabriel and San Bernardino mountain ranges, which act as a barrier between Los Angeles and the rest of California. The climate of the area is semi-desert/Mediterranean with summer drought and very mild winters. Until the early twentieth century it was a farming region based mainly upon citrus fruits, but as water began to be brought into the area the settlement grew, particularly with the discovery of oil and the early developments in the film industry because of its outdoor locations (beaches and mountains) and clear weather. The aircraft industry also benefited from the all-year round flying weather and this grew quickly before, and particularly during, the Second World War. Since then, the population of Los Angeles has grown rapidly to become one of the major population centres in the USA, with over 15 million people living in the full metropolitan area at the end of the

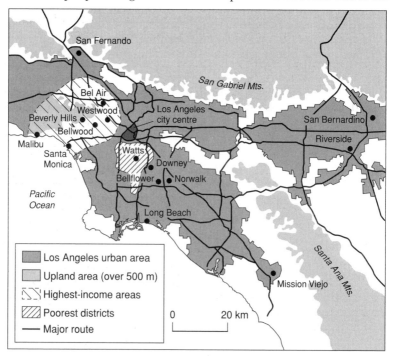

Figure 37 Los Angeles locations

twentieth century. There have been many things that have attracted people to this area, the climate, beaches, snow-capped peaks, sub-tropical vegetation, glamour industries, but Los Angeles is a hazardous region. Many authorities rate Los Angeles as one of the most hazardous areas in the whole of the developed world and it requires effective management if the city is to remain a viable place to live.

Some of the hazards affecting Los Angeles are directly concerned with the physical environment, others are where man has modified the physical environment to his disadvantage and there are also some that occur entirely within the human environment. The ones that will be covered here are:

- earthquakes
- river flooding
- coastal flooding
- drought
- fires
- mass movement (mudslides, landslides)
- smog
- crime (including burglary) and gang warfare
- racial violence.

Earthquakes

A network of active faults underlies the Los Angeles region including the major San Andreas system. The San Andreas is a vertical fault and visible on the surface, but many of the other faults in the area are deep and give no visible sign to their presence. One of these previously unknown faults was responsible for the Northridge earthquake in 1994 (see Chapter 2). Recent investigations carried out by the United States Geological Survey have shown that the basin of soft sediment on which the city sits is much deeper than was originally thought, at least 5 km deep, and as this 'spongy' layer tends to shake more readily during an event, this discovery has dramatically increased the perceived threat to the area. Whilst minor earth tremors are common in the region, there have been five earthquakes since 1933 that have measured at least 5.8 on the Richter scale, the largest being the Northridge event that measured 6.7 and killed 57 people, whilst causing damage estimated at over \$30 billion. The earthquake was not unusually large by world standards but its location beneath a densely populated part of the metropolitan area accounted for the loss of life and the widespread damage. Earthquakes are therefore a certainty in the future within the Los Angeles area with many people fearing the 'Big One', an earthquake that will be much larger than the Northridge event and cause great devastation to the area.

With this in mind, it has become very important that both people and buildings should be prepared for future earthquakes. The following strategies have been adopted:

- **Mapping the geological structure**: it is important to know, in any event, where the strongest shaking will occur. The Los Angeles Region Seismic Experiment (LARSE), established in 1993, has attempted to map all the faults in the area, particularly the hidden ones. Knowing the configuration of the faulting system will help in understanding how earthquakes happen in the region, and information on the thickness and shape of the area's sedimentary basins is essential for predicting where and how the ground will shake during a future event.
- **Land-use planning**: armed with the above information, city planners can identify the most hazardous areas and then regulate. Certain types of buildings such as hospitals and schools should then be put in areas of low risk. Plenty of open space can also be created for potentially safe areas during an event.
- **Hazard-resistant structures**: many buildings in Los Angeles have been constructed with earthquakes in mind. Some have concrete weights that will counterbalance the force of the earthquake, and others have been built on shock absorbers to allow some movement or have been crossed-braced in order to hold the building together. Older buildings and structures such as elevated motorways have been retrofitted with devices giving them a greater chance of withstanding the tremors.
- **Fire prevention**: 'smart meters', which can cut off gas if an earth tremor of sufficient magnitude occurs, have been installed in many buildings.
- **Emergency service readiness**: computer programs have been developed that will identify the exact areas to which emergency services should be deployed. The equipment needed, such as heavy lifting gear, has been placed throughout the city in readiness for the next event.
- **Education and planning**: the Federal Emergency Management Agency (FEMA) has provided a range of advice to residents of Los Angeles, identifying potential hazards and indicating the planning required in order that the dangers of serious injury and loss of life can be reduced. Such advice includes:
  - an indication as to what people should do beforehand such as checking for hazards in the home, locating safe places, teaching the family how to respond, having disaster supplies on hand and developing an emergency communication plan
  - what to do during the event whether indoors, outdoors or in a moving vehicle, and what to do with pets
  - what to do after the earthquake such as preparation for aftershocks, help for those trapped and injured, avoidance of damaged buildings and how to deal with the utilities (gas, electric, sewage, water).

Emergency plans have been drawn up for the evacuation of high-rise buildings, schools and hospitals, the shutting down of nuclear power plants and the lowering of the water levels in reservoirs.

River flooding

Winter storms are a feature of the climate of Los Angeles, and are particularly severe during an El Niño event. Rainfall of over 100 mm per day is not uncommon and, although most of the rivers in the Los Angeles basin are short in length and seasonal, they can transport huge amounts of water during times of flood. Deforestation and numerous wildfires on hillsides have decreased interception rates and this, together with rapid urbanisation, has increased surface run-off. In February 1992, for example, after 2 days of torrential rainfall, floods devastated an area south of Malibu, killing eight people.

The Los Angeles basin is drained by two main river systems, the Los Angeles and San Gabriel rivers (Figure 38). Although the annual rainfall in the basin is often under 400 mm, in the surrounding upland areas such as the San Gabriel Mountains totals are usually over 1000 mm. On the Los Angeles river, the first major flood recorded came in 1815; in the remainder of the nineteenth century there were numerous floods, notably in 1825 and 1861. The 1914 flood caused $10 million in damages and brought a public outcry for action to address the recurrent flooding problems. Some minor attempts at channelisation were attempted, but after the destructive

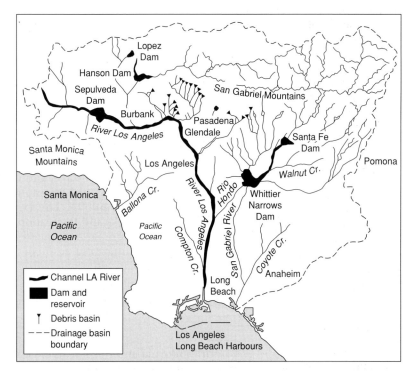

Figure 38 The Los Angeles and San Gabriel rivers

floods of the 1930s, money was made available from federal sources and the US Army Corps of Engineers took a major role in trying to bring the river under control. The following schemes were carried out:

- **Channelising** the entire Los Angeles river (apart from three sections) and its main tributary, the Rio Hondo. This involved both straightening the rivers and paving the beds and banks to put the rivers in completely artificial channels.
- Building **small dams** on the mountain tributaries in order to contain the water near its source.
- Constructing **larger dams with reservoirs** such as the Sepulveda and Hansen dams.
- Constructing **debris dams** near the sources in order to prevent huge amounts of bed load from blocking bridges and other such features downstream. Such blockages can easily lead to more severe flooding.
- Developing an area that could take large amounts of water at time of flood. This was done by building a huge retaining dam across the valleys of the Rio Hondo and San Gabriel river at a point where they come close together. This construction at **Whittier Narrows** is used only at times of the largest floods; normally the rivers flow straight through it.
- Designating large areas as **spreading grounds** for surplus water to be dissipated over it at time of flood.

In both 1992 and 1994, however, the river flooded again. As the flood waters at one time reached within a few centimetres of the top of the channel wall, the Corps of Engineers suggested that they should make the channel wall higher by at least two-thirds of a metre on the whole length of the river and in certain places even higher than 2 m. The Corps insist that any scheme should be designed to get waters to the ocean as quickly as possible as the value of land in LA County is so high, even a minor breach of the present channel would cause millions of dollars in damage to nearby residential and commercial properties. Many people consider this to be a mistake, and it has been suggested that this solution proposes treating the symptom (channel capacity) rather than the cause (urban run-off). The Los Angeles County Departments of Public Works, Parks and Recreation, and Regional Planning are currently engaged in preparing a 'master plan' for the river. Aims of this plan include; improving aesthetics, promoting economic development, preserving and restoring environmental resources, providing a variety of recreational opportunities and meeting flood control needs.

Coastal flooding

The heavy winter rains of southern California and the storms sweeping in from the Pacific that generate large waves that pound the coast have both brought some coastal flooding. The area to the south around Long Beach has also been subject to some subsidence as a result of oil extraction. Sea walls and injections of water to replace the oil have not totally removed the threat.

Drought

Los Angeles has a dry climate, particularly in summer, with an average annual rainfall often below 400 mm. The climate, combined with high evapotranspiration rates, means that run-off is low and rivers tend to dry up in the summer months. This is a real problem to the whole of southern California as the population is over 20 million and water needs to be brought into the region for its survival. Water is brought into the region from wetter northern California and from the River Colorado, and the Los Angeles area has extensive storage reservoirs, but many have pointed out the problems that the area might suffer in future if water demands stay at their present levels or increase. Concerns have already been expressed at the amount of water being taken from the River Colorado that supplies over 50% of the water required in the region. Many feel that the solution will have to be greater water conservation in the Los Angeles area, which will be hard to impress on people used to swimming pools and lawn sprinklers as well as farmers with irrigated crops. In early 2003, the Centre for Urban Agriculture said that '*We are not living within our means, and we are not living within the ecology of our region. A lawn in southern California should be illegal*'. Another solution to the problem could be the construction of desalinisation plants along the coast, although this has high energy costs associated with it. By 2003, the present capacity of all California's municipal sea-water desalting plants represented less than one-tenth of a percent of California's urban water use.

Wildfires (Brushfires)

Much of the Los Angeles basin is covered by drought-resistant chaparral vegetation. As it is too dry for tree growth, scrub vegetation has developed, which after the summer drought (that could last over 6 months) is tinder dry. A typical feature of the area is the dry wind that descends from the mountains, known as the Santa Ana, which tends to increase the dryness of the vegetation to the point where a spark, lightning or a carelessly discarded cigarette can cause a major fire. The presence of the Santa Ana also allows for the easy spread of the fire, which makes it extremely difficult to control. Much of the urban area consists of low-density building where the natural vegetation has been allowed to remain between properties. This means that when a fire occurs, a large amount of property is at risk as it lies within the danger area. In late October and early November 1993, for example, a firestorm swept the area around Malibu, destroying over

1000 homes. The event reached international prominence as the homes of several famous film and TV personalities were affected. There are a number of ways in which the authorities are trying to manage the hazard, including having enough equipment to fight the fires (particularly aircraft) and planning strategies to use it, education of the general public in fire avoidance, clearance zones of vegetation around houses, a voluntary fire watch service, and placing restrictions on people in terms of their movements and activities.

Mass movements (landslides/mudslides)

Landslides and mudslides are common in the Los Angeles basin, particularly during heavy winter rainfall. Mass movement can occur in the softer surface deposits such as sand, silt and unconsolidated gravel, but large sections of the coastal zone are also at risk because of the steepness of the cliffs. The coastal area most at risk is the area around Santa Monica where some of the cliffs are 50 m high. The numerous fires in the area exacerbate the situation as they remove the vegetation, leaving the surface open to rain splash impact and run-off, with few roots to bind the soil. To try to prevent such a hazard, planning regulations attempt to stop building at the sites at greatest risk such as the bottom of steep slopes, and particularly in ravines. The authorities build deflection structures in high-risk areas or insist that such features are incorporated within the design plans for property. On the California Geological Survey's web site, it even gives advice to householders whose property lies at or near the foot of a slope as to which rooms to sleep in for greatest safety if it is raining.

Smog

Despite some substantial improvements in recent years, the people of Los Angeles suffer the worst air pollution in the USA. Several factors have combined to produce this poor air quality:

- **the bowl-like setting**: the Los Angeles basin is surrounded by mountains on three sides, which traps pollution
- **sea breezes**: on the fourth side, sea breezes by day from the Pacific Ocean do not allow pollution to escape out to sea
- **frequent temperature inversions**: subsiding air keeps the 'lid' on the situation, not allowing the pollution to move upwards
- **abundant sunshine**: this energises the reaction transforming gaseous wastes into photochemical smog that contains ozone
- **the vehicle population**: there are over 11 million vehicles in the area, the highest concentration per person in the world
- **reliance on personal transport**: this is a product of the size of the urban sprawl and the poor public transport network up to the 1990s. Over 90% of all journeys are made by car.

During the day, the Los Angeles Public Health Service monitors the smog situation within the basin and issues warnings when the ozone levels become too high. Not surprisingly, there have been many programmes implemented in order to reduce this hazard. In 1989, an Air Quality Management Plan for southern California was approved, its aim being to reduce nitrogen oxides, butadiene and benzene by over 80%, sulphur oxides by over 60% and suspended particulates by 20%. To achieve this, a Clean Air Act was introduced in 1990, which required all vehicles to use specially reformulated petrol and promoted the installation of catalytic converters on vehicle exhausts. At the same time, people have been urged to adopt a different strategy towards cars and their use, including encouraging park-and-ride schemes, car sharing, telecommuting and the staggering of work hours.

In the 1980s, plans were drawn up for a rail-based public transport system to be known as the Metro. This is a light rail system that includes 28 km of underground railway, which links the centre of Los Angeles to North Hollywood. The whole Metro system has lines running for nearly 120 km and there are plans to extend it further during the early years of the twenty-first century. An update to the Air Quality Plan in 1997 stressed the need for new technologies, encouraging the use of electric and LPG (liquefied petroleum gas) driven cars, and cleaner fuels. As a result of all these initiatives, the levels of carbon monoxide, non-methane hydrocarbons, nitrogen oxide and ozone concentrations have all fallen steadily since the 1960s. Ozone, in particular, has seen a very marked decline in peak levels and, in addition, the area subjected to high ozone concentrations has shrunk. Despite all of this, though, there are still nearly 100 days per year in Los Angeles when the air quality is recorded as 'very unhealthy'.

Crime, gang violence and rioting

Like other American cities, Los Angeles has a high crime level. In the city itself (population 3.7 million in 2001) there were 190 000 crimes recorded in 2001, of which just under 600 were murders. Los Angeles has a high murder rate of 15.62 per 100 000 population (2001) compared with the national average in the USA of 9.58. In that same year there were also over 17 000 robberies, 33 000 aggravated assaults and over 25 000 burglaries in the city. Just as in the United Kingdom, there are various schemes, both in the community and within organisations, which are designed to reduce the hazard. Neighbourhood Watch operates, as it does in the UK, with one police department commenting that '*the department has long recognised that citizen crime reporting is the primary means of obtaining information on suspicious activity and crime*'. The Beverley Hills Police Department operates a 'Watchdog' scheme where it constantly reminds residents of how to secure their properties (particularly at holiday time), and on personal safety and general crime prevention.

Gangs are a particular feature of Los Angeles, and in parts of the city, particularly south Los Angeles, they account for a substantial amount of certain types of crime. In 1 month alone (November 2002) gangs were responsible, for example, for 28 murders. In late 2002, the LA police estimated that there were over 400 gangs in the city, with a membership exceeding 50 000, the Police Chief stating that '*the gang situation in the city is unlike anything else in America*', and from time to time the police have operated gang enforcement units in order to control the problem. Gangs are usually organised along racial lines, the largest number being Hispanic, at around half of the total, and this reflects the ethnic mix of the city's population as 47% of people in Los Angeles are Hispanic in origin. The population mix of Los Angeles has sometimes brought about tensions, such as that between African-American communities and Koreans that have spilled over into violence and there have been times when such tensions have resulted in widespread civil disorder. In 1965, there was rioting in the inner area of Watts following the arrest of an African-American drunken driver. Tensions spilled over onto the streets and 6 days of rioting left 34 people dead. A more serious event followed in 1992, when white police officers were acquitted of beating Rodney King, an African-American car driver. The subsequent riots, in which 4000 National Guardsmen had to patrol the city, had fires raging through the streets, innocent bystanders assaulted and looters sacking businesses. This event left over 50 people dead, 4000 injured and a bill of over $1 billion in property damage.

Interrelationships between hazards

In such a large urban area, and with so many hazards, there are bound to be links between some of them. Various forms of relationship can be seen in Los Angeles:

- **A simple direct causal relationship**: one hazard is responsible, in part or whole, for another, e.g. earthquakes → landslides; drought → fires; heavy rainfall → landslides/mudslides; earthquakes → crime (looting).
- **One hazard can be responsible for several others**: earthquakes, for example, can be the cause of many other hazards such as tsunamis, landslides, fires, flooding (dam burst) and crime (looting).
- **Through a central factor**: in Los Angeles, over the last 40–50 years, there has been massive urban sprawl. This may have been a factor in several hazards:

River flooding. As the city has sprawled, more and more land has gone under concrete and tarmac, particularly in the surrounding hills. With far less infiltration, every time that it rains run-off is much more rapid.

Fires. The low-density urban sprawl has left large areas of chaparral vegetation between housing developments. With houses so close to the natural vegetation, there is a great risk in summer of widespread fires when the vegetation becomes dry, particularly if the Santa Ana is blowing.

Smog. Los Angeles is a city that covers a vast area, and this has tended to encourage the use of private vehicles rather than the development of a comprehensive public transport system. Vehicle exhaust fumes have been far and away the major factor in the decline of air quality in the urban area.

Crime/social division. As the city has sprawled, very affluent suburbs have developed (such as Beverly Hills and Bel Air) which tend to be white-dominated, and very impoverished inner areas (such as Watts) dominated by African-American and Latin American communities. The Rodney King affair, and its aftermath, showed the depth of these tensions.

Living in the multi-hazard environment

With so many hazards present, there is a need to produce plans to coordinate responses in times of disaster. The State of California has established the Office of Emergency Services (OES) which coordinates overall state agency response to major disasters in support of local government. This office is responsible for assuring the State's readiness to respond to and recover from natural, man-made and war-created emergencies, and for assisting local governments in their emergency preparedness, response and recovery efforts. At a national level there is the Federal Emergency Management Agency (FEMA) with a widespread brief along similar lines to OES. Figure 39 shows FEMA's representation of the disaster life-cycle, within which the organisation operates. In Los Angeles, in order to respond to events, there is the Emergency Medical Services Authority (LAEMSA) whose brief is to 'coordinate and integrate all activities in the city concerning emergency medical services'.

Individuals within the area respond in three main ways to living with so many hazards:

- Many accept the fact that the hazards exist, but are not prepared to do much about it – 'it won't happen to me syndrome'. The advantages of living in southern California outweigh the disadvantages.
- Some people recognise the severity of some of the hazards and are prepared to do something to protect themselves. At an individual level, they can fit burglar alarms, install gas cut-offs, collect a comprehensive earthquake kit, take out insurance, attend earthquake drills and move house to be above the smog. Such people tend to be the more affluent in the area as they can afford these precau-

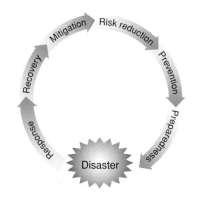

Figure 39 The FEMA disaster life-cycle

tions. They also expect the authorities to act by insisting on smog control, earthquake-proof buildings, emergency services, flood control, etc. They are willing to pay the increased taxes that result from implementing such measures.

- Living in such a multi-hazard environment may become too much of a strain, forcing some people to move away to a less hazard-prone environment. This always tends to happen after a major event, such as the Northridge earthquake and the riots and looting that followed the acquittal of the policemen in the Rodney King affair.

2 Mexico City

Mexico City occupies one of the oldest continuously inhabited sites in the whole of the Americas. As early as 10 000 BC, humans were attracted to the shores of the Lago de Texcoco, which then covered much of the Valle de Mexico. The lake, lying at 2240 m above sea level, began to shrink around 7500 BC and is now represented only by a series of salt pans. The present city sprawls across the former lake bed and is surrounded by mountains that rise to over 5000 m, but which are open to the north and south-west. The site became the capital of the Aztec empire and, by the time the Spanish arrived in 1519, it had a population that was estimated at 200 000. With the fall of the Aztec empire the population declined, but began to grow again under Spanish influence and its population in 1821 of 160 000 made it the largest urban centre in the whole of the Americas. Independence in the late nineteenth century was followed by a great deal of foreign investment and an expanding economy. Mexico City was the centre of much of this development and grew accordingly, so that by 1910 its population was 471 000. The building of a drainage canal finally succeeded in drying up most of the remnants of the Lago de Texcoco, allowing the city to expand further. This, though, brought a host of new problems by causing ground levels to sink, which they continue to do today, with damage to many notable buildings.

Growth continued in the twentieth century, the population reaching 1.75 million at the beginning of World War II. After the war, the city became a magnet for the poor of rural Mexico and it grew at a frightening rate through the 1960s, 1970s and 1980s. At one time, over 2000 migrants arrived in the city every day, drawn by the possibility of work, education, housing and better medical facilities. Since 1940, the city has multiplied in area more than ten times, yet it is still one of the world's most crowded metropolitan areas, as well as one of the most polluted. At the end of the twentieth century the population was put at around 20 million, although some authorities estimate that the real population could be as high as 26–27 million. As with almost all cities in LEDCs, Mexico City is a hazardous place to live and like Los Angeles it requires effective management, something that is not always forthcoming. The hazards of the urban area fall into similar categories as those of Los Angeles. There are those of a physical nature, others where humans have modified the physical environment to his disadvantage and there are also some that occur entirely within the human environment. The ones that will be covered here are:

- earthquakes
- smog
- water supply and sinking ground
- crime.

Earthquakes

Mexico lies in that part of the world where the Cocos Plate is being subducted underneath the North American Plate giving rise to an area that is seismologically very active. This zone creates repeated large-magnitude events with a frequency higher than any other subduction zone in the world. One critical attribute of these events is their ability to cause substantial damage in Mexico City. As the city stands on the old bed of the Lago de Texcoco, long period seismic energy is amplified 5–20 times by the underlying soil, which mostly consists of reclaimed water-saturated deposits. Not only does the amplification of the energy break up these sediments and cause them to lose strength when shaken, but, as they are also prone to liquefaction, this has a serious effect upon the built environment of the city. In the earthquake of 1957, for example, it was estimated that over 90% of the houses built on the lake sediments were damaged as a result of the ground shaking.

On 19 September 1985, Mexico experienced a devastating earthquake of magnitude 8.1 on the Richter scale. The epicentre was located just off the coast of the country, but the seismic waves from the event travelled inland and severely shook the former lake sediments beneath Mexico City, over 350 km away. This caused widespread damage to the city environment and affected thousands of families. Thirty-six hours later, another earthquake of magnitude 7.5 also shook the city. The main effects were:

- the official death toll was over 7000, although some authorities put the actual figure over 10 000
- over 40 000 people were injured
- 30 000 people, at least, were made homeless
- around 100 000 housing units suffered some form of damage
- several important government buildings were seriously damaged including the Ministries of Communication, Employment, Education, Defence and Urban Development
- few buildings in the centre were damaged (less than 5%), the worst damage occurring in areas of high housing density
- the overall cost to the city was estimated at $4 billion.

Smog

The inhabitants of Mexico City suffer from some of the worst air quality in the world. One commentator even suggested that living in the city and breathing its air was the equivalent of smoking 60 cigarettes per day! In the mid-1990s, the World Health Organization (WHO) declared that air quality in Mexico City was only acceptable on 30 days in the year. The city has high levels of carbon monoxide, sulphur dioxide, lead and PM10s and there are also very high levels of ozone, the product of photochemical reactions. Industrial pollution is particularly high in the northern parts of the city where there is a high concentration of industries, particularly oil companies, cement manufacturers and metal foundries. Daytime air flows, though, tend to move this pollution to the rest of the city, particularly the residential areas. The poor air quality is caused by a number of factors:

- the city has around 4 million vehicles on its roads, this number having doubled since 1980
- there are around 40 000 industrial premises, which produce over 12 000 tonnes of gases per day along with particulates and other pollutants
- the surrounding mountains, which trap pollution
- the frequent temperature inversions that result from cold air sinking down from the surrounding mountains
- the altitude of the city with its thinner air (less oxygen)
- plenty of sunshine, particularly in winter
- the vast size of the city means that huge numbers of people travel great distances to work
- the low income level of many of the inhabitants means that they

drive very old cars, which suffer from a lack of proper maintenance. It is such inefficient vehicles that make a major contribution
to the pollution entering the atmosphere
* leaks of unburned LPG, used for cooking and heating.

Around 2 million people suffer some level of disease as a result of air
pollution. Increasing allergies, cardiovascular problems, cancer and a
range of respiratory disease are all seen in Mexico City. In 1993, the
WHO reported that one-third of all secondary school pupils in some
parts of the city showed a 7% reduction in lung capacity while over
90% of the city population as a whole suffer from cell deformation
and inflammation of the nasal passages. Health is made worse by the
large amount of dust in the atmosphere from the bed of the former
Lago de Texcoco and from the huge volumes of waste matter
dumped on open landfill sites. A recent estimate put the health costs
related to air pollution as $900 million per year. Smogs can be so
severe that schools ban all outdoor activities and industries have to
reduce production. It is believed that around 3000 deaths annually
are caused by the city's poor air quality.

There have been a number of attempts to reduce air pollution:

* **driving restrictions**: the 'Hoy no Circula' (Don't Drive Today) programme bans all vehicles from being driven in the city on one day
each week from Monday to Friday. The last digit of the vehicle's
registration number determines the day. Several times a year, when
ozone readings are very high, the scheme bans each vehicle on two
weekdays and one weekend day
* **replacing vehicles**: all taxis when they reach 10 years of age have to
be replaced by vehicles running on lead-free petrol
* **catalytic converters**: have been compulsory on all new cars in
Mexico since the early 1990s
* **the Metro**: this underground railway system has been extensively
enlarged in the 1990s to encourage more people out of their cars.

The amounts of capital available to the city and the government of
Mexico, however, limit the schemes. Huge foreign debts coupled with
the large numbers of poor people in the city means that many more
policies that are environmentally friendly, but expensive, cannot be
implemented.

Water supply and sinking ground

The population of Mexico City consumes at least 90 000 litres of water
per second. Two-thirds of this supply comes from groundwater
(aquifer under the city), the rest is pumped from reservoirs, some of
them over 100 km away. Water enters the aquifer in the mountains
surrounding Mexico City and then is pumped to the surface by means
of wells sunk beneath the city. At the end of the twentieth century, the

rate of extraction of groundwater was estimated as being twice that of replenishment, something which has given the city planners cause for concern.

As the Lago de Texcoco was drained and groundwater extracted, the lacustrine clay that had been deposited in the basin lost its water content and began to dry out, resulting in shrinkage. Following on from this, the ground level began to sink and the city along with it. Between 1940 and 1985, it was estimated that the central parts of the city had sunk by over 7 m. Throughout the metropolitan area of Mexico City the ground level is sinking by between 5 and 40 cm per year, some of the greatest subsidence of any city in the world.

This subsidence has also caused serious sewage disposal problems. The Gran Canal de Desague is the main sewage canal for the city, but as the city sank so did the canal. It now takes 11 pumping stations, which run continuously, to keep the sewage flowing and keep the summer rains from washing it back into the city. Since the 1970s, the city had sunk so much that the water authorities could no longer count on gravity and this has resulted in the construction of a deeper system, transferring the sewage into the El Santo river north of the Guadeloupe Mountains. Through new legislation the authorities are also putting pressure on industries, forcing them to comply with water discharge regulations.

As the groundwater levels fall, the system is becoming affected by polluted surface water. This is causing some concern, as some of the agricultural land close to the city is irrigated by such water and the crops from these areas are then sold in the city markets.

Crime

Reliable crime statistics are hard to come by in Mexico City but it is widely believed that crime between 1994 and 1999 had increased by up to 80%, triggered by the economic crisis of the mid 1990s. Further estimates indicate that only one-third of all crimes are reported, and 5–10% of reported crimes are solved. Many people believe that there is little point taking their grievances to the police as they suspect many of them of being involved in crime themselves, particularly in corruption, where police take money from the many criminal gangs operating within the city. Some police will also demand money just to investigate a reported crime. Major crimes include burglary, violent 'car jacking', armed robbery and kidnapping; tourists are subject to pickpockets in the streets and robberies when in taxis.

With such a problem the city authorities have struggled to find solutions, particularly with a suspect police force. The richer inhabitants of the city employ private security companies, whilst in other areas vigilante gangs have been set up to dissuade the criminals from operating. Both foreign governments and the local authorities issue warnings to visitors, giving advice on the areas and situations to avoid.

In 2002, the city council hired the Giuliani security consultancy to see if the zero tolerance policy, applicable to crime in New York, could be used in Mexico City (Rudolph Giuliani is a former mayor of New York).

Cities in LEDCs

The hazards of Mexico City and other cities in LEDCs are linked because of unconstrained growth, the city authorities having difficulty providing basic infrastructure and services as they struggle with the unplanned and haphazard development of the urban area. Fast growing cities contain increasing numbers of poorly constructed or badly maintained buildings that lead to unnecessary deaths when earthquakes and landslides strike. As a very high percentage of people (20–60% of the population) in cities in LEDCs live in informal settlements (40% in Mexico City), conventional solutions for urban hazards are not easily applicable to the urban poor. Building codes, zoning measures and urban-planning techniques are often difficult to enforce and have had little impact in reducing vulnerability of such people.

The technical knowledge exists, though, on how to reduce the effects of hazards. Structural measures are available, such as making buildings earthquake resistant, and non-structural options, such as limiting types of land use or providing tax incentives that direct development away from hazard-prone areas. Measures need not always be costly. Building earthquake-resistant hospitals, for example, can add less than 10% to construction costs. Nor do all of these measures have to be sophisticated. By planting trees, buildings are sheltered from strong winds, or hillsides are less prone to erosion.

In some cases, this knowledge has been applied successfully. Warning systems installed in many Caribbean cities have reduced the number of lives lost each year during the hurricane season, and after a 1990 earthquake in San Jose (Costa Rica) a retrofitted portion of a hospital survived intact whilst in the section that had not been reinforced, ceilings fell and walls cracked. Technical knowledge alone, however, is not enough as people need to be aware that cities are at risk, and be politically committed to reducing those risks (see Chapter 7).

Summary

- Both Los Angeles and Mexico City suffer from a wide variety of hazards.
- Some of the hazards occur within the physical environment (earthquakes), some are where people have modified that physical

environment to their disadvantage (smog), and others occur entirely within the human environment (crime, gang violence).

- In such large urban areas, and with so many hazards, there are bound to be links between them (interrelationships).
- At an official level, there needs to be a coordinated structure to make sure that the city is in a state of readiness for any event, can respond to it and recover from it.
- Individual responses in Los Angeles to the multi-hazard environment range from 'do nothing' through to 'do something', with many people moving away to a perceived safer environment.
- The hazards of Mexico City, and other cities in LEDCs, are linked because of unconstrained growth

Exercises

1. What sources would you investigate to determine the frequency with which hazard events have occurred in Los Angeles? Comment on the reliability of evidence obtained from these sources.
2. Describe and comment on the interrelationships that appear to exist between some of the hazards that affect (i) Los Angeles and (ii) Mexico City.
3. Discuss the attitudes that individuals have taken towards living in such a multi-hazard environment.
4. What effect will the presence of so many hazards have on the cost of living for Los Angeles residents?
5. Compare and contrast the hazards experienced in large cities in MEDCs with those of cities in LEDCs. Reference must be made to specific examples.

7 Where Do We Go From Here?

1 Living with the Hazard – Kobe Fights Back

On the 17 January 1995, an earthquake measured at 7.2 on the Richter scale devastated the Japanese city of Kobe. This was probably the costliest urban disaster ever, economic damage being put at about $100 billion with over 6000 people killed, 35 000 injured and nearly a quarter of a million people made homeless. Despite being struck by a typhoon 6 months later, the message from Kobe is how well the city and its population have responded to the disaster, bringing capital, technical skills and the understanding of the community to bear on reconstruction efforts.

The scale of the disaster and its complexity posed tremendous economic and logistical problems for the people of the city. There were also enormous emotional problems to overcome with the trauma of a shattered community in which those who lost loved ones, homes and businesses, were struggling to readjust. Many in the city, though, saw this as an opportunity to put into place sustainable development plans that took disaster threats into account. The total bill for this reconstruction was estimated at least $120 billion, but Kobe seems to have coped well and many experts have commented on how impressive its efforts have been. Within a short time after the disaster, Kobe had achieved the following:

- electric power, gas, water, telecommunications, and major road and rail links were restored within months of the event
- within several months, 48 000 housing units had been supplied to take care of the homeless who made up 20% of the city's population after the earthquake
- 70% of port operations were restored within 1 year (Kobe is an important port, handling 70% of Japan's container traffic)
- almost all the debris resulting from the earthquake was removed within a short time, 60% of it successfully reused in landfill sites.

Apart from the reconstruction, it has been regarded as important that the city, as a whole, should learn lessons from the events of January 1995. Since the event, there have been a vast number of conferences and research studies that have analysed the experience from various professional points of view, and the city council considers the most important lessons learnt from the disaster are:

- Improved seismic resistance of existing buildings. Large numbers of houses in the city collapsed in the earthquake and many of those remaining did not meet modern seismic standards. The city council has indicated that eventually all such older houses will be retrofitted.
- Improve the fire-fighting capacity. As a vast number of buildings

were damaged by the fires that followed the earthquake, the city council is determined to explore all possible sources for extinguishing future fires, including rivers and the sea.

- Protecting lifelines. The city council is determined to put into place backup systems wherever possible, despite the cost. With telecommunications, for example, they are constructing a duplicate fibre optic system.
- Community participation. The council now understands that to reduce future risks, the community needs to be better informed through awareness and education programmes. Areas of concern revealed by the disaster were: the stockpiling of resources in readiness for an event; the ability of the ordinary citizen to fight fires; the availability of basic tools for search and rescue. The mayor of Kobe said that '*people pay attention to their own problems, but they must pay attention to the community as a whole*'. The council is also encouraging a range of NGOs, as they seemed flexible during the event in the way that official bodies were not.
- Disaster-resistant measures. A variety of measures have been proposed that would protect the city from the effects of earthquakes and secondary hazards such as fires and landslides. The measures include firebreaks to be established along rivers and roadways, mountain greenbelts to reduce landslides, a new canal project to ensure a reliable water supply and backup systems for hospitals.

2 The Future – Reducing the Impact of Hazards

As we have seen in Chapter 1, the world seems to be becoming a more hazardous place with recorded disasters doubling in number every decade. It is all too easy with so many media images available to be extremely pessimistic about hazards and their impact, but it must be remembered that in almost all cases most people survive disasters. In the example given above, that of Kobe, just over 6000 were killed out of a total population over around 1.5 million, which represents less than 1%. It is true to say that there was a great deal of damage, with over 300 000 made homeless and countless numbers of people still suffering many months after the event, but as we have seen above, there was a spirit in the city that enabled reconstruction to progress rapidly. The IDNDR programme, part of which is given below, will need time to bear fruit, but it will also be costly in monetary terms. The question is will the poorest countries be able to afford to put much of this plan into operation? In another part of Chapter 1, reference was made to the cyclone that devastated Bangladesh in 1991, killing over 130 000 people. The country has shelters for less than 5% of the population, so in such a low-lying country, even with warning, the population would find it difficult to survive such a devastating natural event. The tens of millions people that make up the population of Bangladesh are forced by their circumstances to live on this low-lying river delta and therefore they increase the risk and make themselves more vulnerable to the hazards that effect the area.

Reducing the impact of a wide variety of hazards will not be easy. Solutions may be available but, in many parts of the world, what is needed is a change in people's attitudes, based on the conviction that communities can organise themselves to resist disasters, and the will to act on this conviction. This very much reflects the changes that have taken place in environmental awareness over the last two decades. To make areas safer from hazards we need to build a culture of prevention among society at large. As populations expand into areas prone to earthquakes, floods, volcanic eruptions, landslides and other such natural hazards, they become increasingly more vulnerable. At the beginning of the twenty-first century, at least one-quarter of the world's population lives in areas that are classified as high risk in terms of hazards. According to IDNDR, the dominant approach around the world to disasters is still relief orientated, partly due to the attitude of fatalism that springs from the belief that hazardous events are 'Acts of God.' Nevertheless, as is shown by the example of Kobe, post-event reconstruction is now being carried out in many areas with long-term development and a safer future in mind. Authorities are beginning to recognise that methods to reduce vulnerability are far more cost-effective than large clean-up operations. Not surprisingly, the period immediately after a major event is often the best time to start such programmes, as political will and public awareness are at a their highest levels. From the IDNDR programme, four major policy areas have been suggested:

A. Encourage policies that reduce vulnerability

- **Land use**: plans should be put into operation that limit, or ban, building upon hazardous areas such as steep slopes, river flood plains and faulted areas.
- **Risk and disaster impact assessments**: on the basis of these, special programmes can be designed to reduce vulnerability and to use the results in development projects.
- **Design, construction and maintenance of buildings and other structures**: give advice and financial incentives to encourage safe and cost-effective buildings and enforce construction regulations.

B. Ensure that governments, at national and local level, are prepared to cope with a hazard event

- **Emergency management planning**: roles and responsibilities in emergencies should be clearly identified.
- **Strengthen organisations**: money should be put forward to train disaster managers and to provide staff to enforce regulations. All equipment for handling the impact of disasters should be maintained and updated whenever possible.

- **Communications**: channels should be established for early warnings, evacuations and relief measures. Local decision-makers should be made aware of all scientific evidence, where available, and its value to them.

C. Ensure that the community is well prepared

- **Public awareness and education**: make people aware that they have to protect themselves. Education campaigns should be instituted in order to raise public awareness about hazard risks, and what preparatory and preventive measures people should be taking.
- **Community-based programmes and solutions**: communities, particularly vulnerable ones, should be consulted in order to identify local needs and feasible solutions.

D. Special programmes for high-risk situations

There are a number of areas where special attention should be given as a priority. They include:

- **Essential facilities**: electricity, gas water, telecommunications, hospitals and schools. Existing buildings to be retrofitted, new structures to have disaster-resistant devices built in to them. Back-up systems need to be constructed.
- **High-risk groups**: programmes should focus on groups such as children, the elderly and those on low-incomes, with targeted education programmes, specific financial help and specialised health care.
- **Informal settlements**: within the cities of LEDCs, informal settlements are the areas often most at risk from hazards having been constructed on such sites as low-lying marshy land and steep slopes.
- **Cultural treasures/heritage**: as these cannot be replaced, they will need special precautions to make sure that they survive the hazard event.
- **Buildings with hazardous substances**: buildings such as nuclear power stations and chemical stores should be retrofitted and well maintained. It could be possible to consider relocation of some buildings that fall into this category to less vulnerable sites.

The final word on the future shape of hazard response should be left to the mayor of Kobe who gave this message to other communities facing hazards:

> Wherever you live, city or village, you have to keep in mind that you must protect yourself. You have to prepare to protect yourself, you cannot fight alone. You must have a system to fight disasters, where you must cooperate with relations and your colleagues. Each community has to have its own plan to respond in case of emergency. Your community may not be enough, though, so then you can work with other communities, the government and with other countries. But first, you must protect yourself, for yourself, wherever you are in the world.

Bibliography

Alexander, D., 2000, *Confronting Catastrophe* (Harpenden: Terra Publishing)

Barnett, T. and Blaikie, P., 1992, *AIDS in Africa: Its Present and Future Impact* (Chichester: John Wiley and Sons)

Durschmied, E., 2002, *The Weather Factor: How Nature Has Changed History* (New York: Arcade Publishing)

Elsom, D., 1996, *Smog Alert: Managing Urban Air Quality* (London: Earthscan)

Erikson, J., 2002, *Quakes, Eruptions and other Geologic Cataclysms: Revealing the Earth's Hazards* (New York: Facts on File Inc.)

Ferraro, K.F., 1995, *Fear of Crime* (Albany: State University of New York Press)

Frampton, S., Chaffey J., Hardwick J. and McNaught A., 2000, *Natural Hazards*, 2nd Edn (London: Hodder & Stoughton)

Goudie, A. and Viles, H., 1997, *The Earth Transformed* (Oxford: Blackwell)

McGuire, W.J. *et al.*, 2000, *Natural Hazards and Environmental Change* (London: Arnold)

Middleton, N., 1995, *The Global Casino* (London: Edward Arnold)

Petts, G. and Calow P., 1996, *River Restoration* (Oxford: Blackwell Science)

Skinner, M., Redfern, D. and Farmer, G., 2003, *The Complete A–Z Geography Handbook*, 3rd Edn (London: Hodder & Stoughton)

Smith, K., 2000, *Environmental Hazards: Assessing Risk and Reducing Disaster* (London: Routledge)

Cities at Risk, 2000 (Geneva: International Decade for Natural Disaster Reduction – IDNDR)

Periodicals and other sources

The following periodicals carry frequent articles on hazards and their management: *Geography Review; Geography.*

Numerous issues of the following are also devoted to hazards, hazard events and their management: *Geofile* and *Geoactive* (published by Stanley Thornes Ltd., Cheltenham); *Geo Factsheet* (published by Geo Press, Birmingham).

The Environment Agency. *Flood Warning Campaign Research Sheets* and *Flood Warning Case Study 1999.*

Index